WHEN VALOR MUST HOLD

BOOK ONE OF THE LIBRI VALORIS

Edited by
Chris Kennedy and Rob Howell

New Mythology Press
Virginia Beach, VA

Chris Kennedy/New Mythology Press
2052 Bierce Dr., Virginia Beach, VA 23454
http://chriskennedypublishing.com/

Publisher's Note: This is a work of fiction. Names, characters, places, and incidents are a product of the author's imagination. Locales and public names are sometimes used for atmospheric purposes. Any resemblance to actual people, living or dead, or to businesses, companies, events, institutions, or locales is completely coincidental.

The stories and articles contained herein have never been previously published. They are copyrighted as follows:

DARKNESS BEFORE THE DAWN by Christopher Woods © 2020 by Christopher Woods
THE GAME'S AFOOT by Christopher G. Nuttall © 2020 by Christopher G. Nuttall
THE OGRE'S BROWNIES by RJ Ladon © 2020 by RJ Ladon
DUST IN THE MOUTH by William Joseph Roberts © 2020 by William Joseph Roberts
HANGING BY A THREAD by Benjamin Tyler Smith © 2020 by Benjamin Tyler Smith
SHARD'S FORTRESS by Dexter Herron © 2020 by Dexter Herron
HORSE'S HEART by Sarah A. Hoyt © 2020 by Sarah A. Hoyt
ISLAND OF BONES by William Alan Webb © 2020 by William Alan Webb
GODDESS'S TEARS by Cedar Sanderson © 2020 by Cedar Sanderson
HOLD THE LINE by Kevin Steverson and Tyler Ackerman © 2020 by Kevin Steverson and Tyler Ackerman
WHAT'S IN A NAME by Rob Howell © 2020 by Rob Howell
THE ERRAND by Jon R. Osborne © 2020 by Jon R. Osborne
NO TRADE FOR NICE GUYS by D.J. Butler © 2020 by D.J. Butler
FISTFUL OF SILVER by Quincy J. Allen © 2020 by Quincy J. Allen

When Valor Must Hold/Chris Kennedy and Rob Howell -- 1st ed.
ISBN 978-1950420971

This anthology is dedicated to Christopher J.R. Tolkien

At the beginning, his father's audience, then his assistant, his peer, and finally, the guardian of Middle-Earth. Whether fighting a dragon, on the wall at Helm's Deep, or against Grendel's mother, the Tolkiens gave us heroes whose valor always held.

Preface by Rob Howell

Before I get into the background of *When Valor Must Hold*, I want to thank you, the great readers of Chris Kennedy Publishing, for picking this up and giving all these authors, including me, a chance. Without readers, we are nothing.

Now, let's get to the origin of this anthology. It all started with James L. Young, who actually isn't in this anthology. He made an off-hand comment to Chris Kennedy about publishing alternate history anthologies. Chris said something to the effect of "I will when you put it together."

That led to the Phases of Mars, a set of three anthologies I'm honored to be a part of.

Then I heard about another challenge set by Chris, this one to Jamie Ibson. That became *We Dare*, to which I again was honored to contribute.

All of this made me contemplate the idea of a fantasy anthology. Editing an anthology wasn't something I'd done before, but I'd paid attention to James Young's process and was intrigued. I still have much to learn about writing, of course, and an anthology could be an opportunity to learn a great deal as well as create something new.

On the Thursday night before LibertyCon 2019, we were hanging out at the hotel bar. I had a few IPAs, shocking I know. I realized I could see David Butler, Christopher Woods, Jon Osborne, William Roberts, Benjamin Tyler Smith, and a bunch of other authors.

I did the obvious. "Hey, Chris, when are you going to publish a fantasy anthology?"

"When you put it together."

So I hit up all those at the bar and before night's end well I had lined up over half of the authors in the anthology. I gathered up a few others, like Sarah Hoyt, during the rest of the con, then reached out to a number of others afterward, and suddenly Bob's your uncle.

The writing prompt I had in mind was Akiro the Wizard's speech at the beginning of *Conan the Barbarian*. At the end of the speech, he declares, "Let me tell you of the days of high adventure."

I love that scene. I love the soundtrack by Basil Poleidouris that kicks in right after Akiro. I love the movie. It's filled with vivid scenes and vibrant action. I wanted stories like the movie that told of the days of high adventure.

And that's what I got.

Then I got the basic idea for the title and that's when things got even better. Lines 1508 and 1509 describe Beowulf striving to defeat Grendel's mother despite having no weapon to harm her. And yet, his valor held in that desperate situation. So, *When Valor Must Hold*.

When I passed the title idea on to the authors they all made sure their characters' valor would hold. Even the stories that don't fit the hard-edged style of Robert E. Howard have valorous characters standing up to great foes.

Oh, it wasn't that simple, of course. Some submissions didn't fit. One author had something come up that prevented completing his story. Sadly, one who would have been on the cover had major computer issues.

But what we have here is a bunch of stories I really enjoyed reading. The cover names, of course, gave their usual quality. They all gave me great tales of high adventure.

But the stories provided by Team "And More" might be even better.

The cover art to *When Valor Must Hold* came from "Darkness Before the Dawn," by Christopher Woods. How can one go wrong with a dragon and a water-mage? You can't, so it kicks everything off.

Then Christopher Nuttall's "The Game's Afoot" gives us a magic-wielding infiltrator against a stern and misunderstood foe.

R.J. Ladon's story "Ogre's Brownies" is different from my normal preference, yet her hero held his valor no matter the odds and despite his fear.

If there's any story in *When Valor Must Hold* that could have been written by Robert E. Howard himself, it's "Dust in the Mouth" by William J. Roberts. Swordplay, desperate action, ancient evils, and daring heroes. What more could anyone want?

Benjamin Tyler Smith's "Hanging by a Thread" is a neat combination of mystery, necromancy, and noir. Honestly, I think his Necrolopolis setting would make a great cop TV series.

Dexter Herron was an author I had in mind from the beginning. He's someone none of you have heard of, unless of course, you play in the East Kingdom of the SCA. He tells the tales of Shard, a soldier in the Goblin Army, an army which is all that glittering elven armies aren't. His story, "Shard's Fortress," is definitely PG-13, but left me in stitches.

"Horse's Heart," from Sarah Hoyt, has action, a tragic enemy, and the hint of a world with many stories to tell.

Bill Webb might have been the last person I asked to contribute, but his stuff is perfect for what I wanted. The "Island of Bones" is a great story of a hidden evil.

Cedar Sanderson gave me an origin story in "Goddess's Tears." Her main character pays a price for vengeance that recalls Coleridge's reason to "close your eyes with holy dread."

In "Hold the Line," Kevin Steverson and Tyler Ackerman tell the tale of an heir earning his spurs. It also describes some of the challenges facing the Empire of Minth about a century before their novel *Burnt*, which actually got released the same day as this anthology.

My story in this is "What's in a Name." It's an origin story detailing the first meeting between Edward Aethelredsson and his horse Deor. I got to write about two characters I love beating the hell out of each other and also throw in some of my Old English geekiness.

In "The Errand," Jon Osborne challenges his main character with raiders, invulnerable warriors, and goddesses to test his mettle.

David Butler's "No Trade for Nice Guys" is a spiritual heir to Lieber's Fafhrd and the Gray Mouser, only with sharper prose more reminiscent of Robert B. Parker.

Quincy J. Allen's "Fistful of Silver" has that Man with No Name vibe, but with magic and a Dashiell Hammett-style twist. The perfect ending to a great list.

I thanked you readers first thing in the preface, because we all know we owe our careers to you. That also means we all believe in providing good stories. I had a number of goals when creating this anthology, but that was always the first and overriding goal. Nothing matters if these aren't good stories.

We achieved that, I think. I'm honored to be a part of this anthology and I hope you enjoy it as much as we did creating it.

Rob Howell
Olathe, KS

Contents

* * * * *

Darkness Before the Dawn
by Christopher Woods

"What do you have, there, son?"

"I'm making a jewelry box, sir," I answered and held the box I was sanding out to Galder.

"Those are some fine joints," he said as he examined the box, "and a wonderful design. I think you'll move up to the cabinets on the morrow."

"Yes, sir," I said. I may have been the eldest of his apprentices, but I was also one of the newest. I had tried my hand at several things, and I felt more from the wood than any of the other things I had tried to do.

Stone had been harder work, and metal even harder. I was not afraid of the hard work, but something in the wood just felt *right* to me. My mother used to say I had an affinity for the Elements. She swore I would be an Elemental, but she was fated to be disappointed. All four nodes had rejected me on my testing.

It had been a strange day, for several reasons. The nodes glowed as I approached, just as they did for any of the children with an affinity. The strange part was that each of the stones glowed as I approached. Typically there would be a single node that would react to one of the kids being tested.

I'd seen Dagor, my friend, as he walked past the Elements of Air, Earth, and Water with no reaction. Then the Fire node flared as he neared it. When he touched the obelisk, it had grown bright, and that brightness seemed to flow from the obelisk into him. Dagor had become a Fire Elemental that day.

Not me. I had been rejected by each of the nodes in turn. Each flared as I neared them, but none of them granted me their gift. Everyone was astounded, but the nodes do not lie. I was not going to be an Elemental...not Fire, not Water, not Air, and not Earth. I had been sixteen when it occurred, and all had expected great things of me.

Instead, I was sanding the sides of a small jewelry box for Jenisa. I might not have been an Elemental, but I still had an affinity for the Elements. I could make things. My tools stayed sharp, and the wood was pliable where others couldn't shape it. I could sense exactly where the chisel would need to slide to put the smallest of lines in the design without splintering the wood. I had found that it was a joy to work the wood.

"I think Sammi is ready for some of the smaller things you've been doing," Galder said. "I've never seen anyone learn as fast as you have, but it is hard to move one up without the others. Jarl isn't ready to move forward yet, and Fand is not ready to open his own shop yet. Cabinetry may be the best we can do for you right now."

"Cabinetry will be fine, sir."

"Good, then," he said and handed me the box. "Jenisa will be pleased."

"I hope so, sir," I said. "I would like to gift it to her before her wedding."

"She will love it." He turned to leave the shop. "You spend your day off working in the wood shop. I should put you at the top of the apprentices. You really should get out and meet with people. You cannot pine over what could never be."

"I'm the new guy in Maltos," I said. "I should have known I could never…"

"It is true, Zaro," he said as my voice tapered off. "I thought, for just a moment, it would work out for you, but she was fated for more than a lowly carpenter once she was touched by Water. Destined for nobility are the Elementals. She is out of reach of those such as us."

"You sound like you know."

"I, too, was young," he said. "Sometimes we do what we need to do instead of what we *want* to do."

"But you and Fiona are great, sir."

"Yes," he said. "And if I had gotten what I wanted when I was so very young, I would not have her and four children we both love. What I am saying is that you will find someone else someday, and you will look back on these days with a new eye."

I chuckled. "I hope so, sir. I really liked Jenisa. If only one of the nodes had chosen me."

"Then you would still be in Hallonder, learning from the Elementals of that fine city."

"And I would not have met her, anyway," I finished.

"Exactly so."

"I'll finish this up and go to the square."

"Good."

"Maybe they'll have some of those sabot shanks."

"They're very good with the sauce Fori uses on them," he said.

"They are. I'll bring an extra one back for you. Which is what you were probably aiming for when you told me I should go out."

"Worked, did it not?"

"Yes, it worked. I'll bring your shank back with me."

"Wrap it well so it's still warm when you get it back."

"I'll wrap it, sir. I know you like your shank warm."

He grinned as he walked back out the door of the wood shop.

I lightly sanded the corner of the jewelry box. I wished it could have been me she was to marry, but an Elemental is so much more than any of us. They are imbued with the magic of the world. They live on another plane of existence than we mere mortals.

The Element of Water is one of great power. They are the keepers of the portals, the gateways to the other parts of the continent. Some of the more powerful of the Water Elementals can even open portals to the other continents of Kandria. I had even heard of the High Elemental of Water opening a portal to another realm, but that may only have been a rumor.

My fingers worked across the ornate box, and my eyes closed as I felt the wood under my fingertips. It was smooth and felt warm to the touch. I was certain it was ready for coating with the linseed to preserve it and keep that beautiful color. I figured it would make a nice present for the one I had dared to believe I could marry someday.

But Jenisa had become an Elemental, and that changed everything.

* * *

Thehe square was bright, and there were crowds of people. I had never liked crowds very much. Perhaps it was the initial reaction of most of the people who had been there when I was tested four years back. Nothing prepares you for the derision they show you when you fail. If the stones glow, you are chosen. To have every stone glow and still not receive the gift…

I lost a lot of love for people that day as I watched them turn into a hateful crowd. And hateful crowds were not a thing I enjoyed. But the crowd in the square was not hateful. They were just people doing the things that people do, and I could not hold the feelings I had for all those years as I watched two children playing tag amongst the vendor stalls. Or the couple dancing along to the music being played by the Minstrel at the edge of the square. The last years living in Maltos had gone a long way toward bringing me back to seeing joy in the world.

Jenisa had touched the glowing blue obelisk, and I had seen some of my joy dissolve, but there was still some left, and I would build on that.

"Hello, Fori," I said as I stopped in front of the stall, where a wonderful smell permeated the air.

"Zaroliss Galderson!" she exclaimed. "I would guess that you are here for a shank?"

"Not Galderson," I said. "I am just an apprentice. I could do worse for a father, though."

"All of his apprentices are his sons," she said. "Not all of them are born of his blood."

"Then call me Galderson if you want to," I said with a smile. "And Galder would like one of those shanks wrapped up so it stays warm. I'll take one to eat as I go back."

"Two septs, and you tell Galder he could have a hot one if he would get off of his lazy backside and get his own."

I laughed and handed her the two small coins. "I will tell him, lady."

"I am no lady, young man," she said as she wrapped the sabot for Galder. "No dragon blood in this one."

"Dragon blood?"

"Keakileris blood. The blood of the nobility. My gran used to call it the blood of dragons."

"Ahh, the blood of the ancients. My mother claimed I was Keakileris. I guess I showed *her* when the stones wouldn't choose me."

"There are many with the blood of Keakileris who do not become harbingers of the Elements, young Zaro."

"True enough," I said and took the shank she handed me. It was the leg of a large sabot, nearly five hand spans long. It was, by far, the largest of the shanks on her grill. "Thank you, lady. And whether the blood of the Keakileris flows in your veins or not, a lady is exactly what you are."

"You have a honeyed tongue, young Zaro," she said. "If I were a few decades younger, I would drag you into an alley and show you how unladylike I could be."

I felt my face redden, and she cackled her laughter, which made others look in our direction. I stopped my laughter before it could even start as I heard the screams in the distance.

I turned to the east, where the main gate was located. My head felt like it was on fire as I saw an explosion of black flame erupt from the gate.

"Get down, Fori!" I warned. "Into the buildings! Off the street!"

She nodded and grabbed her coin purse, then ran for the open doors of the Palisade, where the more expensive shops were located. I dropped the shanks on her table and ran toward the east edge of the square. "Into the Palisade! Find cover!"

The gate exploded, and shards of wood ripped through the crowds of people. I felt the one that would have hit me in time to drop to the left and scoop up one of the kids who had been playing tag. I thanked my ancestors for the touch of the blood that had given me the affinity for the Elements. I also grabbed the little boy who had been chasing the girl and ran for the Palisade.

Fori was just inside the door, and took the children. I turned to go back out.

"Stay!"

I shook my head and darted back out the door. There were people in the square who were injured, and they would need help. My head burned again as a bolt of black fire hit the building to the left of the Palisade, and the brick exploded in all directions.

Hallis, whose stall was right in the line of that black bolt, was laying in the center of the square. The bolt had touched his shoulder, and blackness crawled across his body. His scream would haunt me for the rest of my days. As the blackness climbed across his face, the screaming stopped. What sort of magic was this? What did this to people?

I grabbed the young girl who had been dancing. Her partner was dead, and the black covered the upper half of his body.

"You have to come with me!"

She would not take her eyes from his form, so I threw her over a shoulder, and ran back to the Palisade.

I looked to my right to see a guard running along beside me. My head burned again, and I dove to the left. The black bolt hit the guard and sent him somersaulting through the air; his sword tumbled along the street. I regained my feet and grabbed the girl again. As I neared the door, Fori stepped out to grab the girl, but another bolt of darkness blasted the area between us. I heard her scream as it touched her hand.

Throwing the girl in the door, I crouched over Fori.

She screamed as the darkness began to climb her arm. "Take it! Before it goes too far! Take the arm!"

I saw the guard's sword with its nicks and dings. The second I picked it up, it gleamed like a new blade. The darkness was past her forearm, and the blade whistled as I severed the arm in a single stroke. I pulled the strap from my waist and cinched it tight around her arm to slow the bleeding.

There was an immense heat to my left, and Kalib, the Fire Elemental, landed.

He stepped up to Fori as the flames that had surrounded him went out. "This will hurt."

His hand grasped the bloody end of her arm, and I smelled burned flesh as he cauterized the stump.

Then he was covered in flames again and shot into the air. I carried Fori back into the Palisade.

"Stay inside, you damned fool," she muttered as I turned to go back out.

"You stay inside this time," I answered and ran back out into the chaos.

What I would be able to do, exactly, was unknown to me, but I ran in the direction Kalib had flown.

I felt wetness falling from the sky and looked up to see the waterspout as it surged up the street. She wore the blue tunic of the Water Elementals, and her black hair blew back in the wind as she rode the spout toward yet another black explosion.

My heart was in my throat as Jenisa waved her hands in an intricate design that sent bolts of ice in the direction she was traveling. I ran along behind her. I had kept the sword from the guard, and it gleamed as the Water from the spout danced across the surface.

My ears popped as the air changed. Juli sailed through the sky with lightning circling her form. The Elementals were closing on whoever was throwing the dark fire around. The Earth rumbled as several Earth Elementals charged past me toward the fight. Their feet thundered as they strode, and the ground trembled under my feet. A black bolt of fire hit the wall of the building to my right, and masonry exploded in every direction. I swept the sword up and across, knocking several chunks of brick aside.

I followed the Elementals.

A bolt of black fire made it past the earthen shields carried by the Elementals in front of me, and the blackness hit one's chest. It consumed him, and the Earth rocked with his death throes. The throes tossed me around like a leaf in the wind as the blackness consumed his mind.

I finally saw the man who wielded the darkness. He was stocky and wore robes like those worn by the Priests. The Priests wore white, though, and this man wore robes black as night. I slapped aside a chunk of debris that flew at me and charged.

The black wizard threw a bolt at Kalib, who met it with his own fiery bolt. They connected with the thunder of the Gods.

Kalib was a full Elemental with the full power of his element. Still the black bolt approached him. Then lightning struck at the black mage. He blocked it, and his black bolt was split between the Elementals of Fire and Air. Juli was strong, but she wasn't a full Elemental of Air, and she tumbled through the air as her lightning stopped. She plummeted toward the ground, and I ran up a set of stairs to catch the small woman before she could impact the stones. We tumbled across the ground, but she was still alive.

I was on my feet and running toward the black mage again. Jenisa landed and sent ice shards flying toward him. He swatted them aside and raised his hand to point at her. I felt the bolt of blackness coming, and I knew she wouldn't be able to block it. I dived into her, knocking her aside. The bolt slammed into my back, and I knew I was done for. Surprisingly, it didn't hurt as bad as I thought it would. I rolled across the cobblestoned street.

"Zaro!" I heard her yell as she realized who had knocked her aside. "What in the Gods' names are you doing here?"

I staggered to my feet.

"Are you hit?" she asked and spun me around. "What were you thinking? You must have just missed it."

I swallowed.

"Never mind," she said. "We aren't strong enough to stop him."

Kalib tumbled from the sky and struck the building.

The black mage ripped a hole in the side of a building, and I gasped as I saw the black obelisk inside.

"Gods!" Jenisa exclaimed as the mage placed his hand on the obelisk, which seemed to be as dark as the abyss itself.

I could feel the power as it fed into him, and he screamed. The scream grew into a roar, and the darkness began to roil around him.

It spread outward and grew. It settled into a shape I had only seen in the tapestries from the ancients. When the blackness dissipated, there was no longer a man, but a dragon, black as night, his scales gleaming with the power of the black obelisk.

"The Void," Jenisa gasped.

Black fire spewed from the dragon's mouth, and he leapt upward with a powerful thrust of his wings. He rose into the sky with roars of triumph.

I stood there with my mouth hanging open, when Jenisa turned to me. "You saved my life, Zaro, my hero."

She placed her hands on the sides of my face, staring up into my eyes. Just before her lips touched mine, she said, "Thank you, my hero."

"What is this?"

I turned toward the roar of an Earth Elemental. He moved toward me faster than I could actually do anything about. I knew the fist was coming; I could feel it. But it was moving fast enough that all I could do was sidestep the fraction of a hand span it would take to keep that punch from killing me.

It threw me backward into the air, and I tumbled across the floor of the building where I landed.

"Zaro! No!" I heard her scream, but I reached out to the wall I had landed beside to brace myself as I climbed to my feet.

I felt cold in my arm as the wall of black thrummed.

I had braced myself on the black obelisk. The dark power of the void enveloped me in its cold, black embrace, and I fell into darkness. I couldn't see where to go or what to do. I didn't want to be like the man who had just killed those innocent people, but I didn't know what to do.

Something buzzed in my ears. It settled into a voice that seemed to be leagues away.

"Zaro...come back...come back..."

I followed the voice, and saw a tiny spot of light in the distance. I ran toward it. It took a long time, and I was so tired, but the voice was one I would follow to the ends of the Earth. I opened my eyes and stared into the liquid pools of blue that were Jenisa's eyes.

"I'll rip his—"

"You will not touch him, Degos," Jenisa said, "and you will never have the pleasure of touching me again. You will never be wed to me!"

"You cannot—"

"I can, and I have! Come one step closer to me, and I will freeze the blood in your veins! We are through."

He started to make that step until I stood up and made a move toward him. He backed up as he stared in horror at me. I could feel the darkness inside me demanding his blood, but I held it in check.

"This is not over," Degos said as he stepped away from us.

She turned to look at me.

"What has happened to you, my hero?" she asked softly.

"It's inside me," I said. "I can feel the darkness, and it wants to come out and consume everything."

She reached for me, and I stepped back. "I don't think it's safe."

She stopped, and we both turned to our right as a white-robed Priest ran into the building from a door on the far side.

"Gods of light! What has happened?"

* * *

I hungered.

I awoke to find tendrils of darkness flowing from me in several directions. There was the remains of a small creature near the corner of the cell where the Priests had put me. It was blackened, like the people I had seen in the square. The tendrils snapped back into my body as I looked at the dead rodent. I was horrified as I realized the hunger I felt was for *more*. The rodent had been consumed by the darkness.

"It feeds on life."

I jerked around to find the Minstrel from the square sitting in a chair outside the cell.

"What?"

"The Void feeds on life, my friend. It is hungry for the life in the world, and it will take it."

"No," I said. "I cannot let that happen."

"You *are* the Void now. How will you stop it? All the people chosen by the Void succumb to its need. How can you stand up to that hunger at all times? How do you keep it in check when you cannot even control your dreams? The hunger you feel will never go away. The Void always consumes them."

"Them?"

"Those chosen by the Void are cursed, my friend. If they do not consume others, the Void consumes them. If they consume innocents, they have to be put down or imprisoned, and the Void will consume them."

"I don't want to kill anyone," I said.

"I know."

"Who are you?" I asked. "I saw you in the square playing music."

"Just a lowly bard," he said. "Vor is my name."

"What do you know about this?" I raised my hand, and darkness played along my fingertips. "What happens now?"

"The Priests will hold you in a cage until the Void consumes you. They use runes of the Light to keep the darkness inside the cage. It will not take very long. The Void is very strong within you. Most people would have died, being struck by a dark bolt." He cocked his head to the side. "Or have you already been to the dark obelisk?"

"No. I have an affinity for the Elements, but they never chose me. I have never seen a dark obelisk until now."

"Truth, you speak. An affinity, you say?"

"The Elements glowed for me, but none of them chose me."

"Oh, my," he said. "All of them?"

I nodded.

"That is something that has not occurred in a long time. Perhaps you might not perish inside a cage after all."

"What are you talking about?"

The Minstrel jumped to his feet. "I will return. There are things I must learn before I give you hope. Hope is a dangerous thing."

I sat on the cot and wondered about my fate.

The black robed man had not been consumed by the powers he wielded, but he had been pitiless. He had slaughtered any he saw. Perhaps the power had consumed him in another way. My hunger gnawed at me, and I knew how the power would be able to take a person. The gnawing hunger would break anyone down over time. What would I become if I was out there amongst the people of Maltos? Would I slaughter them? Or would I be able to control it? Would it reach out when I slumbered like the tendrils had done to the rodent?

I looked up as someone walked down the hallway. Jenisa sat in the chair.

"I am so sorry, Zaro," she said. "Degos had no right to attack you."

"He is your betrothed?"

"He was until he attacked the only friend I have ever been able to trust with anything. And he has done *this* to you."

"Guess I am an Elemental after all," I said. "It has to be the worst of them, but I am an Elemental."

"My Zaro," she said with pity. "How I missed your humor. Why have you stayed away for so long?"

"The Elements are not meant for a lowly carpenter," I said.

"We could have still been friends," she said.

"Possible, but I could not bear to watch as you wed another because the blood in your veins was different. I am a selfish man. I should not have deserted you."

"You would have been miserable in the Keep," she said. "And you are not selfish. I have seen through the pools what you did in the battle with the Void Wizard. You saved people. You saved Juli, and you saved me. That black bolt should have killed you when it hit you squarely. You had not touched the stone."

"I have an—"

"Yes, I know," she said, shaking her head. "You have an affinity for the Elements. You keep your humor, even in this cell where they will hold you until death. How do you do it?"

"What else *am* I to do?"

Her eyes watered as she fought tears.

"Perhaps things can work out," I said. "The Minstrel seemed to think he had discovered something."

"Minstrel?"

"Yes, he was in the square."

"There was no Minstrel in the square," she said. "I examined every inch of the area with the pools."

"He was playing for the two dancers."

"I will look again, but the pools do not lie. They show what was. They cannot be deceived."

"I was there; I saw him. And I saw him sitting right where you are less than a span ago."

"That is highly unlikely," she said. "The guards said I am your first and only visitor."

I could see the pity in her eyes. She thought the darkness had addled my wits.

"I must return to the Keep. I will come and see you again."

"I will be here," I said.

She shook her head as she walked out of sight down the corridor.

"Unless the Minstrel returns with good news," I muttered.

* * *

"You have eaten another small snack."

I jerked awake at the voice of the Minstrel.

"You."

"Of course it is me."

I looked down to see the tendrils retracting back into my body. Another small form was laying close to the other.

I sighed. "This is how it is going to be?"

"Perhaps," he said. "There is a chance that you may yet survive this, young Zaro. What would you do for the chance to regain your life?"

to the last one. The Elementals charged at me, but they were too late. My hand landed on the obelisk of Water. Ice flowed where Fire had been, and I stumbled backward to land on my back.

All of the Elements raged inside me. The power was unreal, but the darkness still tried to break through. The Void hungered, and I would have to cage that beast.

"You!" yelled the Earth Elemental as he came into view.

Of course it was Degos. He threw a chunk of the street at me.

"I am not the enemy!" I yelled as I melted the chunk of stone with a blast of Fire.

A tendril of black reached out for him, and I latched onto it with my mind, pulling it back inside. A huge fist made of the stone he pulled from the street slammed into me, and I sailed across the plaza to crash through a wall.

A white priest ran to my prone form and lashed white bands around my wrists.

I shook the daze from my eyes and looked down at the bonds, which fell from my arms.

"How did you…"

"I am not the enemy! Just give me some time to get this thing caged!"

A black tendril almost reached the man, and I yanked it back. He screamed and ran for the door. The floor buckled, and a column of dirt and rock slammed into me again.

"Die, you black scum!"

In my mind, another battle raged.

What had the Minstrel said? Earth to cage it. Inside my mind, pillars of Earth surrounded the Void. It flowed through the gaps, trying to come for me. The white of the light flared, and the darkness was pushed back toward the cage.

Then I hit a wall again.

Degos was almost incoherent as he slammed punch after punch into my chest. It hurt, but I had inherited the power of the Earth, just as he had. With it came the durability of the stone. I couldn't keep dealing with Degos and still concentrate on the battle in my head. Earth was his strength, and he needed to stay connected to it. I didn't want to kill him, but I needed him off of me. Air was the only thing I could think of, so I called down a funnel of wind, and jerked him from the ground. The pummeling stopped as he was pulled into the Air, where I left him spinning in a vortex of wind.

"Some people just do not listen," I gasped, with blood running from my lip.

Those hits had hurt like hell.

I returned to the battle raging within my body. Fire. Fire to forge the metal. It felt like I was burning as the Fire rolled toward the cage. Then I realized I was really burning, as Kalib let loose with a bolt of Fire. Fire coated my skin, but it caused no more than discomfort. I returned a bolt of Fire back at him that made him gape.

"What are you?"

"Trying to get this under control! Just let me be!"

"We cannot let you slaughter our citizens, dark one!" He darted in, and his fiery fist slammed into my chest, sending me somersaulting across the plaza.

The fire in my head was waning, and I could see the darkness starting to slide through the bars again.

"Kalib! I am not the enemy! Just let me finish!"

"You would lie, Void Mage? We all saw the transformation!"

He released another bolt of Fire, and I did the only thing I could think of. Water coalesced around him and smothered the flames. His head protruded from the waterspout. I didn't want to kill Kalib. He was a hero and had been protecting the city of Maltos for decades.

I returned to my mind. It was hard to concentrate with the throbbing in my ribs. I think one of my ribs may have been broken. But I kept the flame on the bars.

"Air to fan the flames," I muttered and drew from the Element.

The Fire grew white hot as the Air fed the flame.

I felt wetness on my face as Jenisa landed before me.

"Just...wait..." I said as I dropped to my knees. I couldn't hold all the Elements inside and out. I could feel the crushing weight of all that I held.

"Water...to...quench the flame..."

I dropped the two Elementals and drew from the Water. I left my fate to Jenisa and dropped all my outer defenses. Every ounce of my strength would be needed to bring this to an end. All the Elements flared inside me, and the cage was done.

I felt the massive column of Earth as it plunged downward from where Degos held it. I could not defend from it. I fell to the ground as the cage finished. At least there would not be another dark wizard killing the innocents of Maltos. I had defeated it, even if I did not survive. If I had let it defend me, I would have destroyed the Elementals who came for me. I couldn't live with that.

Why had the column not crushed me?

I opened my eyes to see a dome of ice surrounding us, and Jenisa was on her knees, trying to hold it from collapsing.

I dragged myself from the ground, and with the darkness safely contained, I drew power from the Elements once more. The ice dome dissolved, and I slapped aside the column of dirt and rock. It fell to the ground as a powder. Kalib's Fire just circled around my raised hand, and Juli hovered in the Air behind them with her head cocked to the side. She was staring at something behind me. I turned back to see the Minstrel standing amongst the stones.

"The time of the Gods is coming to an end." His voice was everywhere. It reverberated through the city. "The age of the Keakileris is come, and the dawning of the age of Dragons is upon us. I, Bolivor, God of the Heartstone, have spoken. Zaroliss, son of the Dragon, your true form awaits."

I felt strange as the Elements inside me thrummed their power, and everything *shifted*. Something felt different, and wonderful. I turned my head to look at my body, which should have been impossible. Scales of every color shimmered as my body moved.

"Zaro?"

I held an arm out, and she stepped into the clawed palm with no sign of fear. I raised her to my eye level.

My voice was heard inside the minds of all those around me.

My mother always said I have an affinity for the Elements.

* * * * *

Christopher Woods Bio

Christopher Woods, teller of tales, writer of fiction, and professional liar is the author of multiple series, which include his popular *Soulguard* series, the *Legend* series in the *Four Horsemen Universe*, *The Fallen World*, and *Traitor's Moon* in Kevin Steverson's *Salvage Universe*. He has written nine novels and been featured in several anthologies. As a carpenter of thirty years, he spends his time building, whether it be homes or worlds. He lives in Woodbury, TN with his wonderful wife and daughter. To see what he is doing, just go to www.theprofessionalliar.com.

# # # # #

The Game's Afoot by Christopher G. Nuttall

"I wanted the feeling of romance and the sense of wonder I had known as a kid. I wanted the world to be what they had promised me it was going to be—instead of the tawdry, lousy, fouled-up mess it is."

-Heinlein, *Glory Road*

The hot air stole all the moisture out of my throat.

I forced myself to relax as the horse galloped across the desert, navigating by the distant mountains alone. Navigation charms don't work well near the Desolation, and we were well off the handful of makeshift roads running through the mountainous passes and dry lands of Tidak Bertamadun. Civilisation itself is thin on the ground here; the handful of inhabitants permanently suspicious of anyone from outside their tribal lands. Even the Thousand-Year Empire found it hard to maintain its grip on the region, and *they* had Objects of Power.

We'll get there in time, I told myself as I eyed the storm in the distance. The dust alone would have been a nightmare, but the flickers of raw magic blown in from the east would be worse. Here, on the edge of the Desolation, the merest touch of raw magic could be dangerous. The locals seemed to cope, somehow, but us...? We had only a handful of unreliable charms and our cloaks to protect us. *We have to get there in time.*

The horse whinnied uncomfortably as the wind picked up, blowing sand and dust into our eyes. I adjusted the cloak as best I could, silently grateful the locals believed in covering themselves from head to toe in these formless black cloaks. We'd made jokes about them when we moved our forces into their lands, but I'd come to learn they were practical in more ways than one. No one went out unprotected, unless they were mad or stupid. The closer we moved to the Desolation, the more dangerous it became.

I gritted my teeth as the fortress slowly came into view, sitting on the mountain like a brooding spider. It wasn't a local design. The Thousand-Year Empire had built it, back when it had occupied the country and tried to turn it into a colony. And then it had been abandoned, only to regularly change hands as local kings and princes struggled for power and supremacy. And *now* it blocked our way. We didn't have time for a long siege. We *had* to get through it as quickly as possible.

Well, you wanted adventure, I reminded myself. The spellcaster on my belt, hidden under the cloak, felt heavy. *And now you're going to get it.*

I cursed under my breath. Miles to the north, an entire army was trapped in an unfriendly city. Ruthven didn't like outsiders, any more than the rest of the damned country. I'd been lucky to be away on patrol when the army had been assembled and dispatched, or I would have been with it when the gates closed, and all hell broke loose. If that fool Lord Robertson hadn't thought it would be a good idea to put one of his allies on Tidak Bertamadun's throne…I snorted at the thought. The locals would sooner commit suicide than take orders from a king who took orders himself. They respected power and might, magical and mundane. They didn't respect weaklings. I'd had that drilled into me over the last two years. In many ways, Tidak Bertamadun was just like home.

And Lord Robertson is going to be in deep shit when he gets home, I thought, dryly. Starting a war was bad enough. Starting a war and *losing* it was worse. *If we manage to get him home.*

I rubbed my forehead as the fortress grew closer. General Lord Allen, my commanding officer, had dispatched a relief column at once, but there was no way the troops could rescue the army and fight their way out of Tidak Bertamadun as long as that fortress remained in unfriendly hands. The lines of communication were weak, almost non-existent. The troops had to carry everything themselves, right down to food and drink. Lord Allen had been very clear on the mission. Take the fortress, rescue the army, and fall back to friendly territory. There was no time to teach the locals a lesson. Ancients knew they'd already taught one to us.

We cantered past a handful of local dwellings, a pair of cowled men—or women; it was impossible to tell—watching us with unseen eyes as we vanished into the distance. The locals had a whole string of taboos surrounding men and women, with men doing the fighting and women doing the magic. I didn't pretend to understand it. Everyone could do magic—I knew hundreds of spells myself—but it was rare to find a local man who admitted, openly, to casting even the simplest of spells. They'd rather starve than touch their magic. But I had to admit, they knew how to survive in the wasteland. I knew I'd die within days if I found myself cut off from all help. It was unlikely I'd find anyone willing to help me if I asked.

I glanced back at my four men, their faces hidden behind cowls and cloaks. They were all experienced men; they all spoke the native language perfectly, but the moment we took off our cloaks, we would be exposed. We simply didn't *look* like the natives. We'd cast glamours to hide our true faces, but there was nothing we could do to keep the enemy from looking through them if they realised we were there. A skilled magician would have no trouble spotting us. I hated to think what might await us if we were caught before it was too late.

In the distance, well behind us, I saw dust rising to the sky. The relief column was keeping its distance, advancing slowly toward the fort. They'd pick up speed as soon as night fell, hoping to be there by the time we opened the gates. *If we open the gates.* I knew, all too well, that everything depended on us. There was no *time* to go around the fortress, no *time* to do anything else that might save the army. At best, our men would be forced to walk under the yoke after they surrendered; at worst, they'd all be brutally slaughtered. Lord Allen would take a terrible revenge, of that I was sure, but it wouldn't bring back the dead. And then there would be questions asked about just what we were doing in Tidak Bertamadun in the first place.

We're here to keep our enemies out, I thought as we cantered up the road. *And they're here to keep us out.*

I snorted at the thought. Lord Robertson was an ass. No, that was too kind. He was an aristocrat of a particularly stupid sort, too well-connected to be ignored, and too stupid to be trusted with anything important. And so he'd been sent here, where he'd been told our enemies were on the verge of gaining control of Tidak Bertamadun through the former king. I had a nasty feeling he'd been conned. The locals had no qualms about exploiting the ignorance and arrogance of outsiders. Ancients knew they'd had plenty of practice. They might be primitive—their spellcasting was weak and their forgery skills non-existent—but they were far from stupid. They knew telling Lord Robertson that our enemies were making advances would be more than enough to convince him to send an army into unfriendly territory. And now that army was at their mercy.

The fortress reared up in front of us as we slowed our ride, giving any unseen observers plenty of time to take a good look at us. The local customs forced them to offer hospitality to anyone who wanted it, a tradition that had fallen out of favour in my homeland, but only as long as the guests behaved themselves. It was terrifyingly easy to give offense to the locals, even through something as simple as casting a spell in their house. Thankfully, we weren't going into a local dwelling, not here. The rules would be a little more relaxed.

I held up a hand as the gate opened, revealing a pair of cloaked and cowled men carrying spellcasters that dated back over a hundred years. I wondered if they knew their spellcasters drew on their magic to function, something they should have found utterly taboo. The women *had* to know, I was sure. They'd probably found some way to justify it, if the men had ever bothered to ask. I didn't think *I* would have asked, if I'd suspected the truth. People were very good at ignoring inconvenient realities as long as they weren't rubbed in their face.

"Greetings, friend." Not for the first time, I wondered why the locals stripped all individuality from men and women alike. Outside, it was hard to tell just who was who. "And why are you coming this way?"

"We seek shelter from the storm," I said in the same language. I'd spent three years learning both the language itself and the underlying cultural assumptions that governed how it was spoken. The locals prided themselves on being different from the rest of the continent. "We bring blessings upon your home."

The first man seemed to nod. It was hard to tell. "You may use the guest barracks," he said curtly. "Your swords may be needed later."

"We stand at your service," I lied smoothly. Guests had an obligation to help defend their hosts if they came under attack. It was one I had no intention of keeping. "Our blades stand ready to defend you."

We exchanged a handful of pleasantries, then escorted our horses to the stables and handed them over to the grooms. The young boys were unveiled, surprisingly. I guessed they were slaves, probably kidnapped from other tribes or more settled lands further to the south. They seemed cheerful enough, but I knew they were at immense risk of mistreatment...or worse...if they weren't rescued. Lord Robertson had justified the military deployment by pledging to eradicate slavery. I had the feeling the locals wouldn't let him even *begin* to emancipate the slaves.

I looked around with interest as we walked through the inner gatehouse and into the fortress itself. The walls were made of...*something*, a metal no one had been able to duplicate since the Thousand-Year Empire fell. The interior looked oddly disconcerting, as if the original builders had been giants. They must have been at least two metres tall...I shook my head at the thought. Neither us nor the locals were *that* tall. I figured they'd merely wanted to show off what they could do, back then. A great deal of knowledge had been lost when the Thousand-Year Empire had died.

The locals themselves moved through the lower levels, their faces hidden behind omnipresent veils. It looked more like a small bazaar than the heart of a fortress, a handful of traders trying to make a quick profit by selling everything from cooked food to goods they'd purchased or looted from the neighbouring tribes. The locals had no concept of property rights, beyond an argument that boiled down to *might makes right*. If you couldn't hang onto your property, they argued, you didn't deserve to keep it. That was why we had to keep mounting punitive expeditions into enemy territory. The locals would take anything that wasn't nailed down.

And yet they can barely feed themselves, I thought coldly. *We couldn't rely on them to feed us if we cast compulsion spells on everyone in sight.*

I sensed magic drifting through the air as we walked past the female barracks, the doors firmly closed. Rumour had it that any man who entered female territory was turned into a woman, permanently. Or simply made a eunuch. The women defended their territory with a viciousness that was probably entirely justified. They wielded a surprising amount of power, given they had no formal voice in tribal councils. But then, without them, the tribes would literally become extinct. I tested the magic lightly and smiled to myself. It was strong, but unfocused. My sister could do a *much* better job, even though she'd been sent to a finishing school that specialised in turning young women's brains into mush. I suspected the teachers had their work cut out for them with her.

The male barracks were odd, a cluster of tents pitched within a large room. I guessed there'd originally been bunks for the soldiers, before they'd been removed somewhere in the last thousand years. The fortress itself was practically indestructible, but the interior furnishings had decayed a long time ago. I nodded to my comrades as we picked a corner of the giant room and started to pitch our own tent. The locals would respect our boundaries. I had no qualms about taking advantage of their customs. We were short on other options.

I crawled into the tent, cast a handful of spells to blur surveillance, and removed my hood. Flecks of sand cascaded out of the wool, little sparks of magic flickering as the sand drifted down to the floor. I worked the magic into my spells, ensuring that none of the locals would notice anything *odd* about the magic. If the women went prying, as they could, they'd have no reason to suspect I wasn't *local*. There were charms woven into cloaks and cowls to keep spies from peeking at their wearers. But my spells might feel a little different.

MacManus removed his cowl and smiled at me. "So far, so good."

I nodded and glanced at my watch. "And now we wait," I said. "Five hours to go."

"Yes, sir," MacManus said. "We'd better get some rest."

I nodded as the others started to unpack the rations and hand them round. I took a potions bar and chewed it, trying not to grimace at the taste. I think they make them as foul as possible on purpose. I would have preferred to eat something local—the local food was very good—but the risk of infection could not be ignored. We'd lost too many men to diarrhea and vomiting for me to take the risk, particularly when we were miles from friendly territory. The locals would definitely suspect *something* if they saw one of us throwing up after eating. They had strong stomachs. They were used to the food. We weren't.

You wanted adventure, I reminded myself, as I set a spell to wake me in four hours. *And you got it...*

WHEN VALOR MUST HOLD | 47

The spell jerked me awake what felt like seconds later. I started, grasping for my magic before remembering where I was. MacManus and the others sat up, looking ready for anything. I took a hasty drink of water, then cast a glamour over myself. It would be obvious to anyone who looked too closely, but I couldn't risk wearing the cloak and cowl while we carried out the mission. The robes would simply get in my way.

I looked from face to face. "Ready?"

"Yep." MacManus looked cheerful. He was the only one. "We're ready."

I checked and rechecked my glamour, then inched out of the tent. Snores echoed through the air, coming from a handful of men who hadn't bothered pitching their own tents before going to sleep. I eyed them warily, then headed to the door. Guards, slaves, or lone travellers…it hardly mattered, as long as they stayed asleep. I was tempted to cast a general sleeping spell that should have kept them *all* asleep, but I knew it would be dangerous. There was too great a chance of setting off alarms and rousing the garrison against us.

And that would be bad, I told myself, as I peered through the door. A faint stench hung in the air—the latrines were just down the corridor—but there was no one in sight. *If we get caught before we open the gates, the entire army is doomed.*

I glanced at MacManus and my companions, then carefully altered my glamour as I inched down the corridor. A proper invisibility charm might also have set off alarms, but a simple obscurification spell might *just* keep us hidden for a few seconds longer if no one was expecting to see us. It was astonishing what someone could miss if they didn't expect to see it.

I reminded myself that it would only buy me a few seconds at best. I couldn't afford to forget it. The locals were *sharp*. If they sensed a slight movement in the air, particularly inside the fortress, they'd know *something* was wrong. I kept a wary eye out for trouble as we inched past the female quarters, the doors still firmly closed and warded. I wondered, sourly, why none of the women had accepted the offer of a scholarship to study in our homeland. But then, perhaps we should be grateful. The women were dangerous enough already. Raw magic ran strong in Tidak Bertamadun.

A guard stood at the door, staring into the darkened courtyard. I braced myself, then carefully—very carefully—cast a stunning spell. The power was too low to trigger alarms—I hoped—but the man tumbled to the ground anyway. He'd awaken in a few minutes with a splitting headache, convinced one of the women had hexed him. He wouldn't complain, I suspected. The men and women both would laugh at him, if for different reasons. I stepped over his body and hurried into the darkness, eyeing the handful of men on the walls. The relief force was only a short distance from the fortress, if everything had gone to plan. If it hadn't...

Worry about that problem when you come to it, I thought, as I led the way to the gatehouse and pressed against the metal wall. It felt solid, almost unbreakable. The fortress could be stormed, but it would be costly. The relief column didn't have the time. *Right now, you have a job to do.*

The metal door was closed and locked, a nasty-looking charm drifting over the keyhole. I guessed one of the women had tightened the defences, with or without the men's permission. I studied it for a moment, trying to decide how best to unlock it. But the charm had been woven into a dozen others, ready to trigger the alarm if the charm came undone. I was morbidly impressed. I knew sorcerers back home who wouldn't have done such a good job.

Clever, I thought. *Fuck.*

MacManus tapped my shoulder, then pointed his spellcaster at the metal door. I shook my head—there was no way blasting down the door would work out well for us—then knocked on the door. There was a pause, just long enough for me to think I'd screwed up completely, then the door opened. A young woman—I was sure she was a woman, even though she wore a cloak and a cowl—stared at me. I pushed my way in, lifting the spellcaster to cast a stunning spell. She reacted faster, snapping off a transfiguration spell. I blocked it—I'd learnt how to deflect them in school—and stunned her as hard as I could. Her robes blocked most of the spell, but enough leaked through to send her stumbling to the ground. I smacked the spellcaster over her head, just to make sure. If there was one thing I'd learnt from my sister, it was never to take chances with sorceresses...

My comrades ran past me, firing their spellcasters at the handful of sentries. They reacted quickly, but we'd caught them off guard. Only two of them managed to draw their spellcasters and fire back before we killed them, ensuring they couldn't get in our way. I ducked a curse that would have taken my head off if it had hit me, then killed the caster as we swept through the remainder of the gatehouse. One man tried to hit MacManus, rather than use magic; MacManus punched him in the face, then hexed him as he reeled back. They simply wouldn't surrender.

"Get the gate open," I snapped. Outside, I felt a quiver running through the air. Someone had sounded the magical alarm. The women were already alert. We had bare seconds before they roused the men. "Hurry!"

The locals believed their gate to be impregnable. Under normal circumstances, their confidence would have been entirely justified. It was really nothing more than a thick slab of metal, raised and lowered by a complex system of charmed pulleys that were, in some ways, Objects of Power themselves. But our sorcerers had taken a look at the system when we'd occupied the fortress, briefly, and spotted the weakness. From the outside, the metal slab was practically indestructible. But from the inside, it could be knocked out of place, leaving the gateway open to enemy attack. I clambered into the upper level, keeping a wary eye out for enemy fighters, and inspected the system.

One might as well invest in a suit of armour that blocked everything, but didn't cover one's head or arms.

I pushed the thought aside as I hastily cast a pair of pressure charms, followed by a simple exploding curse. The impregnable metal would become a weakness, channelling the blast into the uppermost structure holding the slab in place. I heard shouting outside, followed by the crackle of spellcasters, as I put the final spell in place, then turned to clamber back down the ladder. I was barely in time. The entire building shook violently, and dust and pieces of debris dropped from the ceiling as the spells detonated. Moments later, a dull thud ran through the compound as the slab of metal hit the ground. I hoped no one had been underneath it when it fell. Friend or foe, it wasn't a death I'd wish on my worst enemy.

"They're coming!" MacManus shouted. I could hear hexes slamming into the gatehouse's walls as the enemy came at us. "They're coming!"

I cast a light spell of my own, informing Lord Allen that the gatehouse was open, then drew my spellcaster as the enemy hurled themselves at the gate. My magic started to drain rapidly as I cast spell after spell, curses and hexes tearing through them...enough to slow them down, but not enough to *stop* them. The gatehouse was a bottleneck. They knew it as well as I did. If they could drive us out, they might *just* be able to keep Lord Allen from breaking in.

"Watch out!" MacManus shouted. I felt a massive spell crash into my wards, fragmenting them. It was barely controlled, as if the casters had lost their nerve halfway through the spell, but powerful enough to do a *lot* of damage. "They're coming..."

I ducked another hex, then found myself grappling with a local who'd thrown himself through the wards and directly into my face. We struggled desperately for a long moment, both of us trying to kill the other. He was strong, too strong. I knew I was going to lose...and then MacManus brought his club down on the man's head, breaking his skull. I pushed the body aside—there would be time to honour him later—as I heard trumpets outside the fortress. Moments later, the first line of infantrymen rushed into the fort.

"Storm the gates!" someone shouted. "Storm the gates!"

I tensed, casting a spell that should identify us as friendly to the infantrymen. After everything we'd gone through, I didn't want to die at their hands. The men kept coming, driving the locals out of the gatehouse, and forcing them to retreat into the fortress itself. A dozen hex grenades exploded, balls of brilliant—and deadly—light throwing the complex into sharp relief. I caught a glimpse of a pair of locals dying in screaming agony as the light burned through them, randomised hexes tearing them apart. Their spellcasters exploded seconds later. It must have been something of a relief.

"Hold the courtyard!" an officer shouted. He wore a red tunic, presumably so the blood wouldn't show and demoralise the troops. I knew him, vaguely. He was of the very highest noble blood and had little time for a natural-born son like myself. But he had nerve. I'll give him that much. "Get the other gate!"

I glanced at MacManus. "They're going to make a stand inside the fortress."

"Looks that way," MacManus agreed. "You think we can get inside first?"

I looked at the men forming up in the courtyard and nodded, then directed him to follow me. The other two could help plan the offensive, if the officer was prepared to listen. I glanced up at a murder hole someone had cut into the metal walls, then levitated myself up and threw a hex grenade into the room. A flash of green light blazed through the crack, sending unearthly tingles down my spine. Someone screamed from inside the room. I hastily cast a twisting charm on myself and glided through the gap, rematerialising myself as soon as I was inside the room. Blood stained the floor, a handful of horribly mutilated bodies lying against the far wall. I felt my stomach twist and forced myself to look away. The lucky ones had died quickly. The men in front of me...

Someone shouted from further down the corridor. I pushed my qualms aside and hurled another grenade in their direction. The flash of light tore through the air. I looked away as the light blazed against my mind's eye, then hurried into the corridor. A man had been caught at the edge of the blast, his lower half twisted so badly he knew he'd die through shock alone. He stared up at me, his dark eyes practically screaming the agony he refused to show on his face. I put a fireball through his skull. It was a mercy.

The building shook down below as the infantry finally began their assault. Caught between two fires, the defenders were unable to either retreat or cover themselves. I allowed myself a smirk, then inched down their stairs and peered into the slave barracks. Young men sat behind bars, watching and waiting. I silently promised them I'd do whatever I could to get them back home—or get them somewhere safer if their families didn't want them. They hadn't had any choice when they'd been enslaved, but it didn't matter. I knew how things worked. Their families would have preferred they committed suicide rather than live as slaves. It was a terrible dishonour.

I liked to think I'd have the nerve to cut my own throat if I was enslaved, but I didn't *know* it. It would be easy to tell myself, time and time again, that I was merely biding my time and waiting to escape. And then I would have become a slave in truth as well as name. *Poor boys.*

I glanced at them, silently noting that they were *all* boys. Girls got kidnapped, too, but female captives were handed straight to the women and never seen again. Or maybe they were…I'd read books on the locals, written by men who'd never actually *talked* to one of the locals, that had babbled about sexual monopolies. The women taught the female slaves how to be one of them, rather than simply giving them to the men. It secured their position within the tribe. Or something along those lines. I had no way to know.

Magic crackled at me as I reached the lower level, the women pressing their power into a single giant *KEEP OUT* spell. I gritted my teeth, marvelling at both the power and its lack of direction. They could have stopped the entire assault force in its tracks if they'd known what they were doing. Even so, they could kill *me*, if they focused. MacManus held back as I raised my hands, dispelling what little remained of the glamour. It was a request for an audience. I just hoped the women were disposed to grant it.

The magic faded as a cloaked and cowled figure stepped into view. The woman moved like my grandmother, but there was more than a hint of solid determination not to show weakness in her gait. Here, so far from civilisation, weakness *killed*. I nodded my head, feeling oddly naked without my own veil. It made me wonder, sometimes, how men and women managed to produce children. Did the locals marry, as we understood it? We didn't know.

"I greet you," I said, carefully. The old woman was untrained, by our standards, but that didn't make her harmless. I'd heard plenty of horror stories from the homeland to know to treat her with utmost respect. A flash of raw magic could *kill*. "The fortress is ours."

The woman's voice was raspy. "And you think *we* will be yours?"

I chose my next words carefully. Local warfare was really nothing more than tribal raiding. It wasn't uncommon, I'd been told, for girls to be snatched from one tribe and inducted into another...the whole system worked, in a manner we didn't pretend to understand. There seemed to be little bad feeling about the raids, as if they were nothing more than games. But now...if they saw us as a bigger tribe, they might think we had a claim on *all* of them.

"We need to hold the fortress," I said. "If you do not impede us, we will release you when we withdraw, and you can go back to your tribal lands. Or claim the fortress for yourself. If not..."

The old woman leaned forward. "We will stay in our domain," she said. "And you will stay out."

"As long as you don't impede us, that will be fine," I said. "It will be our honour."

I bowed once to her, then turned my back and walked away. The woman would tell the other women, and they'd stay hidden away until the fortress was abandoned after the campaign was over. It shouldn't take very long, I told myself. They had food and room to sleep, and hopefully they'd stay out of our way. The only other option was killing them.

We walked down the stairs and reported to Lord Allen, who'd taken possession of the fortress in the name of the king. He took our report, then dismissed us. Dawn was breaking in the distance, the relief column riding through the fortress, stopping for a quick rest and then riding onward to the enemy city. I wondered, idly, if Lord Robertson knew of our approach. It was hard to use communications sorcery so close to the Desolation. But right now that was someone else's problem.

Or so I thought.

"I have a job for you," Lord Allen said after we snatched a little breakfast. "I need you to take a message to Lord Robertson."

I hid my irritation with an effort. There weren't *many* people who had a hope in hell of getting through enemy lines, not without being detected, caught, and brutally executed. I could do it. MacManus could do it. The rest of the army? Not so much, unless they got *very* lucky. It would have to be me.

"I'll go through Hawks Pass," I said to MacManus. "You can go through Eagle's Nest."

"Good thinking," MacManus said. Two men would attract more attention than one. "Good luck, sir."

"Ancients be with you," I replied as I collected my horse. The local horses were already being pressed into service. There were never enough horses in the country. "I'll see you on the far side."

I pulled my cloak and cowl back into place, then cantered out of the gate and headed north to the distant road. The sound of chatter and troopers riding into the distance faded as I headed away from the fortress, spurring the horse onward. I felt alone, even though I knew from grim experience that the desolate—and hazy—wasteland could conceal an entire band of wandering tribesmen. The locals were *good* at concealing themselves, with or without modern spells. An armed man could be hiding behind a bush that looked too small to conceal a toddler, let alone a full-grown man. I kept one hand on my spellcaster, doing my best to look ready for a fight. Sometimes if you looked ready to fight, you didn't *have* to.

The air grew hotter as the sun rose, casting beams of light into the valleys. I was forced to slow as the landscape turned harsher, the mountains narrowing toward me as we cantered into the pass. The valley looked as though it had been carved by water, but I knew there was little water to be found, outside an oasis or two. A handful of white bones gleamed by the broken roadside, the last remnants of people or animals who had tried to run the gap without taking water or food with them. There was no time to mourn. I felt my mouth start to turn to sandpaper as I rode onward, trying to get out of the valley before it was too late. Raw magic hung in the air, mocking me. It was suddenly easy to believe I'd run right into the Desolation itself.

I must have been mad, I thought, as I forced myself onward. *Why are we even here?*

I shuddered. People back home had looked at maps and concluded our rivals would have no trouble establishing themselves if we didn't get there first. I looked around the terrain—the *real* terrain—and snorted in disbelief. The terrain alone was a major headache, even if we didn't have to contend with tribesmen who hated everyone who wasn't part of their tribe. It hadn't been easy to get Lord Robertson's army to Ruthven, even though it had mostly ridden on horseback. I couldn't imagine getting an army all the way to the enemy border without losing half the men during the march. Who needed the enemy? We'd destroy our own army by marching north.

The valley broke suddenly, revealing Ruthven lying below me. I allowed myself a tight smile, even though I could see plumes of smoke rising from the city and hundreds of tents pitched along the edge of the valley. Lord Robertson was still holding out...I jumped as I sensed a flare of magic behind me, then ducked as a fireball shot over my head. A team of enemy horsemen were cantering toward me...I wheeled my horse toward the city, digging in my spurs to convince the beast to run. The horse made a sound of protest but started to gallop anyway as more fireballs rocketed over my head. I kept as low as I could, hoping I'd get to the city before it was too late. I didn't want to die in sight of the city walls.

Everything turned into a nightmare. Fireballs and arrows flew through the air, some of them coming too close for comfort. The horse jerked from side to side, the well-trained beast knowing it had to make us as hard a target as possible. I drew my spellcaster and pointed it over my shoulder, firing a handful of hexes at random. I had no way to tell if I'd actually *hit* anything, but I heard someone shout behind me. I hoped I'd hit him, whoever he was. But it would only make him madder. The horse galloped faster, flanks heaving as it drove onward. I clung on for dear life, trying not to think about what would happen if—when—the horse tripped on the rough ground and I went flying. I readied a couple of spells that might save my life, then hurled a blasting curse at the road behind me. The ground shook, but the volley of fireballs and arrows came to a sudden stop. I took advantage of it to force the horse to gallop faster. The road was *really* starting to crumble. The horse buckled...

I found myself flying through the air, and the ground came up to hit me. I triggered a cushioning spell, but I still landed badly enough to knock the wind out of me. I heard a shout behind me, the tribesmen recovering from their shock and coming to get me. I rolled over, bracing myself for the final battle. And then a hail of spells hurtled over my head, throwing the tribesmen back in disarray. Strong hands gripped me, hauled me to my feet, and half-carried me to the gates. I was safe.

Lord Robertson was waiting just inside the gates. He'd been a portly man the last time I'd seen him. It looked as if he'd lost a great deal of weight in the past few months. He was practically emaciated. His uniform looked ragged. I wondered, grimly, if his tailor was amongst the dead. Lord Robertson had made a point of taking a tailor with him, on the grounds it would impress the locals. They'd be more impressed if he'd wrestled a dragon single-handedly. So would I.

"My Lord," I said, formally. "The fortress has fallen. The relief column is on the way. You have to be ready to break out."

Lord Robertson was too tired to pretend to be anything but relieved. I didn't blame him, even though he was the architect of his own misfortunes. If he'd bothered to read any of the reports from agents like me, the reports we carefully filed every time we returned to HQ, he clearly hadn't taken anything we'd said onboard. There was no way we could impose a ruler by force and expect him to be accepted once our troops were withdrawn. It would have been a great deal better if we'd covertly backed our candidate, without ever openly showing our hand. But that would have been too quiet for Lord Robertson. He could hardly have bragged about it without giving the game away.

And I would have felt sorry for him if he hadn't gotten so many of his men killed and put the rest in immense danger, I thought. The army was small, as armies went, but…it was the largest army outside the homeland itself. *And he might have gotten one of my men killed.*

Ruthven was an interesting city, although it had changed in the year since I'd last visited. I'd been in disguise last time, studying the terrain. It was clear that Lord Robertson hadn't bothered to read those reports, either. There had been bazaars and homes that were oddly modern—if firmly separated into male and female sections—and even a handful of schools. Now the modern buildings were piles of rubble, the bazaar was firmly closed, and the schools were scorched and pitted with spellfire. There were only a couple of people on the streets, apart from our soldiers, but I could sense a looming air of menace pervading the city. Lord Robertson hadn't made himself popular. I supposed that nothing short of not occupying the city in the first place—if that—could have done it.

I forced myself to take a sip of water and relax as the troops rushed into position, ready to march out and do battle with the tribesmen one final time. MacManus hadn't appeared, which meant…what? I knew from bitter experience that a man could get lost or simply discover that it took days or weeks longer than expected to reach his destination. Or he might be dead. I tried not to think about it as the signs of Lord Allen's approach became obvious. A green flare appeared in the air, visible even at noon. The relief column was in position. It was time to go.

Lord Robertson had the same idea. "It's time to go home," he said as he mounted his horse and raised his sword. "Let's go."

The men cheered and followed him. I sat back in the saddle, watching as the tribesmen fired a handful of spells and vanished into the undergrowth before the troops could close with them. They disliked pitched battles, thankfully. A warlord with a small army under his command was a major player, but not if the army got chewed up and spat out by a modern force with grudges to pay off. They'd snipe at us as we left, I was sure, but not much else. The odds were in our favour for once. I hoped they'd stay that way until we got back to the fortress, then home.

You should leave playing the game to the people who know it, I thought as I stared at Lord Robertson's head. *And be prepared to lose...*

I shook my head. There'd be people who'd say, back home, that we'd been defeated. And in a sense, they'd be right. We had failed to achieve even *one* of our objectives before we headed home with our tails between our legs. There were going to be inquires and inquests, and public demands for explanations they didn't want to hear, and scapegoats who were unlucky enough to be in the wrong place at the wrong time. Lord Robertson would get away with his mistakes, I was sure. On paper, his plan had been perfect. Reality had been much less obliging.

But it didn't matter. All that mattered was that we'd gotten the army out of a trap...

...And now, thankfully, we were on our way home.

* * * * *

Christopher G. Nuttall Bio

Christopher Nuttall has been planning sci-fi books since he learned to read. Born and raised in Edinburgh, Chris created an alternate history website and eventually graduated to writing full-sized novels. Studying history independently allowed him to develop worlds that hung together and provided a base for storytelling. After graduating from university, Chris started writing full-time. As an indie author, he has published fifty novels and one novella (so far) through Amazon Kindle Direct Publishing.

Professionally, he has published The Royal Sorceress, Bookworm, A Life Less Ordinary, Sufficiently Advanced Technology, The Royal Sorceress II: The Great Game and Bookworm II: The Very Ugly Duckling with Elsewhen Press, and Schooled in Magic through Twilight Times Books.

As a matter of principle, all of Chris's self-published Kindle books are DRM-free.

Chris has a blog where he published updates, snippets and world-building notes at http://chrishanger.wordpress.com/ and a website at http://www.chrishanger.net.

Chris is currently living in Edinburgh with his partner, muse, and critic, Aisha.

# # # # #

The Ogre's Brownies
by RJ Ladon

The snap of a branch grabbed Dogumrik's attention. He shifted his spear from one hand to the other. Pulling his dagger, he tossed it at Panao. The tip of the blade thunked into the wood, waking his companion. "Noise near the center of the village," he told Panao.

Panao nodded as he stared at the quivering dagger. He opened the door. "Noise at village center!" he shouted.

Bioluminescent insects buzzed awake, and their glow filled the barracks. Grunts and groans emanated from the bunks. Some brownies stirred and donned their leathers. Others sat up, sleep still thick in their eyes. Another loud crash echoed off the trees, followed by a startled scream.

"Rangers, get your gear." Shomede, Warden of the Glade, directed the seasoned brownie warriors. "Dog, you and Panao help with their armor and weapons."

"But, Father," Dogumrik complained. He had two cycles of coursework and training, plus countless cycles learning from his father. He was ready for action.

Shomede raised his spear, pointing it at him. "Do as you are told."

Dogumrik and Panao fetched equipment and weapons, helping to prepare the warriors. Once satisfied, the warden left the barracks with thirty experienced rangers.

The two youngest brownies in the Ranger Corps put on their fighting leathers, grabbed their spears, and went to find the excitement.

The direction the rangers took was lost to the night. The moon was new, and with only the stars to light the way, the two brownies continued to the center of the village. Shadows seemed to be everywhere.

Ferns that once grew thick were trampled and flattened. Huts and homes were tossed aside like twigs. Smoke and pitch fill the air. Brownies never used tar for torches. That was something a human would bring into the woods.

Panao pointed. Movement. They crept toward the activity. A twig snapped behind them. Dogumrik turned. He pressed his back against the smooth white bark of a birch tree. Something hunted them. He felt it in his bones. When he turned back, he saw Panao moving toward a mushroom hut.

Green eyes flashed, and Panao was in the maw of a black cat. The cat bit down, crunching, and disappeared into the shadows with its prize.

"Skunk piddle!" Dogumrik pressed his body against the tree trunk, trying to remain hidden. In the distance, light from a single torch held high threw unnatural shadows and light. Muffled screams of pain and fear seemed to move along with the flame, as if a giant carried the villagers.

Leaves rustled nearby, drawing his attention back to where he stood. *Was that a shadow, or the cat?* He held his breath as the very darkness seemed to move. Dogumrik darted away from the birch and hid under a shelf mushroom growing on the side of a fallen log. He needed to find his father. Shomede would know what to do and how to fight off their giant attacker.

Dogumrik worked his way toward the light and the tiny cries for help, taking advantage of the ferns that grew thick where trees fell and rot worked its magic. As he crept, his spear was poised to throw at the cat's green eyes.

The cries quieted, and the torchlight dimmed; the beast was leaving the area.

My clan! Dogumrik ran toward the voices, more afraid of losing his family than the cat.

"Dog, stop!"

Dogumrik flinched. He was no dog. He was a brownie warrior. Still, he slowed and turned to the familiar voice. "I must free our people."

"Don't be a fool. We must gather our remaining forces and attack at full strength."

Dogumrik bowed his head. "Yes, Father."

The old warrior bled from a head wound, and his brown leather sleeve was torn. "Come with me to the fortress," Shomede said, pulling his son to his side, leaning into him when it seemed his ankle might give out.

"What happened? Was it a great battle?" Dogumrik blurted out, unable to stop his curiosity.

"No battles are great, son." Shomede shook his head. "We heard the cries from the villagers, and we ran toward them. Weapons ready, we expected to find the enemy, but as we entered the clearing, a wicker net swooped down."

"How did you escape?"

"I didn't. The net hit me." Shomede gently touched his wounded head. Mud and blood caked his light brown hair. "I must have blacked out. I woke when I heard you approach."

"What attacked us?"

"I don't know."

They walked in silence, studying the damage. Branches and twigs were broken high in the trees. Scorch marks on the leaves indicated torch height. Footprints in the mud revealed the giant's weight and size.

"Human?" Dogumrik poked his spear into the footprint, losing roughly half its length.

"No, it was bigger, heavier than a human." Shomede pointed. "Look, see the toes? It was barefoot. Human feet are tender. They wear boots."

Dogumrik nodded. He had never seen a human, but he knew the tales. They were monsters without magic who used brute strength to force nature to do their bidding. They planted vegetation in straight lines, breeding grains and vegetables into strange and horrifying abominations. They harnessed animals and whipped them into submission. They were frightful monsters of nightmares. "What do you think it was?"

"An ogre, or troll."

"It can't be a troll," Dogumrik stated.

"Why?"

"Because it had a torch. Trolls have excellent night vision."

"Very good," Shomede said. "You were paying attention. What else did you notice?"

Dogumrik frowned. "I saw Panao get eaten by a cat." Fear and anger flooded his mind, threatening tears.

"A cat?" Shomede shuddered beside him. "Raven carcass," he hissed. "That is bad news. We must find the queen and tell her."

Cats were creatures of magic, often used to hunt fae. When a feline was spotted within the forest, brownies watched and gave warning until it left. A cat working with an ogre or human could bring disaster to any fae clan.

They climbed the enormous burr oak tree and entered where a branch had broken off. Phosphorescent moss and insects lit their way into the heart of the tree, the meeting hall. The dome ceiling echoed with cries and whimpers of the scared and the wounded. A handful of elders huddled together, whispering.

The old shaman, Immat, and his acolyte walked among the injured, applying salves, tinctures, and bandages. The young acolyte had arrived in the village alone, with few belongings, and a raccoon as her companion. There was something odd between Immat and her. People whispered that she possessed Immat's mind, as he never had an acolyte before.

"Shomede, Dogumrik. You're alive." An older woman approached, hugging them. She gestured around the room. "We lost many." Her eyes were red. "You are the only warriors to return." She sniffled, but no more tears came.

"My queen," they said in unison.

"None of that nonsense." She frowned. "Come, we must decide what to do." She shuffled to the circle of elders.

Dogumrik blurted, "I'll tell you what we need to do. We need to rescue our clan." The young warrior thumped his spear butt against the floor.

"How?" Shomede glared at his son. "You and I are the last warriors. And if you saw a cat tonight, then the rumors are true."

"A cat?" the queen hissed. "Mother Moon, it can't be!" She shot a look at the shaman and his acolyte. "We were warned."

The circle of elders stared at each other in silence.

"We must gather what we can and move south," the queen said. "We must let the gods determine our people's fate."

"Our people are still alive!" Dogumrik shouted. "I heard their cries for help. We can save them."

"Don't be a fool, boy," his father admonished. "The ogre cannot be stopped, not by a warrior such as you."

"That's it? You're giving up?" Dogumrik snapped. "We could join forces with other fae and bring the battle to the ogre."

"No," admonished the queen, fear etched on her face. She looked more child than monarch. "The other fae have left the region, and we must also."

"Perhaps you need more than muscle and steel."

Dogumrik turned to see the young acolyte, Maramalik. Her soft green-leaf dress swayed as she fidgeted. Her mouse-head hat appeared to be staring at him.

"Don't listen to my acolyte. She's young and foolish." Immat scowled at her.

"I will not lose more of my people." The queen shook her head, then pointed to Dogumrik. "You search for survivors." She turned and pointed to Maramalik. "And you attend the wounded."

Dogumrik looked to Shomede. "Father," he begged.

"You will do as your monarch says. Do not humiliate me or your family with your insolence." Shomede leaned into the circle and talked with the others in undertones.

Dogumrik turned on his heel and stomped out of the chamber.

* * *

The morning sun revealed the carnage. Pristine ogre footprints contrasted sharply with the toppled and crushed huts. Dogumrik found blood, but no survivors. It appeared that the ogre prized even the dead. *To what end?*

He entered a partially crushed log. Maramalik was inside, collecting herbs and bottles from the disarray.

"What are you doing?"

Maramalik hissed, surprised. "You weren't supposed to see me." She continued to put items into a backpack. "If you must know, I'm going to track and kill the ogre."

"Immat would not approve." Dogumrik knelt in the clutter and looked for more intact items. He held up a bottle of purple liquid.

"Immat." She spat on the ground. "I've more experience and skills then he'll ever have." She shrugged. "I've used him to get what I want." Maramalik snatched the bottle from Dogumrik's hand and put it in her bag. "Immat will shed no tears for me." She flung the pack over her shoulder, then studied him. "Well, are you coming?"

"What?"

"Didn't you want to hunt the beast?"

"Yes." Dogumrik stood tall, trying to appear brave.

"Gather weapons and meet me by the rose bramble at high sun." Maramalik left the crushed log.

Dogumrik grabbed a bag from the floor and followed, but she was gone. He shrugged. Acolyte or not, shamans had powers he didn't understand. He went back to the barracks to collect weapons and food.

When the sun reached its zenith, Dogumrik arrived at the old rose bush.

"You're late." Maramalik tightened a braided-grass strap under the raccoon's chest.

"It's high sun." Dogumrik pointed.

Maramalik shaded her eyes and frowned at the sun. "Sun Father lies." She waved her arm and directed with her quartz-tipped staff. "We must hurry. Do you need Shelia to carry anything?"

Shelia curled her lip, showing her teeth, smiling, making a soft chattering sound. Her muzzle was grey with age.

"No, I prefer to carry my weapons. I have little else." Dogumrik studied the raccoon and wondered why the young shaman would have one as a companion. As pack animals, they had a reputation for breaking what they carried. "I should scout."

"There's no need." Maramalik pushed the ferns aside. Beyond was a path of destruction like a herd of antelope had crashed through the forest. Broken branches, footprints, and bent vegetation indicated the direction. "It's as if the ogre is inviting us." She shadowed the trail, Shelia following close behind.

"This isn't a good sign," Dogumrik grumbled, staying close to the acolyte. She was short, only reaching his shoulder, and appeared to be just a babe.

"Neither is the cat."

"Then why follow a trail that is so clearly marked? Are we not walking into a trap?"

"Knowing of a trap is the first step in avoiding it. Besides, time is of the essence." She picked up her pace.

Dogumrik trotted beside her. "You sound much older than you appear. How many cycles have you seen?"

"Eleven."

Dogumrik stumbled. He had seen twenty cycles, and some, like his father, still saw him as a child. Eleven cycles? He should return her to the village. Still he kept pace with her, unwilling to turn back. She knew the ogre or cat might kill her. Yet she persisted.

They continued for hours in silence. The trail never wavered from its direction. Eventually, Father Sun's red body fell toward the horizon.

"We need to set up camp for the night," Maramalik said. "It must be in a clearing with the sky open above, no trees."

Dogumrik had heard similar requests from Immat in the past. Even though he was surprised by her request, he knew what to look for. *Could a child so young be a full-fledged shaman?* He had doubts. A shaman took cycles of training, Maramalik couldn't be any different.

"There." He pointed. "From the sound of it, there is a stream, too."

Shelia stood upright, her nose twitching in the slight breeze. She chittered her approval.

"A stream would add to our good fortune." Maramalik glanced at Shelia, patting her shoulder. "Hurry," she called. The girl ran toward the stream. "Race you!" she shouted, giggling. The raccoon bounded, lumbering after her friend.

Dogumrik smiled, trotting after them. The acolyte could behave like a child, after all.

The shaman stopped at the stream's edge. Maramalik removed the raccoon's harness and set her belongings on a wide log that jutted into the stream. "Don't go far," she said to Shelia, giving the raccoon scratches where the harness rubbed.

Shelia waded into the stream, feeling under the water and mud for tidbits to eat.

Maramalik pulled a small drum from her bags, then sat with her back to the flowing water. The staff with the quartz crystal pointed to and caught the last rays of sunlight. The drum rested in her lap.

"Once the sun sets, I must ride my horse to the first world below. Do not light a fire. Do not talk. Do not stop me." Maramalik paused and raised a finger. "If my horse stops, you must wake me."

Dogumrik was uneasy being so close to a spirit-walking ritual. "To wake a shaman is unwise and dangerous," he said. When a shaman rode their horse to the world above or below, they were spending time with the dead. If the ritual was interrupted, those spirits could follow the shaman back, entering the world of the living, cursing anyone unlucky to witness.

"This trail is dangerous. If you do not wake me, then the secret of the ogre's defeat will remain with the dead." Her cold, dark eyes bored into his with an intensity he had never experienced before.

"You want to save your clan, do you not?" She pulled off her mouse-skin hat and set it beside her.

Dogumrik swallowed hard and nodded. "I will do as you request."

"Excellent." Maramalik began the ritual with prayers to the old gods. Three green leaves went into her mouth. She chewed them, allowing the sacrament to focus her mind and soul. The acolyte played the drum with a four-time rhythm. Her head and shoulders dipped and swayed with the sound.

The drum reminded Dogumrik of the beating hooves of steppe horses and buffalo. He felt the beats roll across his body and soul like Sanu, the children's nightmare. The cold fingers of fear tapped on his spine in time with the drum, drawing memories of his youth.

Dogumrik's eyes dipped closed. He slapped his face to stay awake. Still, his eyes weakened. The steady rhythm of the drum pulled at his sleeper's mind. *Sleep*, it told him, *sleep*. "No," he mumbled. He stood and stumbled away from the drum and the stream. Lighting bugs flashed, keeping the tempo of the drum. Even though he stood, his eyes closed.

Silence.

His brain screamed, and his eyes snapped open. He had not wandered off as he'd thought. He still perched on the log above the stream. Maramalik sat before him, unmoving.

Unmoving.

The drum.

Dogumrik jumped to his feet. *How long has the drum been silent?* He moved to Maramalik's side. She was not breathing. "Wake up!" he screamed. He shook her shoulders. Her head slumped forward.

He lifted her small form, surprised by her massive weight. He shook her. "Maramalik!" He raised his hand to slap her across the face. Her bodyweight shifted and wrenched free from his grasp, falling into the stream. She sank below the surface and didn't return.

"Skunk piddle!" Dogumrik jumped into the stream where Maramalik had disappeared. His hands flailed in the murky darkness until he touched something long and stringy—her hair. He pulled, then grabbed her clothing, heaving her to the surface.

She didn't wake or breathe.

Dogumrik carried her back to the log. He put the drum in her lap and set her hands on its leather surface. The drum thumped under her fingers. Maramalik's eyes snapped open, and she inhaled sharply.

"Why am I wet?"

"I panicked." Dogumrik fidgeted. "I didn't know how to wake you."

Maramalik laughed, warbling like a bird. She set the drum aside.

He sighed in relief. "Did you learn how to defeat the ogre?"

A yawn escaped her lips. "Yes." Her eyes blinked slowly and drooped. "We must befriend the lion, clean the beast's ears, and the wolf will conquer." She fluffed her hat and lay her head on it.

Fearing the dead had followed the shaman, Dogumrik searched for a better campsite, a better place to hide. Near the water's edge grew a sentinel, a tree with weeping limbs. The evergreen would provide cover from wind, rain, and prying eyes. Dogumrik collected soft grasses for bedding. When he returned to move Maramalik to the protection of the tree, she was missing. Shelia had pulled her onto the bank and curled up, covering the shaman with her tail.

When Dogumrik approached, Shelia growled. He stopped and took a step back until the raccoon became quiet. "Shelia, I need to move her to the shelter of the tree." He pointed to the sentinel. "You can come and sleep with us." As he spoke, he moved toward the raccoon and petted her muzzle.

Shelia relaxed, allowing him to carry Maramalik. The raccoon followed, chattering as if nervous. When he set the shaman on the bedding, Shelia curled up around her once more.

* * *

Maramalik stirred and sat up. She stroked Shelia's muzzle and scratched behind her ears. They chatted at each other.

Dogumrik watched, curious.

"Did you sleep?" Maramalik turned to look at him.

Dogumrik slid a flint arrowhead into an arrow shaft and secured it with nettle twine. "I dozed." He shrugged, not worried about sleep. He added the arrow to the growing bundle at his side.

"Did you bring food?"

He tossed a small woven grass pouch to her. "There's fruit leather and nutmeat in there. If you need anything else, you'll have to forage."

Beyond the sentinel's branches, the world grew lighter. "We ought to get moving. We don't know how far we have to go." Maramalik pulled out a strip of strawberry leather and put it between her teeth, then gave the pouch back. She combed her long hair with her fingers and stuffed her mouse hat in place.

Dogumrik bundled the arrows with a tie, setting them aside.

Maramalik eyed the large bundle of arrows. "How many weapons did you bring?"

"Four spears, two bows, and many arrows."

"Why so many?"

"A bowstring can break, and a spear can crack. I want to be prepared."

Maramalik nodded. She put the harness and her things back on the raccoon and walked the way they had come the night before.

Dogumrik trotted to catch them. "Did the queen or Immat tell you about this ogre?"

"No, I told them." Maramalik adjusted her hat. She looked away, refusing to say more.

"I don't understand."

She sighed. Maramalik pulled off her hat and looked into its beady eyes. She smoothed the fur on the nose. Tears welled up, running down her cheeks. "This was my father's hat." She hugged it, looking more her age than ever before. "He gave it to me the day I completed my first transformation."

Dogumrik continued walking, eyes focused on the path ahead.

"My clan, like yours, was taken during the night." She sniffled. "My father, too. Shelia protected me, hiding me under her tail and among her kits. Later, Shelia took me to him. The ogre had flayed him, pulling his organs to divine the future. He was barely alive." She took a shuddering breath, as if reliving the scene. "He asked me to avenge him. To save other clans." She stuffed the hat back in place, pulling the nose down. "It is my calling, my duty, to finish this monster."

"How old were you?"

"Eight." She shook her head. The mouse hat bobbed, threatening to fall.

"Raven carcass!" Dogumrik kicked a pebble out of his way. *It's no wonder she acts older than her cycles. She rides the demon horse, Sanu, living the nightmare.*

"I've been tracking the ogre ever since."

"The cat?"

"The cat is an unwilling servant."

Dogumrik raised his eyebrows. "How do you know?"

"The spirits told me. They share many things, knowledge of the past and future." Maramalik nodded as if deciding to tell a secret. "My mother and I died in childbirth. I returned. She did not. I'm a born shaman." She pulled her hat tight to her head. "My father was a great shaman. He taught me much in this world. He teaches me still."

A chill crept over him. Dogumrik frowned. "That explains why you speak as if you've seen thirty cycles."

"I've always talked this way."

Dogumrik ruffled her hat, messing her hair underneath. "I would be surprised to hear otherwise."

They continued until high sun. Dogumrik shaded his eyes. "We ought to be more careful. We've got to be close." He looked around. "That cat could be stalking us, and we'd never know."

"We are safe. The spirits said we would reach the ogre's hut unscathed." She patted Shelia's shoulder. "Shelia will warn and protect us."

The trail they followed had more grass than ferns, and fewer trees and bushes. For vast distances, the brown grass extended. Fewer birds sang, and rodents were conspicuously absent—cat sign.

Dogumrik chewed on his bottom lip. "I would feel better if we followed the trail at a distance. There's no cover here."

"The spirits said we'd be safe," Maramalik insisted.

"I trust my gut, not your spirits."

"Then you're a fool."

"Our safety is important."

"Time is of the essence," she argued.

Dogumrik held up his hands. "I hope you're right."

"I'm always right." She placed a hand on him. "If you'd feel safer, go to the trees. Shelia and I will continue on the path."

Dogumrik stopped. He could pick her up and force her into the trees, but the raccoon would stop him. Shelia might hurt him in the process, and then he would be useless when they came upon the ogre. He sighed and followed the raccoon's striped tail.

It was twilight when they saw the light of the ogre's house. It wasn't the dilapidated hut Dogumrik had expected. Instead, it was a square structure of human design. He'd heard stories of human dwellings. They forced the wood to take the shape they needed. He curled his lip, disgusted.

Not far from the house was another building that smelled faintly of cows, pigs, and clover. An animal house; if he remembered right, humans called it a barn.

She grabbed his arm. "Do you smell that?" Maramalik's nose pinched. "Smells like death." Her eyes widened, and she pulled Dogumrik toward the house, stopping under a tree midway between the buildings. She pulled her bags from Shelia's back, then cut the harness.

"What's wrong?"

She raised her finger to silence him. "Remember what I said about the ogre using entrails to divine the future? Suppose that's how he got the house and barn."

"Human entrails?"

"And cows. And pigs." Maramalik added, fear sparkling in her eyes. "We're at the right house."

Shelia growled, making them jump. She chattered at Maramalik and backed toward the barn. The raccoon sat on her hind legs and pulled her arms toward her belly.

"You can't protect me forever, Shelia," the shaman said to her friend. "Go, if you must. This is something I must do."

Shelia barked and hissed, then waddled toward the barn. Night swallowed the raccoon.

The snap of a twig jerked their attention to the house. They saw a supple black shape moving towards them. "The cat! Climb." Dogumrik pushed the shaman toward the tree trunk.

Maramalik climbed, deftly finding purchase on the rough tree bark. "Cats climb, too!" she shouted at Dogumrik, ascending beside her.

The black feline jumped on the trunk, scaling quickly. The brownies moved to separate branches, dividing the cat's attention. The cat followed close to Maramalik's heels. Dogumrik felt helpless as the cat moved closer and batted at her. The shaman jumped to a thinner branch. Perhaps it was too small. He rubbed his eyes. *Did*

Maramalik turn into a mouse? The cat followed. The twig broke under their combined weight. Both cat and mouse fell into the shadows.

"Skunk piddle!" Dogumrik swore under his breath. He couldn't see the black cat or mouse-shaped shaman in the darkness below. If he climbed down, surely the cat would attack him. He couldn't call out to Maramalik. If she responded, the cat would find her. He held onto the hope she had outwitted the feline and went toward the house.

He climbed from one tree to another until he was near the house. A branch, low on the trunk, reached into a wound on the side of the building. The crunch of paper and leaves greeted Dogumrik as he tumbled through the broken and missing boards. Spiders had woven a tapestry of nets and curtains between the attic rafters. Light filtered up through holes, allowing Dogumrik to see into the room below.

A gigantic creature paced around the overturned furniture like a trapped animal. He was shirtless, but that mattered little, due to the length and depth of the black hair growing on his back, chest, and arms. His bald, sickly green head seemed tiny when compared to his barrel chest and round belly. A dirty and torn pair of leather pants covered the rest of him.

"So that's what an ogre looks like," Dogumrik mumbled.

The ogre strode into a room and out of sight. A door opened and then closed. Metal scraped across glass. The ogre belched, then reentered the room. His grotesque grin exposed his curved canines. The beast settled into a soft-looking chair. He closed his eyes, but the smile didn't leave his face.

The black cat crept into the room. It walked past the ogre to some cabinets near the fireplace. Had it dropped something? A mouse slipped under the cabinets. *Was that Maramalik? The spirits told her to befriend the lion. Perhaps she's done precisely that.*

Something substantial fell inside the cabinet. Dogumrik held his breath.

The ogre stirred and grunted to the cat, "Onyx?" The cat meowed, raised its tail, and padded to him. The ogre patted the cat's head, stood, and opened the cabinet. He picked up a candle from the fireplace hearth. He raised it high, then moved boxes and bottles, checking for an intruder.

At the very top of the cabinet was a cage with five kittens. They meowed at the ogre, kneading the cage, begging to be let out. Onyx meowed and jumped on his leg. The ogre kicked her off. *Is that why the cat works for the ogre? Does he hold her kittens hostage?*

Dogumrik sucked in his breath. He saw a mouse hide behind a metal container. A mouse that looked vaguely like Maramalik. The ogre grunted, slammed the door shut, and latched it.

The warrior brownie moved quickly across the ceiling, through cobweb veils, and stopped above the cabinet. Dogumrik pushed at a knot in a board face and slid it free. He left his pack and weapons on the attic floor and dropped into the cabinet.

He landed on the metal cage, and his leg slipped through the bars. The kittens hissed and clawed at him. Dogumrik rolled off the pen, avoiding the dagger-thin claws. Their paws were the same size as his head. Even a kitten could kill him. He frowned. *How can two brownies defeat the ogre?*

Suddenly Maramalik stood next to him. "Seems that *Dog* fits you," she said, nodding at the hissing kittens.

"How do you know that name?" Dogumrik folded his arms.

"Everyone knows it. No one but your father *says* it." She patted his arm. "We've got to save the kittens. The spirits demand it."

"Your spirits are insane. These kittens are bigger than me." Dogumrik was four walnuts tall, which was average for a brownie.

"Not for long," Maramalik said. She pulled the purple potion bottle out of her bag. "See, the spirits want you here. Without you, we wouldn't have this bottle, save the kittens, or succeed."

Dogumrik stepped back away from her. "We?" He looked around the cabinet shelf, conspicuously devoid of any other brownies. "We who?"

"You're in too deep now." Maramalik reached and bonked him on the nose. "The spirits told me that a dog would kill the ogre, and they haven't been wrong."

"You said 'the *wolf* will conquer,'" Dogumrik protested.

"I stand corrected." She grinned at him, then turned to the cage.

The wide-eyed kittens backed into a corner, away from the brownies. Maramalik rolled her tongue, making one cat-like noise after another.

One black kitten stepped away from its siblings and approached the shaman. Maramalik continued her cat-speak, coaxing it to her side. Deftly she tipped the bottle. A tiny drop of purple liquid fell into the kitten's ear.

After a few moments, the black kitten reduced in size until it fit through the bars. Maramalik lifted the feline and placed it into her bag, all the while she talked to the other kittens. Once they saw their sibling leave the cage, they seemed more willing to listen to the shaman's cat-speak. Eventually, she shrank all five kittens to walnut size.

"Think you can handle three?" Maramalik raised an eyebrow. "Where's your pack?"

Dogumrik pointed to the hole above the cage.

"Well, get it."

Dogumrik scowled. *She's only eleven. How can she be so bossy? Why am I so inclined to listen to her?* He climbed the cage and returned with his weapons and bag.

Two black kittens were tucked into her pack, their heads sticking out. The other three romped at her feet. Their meows sounded like mouse squeaks. Maramalik took Dogumrik's bag and put two tabbies inside, loosely cinching up the mouth around their necks.

"What about that one?" He nodded to the tortoiseshell running around their feet.

Maramalik caught the kitten and shoved her into Dogumrik's arms. "You'll have to carry her."

The kitten licked his chin with her scratchy tongue. He tried to pull the tortoiseshell off his chest, but she wouldn't budge. Her claws dug into his leathers, and she shoved her head under his chin. The kitten clung like a cocklebur; the more he resisted, the tighter she held.

"Come on." The shaman waved her arm and ran to the corner of the cabinet. A mouse had chewed an opening some time ago. She placed the bag near the hole. "Once I'm through, drop the bags, and I'll catch them."

Maramalik jumped through the hole. He dropped the bags into her arms and slipped through the mouse hole, kitten still attached. Dogumrik stroked the tortoiseshell's fur, glad she was unharmed.

The shaman picked up her bag, and they continued to the next level, ever downward.

The space between the cabinet and the floor was too tight to walk. Dogumrik crawled on his hands and knees. The decorative feet and bottom edge allowed them to peek out and observe the ogre. When the kittens saw the beast, they hissed their disapproval.

The ogre moved from his soft chair, walked through a door, and out of sight.

Big black paws dropped in front of the cabinet. The cat's bright green eyes looked underneath. Dogumrik touched Maramalik's shoulder. "Once she has her kittens, will she kill us?"

"The spirits wouldn't have instructed us to help if it would end our lives." She gave a reassuring smile. "Come, there is no time to think, we must move." The shaman crawled out from undercover and spoke to the cat with various purrs, meows, and chirps.

Onyx lay on her side, exposing her back to the cabinet. Maramalik waved Dogumrik to come close. "Climb on, grab her fur."

As he approached the cat, the sound of rumbling filled his ears. *Was the cat growling?* He held his fear close, knowing it would serve him well if he had to fight. Dogumrik did as Maramalik instructed, wrapping his hands in the long black fur.

The cat lurched to its feet, jumped on the soft chair, and out a broken window. Dogumrik's stomach flipped and turned with the cat's fluid movements. He giggled, delighted, as the wind pulled tears from his eyes.

The cat stopped at the tree midway between the house and barn. The feline made a funny sound. Maramalik released the black fur and slid to the ground. "Dogumrik, it is safe to dismount."

If he dropped to the cat's level, he could be eaten, like Panao. The sudden remembrance and fear made his body seize. The kitten on his chest nuzzled his chin. *Surely not while her babies are attached.* Dogumrik released his grip and dropped to the ground.

The black cat whirled to stare at him. Onyx continued to make a deep rumbling noise in her throat and chest. Her eyes narrowed, almost closing. Dogumrik swallowed hard, expecting an attack. She approached and rubbed her head on his body, striking him solidly on his forehead, knocking him on his rear. The cat sat back, licking her paw.

"What now? Is she going to eat me?" He stared at the sinewy muscle under the cat's fur. Her white teeth looked sharp.

Maramalik laughed. "Are you not a brownie? Don't you know animals and their behavior?"

"Not cats, they kill our kind. They are friends to humans and ogres." Dogumrik looked away. It wasn't true. Onyx wasn't the ogre's companion, not by choice.

"Onyx marked you as her friend. She gave you the blink of trust. You're not in danger here." The shaman rubbed the cat's chin. "Listen, she purrs to us. She's happy."

Maramalik opened her bag. The black kittens scrambled out, mewing in high voices. Deftly she opened a bottle with orange liquid and placed one drop in each of the kittens' ears. They grew, returning close to their original size.

The kittens in Dogumrik's bag wiggled and twisted, mewing for their mother. He shrugged the bag into Maramalik's arms. She treated them with the same liquid, then peeled the final kitten off

Dogumrik's chest and enlarged her, too. The tortoiseshell scampered to join her nursing siblings.

Dogumrik pointed to the kittens. "Will they stay that size, or will they return to normal?" His eyes lingered on the tortoiseshell, who seemed to be smaller than before. In some visceral way, he felt responsible.

"The potions I used will last a day at most. To make them permanent, blood must be added."

"Blood magic?" Dogumrik frowned. He had heard stories of blood magic. Fae councils always forbade it. Anyone who used blood magic was banished or killed. Surely those were only tales told to children. *Could magic be evil? Even if the intent was noble?*

Maramalik patted Onyx on the head, then turned and walked back toward the house.

Onyx meowed, adding a purr at the end. As a group, the kittens stopped nursing. Onyx issued another cat command, and the babies followed her into the dark.

Dogumrik watched her go. "We're on our own, aren't we?"

"We always were. Onyx was a barrier, remember?"

He remembered watching his bunkmate disappear, and the snap of breaking bones. He shook his head. "There's no way she killed Panao."

"What?"

"I saw Onyx grab Panao, and I swear I heard his bones break. But she couldn't have." Dogumrik lowered his head, hoping he was right.

"Let's save Panao and all the others." She guided him toward the ogre's house. Numbly, he obeyed. Suddenly the shaman stopped and turned around. A large shape waddled out of the darkness, chattering.

"I told you, I have to do this," Maramalik said to the raccoon.

Shelia patted Maramalik like she was a tasty morsel she'd found underwater. She purred and clicked her teeth together.

"You're more than welcome to come with us," the shaman encouraged.

Together all three climbed through the broken window and into the house.

The ogre lay in a stupor in his soft chair. His head turned as they made crunching noises treading on the broken glass.

"Onyx?" The ogre's eyes rolled back, and his head fell against the chair. Shelia walked under the ogre's hand, allowing him to stroke her fur. "Kitty," the ogre said, with massive pats to Shelia's masked head. He snored, and his hand went limp.

Dogumrik made a motion with his hand as if holding a glass and drinking.

Maramalik shook her head, and worry lines creased her young face. She looked away from the ogre and ran into a different room. Dogumrik followed.

They entered a room meant for food preparation. Cabinets filled the walls, high and low.

Onyx sat on a countertop, twisting her head, whiskers forward, peering down at them. She meowed.

Maramalik meowed back. "Where are our people, Onyx?"

The black cat jumped to the ground, tail in the air, and padded to a large floor-to-ceiling cabinet. Onyx placed her forepaws on the door and mewed.

The brownies gaped at the massive wooden door. They seized the edge, heaved and strained, but the door remained closed. Shelia chattered at them, then shoved her muzzle between the door and the jamb and pulled with her paws until it opened.

Tapping emanated from the top shelves.

The brownies looked up. Glass jars with metal tops filled the shelving. Inside each was a fae, striking the glass wildly and shouting.

"We need to get them out!" hissed Maramalik.

"How? We're too small."

Maramalik grabbed Dogumrik's arm and pointed. "What's that?" Scattered across the bottom few shelves were hundreds of jars. Fae objects sat inside the glass, like torn fairy wings and smashed gnome hats.

Shelia climbed into the cabinet among the open jars, pushing them aside, sniffing.

"What the hell's going on?" Dogumrik looked at Maramalik. She avoided eye contact.

"When I ride my horse to the world above or below, I hear spirit stories…I didn't want to believe them." She closed her eyes, taking a deep breath. "There are non-magic creatures who eat magic creatures to gain their power."

"What?" Dogumrik looked at the copious number of jars. "Are you telling me that the ogre has all the power of a few hundred fairies, gnomes, and brownies?"

"Oh, no." She placed a consoling hand on his arm. "Magic can't live in a non-magic creature. Over time, the power dissipates. The euphoric feeling and the illusions are potent. Non-magic will do anything to feel magic course through their bodies, even if it is fleeting."

Dogumrik stared at her, mouth open. "That ogre is *eating* fae to become intoxicated?"

Maramalik nodded. "There's more. The ogre has eaten so many, he can't stop. He will hunt our kind to extinction." She turned to look Dogumrik in the eyes. "You have to kill him."

He stepped back. "Me? Have you seen the size of that ogre?"

"The spirits said…"

"I don't care what they said!" Fear made his voice quaver.

Maramalik shook her bag. "I have magic. I will shrink him." She pulled the nearly empty purple jar out of the bag and frowned. "If I can add his blood to the potion, then put it in his ear, he will shrink more than the potion alone. And the change will be permanent."

"Will it be enough?"

"Yes. It has to be. Otherwise, the spirits would be wrong, and they're never wrong. Never." Maramalik shook her head with conviction.

Shelia pushed a fairy-filled jar from the cabinet. It clunked and rolled across the floor. The male fairy inside yelled at the raccoon, making twisting motions with his hands. Shelia chattered at him, showed her toothy smile, and then wrenched on the lid.

From the other room, the ogre grunted. The brownies looked around the corner. The beast was still asleep, but he tossed and turned as if he would rouse at any moment.

"I need his blood, but if I cut him, he'll wake, and getting to his ear will be impossible."

Dogumrik saw fresh scratches on the ogre's leg. "Look! When Onyx begged him for her babies, she scratched him."

Maramalik asked Onyx to lay on her side and examined each claw. The shaman set her bag on the floor and opened the purple bottle. Using the dagger at her waist, she scraped the underside of the nails, dropping the debris into the flask.

"Was that blood?" Dogumrik asked.

"I don't know. But I have to try." She gave her shaman's bag to him. "Put it in a safe place." Maramalik ran toward the sleeping ogre.

The shaman scaled the soft chair, creeping along its arm. She gently climbed onto the ogre's shoulder and poured the liquid into his ear.

The ogre thrashed his head as the liquid took effect.

Maramalik jumped back, narrowly avoiding his arm.

The ogre opened his eyes and roared. He swatted Maramalik.

She flew to the floor, landing on her back, the wind knocked out of her. She sat up, wheezing and coughing.

The ogre looked over the arm of the chair, recognizing the shaman for what she was. "Vitu see you, magic brownie; Vitu want," the ogre said in broken fae. He moved to get her, his body shrinking with every action. He roared with rage. "You make Vitu small!" The ogre threw objects aside as he chased her.

The ogre stopped shrinking; he was smaller, but still a formidable opponent. Vitu reached down and grabbed Maramalik. "Make me big and strong. Or I eat." He motioned to place her inside his mouth. Desperate, Maramalik bit the ogre's hand.

Onyx yowled and ran into the room, attacking the ogre, scratching his legs. The ogre dropped the shaman and kicked the cat, sending her into a wall. Her limp form slid to the ground.

"Where magic brownie?" Vitu roared. "You make Vitu big, or me eat." The ogre threw furniture, trying to find Maramalik.

Another glass fell out of the cabinet. The male fairy, free from his prison, directed Shelia to open the jar, setting a brownie warrior free.

Hope jumped in Dogumrik's heart. Shelia could free their people, but she would need time to open all those jars. Time was something the shaman and Onyx didn't have.

He searched Maramalik's bag, looking for the orange bottle. Dogumrik swallowed hard, then cut his finger and added his blood to the potion. He poured a drop into his ear and waited. His body stretched and grew, tearing his clothing and armor.

Nothing seemed right. The ceiling was too close, and the floor too far away. Dogumrik felt woozy, like a child who had spun around too fast for too long.

Permanent.

He spotted his spear and bow and arrows, but they were now too small. Dogumrik looked for other weapons and spotted knives in a wooden block. He pulled one and threw it at the ogre, sinking the hefty blade deep into his back.

The ogre roared in pain and turned to face his attacker. "You, big brownie. I cook you like pig with fire." Vitu's canines glistened as if he were salivating at the idea.

Dogumrik threw another knife, but the ogre batted it out of the air. He felt something small in his hand, the orange potion bottle, and it still had liquid inside. He tilted his head and poured more into his ear. His body stretched, creaking with resistance.

"Vitu want magic!" The ogre lunged at Dogumrik, intent on the bottle in his hand. He grabbed the brownie's wrist, then landed punches to his face.

Dogumrik wasn't ready for the speed and power of the ogre's attack. His warrior training hadn't prepared him for such brutality. He fell backward, striking his head on the cabinets in the center of the room.

The ogre sat on Dogumrik's chest. His shin pressed into the brownie's throat. Vitu attacked his hand, trying to pry the bottle free.

Dogumrik gasped for air. He tried to lift the ogre but wasn't strong enough.

Vitu held up the tiny bottle in his greenish hands. "Vitu win." The ogre swallowed the bottle. "Now, Vitu grow." He jumped off the brownie as if movement upward would encourage growth. "Grow, grow, grow." He hopped with every word.

An empty jar rolled into Dogumrik's hand. Panao and a gnome peered over its edge. He smiled at his friend, relieved to see he was alright, then grasped the jar and threw it. The glass struck in the center of Vitu's face. Blood erupted from the ogre's nose.

Dogumrik scrambled to his feet. He glanced toward the cabinet and the small fae army, growing with every empty jar. Another container rolled to a stop, bumping his ankle. He bent and grabbed it, preparing to throw it at the ogre.

Vitu wiped the blood from his face with the back of his hands. His eyes locked with Dogumrik. "Big brownie, die!"

Dogumrik threw the jar.

The ogre knocked it aside.

A fairy swooped into the foray and threw dust into the ogre's face.

The ogre swatted at the fairy, but his charge didn't lessen. Vitu struck Dogumrik low, driving upward and forward, throwing the brownie to the floor, knocking the air from his lungs.

Dogumrik wheezed.

"Die!" Vitu yelled as he rained blows down onto the brownie.

Dogumrik covered his face with his arms, curling into a ball.

"Die!" the ogre yelled. His weight and strength were behind each strike.

The ogre grunted and then stopped hitting Dogumrik.

The brownie warrior looked through his arms. The fairies dropped anything they could find onto the ogre's head. Brownies and gnomes had taken Dogumrik's weapons. Some shot arrows. Others stabbed the ogre's legs with spears.

The ogre turned away from Dogumrik. He kicked and swatted at the little people. The knife stood tall, like a flag in Vitu's back. The fae army were distracting the ogre, but they couldn't kill him.

The wolf will conquer! Dogumrik stood and pulled the knife from the ogre's back.

Vitu roared and spun, flailing his arms, trying to strike Dogumrik.

The brownie dropped low, slicing across the ogre's bulbous gut. Viscera and thick gray ropes of intestine spilled from the wound.

Vitu looked at his belly, unable or unwilling to comprehend the damage. The ogre moved to attack Dogumrik but slipped in the pooling blood and liquid. He fell forward, crushing a small table. "Magic brownie!" Vitu cried. His arm slipped under the chair near his head. He pulled out Maramalik. The shaman screamed defiantly as the ogre moved her to his mouth.

"No!" Dogumrik yelled, landing on Vitu. He pulled the ogre's head back and slid the knife across his throat. Bubbles and gurgles issued from the ogre. The greenish hand relaxed, and Maramalik wriggled free, then ran back under the chair.

Dogumrik lifted the chair and moved it. Onyx lay on her side. A trickle of blood came from her mouth and made a small puddle.

"Can you save her?" Dogumrik asked.

"She has a collapsed lung. Lift her and place her in the chair, but turn her so she lays on her other side. It will help her breathe."

Dogumrik carried Onyx to the chair, carefully placing her on the cushions.

"And, Dogumrik," Maramalik said between fits of giggles. "You ought to check for clothes."

Human clothes. Forever human.

Dogumrik went through a closed door and found a room with a bed and a chest of drawers filled with clothing. He slipped on a pair of pants that were a little too big and returned to Onyx and Maramalik. "Will she make it?" he asked again.

"Yes, I think with time, she will."

"This is my home now. I can't live with the clan, not like this." Dogumrik threw his hands up, indicating his enormous size. "Now that I'm *human*." His lip twisted with disgust.

"You're still a brownie," Maramalik assured him.

"Am I?" Dogumrik shook his head. "Onyx and her kittens can stay here as long as she wants." He looked around at all the fae that milled around. "You all can stay."

"I'll find a way to bring you back to the right size," Maramalik said. Her tiny hand patted his enormous mitt.

"It's alright. I knew it would be permanent when I added my blood to the potion. I'd do it again." He nodded. "Your damn spirits were right. The wolf did conquer."

He stood and went to the cabinet. Many empty jars were on the floor, laying on their side. Shelia sat among them with her hand in a glass filled with nut butter. She smiled at Dogumrik and chattered her teeth. "Taking a break?" He stooped to pat her head and scratch behind her ears.

The cabinet still had fae-filled-jars on the upper shelves. "We didn't want the raccoon to drop those jars. It's too high." The male fairy fluttered near Dogumrik's shoulder. He carried a mandolin on his hip and a flute in his belt. "That was a brave and foolish thing you did." The minstrel fairy bowed to him in midflight. "Without you, we would have died. We owe you a debt of gratitude. Your parents, your clan, ought to be proud."

"I'm not sure they will be," Dogumrik commented, thinking how his father hadn't wanted him to hunt the ogre. He picked up a jar and freed the occupant, a gnome. Dogumrik continued, going at a faster pace than Shelia.

"Might I know your name?" the minstrel asked.

"You can call me Dog."

* * * * *

RJ Ladon Bio

RJ Ladon is a nightshift writer (by choice) and a dayshift design engineer (by necessity) to pay for the aforementioned writing addiction. She is a self-proclaimed tree-hugger and animal-lover. If she is not in her garden, pasture, or woods, you can find RJ watching movies or reading books. She lives with her husband, children, and a variety of animals on a farmette in Wisconsin.

Writing a novel has always been on RJ's radar, and it will soon become a reality this year (2020) with the first book in the series Bloodstone (new adult, urban fantasy). In the meantime, you can find her stories in multiple anthologies. Two horror stories: *Gwen's Gamble* and *The Poppet* in *Sha'Daa—Toys*. One military science fiction: *The Felix* in *Tales from the Lyon's Den—Stories from the Four Horsemen Universe* (Book 4). One non-fiction: *Invisible Battles* found in *Impossible Hope*. And *The Ogre's Brownies*, in *When Valor Must Hold*. A list of books, anthologies, and other oddities can be found at www.RJLadon.com. On Twitter: @RJLadon, and on Facebook: RJLadon.

# # # # #

Dust in the Mouth by William Joseph Roberts

Afire's light slid through the fading greens of early autumn. Draven had marched along a well-beaten game trail over the rolling hills of Angara for weeks. Just ahead in the dimming evening light, the fiery glints of the setting sun reflected in the frothing whitecaps of the rushing stream. Weary and worn from his long trek, he had hoped for a trout or some other easy prey as it drank from along the water's edge.

He quietly knelt down and retrieved two fist-sized stones from the ground, then, crouching low, he moved as if he had been transformed into a wolf stalking its prey. Slowly, he pressed forward around obstacles to find an opening in the undergrowth, off the side of the game trail.

There before him, bathing in the frigid mountain stream, a voluptuous beauty sat stark naked on a worn boulder at the water's edge. Gooseflesh rippled upon every part of her supple white flesh. She faced away from him and looked in the direction of her camp, which was set beneath a rock ledge that protruded from the face of the mountain. A familiar scent drew his attention to where a hare or river rat roasted over the fire.

Draven turned his attention back to the woman. Long, dark hair hung down her flawless back, where it brushed the well-formed top of her curvaceous rear. Draven could barely make out the familiar tune the river vixen hummed over the rushing torrent of the mountain stream. Lifting one of her ample breasts, she continued to wash, unaware of him.

He watched from the concealment of the underbrush. Both the scent of cooking meat and the sight of the softly pale olive flesh struck long denied chords of hunger within his soul.

"It is impolite to spy on another unawares, warrior," a wizened old voice said from behind him.

Draven whirled to face the unseen voice. Beneath the boughs of an ancient grandfather oak, an old man sat cross-legged on a bed of thick heather.

"By Morrag's beard. You startled me, old man," Draven said quietly as he stared. The ghastly white of his clouded eyes seemed to glow from behind his large, hawkish nose, which was the dark brown color of tanned leather. He wore ragged and muddy furs that were draped over his shoulders and hung loosely over his gaunt frame. "Who are you? And how do you know me to be a warrior? I could be a huntsman or a simple beggar, and you would never know, for you cannot see me."

"Naught but an old blind pilgrim on his way to the temple of Su-rath-Durgra," the old man said in a dry, raspy tone. "As for your second question, my boy. To these old ears, you tromped through the forest like a wild bull. A huntsman is quiet, soft of sole and mindful of his surroundings. Now if I may ask you a question, young warrior."

"By all means, Seer, ask away."

"Why do you spy on my daughter?"

"A man would be a fool not to gaze upon true beauty when he comes upon it. I merely admired from a distance, and did not soil her with my touch."

The old man smiled and laughed with a heavy breath. "I cannot blame you, son. My very own lustful gaze has caused me more trouble than I have cared for during my years." He let out a bellowing bout of laughter, then stretched forth a withered hand. "Help me back across the river. Come, share our fire and sup with us, young warrior."

Help the old man he did. Through the briar and brambles at the water's edge they emerged, startling the girl, who stood and stared, doe-eyed, before realizing the warrior was aiding the old man across the flowing waters.

After a time they sat and supped and shared the roast rodent. The old seer introduced himself as D'Bia of the Azkateri, a people from far to the east. His daughter he named Branwen. She looked up at Draven, then averted her eyes shyly and stole glances of interest. The thin silks she wore left nothing to the imagination. Each delicate and soft curve of her pale olive skin called to the flames that burned within Draven's heart and loins.

Feeling somewhat obligated to contribute to their meager meal, Draven passed his wineskin to her, and she eagerly let the sweet liquid pass between her parched but otherwise thankful lips. He removed his cloak and draped it over her shoulders. She thanked him. The old seer told of how they had traveled from far in the south with a trade caravan.

"Three days ago, we were set upon by bandits," the old man growled. "If not for my Branwen's sharp eyes and quick wits, as sure as we sit before you now, I would be dead, and she'd be a slave or whore." D'Bia spat to the side.

"Then for the sake of your kind hospitality, let me guide you to your destination," Draven demanded.

"We could not impose upon another during our pilgrimage," Branwen said softly. She looked up at him with innocently imploring amber eyes that melted Draven's heart. "We must endure the trials which both the goddess Surath and her king consort Durgra impose upon our mortal shells in order to seek purity by the time of our arrival."

He hung on her sweetly spoken words, which gently glided on the air as brightly as the fresh golden honey of an early spring harvest.

"I have neither obligation nor set path before me," Draven announced. "I am free to wander the world and experience all that it has to offer. By the Morrag and his witches three, I willingly pledge my blade and my arm to the two of you, to see that you arrive at the end of your pilgrimage otherwise unmolested."

The next morning Draven set a fair pace, scouting ahead, while Branwen guided D'Bia along the game trails of the Angaran forest. By early evening, the trio tread upon the open grasslands of rolling hills that bordered the lands of the Nos'Bigyle. Beneath the boughs of a poplar grove, they stopped to camp for the night. Draven gathered wood for a fire as Branwen tended to her father and settled him in for the night. By luck while gathering wood, Draven stumbled upon a growth of root vegetables. Once the fire had been started, he sliced the roots and placed them on a stone amid the hot coals and flames.

Quietly crouching beside the fire, Draven stared into the hellish red glow of the coals as he stirred them about, careful to evenly heat the stone.

"You are a kind soul, warrior," Branwen said as she placed Draven's cloak over the old man as he dozed. "Not many would go out of their way to help a stranger without expecting something in return."

"It was merely luck that I happened upon the two of you when I did," Draven said. "My course has not been steadfast in months. I set my rudder by the winds of change, to sway to and fro as is necessary."

She smiled and looked away into the orange glow of the fire. "You speak as if you were a poet as well as a warrior."

"I've never been anything, really." Draven took a long breath. "I've learned many a thing in my time, but never will I be a master of any skill or trade. The fates see to it that my stars change and a new adventure begins before I can settle down. I sometimes fear that I am cursed to wander the world for eternity, never able to find my peace in one place."

"Then let us test the fates," she said excitedly in a hushed whisper. "When we reach the temple and join our brethren, you must stay and join us." Branwen sat behind the fire-haired warrior, resting her breasts against his stooped back. She draped her arms over his muscular shoulders and around his neck, holding him in a firm embrace. "We will not go hungry in the service of the Surath-Durgra." She nuzzled the side of his face and nibbled on the tip of his ear lobe. "It is said that *all* the hungers of man and beast alike are satiated and fulfilled in the service of the earthbound gods," she whispered into his ear.

Draven leaned to the side and drew Branwen down into his lap, where he embraced her, smothering her with a passionately deep kiss before the long howl of a wolf in the distance struck at his soul.

A low growl escaped Draven's throat as he located the direction of the howl. Lifting Branwen with ease, he placed her back onto her feet, then stood and pushed a heavy stone into the girl's hand. "Stay close to the old man, and try not to move unless you have no choice. Let them focus on me. If you move, you become prey."

She swallowed a dry gasp and nodded before returning to her father's side and kneeling on the ground where he slumbered.

Draven withdrew his dagger from its sheath, and gripped its familiar form in his right hand, while wielding a makeshift cudgel of firewood in his other. He circled the small campfire, keeping his back to the flames. Shadows danced and leapt about amid the ancient poplars in the dimming light of dusk. His gaze scanned the dimly lit forests that surrounded them.

The howls grew closer, the darker the sky became. Movement darted about at the edge of the firelight. Leaves rustled on all sides.

Draven could hear Branwen's frightened breaths over the pounding of his heart. He circled around the fire to his left and froze at the sight of two burning green orbs in the black distance. They moved and swayed with the hypnotic dance of a stalking predator.

Two other pairs joined the first, followed by three others that had flanked them. Gooseflesh rippled up his neck at the long howl of a wolf from his left, then the growling charge of the pack into the dim firelight.

Draven batted away the first and dove beneath the second beast to leap at him, sticking the creature in the haunch with the blade of his dagger, before rolling back to his feet in the face of another massively wooly beast that stood as tall as the warrior himself. He swung and dove at the creature, landing a crunching blow to the side of the wolf's sensitive snout.

All but one of the husky beasts kept their distance. Some whimpered, some limped, but the pack continued to circle. Draven roared and stomped at the ground. His coppery locks burned with the glow of the fire behind him. A massive wolf with fur as red as fresh blood answered his war cry. The mottled dark fur of the beast's face made it look as if it wore a black-masked helm, like a warrior prepared for battle.

Draven sprung backward as the great wolf lunged forward. He swung the cudgel in a circle above his head and brought it around with all of his might, only to have it stopped as if he'd stuck a stone wall. The beast clamped down on the makeshift club and shattered the seasoned branch as if it were nothing more than a twig.

"Alkahi!" Draven roared at the forest as he stepped back from the beast. "Call home your pet before I send him to sit at the side of your cousins in the nethers of the great Underdark!"

The beast charged again, only to be met by both blade and fist alike. It whimpered and staggered from a powerful left hook to the side of its head.

It snapped, barely missing, as Draven stepped aside and forced his blade down into the gullet of the heaving beast. Its body constricted and wrenched as it reflexively attempted to expel Draven's arm. He twisted the blade wildly about on the inside of the retching monster, carving out the beast's innards. The massive red wolf heaved and contorted, then suddenly slumped and went limp before it dropped to the ground and slid free from the warrior's blood-soaked arm.

Sorrowful howls erupted from all around them. The pack paced and barked at the warrior who had felled their leader.

Draven grabbed the leader by the scruff, cut its massive head free, and held it high for all to see. He roared and howled at the pack, stomping ferociously at the ground as he leapt toward other members of the pack. With reluctant whimpers, the wounded animals grumbled and growled, then slowly they melded back into the darkness of the night.

Draven broke the top of a large sapling and mounted the massive head atop the living pike. He roared, then cried out to the things that lurked in the dark of night. "Neither man nor beast nor god alike matters to me. I swear to the universe that you will all bleed equally by my hand should you cross me!"

His menacing gaze swung around to bore into Branwen's soul. She breathed in, about to speak, but then froze at the sight of Draven's fiery gaze. Without another word, he stoked the fire, then rolled the carcass to the side, and with a quick flick of his blade, he separated fur from flesh.

By early evening three days later, Draven strode into the outer courtyard of the temple of Surath-Durgra. Columns and statuary of gleaming white marble burned with the hubristic reds and oranges of the setting sun. A loud drumming gong resounded throughout the courtyard. A midnight black beast of a man who stood at least two hands taller and better than four hands wider than Draven struck an intricately cast bronze gong. It hung suspended by chains between two of the white marble columns. The two heavy wooden doors of the temple entrance opened, and attendants dressed in loose-fitting wraps of white fabric emerged from within.

Attendants ran to welcome Branwen and her father. Branwen explained the exploits of Draven the Red Wolf during their journey and begged that he be given a hero's welcome.

And so he was led away by a half-dozen women that, to the best of his knowledge, were each of a different land. One had the midnight black skin of the Tuathakan jungles far to the south, another with the buttery-colored hair and complexion of a woman of the ocean-going Angeraine. There was a redhead of the Juentheim, a hawk-nosed brunette of the Azkateri, a deep brown goddess of curves with eyes as dark as the pitch of night and a petite, flat-faced lass half the size of the others of the Bergarum people from the frozen deserts far to the north.

They led him deep into the temple to a steamy chamber of cerulean blue tile, where each of them disrobed before stripping him of his garments. He slid into the soothingly hot water, where they bathed and oiled and pampered him beyond anything he had ever experienced in his short eighteen seasons.

Once finished with him, the six carefully dressed him in a white linen wrap and brought him into a torch-lit great hall. Dozens of onlookers stared at him in complete silence as he entered the spacious chamber.

The scent of roasted pork hung heavy amid the pitch-scented air. Eight long feast tables were arranged in the center of the hall to face one another, forming an octagon. At the head of the room sat the old man, D'Bia, in a throne-like seat, dressed in rich red velvets and expensive furs. To his right sat Branwen, dressed in a silken gown the color of a man's blood. The thin layers of the gown did little to hide the voluptuous curves of her body. Each of the six attendants nudged Draven forward to be seated at the head table next to Branwen.

"I thank each of you for your service," Branwen said as she stood and nodded a bow to the attendants. They reciprocated the bow with giggles and blushing smiles as they rushed to take their seats around the hall.

D'Bia arose with an outstretched hand as a gong resounded from deep within the temple. Musicians plucked at harps and tapped lightly at drums as a mass of roasted meats—ribs, shanks and the like, surrounded by enough exotic fruits and vegetables to feed a small army—was carried in by two muscular men upon a thick wooden plank. A pack of boys rushed ahead of the pair to place the supports in the center of the tables. Once set in its place, the two hefty men exited the room. The small army of boys began to serve the meal to those seated at the tables, starting with D'Bia, Branwen, and Draven.

"From His great hall on high at Jut'athal'akan, where *He* slumbers and awaits the next coming, may He bless us again on the morrow as we are now, with full bellies and the protection of His great embrace," D'Bia said aloud as he held his goblet high, then drank deeply.

Draven followed suit and choked on the heavy, coppery tang of the sweet drink, but swallowed so as to not offend his hosts.

At one point midway through the meal, a small man in finely colored silks, equal parts jester and bard, plucked at a small harp while he sang and joked and poked fun at the audience gathered about the tables. The meal continued for some time, with light chatter, laughter, and the accompaniment of the music before the first of the attendees rose.

Two beautiful young women, one of the Angeraine and the other of the Reklaw people who dwell in the hills south of the valley of the Mauga, Draven's own homeland, tugged at a strapping lad not much older than they. They teased and beckoned him to follow as they embraced one another then disappeared from the room.

Branwen leaned over and laughed as they watched the young man arise and leave the hall. "It looks as if the evening's real festivities have begun." She giggled and flashed a knowing smile at Draven.

"By the grace of Del and Corimaen," Draven cursed. "The lad may be at the edge of death's door by the time those two are finished with him."

"That is quite a goal to strive for, is it not?" Branwen said, then toasted Draven.

"Aye," he said, returning her toast with a clank of goblets. "Aye it is, and it is quite a good goal to have, if I do say so myself."

They quietly finished their meals, each giving the other teasing glances as they watched the others slowly slip away by ones and twos. When only a few remained, and the kitchen boys had returned to collect the remains of the meal, Branwen placed her hand over Draven's thickly calloused hand.

"Come, let us not miss out on all that the evening has to offer." She smiled wide and stood. Hand in hand, she led him from the room in pursuit of the ones who had gone before them.

They ducked through the low entryway that led into a long dark hallway. The scent of lavender roses hung heavy in the air. Draven could feel the effects of the wine as they strode forward into the darkness, where the corridor arched around to the left. The air seemed to undulate with the slow, rhythmic beat of drums and moans that emerged from the end of the corridor as they approached.

Braziers burned at five points around the circular room, the acrid smoke rising high overhead to the tiled dome of a ceiling above. Two gilded thrones sat atop a raised dais to the left and overlooked a massive bathing pool that took up the majority of the room. Linen wraps littered the floor leading to the steaming surface of the water. Stairs climbed either side of the wall that backed the pool and ended at a platform twenty feet above the writhing mass of nude bodies below.

Branwen looked back over her shoulder as she released Draven from her grip and slipped the red silk gown from her shoulders, where it fell in a heap on the tiled floor of the chamber. She flashed a teasing smile at Draven, then descended the steps into the pool.

Eagerly, Draven let his own cloth wrappings fall free as he pursued her into the waist-deep water of the pool. He caught her up in his grasp and pulled her tightly against his bare, muscular chest. The warm scent of vanilla filled his nostrils as he sniffed at her long, dark tresses. Others pawed, kissed, and groped at the pair, and his hunger intensified as he tasted her neck, then spun her about and pinned her against the carved stone wall, where he partook of her full, thick lips. Draven rose for breath and glanced upward at the strange carving. *A seal of the cults' elder god no doubt,* he thought, but he had other matters to attend to.

Branwen looked up, following his gaze. "There are many other benefits to being a believer," she said softly. She pulled her wrists free and draped her arms around his thick neck. "The old ones," she said, nodding behind herself, "they hold our eternal souls in balance among the universe, to be devoured by the void, or born again on this unholy plane."

She tiptoed and kissed him so deeply it felt as if his soul were being pulled from his mortal form.

A trio of other attendees stumbled into the pair, separating them. A pert and healthy blond all but climbed onto Draven's form. He pushed the blonde aside and went back to Branwen, wrapping his thick arms about her small waist, as he lifted her high and ravenously suckled at her breast. Her back arched as she let out a long, entreating moan.

The world suddenly lurched and spun out of control. Her breast crumbled to dust in his mouth, then became whole once again. He tightened his grip, holding on to her to steady himself, but only heard the dry crinkle of leather over the cacophony of rushing wind that roared in his ears. The universe coalesced and reformed into reality as he released his grip and dropped the shapely lass into the steaming pool. Pushing her away he leaned back against the great carved seal.

"Come, lover," Branwen said in a sultry tone that rattled in his skull. "Tell me, what is wrong? Don't you like me? Embrace me and submit," she beckoned.

Sight and sound alike failed him, and the universe became a dark, perpetual silence to Draven. He retched at the overwhelming scent of electric purple ozone that felt as if it danced across the entirety of his being. An indescribable inky blackness became the eternity of existence in the absence of all other things.

Reality snapped back at her gentle touch. Branwen stepped closer. Pressing herself against him, she wrapped herself about his thigh. Draven shook his head and attempted to clear the charm that had overcome him.

"What are you?" Draven growled.

Branwen pulled herself close and, standing on tiptoes, gently kissed Draven's spasming brow. "Quiet, lover," she said with a shush.

"I asked you a question, witch!" Draven roared as he attempted to push her away. He could feel the strength of his limbs ebb away and they began to fail him.

"Your soul is stronger than any I have encountered in a millennium," Branwen said with awed reverence. "Jut'athal will be pleased. Guards! Take him to the cells while we await D'Bia's arrival." She reluctantly untwined herself from the warrior and stepped away. Draven struggled to stay where he was, slumped against the stone wall. He watched helplessly as Branwen strode to the dais and sat in one of the thrones. She beheld all who bowed in reverence to her commanding gaze.

In moments, two large guards rescued Draven from slipping beneath the water's soothing surface and carried him to a holding cell with no other exit than the steel-grated entrance the pair tossed him through. He lay there for some time in the near darkness, unmoving, surrounded by the sounds of shuffling feet on stone as they moved about the cell.

"Welcome to the remainder of the rest of your life, warrior," a smooth voice said with a shaky laugh. "Do not fear for your limbs my good man; they will work again in a short time. Each of us who remain here has been face down in that same place at one time or another. Jaleel, the one in that dark corner over there, didn't learn the first time, and thrice did he find himself face down in that spot."

The disembodied voice laughed and grew closer. "Slowly," the voice said as a figure knelt beside Draven and rolled him onto his back. "They take us out from time to time to meet their god or some such thing. One past inhabitant of this place speculated on the idea that they were beings of another realm. Then again, he also talked as if they were daemons or succubi sent from the lowest pits of the twelve hells."

Draven strained with every ounce of his being to sputter and form his lips into words his talkative cellmate could understand. "What is Jut'athal?"

The young man smiled down at Draven. Old eyes stared out from a smooth, boyish face. "That, my friend, is the mystery of this place, but from what I have ascertained, Jut'athal is the God-thing these cultists serve and worship." He spat to the side. "Something along the lines of 'service leads to immortality' or some nonsense. You look as if you've been about the world a time or two. I'm sure you've run across the type in the past."

Draven sat up with the young man's help. "Branwen mentioned introducing me to her god."

"Oh, did she now?" The young man scoffed. "You should feel a might privileged, my friend."

"I don't think that's something I care to stay here for."

"Neither do I," the young man said, laughing as he extended his hand. "I am known as Callum the Atlantean. Poet, minstrel, and scribe to those with the silver for such luxuries."

"I am Draven of the Mauga," he said, then forced his arm to do his bidding with all the power of his will. He reached up and locked arms with Callum.

"It's a pleasure to meet you, Draven of the Mauga."

Some time passed before the effects of the charm fully wore off, and Draven climbed to his feet. He tested the cell for any weakness.

The only light in the room was that which filtered through the barred window set in the thick wooden door. The walls were of solid stone, carved into the bedrock itself. The locked door must have been two inches thick. He tugged and tested the rings that were set into the stone walls and connected the shackles to the chains that dangled down the cold hewn surface. One such ring they found to be loose in its setting. Both Callum and Draven worked at the ring, then with their combined might, the spike released its grip and pulled free from the stone. The other prisoners cowered in the darkest corner of the room, out of sight should one of the guards look in.

"This should be all we need to pry the hinges on that door. But what of the guards?" Draven asked.

"Most times the guards are nowhere to be found," Callum replied. "We've been lucky to be fed at all, but it seems to me there is more noise from above as of late. And the guards have been more active in the last two days. So there's no telling when they may be back."

"Then let us be swift." Draven strode toward the door. "It is time to leave this forsaken hole."

Using the freed spike, the pair took turns digging at the iron bars set into the window of the wooden door. Removing two of the bars, Callum held onto them for later use. Able to reach his arm out through the portal, Draven lowered the chain, and was able to hook the crossbar that restrained the cell door, which he lifted and held tight as he freed it from its cradle.

Silently the pair pressed forward, down the carved stone corridor, back the way they had been brought, and stopped at the first turn in the path. Draven calmed himself and slowed his breathing to little more than short, shallow gasps. They both went rigidly still as they listened intently to the festivities above.

"Do you have any idea of how we'll get past that?" he said, pointing in the direction of the revelry with the iron bar.

Draven held up the chain and let the shackle drop before Callum. "Aye, I know exactly how we'll get through that. We'll cut our way through it using whatever we have at hand."

He peered around the corner of the corridor, then turned back to Callum. "We've two guards only a few feet away around the corner, but they look to be sleeping." Draven looked Callum over, then to the weapons that they each held. "Here lad, you strangle the life out of one of them, while I snap the other's neck." He handed Callum the chain, took one of the cold iron bars from his hand, and rounded the corner without another word.

The pair moved swiftly, both upon their quarry in the breath of a moment. Callum wrapped the chain around one's neck and pulled backward with all his might. The other guard turned and drew his sword just as Draven's calloused hands gripped the man's skull and snapped his neck as if it were a piece of dry tinder. He clasped the guard's short sword before the man could hit the floor and sliced across the other guard's throat in one swift movement.

"Come, let us hurry from this place," Draven said. He turned and continued down the corridor in the direction he knew led back into the great hall. Both men gagged at the heavily sweet odor of rot and decay.

"What in the hells is that stench?" Callum coughed, covering his face in the crook of his arm.

"Nothing for us to concern ourselves about, if I have my bearings right. We've to climb these stairs, then cross the great hall to a corridor that leads directly to the outside." He turned back to Callum and smiled. "How fast can you run?"

"Fast enough to keep up with you, at least," he said, then flashed a challenging smile back at Draven.

The red-haired warrior leapt forward at a blinding pace and climbed the stairs before Callum even began. Callum reached the top and skidded to a halt beside Draven.

"How convenient," a large guard said with a sarcastic smile at the pair. "We were just sent to fetch you back to our mistress." He motioned with outstretched hands to either side at the dozen other guards armed with crossbows who stood about the great hall. "Please. Do resist. It's been some time since my men had more than stuffed targets to fire at."

Draven glanced at Callum with the look of experience. He nodded, and both men dropped their newly acquired blades to the stone floor of the hall.

Flies swarmed about them as they were urged into the room by the guards that circled behind them. The scene in the great hall had changed, from the decadent magnificence of earlier, to a grotesque disfigurement of its previous self. Rotten fruits, molded by what looked like time itself, lay alongside the fettered carcasses of man and beast alike. Clouds of black flies swarmed over everything. The buzzing of wings and the sickly wriggle of maggots resounded as a deafening discord within the chamber. Atop the tables, cadavers of questionable origins lay flayed open and left to ferment over time, forming into oozing puddles of putrid rancor that collected on the cold stone floor below.

Callum involuntarily heaved as they were led from the room in the direction of the inner sanctum. Draven growled and spat at the scene, cursing under his breath at all the gods that came immediately to mind.

They were marched into the inner sanctum, where D'Bia and Branwen both sat on the thrones atop the dais. A massive guard stood to one side of the thrones, and with rhythmic regularity stamped the butt of his glaive on the floor. Joined by the wooden beat, a low-toned drum echoed through the chamber, its resonance droning, beckoning to all within earshot. Most figures stood stoically among the shadows of the dimly lit chamber, while a few shifted and swayed in time to the drumbeat.

D'Bia stood and stepped to the edge of the pool, its waters now stained dark with the blood of the bodies that floated aimlessly about. He turned his white-eyed gaze upon Draven and laughed.

"You have such great energy, untapped and raw as it is; the power within you is majestic, my son. My master will be very pleased."

A guttural chant emanated from deep within D'Bia's throat and joined the cadence of the room. Others joined in, humming to the tune, as the old blind seer sang a deep, throaty chant. At the point of their crossbows, the guards urged both their prisoners along to the stairs leading to the upper platform.

Branwen's voice continued the low chant as D'Bia spoke the unknown words of a long-forgotten tongue. The guards shackled Draven at the edge of the platform overlooking the pool below. The cold steel grip of shackles upon his flesh was an intimate reminder of his past indiscretions. He smiled as he held up his wrists and gazed at the metal bindings.

"Hello, my old friends. We meet again." Draven laughed so loudly as to overpower the measured time of chant and drums, then let out a whooping howl.

D'Bia began a new incantation as the beat and throaty chants continued from all around. The old man's white eyes glowed brighter with the pronunciation of each ancient word. The skin of his face cracked and began to flake away, as if a thousand years had suddenly reclaimed their grasp upon him. Dry, desiccated flesh fell away from the bone in places. His robes now showed the ages since their creation, rotten and moth-ridden as they were.

"Blessed be the grace of Del and Corimaen," Callum cursed.

"Krull!" Draven shouted, then began to growl and stomp to the time of the drumbeats. "Sorcerer or daemon, makes no matter to me, beast! You'll bleed the same by my hand!" Draven roared and let out a barking howl that echoed through the chamber.

Branwen stood alongside the old man with her arms raised. Her eyes began to glow as she joined him in the sing-song incantation. Her voluptuously beautiful nude form sloughed away, leaving the husk of a rotted corpse behind as the pair praised and called upon Jut'athal the Ancient, Jut'athal the Magnificent, Jut'athal the Old One Himself.

A great rumbling shook the platform beneath Draven's feet. The roar of falling rocks became a cacophony of noise that drowned out the rhythmic beat of chants and drums. Flashes of purple light reflected in the blood-filled pool below. The undead undulated in the dark waters. Decayed and bloated flesh writhed about atop one another in an orgy of necrophilic ecstasy.

"Kill the lich and his queen!" Callum shouted, then elbowed the guard who restrained him. He took up the guard's sword and skewered the second guard atop the platform, then with one mighty swing, he cleaved through the iron chain that bound Draven to the floor.

The fire-haired warrior dropped from his perch into the waters below. Without hesitation, Draven leapt upon his prey. He grabbed the first ghoul by the head and twisted. With a sickly snap of bone and sinew, he decapitated the animated corpse, then smashed its fleshy skull into the face of another fiend.

With his bare hands Draven rent flesh from bone, and two more of the things dropped to float helplessly in the darkened pool. Guards charged into the fray, surrounding the warrior. A blinding flash of purple light filled the room as a portal came into being, followed by the frantic screams of a guard.

He dropped his sword and pounded at a slick black tentacle that extended into the chamber from the great abyss itself. It grabbed one of the guards, knocking his sword into the air to splash near Draven. Gurgled screams and the cracking of the man's ribs accompanied the chanting and drums before the appendage dragged the man through the iridescent purple portal.

Draven dove beneath the surface of the red-stained waters. His grasp found its mark, and he burst forth from the water. The leaf-bladed sword in hand, he began to cut a path through the roiling throng of undead. With quick, accurate strikes, the short blade found its mark and cut down ghoul and guard alike.

He reached the edge of the tiled pool and gripped the ankle of the thing that had once been Branwen. The she-creature's foot was held fast to the ground, as if staked through with an iron rod. Neither D'Bia nor Branwen attempted to evade; instead, the sing-song incantation continued to repeat from the depths of their seemingly hollow forms.

Another of the inky black tentacles shot forth from the portal and wrapped itself about the warrior's leg. Blood rushed to his head as he was spun about and dangled upside down before the great maw of the beast that now emerged from the portal. Its muzzle splayed open into four equal section, like the budding of a flower, to reveal thousands of teeth lining the inside of the thing's gaping jowls. The stench of a thousand dead souls flooded the inner sanctum as the thing roared its arrival.

Draven struck at the appendage with his sword, stabbing deep into the thing's rubbery, black flesh. It jerked him about so violently that the sword flew from his grip. Digging deep, he drove his fist into the gash made by the sword and gripped the thing from the inside. He reached with his other hand into the opening and forced it wider.

The beast let out a primordial shriek unlike any earthly beast Draven had ever heard before. The sound sent waves of gooseflesh rippling up the back of his neck. The tentacle let loose of his leg and retreated back through the portal, dropping him headlong into the pool below.

Without hesitation, Draven climbed out of the water's sticky depths to face the largest guard he had ever seen. The man towered above Draven with shoulders at least twice as broad as his own. The honed blade of a massive great axe sang a wailing tune as it sped in a killing arc that grazed the hairs of Draven's nose. The fire-haired warrior pounced upon the massive guard before he could recover and swung about his neck to land on the man's broad back. He dug his heels into the man's kidneys and, holding onto the guard's throat with laced fingers, pulled with the entirety of his being. The guard reached overhead and flung him down into the water.

He scrambled to get his head above the waist-deep water, but before he could turn, a mighty fist came down onto his shoulder. It felt as if an anvil had been dropped onto him from a great height.

He spun and pounced at the guard once again and slammed his fist into the guard's thick jowl. The mountain of a man staggered, and, before he could shake the fog from his head, Draven was upon him. His hands clamped around the guard's throat, and Draven chortled like a mad man as he and the giant plunged back into the ruddy pool.

Draven burst forth from the water once again, the titan's great axe in hand. A scream immediately drew his attention upward. Above him dangled the nude, flailing form of a young woman. She beat at the thick black tentacle that gripped her legs with no result. It lowered the girl into the maw of the great beast, and with the suckling sound of a thousand ravenous pit fiends, the being consumed both flesh and bone.

"We have to flee!" Callum shouted from the far side of the chamber. He kicked at a guard, drawing his blade from deep within the man's gut, where it had lodged.

"No!" Draven shouted. "We can't let that thing loose upon the world! We have to stop it here and now!"

He let out a roar that was both deeper than that of a great saber-toothed beast and more shrill than the cry of a harpy eagle, then charged for the stairs that led to the upper platform. With little effort, he swung the great two-bladed axe in a wide arc that cleaved another of the guards in twain. Careful not to slip in the spilling entrails, he retrieved the man's spear and continued up the stairs.

"What do you propose we do?" Callum shouted from across the room.

"We kill the wee beastie!" Draven reached the upper platform and stared down over the edge at the exposed top of the creature where it extended from the portal. He hefted the spear in his right hand to test the weight of the thing, then hurled the missile downward, plunging it deep into the thing's rubbery flesh. Black ichor flowed freely into the already dark pool as the thing howled and thrashed about.

The creature screeched with a sound like the lost souls on the winds of the nether.

The black tentacles of the thing lashed out, grasping for anything within reach. The remainder of the guards fled as the god-beast snatched and devoured two more of them.

Draven crouched low as another of the thing's appendages reached onto the platform. It swung about and connected with a frightened worshiper. The strike sent him flying into a wall, cracking his bones.

Draven reeled forward, blindsided by the limb as it whipped about in search of prey. He shook the fog and spinning stars from his head, forcing himself back to his feet.

"By all the gods," Callum shouted. "Draven! Kill the Lich!"

A mighty laugh drew Draven's gaze back to the platform, where heavy muscles flexed beneath a guard's ebony skin. He spoke in a tongue full of clicks and forceful grunts, which Draven did not understand. In an overhead swing, he slammed a great maul down. Draven leapt out of the way, and the weapon crashed into the stone floor. The man swung it around in a wide arc with a single hand, bringing the castellated hammerhead around at Draven.

He ducked and rolled to the side just as the hammerhead struck the edge of the platform, knocking a number of the stones loose to drop into the pool below. With muscles bunching, the guard reversed his strike and brought the bladed edge back around in another blow.

Draven lunged backward, arching his back, and he could feel the wind of the blade as it passed by his naked groin.

He dove forward at the black warrior's feet, gripped the man by the ankle, and lifted with all his might. The ebony guard tumbled backward. Draven grabbed the great axe and swung it in a killing stroke that chopped through the guard's chest and into the stone floor.

"Kill the Lich!"

Draven worked the axe free from the chest of the corpse and stepped to the edge of the platform to take in the scene before him. Callum batted at undead things that lunged forth from the pool. D'Bia the lich and his daughter-queen continued their chant to the god-thing that slipped ever farther through the portal.

"Hurry and kill the bastard already!" Callum yelled as he severed a ghoul's leg at the knee.

Draven stepped back to the wall of the upper platform, then he turned and sprinted over the crumbling edge. He soared downward across the distance with the great axe raised high and brought it down on the lich. The blade found its mark and split cleanly through the ancient skull of the lich king, stopping only at the abrupt meeting of steel and the cold stone floor. The desiccated corpse of the old man slipped to either side and fell away to the floor.

The world exploded into a dissonance of bestial aberrations as the portal closed upon the great god-thing. The tentacles that remained fell limply to the ground, augmented by momentary muscle memory that sent contorted spasms through their dying limbs. The head of the great beast slid down and separated at the carved stone wall that had been the portal to some unknown hell dimension just moments before. Thick ichor and entrails forever stained the waters an inky black, overflowing the pool of the inner sanctum.

Draven stood tall and gazed down on what remained of the old man. *Perhaps that was who he was, once, before the evil of the undead took hold of him. Perhaps,* he thought.

"They stopped," Callum shouted. "You did it! The ghouls fell silent as soon as you split the lich's skull."

Draven held up the great axe and examined the edge of the blade. He brushed his thumb against the edge, seeing it still keen despite it being slammed into the stone.

Motion to his left caught his eye and pulled him out of his contemplation. He looked up to find Branwen sprawled out, moaning and writhing in pain on the cold stone floor. Even now her shapely nude form called to a hunger deep within him. A wave of dizziness and nausea washed over him. He leaned over and placed his hands on his knees to steady himself, but could not take his eyes from the woman's form.

Branwen sat up and turned to face him. She leaned to one side, arched her back, and presented her pert round breasts. "You have freed me of my curse, warrior. The throne is yours to claim, and I am your eternal prize."

Draven watched, transfixed on her thick full lips as a teasing tongue darted out and licked their deep red surface. All the world suddenly fell away, except those plump, ruby lips.

"Come to me, my love. Come to me and rule by my side," the lips said in a soft, sensual tone.

"She's bewitching you! Draven! Kill her!"

Draven shook his head and looked over in the direction of the familiar voice. Callum struggled to free himself from the grip of one of the beast's spasming limbs.

"By my side for all eternity," the soft voice seemingly whispered into Draven's ear. "My love...my king."

Draven turned back in the direction of Branwen's voice. She sauntered toward him slowly. Her round, enticing curves bounced gently with every step and begged for his touch. He wiped at his eyes and shook his head, but it did not clear the fog from his mind.

"Become one with me, lover," she said as she gently took him by the chin and tipped his head upward to look into her eyes. "Together we shall rule all."

Draven laughed. He let out a guffaw so loud and defiant that the gods themselves cringed at its sound. With all his might, he slammed his fist into the side of his head to clear his muddled mind.

He blinked and stared up at the desiccated, leathery flesh of the corpse bride that held his chin in her hand.

"I will not be shackled by you, nor by anyone!" He jerked his chin free and kicked her in the chest with his bare foot. She stumbled backward from the forceful blow, but regained her footing and began a low guttural chant.

Without hesitation Draven lunged forward, bringing the great axe around in a whirlwind arc that split the lich queen in two, from her right shoulder to left hip. Before the halves could slip and separate, her cadaverous form shattered and crumbled to dust that exploded into motion. A dust devil formed and undulated on the stone floor. It danced and swayed in time to a cackling scream that drifted out of the room as if it were smoke on the breeze.

"Del and Corimaen protect us," Callum said as he approached.

"Oh, aye," Draven said with a grunt. "And the Morrag's witches as well."

"I'm indebted to you, Maugan," Callum said as he flipped his sword, gripping it by the blade. He held it out to Draven and knelt. "You've freed me from a fate worse than death itself. I pledge my fealty and my steel to you, Maugan. Bound to you by my own willing honor and oath."

Draven gripped the handle of the blade and took it from the man. He admired the intricately engraved details along the lines of the fine steel, then flipped it in his hand. Holding it by the blade, he handed it back to Callum. "I'll not be master of any man, whether he is bound to me by either debt or oath. I'll claim a friend, though."

"Then your friend I shall ever be."

With a great laugh, Draven clapped the bard on his back, nearly knocking him over. "Come, let us leave this place, my friend."

Callum took the blade back and stood. "Where will we go?"

"Wherever adventure may lead us," Draven said, then smiled wide.

"Then I hope it leads us to a tavern with cold ale and pretty wenches," Callum said.

Draven laughed. He lifted the great axe to his shoulder and headed toward the exit. "Oh, aye. I'm sure there will be many an adventure begun or finished within the depths of a dram of ale."

* * * * *

William Joseph Roberts Bio

In a previous lifetime, William Joseph Roberts was an F-15 mechanic and Staff Sergeant in the United States Air Force. During this lifetime, he has traveled the world, been called a Jack of all trades, a Renaissance man and an insane squirrel wrangler by his peers. Since his enlistment ended, he has perused careers as an industrial and architectural designer, design engineer, and now, eclectic writer. William Joseph Roberts currently resides in the quaint southern town of Chickamauga, Georgia with his loving wife, three freaky-smart nerd children, and a small pack of fur babies.

Web page link: https://williamjosephroberts.com/

# # # # #

Hanging by a Thread by Benjamin Tyler Smith

"Mr. Kilaran, why is there an outhouse next to your tomb?" I pressed the sleeve of my black robe to my nose. "And what's with the pigs?"

A snort echoed from the three holes in the floor.

"It's a *joldka*, Mr. Adelvell, not an outhouse." Kilaran spread his skeletal hands to encompass the cramped room and its three stalls. The blue fire in his empty eye sockets glowed brightly in the gloom. "It's an innovation of the Treingar people: a self-cleaning privy. The pigs take care of everything." He pointed at the bone-handled shovel in my hand. "You won't be needing that here."

"This is for protection." Treingar must have been far away, if Kilaran didn't recognize the shovel for what it was. I didn't normally carry it with me, as it had a bad habit of unnerving the citizens I served. But with everything going on in Necrolopolis these days, I wouldn't leave the office without it.

"Protection?" Kilaran shrugged. "If you say so."

My eyes burned from the stench permeating the wooden structure. "What does a skeleton need with an outhouse?"

"*Joldka*. It's for through traffic. From the Mortal Quarter. And what's the problem? It's not going to hurt the ambient odor."

"Well, it's certainly not going to help."

"You mortals and your petty complaints." Kilaran crossed his arms in a clatter of humerus on rib. "Wait 'til your nose rots off your face, necromancer. I'd kill to be able to smell anything, even this!" He glanced at one of the holes in the floor. "Well, maybe not this."

Yeah, I didn't think so. I retreated outside, but waited until I was halfway down the steps before drawing a breath. The dank, musty stench that permeated this section of Necrolopolis was a blessed relief in comparison.

Kilaran followed me down. His tomb stood in the middle of the Bony Barrows, one of the poorest neighborhoods in the city's Skeleton Quarter. Crumbling tombs and weed-choked burial mounds lined the cobbled street on either side.

I held up a piece of parchment. "Mr. Kilaran, your neighbors complained about the noise your outhouse—"

Kilaran glared.

"Your *joldka* has been generating. They say people are coming and going at all hours."

"I'll keep the customers quiet," Kilaran said. "The pigs, though…They do like to make a racket from time to time."

Customers? "Wait, you *charge* people for that monstrosity?"

"Addy!" a husky voice called, before Kilaran could respond.

Down the street, a woman clad in a chainmail tunic and wielding a long-handled billhook approached at a trot. She bulled her way through the foot traffic. "Make way, make way! Constable coming through!"

Kilaran shrank back. "In Pusco's name, what does *she* want?"

I tried not to laugh. Most undead had a healthy fear of Necrolopolis' husband-wife constable team, and for good reason. I waved. "Henrietta! How are you this fine—"

"Got another limbless one for you." Henrietta settled the bill-hook's shaft against one shoulder and hiked a gloved thumb over the other. "At the Temporal Gate."

Again? That was the sixth one inside a month! "Lead the way."

She spun on her heel to leave, then sniffed the air. "Pigs?"

"Long story. Stinks, doesn't it?"

"I smelled worse back on the farm." Henrietta marched up the street. "Shake a leg, Addy! We're burnin' daylight!"

I handed the complaint letter to Kilaran. "Keep the noise down. The restless dead need their sleep." I sucked in a breath and grimaced. "And burn some incense with that coin you're earning. You owe your customers that much, at least."

Kilaran stared at the constable's retreating back, his eye sockets dim. "I'll see what I can do."

I jogged after Henrietta. One didn't keep the infamous Hook and Pitch waiting.

* * *

The iron-shod butts of our weapons clicked against the cobblestones as we walked along Mortus Way, the main street of the city's Mortal Quarter. People gave us a wide berth. Henrietta was intimidating enough on her own, but my presence enhanced the effect. Generations had passed since the Fallen War, but memories were long where black magic was concerned. That was especially true in Necrolopolis, a city of some four million undead awaiting their chance to cross to the other side.

The street opened into a wide square with a tall obsidian gate-house on the far end. A crowd of onlookers had gathered around a covered wagon near the massive gate. Most were townspeople or denizens of the undead quarters, but there were at least a few visitors in the mob, if their dust-covered clothing was any indicator.

"Make way!" Henrietta roared, opening a path.

A gnome slumped on the rider's bench of the wagon, reins held loosely in one gnarled hand. A shirtless, dark-skinned ghoul rested next to him. His shoulders ended in two stitched wounds where his arms used to be, and his trouser legs were empty. He cringed when he saw me. "A necromancer!"

"Merchant Walenty, Mr. Ranvir," Henrietta said, "this is Adelvell, assistant to Director Grimina, chief administrator of Necrolopolis. Share your story with him."

The gnome wiped his forehead with a sweat-soaked handkerchief. "I was about a mile from the city when I happened upon Mr. Ranvir." He nodded at the stricken ghoul. "He was as you see him now, except with a sack over his head."

"I could've taken them!" Ranvir spat at the ground. "I could've taken them, but they blindsided me."

"Did you see your assailants?" I asked.

"No, but as I told your constable, I did hear voices: a gruff-sounding man, and someone higher-pitched. I couldn't understand them with burlap stuffed in my ears, but it sounded like they were arguing."

"No idea at all what was said?" Henrietta removed a notebook and charcoal pencil from her belt pouch. "Even a single word could be helpful."

Ranvir shook his head. "Apologies, but no."

At least we had a little more information. Two assailants at least, but what was the motive? Undead flesh was a reagent in certain alchemical processes, but it could be legally purchased from ghouls wishing to join the ranks of the skeletal populace. And at cut-rates, too.

No pun intended.

There was also no need to take entire limbs for that. A sliver of skin went a long way. I was starting to wonder if the city had been infiltrated by a gang of necro-cannibals, or some kind of fringe faction of the Cult of Mortus.

"In my younger years, I was a mercenary, protecting caravans across the continent." Ranvir barked a laugh. "Look at me now: jumped by some limb loppers and left to rot." He looked at Walenty. "Most wouldn't help a ghoul. Thank you."

Walenty patted Ranvir on the head. "One of my sons is interred here. I couldn't imagine this happening to him." He glared at us. "You'll find those responsible, won't you?"

"That's our aim," Henrietta said.

I stood on my toes to get a closer look at one of Ranvir's shoulders. The arm had been neatly severed at the joint, and the wound sewn closed with golden thread. The flesh around the stitching looked healthy, unlike the rest of his wasted frame.

"Same as all the others," I muttered.

"'Tis just like the others," a lyrical voice said.

I jumped, startled. A pixie floated overhead, her silvery wings fluttering. She wore a tight-fitting leather tunic and trousers, both dyed a light blue. A brown bag was strapped to one hip, and what appeared to be a brass thimble hung from the other. Her lavender eyes bored into Ranvir as she scribbled in a notebook with a quill.

"Arrived in Necrolopolis," she murmured as she wrote. "Met a ghoul—What's yer name, good sir?"

"R-Ranvir," he stammered, glancing from the pixie to me. I shrugged.

"Met a ghoul named Ranvir. All limbs amputated. Judging by the limited signs of necrotic regression, I estimate removal occurred within the last day. Two, at most. Suturing is excellent, but conducted in haste."

Henrietta craned her neck upward. "Can we help you, Miss—?"

"Pray, forgive me. I've yet tae introduce myself." The pixie closed her notebook and bowed. "Chief Apprentice Dymphna, at yer service."

"Chief apprentice of what?" I asked.

"Chirurgery." Dymphna dropped the notebook into her hip bag and produced a scroll. "My writ of licensure, from the Parlor Lord himself."

I wasn't sure who this parlor lord was, but he had horrible handwriting. I squinted. "Couldn't you have made this bigger?"

"Oh, ha." Dymphna rolled her eyes. "Tell me, do all middle folk make the same stupid remarks, or just bureaucrats like yerself?"

Tell me, are all small folk as insufferable as you? I held my tongue and read the scroll. "'Dymphna Gaelen is hereby granted the title of Chief Apprentice Chirurgeon. She is to have access to and use of the healing thread produced by the Parlor Spinners, in the quantities needed by her or her maester.'"

"Healing thread?" Henrietta asked.

"The sutures around Mr. Ranvir's wounds." Dymphna rolled the document and returned it to the hip bag. She drifted down to the ghoul's shoulder and pointed. "See how it glimmers? It's the same with all the others."

"You're saying a pixie did this?" Henrietta stepped closer. "A pixie like you?"

"How rude!" Dymphna glowered at the constable. "If I was involved, d'ya think I'd be conversing with ya like this?"

I stepped between them. "You mentioned 'the others.' You've seen the other victims here?"

"Nay. You mean there've been more in Necrolopolis?"

"Just so." Henrietta returned the glower. "Where'd *you* mean?"

"We've been following this trail for the past two moons, since leaving Firinor. We've counted nine victims, including Mr. Ranvir."

My stomach clenched. "Make that fourteen. He's the sixth in Necrolopolis alone."

"So many?" Dymphna balled her tiny hands into fists. "This is where we'll find him. I'd bet my scalpel on it."

"Him? We? Who are you talking about?"

Dymphna rose into the air and whistled. Six pixies flitted in from every direction and gathered around her. Each was clad in matching leather tunic and trousers, complete with bag and thimble. "We are the crew of Maester Faolan, the greatest chirurgeon of the age." She smiled. "Give my father needle and thread, and he'll fix a man cut near in half."

Henrietta jotted in her notebook. "And where is your father?"

The smile vanished. "Gone. Nay." Her lower lip trembled. "Taken."

"Taken?"

"The maester went missing when the mutilations began," another of the pixies said. He studied us, his expression hard. "We believe he's being forced tae conduct illegal chirurgery."

Excitement stirred within me, along with a pang of guilt. I felt bad for Dymphna, but this could be the clue Henrietta and I desperately needed.

"I want to rescue my father." Dymphna dabbed at her eyes, then looked down at me. "Will ya help us, Mr. Adelvell?"

* * *

I knelt in the dirt, my hands supporting Ranvir as Walenty strapped him to my back. "This'll just be until we get to the constabulary," I said. Henrietta had already gone ahead to wake her husband Paul, who worked the nightshift.

"I hope so." Ranvir heaved a sigh. "This is most embarrassing."

"For you and me both," I muttered. There were fewer gathered around the wagon now than there had been before Dymphna showed up and Henrietta took her leave, but the few remaining looked at me as if I had two heads.

Bad analogy, I know.

"And don't try to compel me."

I grunted as Walenty cinched the rope tight. "It doesn't work that way. My blood needs to get on you before I can do anything. Besides, it's forbidden in Necrolopolis." I wasn't even allowed to draw on my magic without permission, except in self-defense.

Walenty clapped me on the shoulder. "All done. Get on with you, and stop these malcontents."

We left Temporal Square and walked toward the constabulary. Well, *I* walked, Ranvir rode, and Dymphna and her pixies flew. "You could've gone ahead without me," I said.

"Mr. Ranvir's a patient. Once father touched him, he became our charge."

I used my shovel as a walking stick and leaned into it with each step. Even without his limbs, Ranvir was heavy. "How do you know it's the work of your father?"

"The healing thread." Dymphna landed on my shoulder and touched Ranvir's stump. "Chirurgeons weave their magic into both flesh and fabric. Call it a maker's mark."

"And it's the combination of thread and magic that revives the dead flesh?"

"Nay. It's been restored tae the moment of death, but no further. Eventually the tissue will rot, unless the thread is reapplied."

"Careful who you say that to here." If word got around that pixie healers could restore decaying flesh, we'd be up to our ears in requests for maesters. And if my demigoddess of a boss couldn't provide them, the city's seedy underbelly would step in by any means necessary.

Dymphna flapped her wings and rose to join her companions. Sunlight glinted off the thimble bouncing against her hip. I pointed. "What're those for?"

"Oh, this?" She patted the brass surface. "A tool fer the healing trade."

"How can it be used for healing?" It looked much too big for her to use when working with a needle.

"A secret of the trade. Pray that ya never learn more than that."

"That's…ominous."

She smiled, but said no more.

We passed through a small square with a fountain at its center. A crowd not unlike the one at Walenty's wagon had gathered, and over the tinkling spray of water I heard someone singing baritone. I grimaced and quickened my step.

"Such a lovely voice." Dymphna hovered higher to peer over the crowd. She gasped. "'Tis a *ghoul!*"

"Velvet-Tongued Cecil," I said, not slowing down.

"I know this name." Ranvir stirred on my back. "He was a traveling minstrel. We crossed paths a few times in my caravan days."

In life, Cecil had been renowned throughout the continent as a musician and singer without peer. In death, his reputation was no less storied, and he was just as popular in Necrolopolis as he was in the music halls of Penrose and Montsanten. Every faction of the undead was happy to host him. Even Ashwarden, and *he* hated anyone who wasn't part of his Cremainder gang.

"Gods!" Dymphna put a hand to her chest. "His limbs are gone!"

"He was the first. A month ago, he was found like that near Columbarium Tower in the Ashling Quarter. We had no idea who attacked him."

"How awful. And the others?"

"A dwarf gem cutter named Dolgir was found a week later, outside the shop he runs from the first floor of his mausoleum. At first, we thought this was a coincidence, until seamstress Hiliana lost her arms a few days later. That's when we realized there was a pattern. Cecil we could have passed off as some kind of lovers' quarrel gone horribly wrong, but with two others?"

Mina had been furious. She had called Henrietta, Paul, and me to her office on the top floor of Necrolopolis Hall. She didn't pound her bloodwood desk with her petite hands, nor did she threaten us with her father Mortus' reaping scythe. Instead, she just quietly stared at us for a time, her red irises aglow. Finally, she said, "I won't have this in my city. Find the culprits and send them to Father for judgment."

As I described the remaining victims to Dymphna, I hoped we could finally carry out Mina's will.

We turned up a narrow side street, this one crammed with shop stalls and packed with prospective buyers. I plunged ahead. Even on market day, this was the quickest route to the constabulary. The crowd tried to let me by, but the crush of bodies made that impossible. Instead, people just flinched and pressed themselves against whoever wasn't me.

Sometimes being a necromancer paid off.

Dymphna and her pixies hovered above, taking in the sights and sounds. "Who would kidnap your father?" I asked, raising my voice over the din.

"Who would gain from stealing limbs off ghouls?" Dymphna called back. "That's who we should be looking for."

That was the problem, wasn't it? Someone stood to gain from this, but who? None of the city's faction leaders would dare try something this heinous. If not out of respect for their fellow undead, then out of fear of Mina or her divine father.

Besides, why bother selling undead parts when a pixie chirurgeon could just stitch up a ghoul's own limbs? That thought troubled me. The addition of Dymphna's maester to the mix spoke of much more elaborate planning than any of us had anticipated.

"Mr. Adelvell, behind you!" Ranvir shouted.

I spun and tried to bring up my shovel, but Ranvir's weight shifted. I stumbled and went down to one knee. Something shiny streaked over my head.

The pixies screamed as a metallic net covered them. They struck the cobbles with a loud thump. "Get us out of here!" Dymphna cried.

A jolt of anger shot through me as I scrambled to my feet. Who in the thirteen hells—?

"Nice toss, Clesk!" a feminine voice called.

The panicked crowd scattered, and four individuals in various states of vitality or decay stepped in front of us: two living men in traveler's cloaks, one orc ghoul, and one skeleton. The leaner man wielded a short spear in his gloved hands, while the larger one brandished a heavy cudgel. The ghoul and skeleton each carried a sword.

"Thanks, Eshe." Clesk twirled his cudgel and flicked his free hand up. "It's all in the wrist."

Eshe cackled, her eye sockets burning purple. "Boss Gualter'll love this haul."

The orc ghoul gasped and pointed at me. "It's a necromancer! We can't fight him, Hul!"

"That's what *we're* here for, Borgas." Hul leveled his spear at me. "We don't want any trouble, necro. Just the pixies."

Road dust covered Clesk and Hul's clothes. My eyes widened. "You were at the Temporal Gate!"

"Yeah?" Clesk smacked the flat of his palm with the cudgel. "And what if we were?"

"That voice!" Ranvir thrashed against my back. "He's one of the ones who carved me up!"

I stepped between the thugs and the stricken pixie crew. "Lady Dymphna is under the protection of Director Grimina. My boss won't stand for anyone being harmed inside her father's city."

"Good news for you and your boss, then." Hul advanced, Clesk a step behind. "We're almost full up on parts. Once we get these new pixies underground, we're out of here."

Only an outsider would fail to see the threat posed by my boss. Mina was happy and bubbly most days, but she wasn't called Lady Death for nothing. "It's your funeral." I widened my stance and raised my shovel. "Hope you brought your interment fee."

Clesk snorted. "You want to fight us with *that?*"

Definitely outsiders. It might not look like much, but the shovel had been a gift from my mentor. He and his fellow necromancers had carried them into battle during the Fallen War, to be used as weapons and magical foci. I was out of practice, but I kept the blade sharp. It would be enough for these louts.

I hoped.

Hul thrust his spear at my chest. I parried with my shovel, then countered. He danced away. Clesk rushed at me from the right. I ducked the clumsy swing and kicked him in the gut. The big man fell on his rump, the wind knocked from him.

"To your left!" Ranvir cried.

I spun and tried to dodge Hul's lunge, but Ranvir's weight slowed my movement. Pain lanced across my side, and I gasped. Mortus, it hurt! I slashed at Hul's midsection, but he jumped back.

Eshe brushed past Hul as she charged, her sword held high. Borgas was a pace behind her, his puffy lips pulled back in a snarl.

Three against one? Time to even the odds. I tapped into my power. A translucent black orb bubbled out of me and slammed into

Eshe and Borgas. Skeleton and ghoul sailed backward and crashed into a baker's stall. The structure collapsed in a heap of splinters and ruined pastries.

Hul struck the ground at the same time, his right arm hanging at an odd angle. He cursed. "Bloody hell!"

I frowned. Only undead were affected by my spirit shield, and Hul was very much alive. Had Borgas' bloated girth clipped the spearman?

Ranvir jerked his weight to the left, and I fell on my side. Clesk's cudgel cracked the cobblestones I'd just been standing on. The big man stepped my way, his weapon poised to strike. I tried to bring up my shovel, but the handle was trapped beneath me. Fear seized my heart.

A shrill whistle pierced the air. "The constables are here!" someone shouted.

Clesk looked down the street and snorted. "One more fool won't make a difference."

"Make that two!"

Clesk whirled around just as Henrietta struck, her billhook's blade flashing. The weapon separated the giant thug's head from his shoulders. Blood fountained from his neck as he teetered, then fell.

"It's Hook and Pitch!" Borgas cried. He scrambled to get his bulk free of the baker's cart.

Cherry pie filling covered one of Eshe's eye sockets as she turned toward Henrietta. "It's you!"

Hul scrambled to his feet. He tucked his broken arm against his body and darted down a nearby alley. "Run for it, you two!"

Borgas jumped up and ran, his green backside covered in icing and fruit jam.

Eshe glared at us for a moment before following after Borgas. "Wait for me!"

Where do you think you're going? I channeled my magic into a black ball the size of my fist. I pulled my arm back and hurled the dark sphere at the retreating skeleton. I still lay on my side, so the throw was awkward. The ball nicked her collarbone and shot past her. She and Borgas disappeared from view.

A man in the same type of mail as Henrietta broke through the crowd. He charged into the alley, his pitchfork held in both hands. "Halt! In Grimina's name, halt!"

Henrietta bent over me and extended a hand. "I can't leave you alone for even a quarter-hour, Addy."

"Thanks." I nodded toward Clesk. "Shame you couldn't spare him."

"He called my husband a fool." She grinned. "Only I get to do that."

"You could've killed him *after* we questioned him."

"Can't you just…" She wiggled her fingers at me.

It was that kind of attitude that perpetuated necromantic distrust. I wanted to admonish Henrietta, but she had just saved my life. By chopping off a man's head, no less. "His soul's already gone, on its way to the Isle of Passage. I can't question an empty shell."

Dymphna flew over to us, her hair a tangled mess. Behind her, the rest of her crew pulled themselves from the metallic net. More than one held a bone saw or scalpel.

"You're bleeding." She dropped down to inspect my side. "I'll have that sutured in a moment."

"Don't let his blood get on me!" Ranvir snapped.

Well, excuse me for being mortal. I bit back the retort, and said, "You saved my life, Ranvir. Thanks."

"If I had my limbs, these thugs would've been nothing." He spat on the ground. "Nothing!"

I glanced at Clesk. "Dymphna, can you reattach limbs like Maester Faolan?"

"My skills pale in comparison to his, but yes." Her eyes narrowed. "What d'ya have in mind?"

I grinned. "Oh, nothing you can't handle."

* * *

Paul spread a detailed map of Necrolopolis across the table's surface and placed five crudely-carved toy soldiers at different points. "This is where the original victims were found."

He and I stood in the main work area of the constabulary, a squat fortress of a building in the center of the Mortal Quarter. The structure was capable of housing an entire company of watchmen, but so far only Henrietta and Paul had been brave enough to join. Mina hoped having the famous Hook and Pitch would attract more recruits to help police the city's living residents. Until then, they were in the same boat as me: overworked, underpaid, and feared just enough to keep things interesting.

Paul placed a sixth figure at the Temporal Gate. "Mr. Ranvir was somewhere within eyeshot of the city when he was attacked. I'll also need the locations of Lady Dymphna's eight victims."

"Shouldn't we keep our focus within Necrolopolis?" I asked.

"For now, but this is a much bigger problem. There are more victims than even our pixie healer knows about." Paul picked up another figurine and ran his thumb along the toy's painted helmet. "There always are," he added quietly.

I grunted. He was right. Whoever was doing this had a far-reaching operation, one that could affect undead across the continent.

A door on the chamber's far end opened, and Henrietta appeared. Ranvir followed after her, moving unsteadily on his legs. *Clesk's* legs, to be more accurate. He flexed the dead bandit's pale arms. "It'll take some getting used to, but this is remarkable work."

Dymphna floated into the room. "Go easy for the next little while. I'll not have any of yer new limbs popping off."

"Yes, Lady Dymphna."

She landed next to one of Paul's toys and crossed her arms. "I don't much enjoy mutilating the dead, Mr. Adelvell."

"If it makes you feel better, Clesk's soul wasn't around for the mutilating. Unlike his victims."

"Fair point."

Paul wrinkled his nose. "Mr. Ranvir, go scrub your new limbs. They reek of pigs."

"What're you complaining about?" Henrietta asked. "We smelled worse back on our farm."

Wait. Pigs? "Ranvir, where would you say Hul and the others are from?"

"Considering their style of dress and accents, a few countries come to mind." Ranvir counted off his borrowed fingers. "Yulnan, Ecklo, and Treingar."

I sighed. "Great. Just great."

"What's the matter?" Dymphna asked.

"You'll see." I grabbed my shovel. "Come on. I think I know where the enemy lair is."

* * *

"Addy, why are we in an outhouse?" Paul pressed a handkerchief to his nose. "And what's with the pigs?"

"It's a *joldka*, not an outhouse." My eyes stung as I walked to the rear of the cramped room. A trapdoor with a ring-shaped handle had been cut into the corner, large enough for a man to climb through. "It's a self-cleaning privy. The pigs take care of everything."

"My nose would argue otherwise."

Dymphna coughed. "On that, we agree." She and her crew wore perfume-laced cloths around their faces. "All I smell is floral-scented excrement."

I grabbed the handle and pulled. The trapdoor lifted on well-oiled hinges, revealing the top rung of a ladder. Snorts and squeals rose from the darkness below. I leaned over the hole and held my aether-lantern to see, but Paul yanked me back. A crossbow bolt snapped past my face and embedded in the ceiling.

A curse drifted from the pigpen, followed by a clatter.

Ranvir jumped down the hole. The pigs screamed in fright, as did a familiar voice. "Get away from me! Help!"

Paul clambered down the ladder, followed by Henrietta, then me. The green light from our lanterns reflected in the eyes of five fat pigs hiding in the corner of the smelly room. A multitude of flies buzzed through the fetid air, a result of so much waste on the floor. This was a rare sight in the undead section of town. Protective magic kept most carrion insects at bay, which greatly decreased the rate of decay for the city's fleshier citizens.

It did nothing for the stench, though.

Kilaran struggled against Ranvir's iron grip, his eye sockets blazing with blue light. "Let me go! I'm a citizen!"

"A citizen who attacks civil servants?" Henrietta picked up a crossbow. "Or were you shooting at flies and one went wide?"

An open doorway stood next to Kilaran, revealing a wooden stairwell leading down. I took a step toward it, and my boot crunched against something hard: A broken femur, its jagged ends covered in teeth marks.

Bone fragments lay scattered across the filthy floor. "Gods, how awful," Dymphna said as she descended into the refuse pit, her lavender eyes aglow. "There must be dozens of limbs here!"

I tightened my grip on the shovel. "What's going on here, Mr. Kilaran?"

"You heard Mr. Adelvell." Paul patted the mallet looped in his belt. "Start talking, before we remember how much we hate your misbegotten kind."

"Skeletons overran our farm." Henrietta slammed the crossbow against the wall, right next to Kilaran's skull. "Skeletons killed our children. Skeletons pierced my womb and left me barren!"

Kilaran squeaked. "Mr. Adelvell! Help me, please!"

"And why should I do that?" I hooked my lantern to my belt and tapped my forehead. "Remember that crossbow bolt? Because I do."

Ranvir pounded the floor with Clesk's cudgel. "None of these limbs better be mine, you stinking toilet troll!"

"Toilet troll? How dare you—"

Ranvir's next blow splintered the wooden floor.

"N-n-no, of course not! These are the discards. Your limbs are of much better stock than this, to be sure."

Mortus, how many "discards" are there? We were looking at dozens of victims, many who would never get their limbs back. I wanted to let the pigs chew on Kilaran, but we had more pressing concerns.

I pointed at the stairwell. "What's below?"

"Access tunnels the Collectors once used for the Catacombs of Final Rest, before the section beneath this quarter filled up. Lord Gualter's using a storehouse deep inside as his lair." Kilaran raised his skeletal hands. "He pressured me into doing this. I swear I'm not involved!"

"We'll see." I channeled magic into my hand and shaped the energy into black manacles. They fit tight against Kilaran's ankle bones. "Take us to this storehouse."

"And you best not lead us astray." Henrietta grabbed Kilaran and shoved him toward the stairs. "Or it's coming out of what's left of your hide!"

The staircase connected to the broken wall of a damp, dark tunnel. Rubble blocked one direction, but the other direction extended well past the range of our lanterns.

We splashed through puddles of muddy brown water as Kilaran stumbled down the tunnel. Henrietta and I walked right behind him, with Ranvir and Paul bringing up the rear. The path twisted several times, and we traveled through so many side passages I feared getting lost on the return trip.

The pixie crew hovered between Henrietta and me. "How's your wound?" Dymphna asked.

I touched my side. "Much better. Thank you."

Her face flushed. "My thread won't heal as quickly as father's, but it'll prevent infection and scarring."

Kilaran staggered into the wall. "These twice-damned manacles," he complained loudly, his bony digits running along the wall. He pushed himself upright, and a series of clinks and clanks reverberated through the tunnel.

Something shifted in the ceiling.

I shoved Henrietta back. She tripped on her billhook's shaft and fell with a loud splash. Before she could recover, a grate of rusted iron slammed down between us.

Kilaran tried to run. I concentrated on the manacles around his ankles and clenched my fist. The black energy sprang from his legs and coiled about his body. He struck the floor with a dull smack and rolled around, throwing curses my way.

Paul helped Henrietta up, then punched the grate with an armored fist. "It's rusted, but strong."

"Can you destroy it, Mr. Adelvell?" Ranvir asked.

I shook my head. "Necromancy only affects the dead and undead."

"And these bars are too thick for us to cut through," Dymphna said.

Henrietta spat on the grimy floor. "We'll have to find another way in."

Kilaran laughed. "Good luck with that!"

I stabbed my shovel blade through Kilaran's exposed neck and scooped up his skull. "That's where you come in, my bony friend."

"Stop! My body!"

"I'll put it somewhere safe until this is over."

"What happens if you get killed?"

I shoved Kilaran's skull between the bars. "You better hope that doesn't happen."

"Hey, watch the cheek bones!"

Henrietta took Kilaran's skull. "Don't string us along, criminal. If anything happens to Addy, we'll smuggle you out of the city and take you to the exorcists. You'll never see the other side."

I shivered. Banishment was death of the soul itself, and the worst thing that could happen to anyone, undead or otherwise. I hoped she was bluffing. As much as Kilaran's actions sickened me, he deserved better.

"You're injured, Mr. Adelvell," Ranvir said. "Will you be all right on your own?"

"He won't be alone!" Dymphna reached into her hip bag and drew her scalpel. The other pixies brandished needles, knives, and bone saws. "We're in this to the end."

"Doesn't this violate some kind of healer's code?" I asked.

"'Do no harm, unless someone tries tae harm ya.'" Dymphna grinned. "Then ya mess up their guts so they can't harm anyone again."

"Fair point."

Paul, Henrietta, and Ranvir jogged back up the tunnel. "We'll join you soon!" Paul shouted.

"Like the proverbial cavalry!" Henrietta added.

Dymphna watched them leave. "They have a guide, but what about us? 'Tis a maze down here."

"Let me try something." I closed my eyes and focused my energy into the shovel's handle. It had once served as a necromantic divining rod, to find corpses and souls to enthrall. More grist for the Fallen War's mill. My stomach soured at the thought, but I pressed on. The victims were counting on us.

The shovel tilted left, toward the grate barring our retreat. Through the magic, I sensed a pair of undead. That had to be Kilaran and Ranvir, and they were moving fast. Hook and Pitch set a relentless pace on the hunt.

I poured more energy into the shovel to expand its radius. Sweat beaded along my brow, and my head ached from the effort. There, up ahead—more than twenty undead clustered together. Since these tunnels were sealed, that meant only one thing. "I've found them."

"We should hurry," Dymphna said. "They may be preparing to leave."

I ran down the corridor. My lantern bobbed up and down, casting its beam of green light in a dizzying pattern as we turned left, then right. Dymphna rode on my shoulder, while the other pixies hovered around us in a protective circle. Their beating wings buzzed in my ears as we followed the shovel's guidance.

The tunnel widened into a vast chamber illuminated by wall and column sconces. Row upon row of shelves filled with moldy crates and crockery lined the place. Some of the shelves contained boxes that looked new, while others lay barren.

In the center of the room, silhouetted figures laughed and cursed as they moved about. I shuttered my aether-lantern and crept forward, keeping to the shadows. The figures resolved into men, ghouls, and skeletons. Some stood guard, while others carried boxes to a pair of wagons on the room's far side.

"You'll do as you're told!" someone bellowed. "Or shall we kill her? My people have your daughter and her precious crew. With a snap of my fingers—"

I couldn't make out the murmured reply, but Dymphna went rigid. "Could it be? Father!"

She leaped off my shoulder and soared toward the voices. Her crew hesitated an instant before winging after her. I cursed and broke into a run.

Screams and shrieks pierced the gloom, along with the crashing of crates and scrambling of boots on stone. I put on a burst of speed and entered the open space. Several gang members writhed on the ground, clutching at sliced hamstrings or missing fingers. The others swatted at the pixies flying overhead. "Get the nets!" one yelled.

An orc ghoul covered in icing and pie filling pointed at me. "Boss Gualter, it's him!"

"Hello, Borgas." Black energy crackled along my fingertips. "So glad you remember me."

Borgas backed away, eyes wide.

A tall man stood in the center of the room, surrounded by Hul and several well-armed thugs. He wore a sleeveless shirt, and the muscles in his arms looked like they were made of tanned granite. One of his hands clutched the short handle of an axe, and the other held a birdcage with a white-haired pixie inside.

He bowed. "Welcome, Mr. Necromancer. I'm Gualter. Thank you for bringing the pixie crew to me." He shook the cage. "This one needs more...motivation for the next phase of the operation. Having his daughter should do the trick."

"Father!" Dymphna cried. She swooped down from the ceiling. Hul jumped in front of Gualter and stabbed at Dymphna with his knife. She dodged the blade and lashed out with her scalpel.

Hul's knife clattered to the ground, along with his thumb and index finger. He shrieked in pain.

"Don't worry, Hul," Gualter said. "We'll make her reattach them. Or we'll get you a new hand. Something to match your other arm."

That was why my spirit shield had affected Hul. "You're not selling these limbs to other undead. It's for the living!"

"Very astute." Gualter nodded at the wagons. "This will be enough to get us started back in Treingar. Once established, people will come from all over for replacement limbs. For most amputees, anything will do, but for the discerning eye, we'll have the arms and legs of athletes, warriors, artists, and craftsmen."

Anger boiled within me. It all made sense now: Ranvir the mercenary; Cecil the minstrel; Dolgir the gem cutter; Hiliana the seamstress. They and the others had been targeted for the muscle memory stored in their limbs. With just a bit of golden thread, anyone could be a master of whatever craft they chose.

I ground my teeth together. "You'd mutilate dozens of people for money?"

"Dozens?" Gualter laughed. "It'll be hundreds—no, thousands—before we're through. My boss is quite demanding."

I slammed the iron-shod butt of my shovel against the stone floor, the metallic clang like the toll of a funeral bell. "Death is too good for scum like you. I won't allow you to harm anyone else."

Or so I said. Mortus, how were we supposed to fight so many?

A door burst open. Henrietta, Paul, and Ranvir charged in. Henrietta hurled Kilaran's skull and smacked one of the guards square in the jaw. She jumped over his unconscious body and lopped a ghoul's head off. "In the name of Lady Grimina, surrender at once!"

I grinned. Like the proverbial cavalry, indeed.

Paul stabbed a skeleton in the ribcage with his pitchfork, then flung it over his shoulder. The undead exploded against a nearby column. Its skull rolled to a stop next to Kilaran. The two skulls screamed.

Ranvir swung his cudgel at a dwarf ghoul and mortal human. The pair smashed into a group of crate-laden skeletons. Arms, legs, and bones flew everywhere.

"Kill them all!" Gualter shouted. "But keep their limbs safe!"

A familiar laugh answered Gualter, and Eshe strode out from behind a column. "Can you imagine what we'd get for the arms of Hook and Pitch?" She tossed her sword from one skeletal hand to the other. "It might make up for what they did to my lovely horde all those years ago."

Paul's head snapped toward Eshe. "Oh, ho. I guess we didn't put all of you in the ground, did we?"

"We'll fix that!" Henrietta sheared the arm off a ghoul with her billhook, then lopped off his leg with the reverse swing. She kicked the crippled undead over and charged Eshe.

"Stay together!" Ranvir shouted.

The ghoul mercenary was hard pressed, fighting against four opponents at once. A skeleton tried to stab him in the back, but I blasted it apart. "Ranvir's right! Don't get separated!"

"Save the Maester!" Dymphna cried.

She and her crew swarmed the thugs closest to Gualter. They flew above, beneath, and between the gang members, swarming them like gnats. Mortal and ghoul alike cursed and cried out as they were slashed again and again. One tried to run away, but he tripped and fell, dragging another down with him. Golden thread tangled their limbs. One of the pixies laughed. "The bigger they are—!"

A net covered the pixie and dragged him to the floor.

More nets sailed through the air. Dymphna and one other pixie reached the rafters in the high ceiling, but the others were captured.

Paul pitched another skeleton into the air. A ghoul lunged at him with a club, but my energy bolt caught her in the chest. She collapsed, her rotting body paralyzed.

"My thanks!" Paul drew his mallet and whacked a bandit in the temple. The man dropped on top of the ghoul, unconscious or dead, I couldn't say.

Henrietta and Eshe danced across a tight space in the underground storehouse, trading strikes, blocks, and parries. I tried to aim for Eshe, but the two moved so fast I couldn't get a clear shot. "Stay out of this, Addy! This is between her and me!"

Movement caught my eye. I spun and blocked Gualter's axe with my shovel handle. The force of the blow pushed me back. I countered with a slash, but Gualter deflected it. Back and forth we went. I swung, he dodged. He chopped, I deflected.

My next attack went for his neck, but he ducked and backed away. I followed with a thrust to his chest. He raised the cage holding Maester Faolan. I stopped short. "Damn you, coward!"

"I fight to win, Mr. Necromancer." Gualter lifted his axe, and I readied myself for the next set of attacks.

Then Gualter did something I hadn't expected: he turned and ran. I sprinted after him. So much for all that bluster and—

He whirled about with terrifying speed. I tried to jump clear, but his axe tore into my left side. He pushed me away and wrenched the blade free. I collapsed to my knees, my ruined side ablaze with agony.

"Mr. Adelvell!" Dymphna shrieked from the rafters.

"Addy!" Paul shouted. "Filthy rotters, get out of my way!"

I tried to stand, but the searing pain forced me down. My vision swam. Mortus, it hurt!

Gualter flexed his bloody arms. "These came from the great Jiltor, a gladiator in Treingar." He studied me. "We wouldn't get much for your limbs, but they'll make fine trophies."

Jiltor? Those weren't his? I reached deep into my faltering magic and focused on Gualter. The pixie's healing arts masked it, but his arms were definitely dead. And they had my blood on them. I grinned and thought a simple command that even my foggy mind couldn't get wrong.

Gualter's hands released axe and cage, then clamped onto his throat. His eyes bulged as the great Jiltor's strength crushed his windpipe. He fell onto his backside and rolled around, trying in vain to control arms that weren't his, trying in vain to draw breath that would never come.

"There." I spat blood. "Not as out of practice as—"

I passed out.

* * *

I woke to pain all through my body, and a coppery wetness in my mouth. Mortus, what happened? I opened my eyes, but blinding light forced them shut again.

People spoke in hushed whispers all around, in a singsong language I was familiar with but didn't understand. The conversations were drowned out by a strange sound that repeated at regular intervals. *Clunk-whoosh. Clunk-whoosh. Clunk-whoosh.*

Belatedly, I realized I lay on my right side. I cracked my eyelids open. Lanterns had been hung from several nearby columns, bathing this section of the storehouse in noontime light. Blood pooled around me. A lot of blood. Was all that mine?

My robes had been cut away, revealing a ghastly wound on my left side. Maester Faolan stood next to the opening, watching as a pixie tied golden thread around what looked like an exposed rib. She wore a brass thimble on her head. No, not a thimble: a helmet. A hose ran from its shiny dome to a small bellows resting on my thigh. Another pixie worked the bellows steadily, pushing the lever high before pulling it down.

Clunk-whoosh. Clunk-whoosh.

The helmeted pixie wrapped her wings around her body like a bat, then she slid down into the wound, using the rib as an anchor. The ache in my side flared, and I groaned.

Faolan looked at me. "Ah, Mr. Adelvell, welcome back."

Dymphna appeared at my side, a brace of tiny skins in her hands. She poured their contents down my parched throat. I coughed, but managed to swallow the bitter liquid.

"The potion will dull the pain," Faolan said. He held up a pair of brass helmets. "We're just about ready tae work."

"How bad?" I croaked. Speaking hurt. Breathing hurt. Mortus, just *living* hurt.

"You have several broken ribs and a punctured lung, yer stomach and small intestine might as well be fused together, and there's a nasty boil on yer hip we'll be wanting tae lance."

"So pretty good, but for the boil." I coughed again. When was that potion going to do its job?

"We'll get ya sewn up right quick, Mr. Adelvell." To his daughter, he said, "Dymphna, it's time."

Dymphna took a helmet from Faolan and looked at me, her eyes glistening with unshed tears. "I said it'd be best if ya didn't find out what these were for, didn't I?"

"You also said your father could fix a man cut near in half," I whispered, my words slurred.

Dymphna laughed and kissed the tip of my nose. "Ya didn't have tae make us prove that, ya know."

Another of Faolan's crew attached hoses to their helmets. They waited a moment, then waved at the pixie working the bellows.

Clunk-whoosh. Clunk-whoosh.

The potion hit me just as Faolan and Dymphna took the plunge into my insides. Darkness swallowed me.

* * *

I set the large crate down in the back of merchant Walenty's covered wagon. "These should be the last." I wiped my forehead with a sleeve and was thankful for the cool, early morning air. Who knew severed limbs weighed so much?

Ranvir set another crate into the wagon. With his true legs restored, the ghoul towered over me. "Thank you for the help, Mr. Adelvell." He bowed low. "For this, and everything else. I'll never be able to repay you."

Faolan and Dymphna floated from the back of the wagon. "We also owe a debt of gratitude to ya," the maester said.

"After what you did for me, consider the debt repaid." It was hard to believe only a week had passed since the storehouse battle. My horrific wounds were gone, even the scars. Pixie magic was great.

Dymphna landed on my shoulder. "Just be more careful, Mr. Adelvell. We only have so much healing thread, and we've a long journey ahead of us."

"Ain't that the truth!" a husky voice called.

Henrietta and Paul appeared from the mist blanketing the square. She was clad in her customary armor, but Paul wore a rucksack and traveler's cloak. "I trust my husband won't prove a bother if he tags along?"

"I'll pull my weight, woman. Enough for us both."

"And I'll do the same here." She reached out and clasped his free hand. "See justice done, and avenge our children."

"Aye," Paul said, his voice tight.

"All right, get going." She thumped his leg with the butt of her billhook. "I hate all this weepy stuff."

"We're glad to have an experienced lawman with us." Ranvir extended an arm that Paul clasped. "I look forward to working with you."

"Likewise."

The pair mounted horses provided by Mina. I climbed onto the rider's bench next to Walenty. Inside the wagon, Faolan and Dymphna settled in with the rest of the crew. Some napped, others tended to chirurgical equipment, and one plucked at a tiny harp.

Walenty snapped his reins. A mixture of excitement and trepidation bubbled up inside me as we passed through the Temporal Gate. My first trip outside Necrolopolis since my tenure as Mina's assistant began, and it was for city business. Returning the stolen limbs to the victims was only part of our purpose. Eshe, Borgas, and several others had escaped in one of the wagons. Doubtless they were on their way back to Treingar and Gualter's boss, whoever that was.

Mina's orders had been explicit: "Root out this gang, and bring them to final justice."

Oh, we would do just that.

* * * * *

Benjamin Tyler Smith Bio

By day, Benjamin earns his bread as a necro-cartographer (which is a fancy way of saying he makes digital maps) for a cemetery software company, and by night, he writes about undead, aliens, and everything in between. *Blue Crucible* is his first novel. Other works include short stories set in Chris Kennedy Publishing's Four Horsemen military sci-fi universe, and the Sha'Daa dark fantasy/horror universe by Copperdog Publishing. He had stories that were Baen contest finalists in 2018 and 2019. He is working on the sequel to *Blue Crucible*, as well as a Four Horsemen novel, both of which will be finished by the end of 2020.

# # # # #

Shard's Fortress by Dexter Herron

The pounding rain fell insistently as the Goblins crawled their way along the tenuous trail turned roaring river. Their flat noses just poked above the black, frothing water as they struggled to follow the thug ahead. In the lead, their captain moved, unrelenting. His toes scrabbled for purchase in the slick clay as his black eyes squinted in the harsh spray, scanning the darkness ahead.

Captain Wiggletooth Shard was on a mission of mayhem.

Specifically Mayhem. Shard had never done a Mayhem mission before, and he wasn't quite sure what it meant. It sounded much like, "go over there and fuck those guys up," but Major Bark-Bite was emphatic about involving Mayhem.

Mayhem, Bark-Bite had explained, was what Shard was known for.

"It's your theme," Bark-Bite said, appearing next to him in the latrine.

"By Roberta's rubber-spiked cock!" Shard screamed, startled. "Where the fuck did you come from?"

Bark-Bite looked around distractedly. "I've always liked these two-seaters. You could encourage the thug next to you, you know,

159

cheer him on." The major's thick glasses glinted dully as he eyed his captain. "How goes it? All well?"

Shard looked around slowly. He was in a dark, confined latrine with one door and two holes, one occupied by his bum. He had been alone with his thoughts, a rare, precious moment for a Goblin officer. An eye blink later, his major sat next to him, the intoxicating wreath of halitosis and chaw from his heavy, rum-soaked breath overpowering the latrine's stench.

"All good, sir," Shard mumbled. "You literally scared the shit out of me."

Bark-Bite smiled with remarkably straight teeth. "See how well these latrines work?" He leaned back, his eyes flashing with memory. "The twelve-seaters, gah, that was too much pressure. Thugs all around you." He glanced at Shard. "And the smell!" He touched the rough-hewn wall affectionately. "Granted, it cut down on the wait time, but I had to smear a bit of menthol ointment under my nose to mask the horrific odor. It did nothing to alleviate the stench, and I was forced to endure it, now mentholated." He looked at Shard, his eyes huge behind his glasses. "But short lines, right?" He nodded to himself. "Thank Toddleham's ruby nipples the random explosions put an end to that."

"Uh, Major," Shard said carefully, remembering Major Bark-Bite had murdered several Goblins to find the right one with his particular eyeglass prescription, "I'm done now, so I'm just gonna wipe my ass, pull up my pants, and run like hell, okay?"

Bark-Bite's hand was like an iron shackle on his arm. "No, Shard. Not okay." His eyes narrowed into thin blades. "Did I not instruct you in the proper protocol for meeting with a senior officer?"

Shard felt his breath light in his lungs as his heavy mono-brow lowered over his eyes. "Yes, sir, but in all fairness, I'm in the fucking shitter. I didn't bring anything."

Bark-Bite's eyes hardened. "Don't you think I bloody know that, Shard? I'm not here randomly talking about latrines! Of course I'm aware of where we are." He glanced around, his face filling with mock surprise. "Oh, look Shard! We're in the shitter!"

"Major, with all respect, fucking order me what to think," Shard growled, anger tinting red in his black eyes. "We both know I'm just a thug with a big sword, and you, sir, respectfully, are a crazy fuck."

Bark-Bite smiled, his face filling with pride. "There's the Shard I broke into a latrine looking for. There's the Mayhem I need." Bark-Bite pulled a flask and two tin cups from his voluminous coat. "Of course I came prepared." He shoved the items at Shard.

Shard fumbled with the flask and cups, gripping them as he remembered the routine. "Ah, Major!" He exclaimed, pretending to just notice the Goblin sitting next to him. "Might I offer you a libation?"

Bark-Bite's head swiveled sharply. "A libation? Shard, can't you see I'm already cocked off my ass? Well, if you insist." He grabbed a cup, and Shard quickly filled it. Bark-Bite eyed it, the dark rum sloshing in the cup. "Shard! You are quite generous with your rum!"

Shard lined his own cup. "Yes, sir." He raised his cup. "To God Emperor Spinecrack!"

"To the emperor!"

Knocking back his rum, Shard grimaced as the sweet burn rolled down his throat like fighting red ants. "May I pull up my pants now, sir?"

"Mayhem, Shard," Bark-Bite grumbled. "Mayhem."

"I'll take that as a yes."

"There isn't enough room in here for you to be diddling with your britches, Shard." Bark-Bite sipped at his rum. "I've a mission for you and your Chosen Thugs." His eyes loomed large as he smiled. "A mission of Mayhem!"

"You mentioned that."

"A *secret* mission of Mayhem." He slurred the word 'secret.'

"I really think I can get my pants up without too much trouble."

Bark-Bite scooched over slightly, giving Shard a bit of room. "The Wolf Claw Dwarves have announced the release of ten casks of their Dark Fire Rum. You remember them, right?"

Shard knotted his drawstring. "Weren't they the fucks who lost half their numbers in a yearlong war against Orks who didn't exist?"

Bark-Bite smiled brightly. "Yes! That's them."

Licking his lips, Shard finished off his cup of rum, suddenly finding it as pale as white toast to the memory that washed over him. "That was some good rum."

"I want you to go steal some."

Shard stared into Bark-Bite's unblinking eyes, wild and round. "Begging the major's pardon, but the human army has us trapped against the shore, to either fight to the last thug or drown, and you want me to take my company leagues behind enemy lines on a secret mission to steal a couple casks of hallucinogenic rum?"

Bark-Bite's perfect teeth shone like aged ivory as he smiled. "Yes!"

Shard blinked, his mono-brow a wave of confusion. The latrine was hot, cramped, and stunk with potent Goblin mud. "Yeah, sure."

"Mayhem, Shard!" Bark-Bite leaned close, his breath harsh. "Mayhem!"

Mayhem indeed, Shard remembered as he slipped up out of the water to solid, but muddy, ground. Still crawling, he made his way, following the distant lights of the massive fortress up ahead. Finding solid rock, he sloughed off the mud with a shrug and stood, poised like a banner for his Thugs to focus on. Shard eyed the distant towers as his Thugs filed onto solid ground behind him. It was sheer discipline to get his company, the Black Dragon Company of three hundred *Chosen Thugs*, followed by ninety Thugs of the *Other* Black Dragon Company commanded by Lieutenant "Smiley" Gralfange, forty-five Thugs of the Queer Purple Fucks Company led by Lieutenant Christina 'That Bitch with the Fucking Axe' Splinthrax, and a dozen Troll Rawque Chuquers led by a troll who Shard was pretty sure was named Squiff, but quite possibly Piqurd, across one hundred and twelve miles of human-controlled lands to an out of the way, nearly forgotten fortress, without a single engagement with an Elf, Gnome, Human, Hobbit, or Dwarf.

Now, as the rain dribbled onto Shard's head, running down and across his heavy monobrow, he glared at the stone walls, tearing them down with his anger.

They were there for rum.

The good shit.

The Goblins seethed, nearly crazed with battle lust after tiptoeing past enemy after enemy without so much as a wet fart barrage. They had gone through every bog and lowland, lured by the promise that each thug would receive a canteen full of Dwarf Crazy Juice and the terrorizing bark of Sergeant Major Whoretwang Ribsplitter-Jones, the legitimized, despised, and unloved bastard son of Field Marshal Ribsplitter.

"E'rats!" Ribsplitter-Jones' voice cut like a rusted saw just loud enough to be heard over the sound of the rain. "Ya useless fuggin' dribbling cock-draggers! Dress those lines! Falls in! 'Ere we ares, be ready nows to fight, ya fugs!" His eyes blazed red as he scanned the line. "Gunny Glenkar, Ah's needs a count! First Sergeant Shiro! Take the right flank! Ah needs ya to rein those fugs tight! Yer gonna be the 'inge to the door!" He grimaced in simmering fury, his eyes spotting the officers. "E'rats! Smiley! Axe Bitch! Officers up 'ere!" He then added under his breath, "Outta the fuggin' way."

Lieutenant Splinthrax slid past the sergeant major, shaking her waxed cloak and showering him with more rain. "Fuck you, Sergeant," she said calmly, eyeing him carefully.

"At ease, you two," Shard hissed. "I don't have time for you fuckwads measuring your cocks." He glanced back. "Sergeant Major, where the fuck is Smiley?"

The sergeant major reeled back. "E'rats! Fugs should I knows where yer little piss buddy is? Fuggin' drowned in a puddle, probly." He caught Shard's glare and relented. "Eh, I'll see where he fuggin' wandered off."

As the sergeant major turned away, Shard motioned Splinthrax over. "Lieutenant," he began quickly, his voice sharp, "when I fucking told you Ribsplitter-Jones likes killing Goblin officers, that was not a challenge."

The sergeant major's misshapen head swiveled back. "E'rats! 'Cause whens I shanks an officers, I shanks him dead...unlike *some* fugs ahs knows."

Shard flashed his tusks. "Have you found Smiley yet?"

"E'rats!" Ribsplitter-Jones knuckled. "Ya stupid fug can't keep an eye on yer own officer." He turned, peering at the Goblins amassing.

"There! I sees his stupid face." The sergeant major stepped off, calling, "Smiley! E'rats! Ya fuggin' useless fug! I should'a shanked ya whens I had the chance."

A Goblin with a mass of teeth like a busted picket fence that twisted his face into a permanent smile looked up, squinting from the splatter of rain. "Oh! Sergeant Major! There you are!" Smiley tried unsuccessfully to push through the crowd of moving Goblins. "If you kill me, you'll undo saving my life, that you would."

Ribsplitter-Jones' face tightened. "E'rats! Ya fuggin' useless twat! Say that agains out louds and I'll fuggin' gack you fer a week!" He grumbled, "Get over heres! Didn't I fuggin' tell you to stay close?"

Smiley tried moving through the line of Goblins, only to be pushed back. "I tried, that I did, but it didn't quite work out."

Grumbling, the sergeant major barked at the Goblins, forcing open a path for Smiley.

On the knoll, under the awning of a tree, Shard and Splinthrax watched.

"Lemme kill him," she said, nodding to Smiley. "He's a little twit, and I need to add a Goblin officer kill to my resume."

"We need him," Shard said.

"For what? To look competent in comparison?"

Shard sighed, then held up three fingers. "How many is this?"

Splinthrax looked at the fingers, then looked at her own hand before looking back at Shard's fingers. "Grapevine?"

Shard nodded slowly, almost sure the answer wasn't grapevine. He wiggled his fingers, holding up three again. "And how many is this?"

"Octigren?"

"That's not a word."

"It's metric."

"That's why we need Smiley," Shard said, turning to greet his second-in-command. "About time, fuckhead."

"It's two hours after moon, that it is," he said brightly.

Splinthrax snorted. "He's so stupid, it's cute." She looked at Shard. "Now, *sir*," she emphasized the word, "what's the plan?"

"I already went over the plan!" he growled. "I drew a map!"

She nodded, relenting, her eyes rolling back. "Yes, but it made no fucking sense, and now that it's raining, it makes even less sense. You want us to carry torches, and charge Dwarven ramparts...waving torches at them."

"Yes," Shard said hotly, annoyed she was questioning his plan.

"Stating the obvious," she stressed, "we and the Dwarves can see in the dark. They're in an indestructible Dwarf-built fortress, which is immune to torches. Most importantly, they're in an indestructible fortress built by Dwarves which is immune to torches, *and they know it!* Finally, it's raining, so how are you going to light torches?"

Shard sighed, trying to calm down. "What I need you to do is follow the plan and make sure your Thugs follow the protocol."

Splinthrax stiffened. "Captain Shard, with all due respect, sir, my Thugs understand the concept of rape, pillage, plunder, *then*, when all that's done, burn."

From the crowd of Goblins one of them spoke up. "Burn?"

Ribsplitter-Jones launched a massive fist into the face of the closest Goblin, knocking the thug to the ground. "E'rats! Ooo says that?"

"Said what?" came a voice from the crowd.

The bone-cracking sound of the sergeant major's fist impacting another Goblin's face echoed into the night. "Anyones else?"

The hiss of rain and distant, trembling thunder was the only sound.

Lieutenant Splinthrax nodded, admiring the sergeant major's work, then turned to Shard. "Rest assured, Captain, the Queer Purple Fucks Company understands protocol and stands ready." She reached into the folds of her waxed cloak. "Here, I'll show you."

Like the drawing of a sword, Lieutenant Christina 'That Bitch with the Fucking Axe' Splinthrax pulled out a codpiece of polished Goblinwood. Quickly she strapped it about her waist and brandished it at Shard. "The Queer Purple Fucks Company is ready for inspection, sir!"

Upon hearing their lieutenant, the Thugs of her company pulled out their hand-carved codpieces and strapped them on.

Shard and Smiley stared, blinking in amazement.

"Fuckages, Lieutenant," Shard said, coughing into his fist. "I didn't know you had a field dildo."

Smiley was transfixed on the codpiece. "It's as big as my leg," he whispered in awe. "That it is."

"Shut up, Smiley," Shard said.

"It's almost as big as your Dad's."

"Shut up, Smiley. That means stop talking now."

Splinthrax's face flashed with confusion. "What do you mean, *almost* as big?"

Smiley brightened. "Oh, his Dad's was a religious relic, claimed by Princess Hiroki herself, that she did."

"His codpiece?"

"Oh, no!" Smiley exclaimed. "His actual...oof!" Smiley doubled over as Shard kicked him in the crotch. "I deserved that," his voice whined. "That I did. You warned me twice."

Splinthrax threw her hands up. "Well, I'm confused. Are you saying that Shard's father's cock is actually a holy relic?"

Shard's monobrow lowered over his eyes as he focused on Splinthrax. "We're getting off track. I need you to take the torches and ready your company."

"Sir," Smiley wheezed, "you shouldn't feel bad. You're pretty big too, that you...ooooof!" Smiley dropped to one knee after Shard kicked him again. "Oh, I'll shut up now." He slumped and fell over to his side, curled in a fetal position. "Maybe I'll take a nap, that I will."

Lieutenant Splinthrax shook her head confusedly. "Wait, is there a holy relic or not?"

Shard spun, launching his foot up between Splinthrax's legs, lifting her off her feet. As she landed, she dropped to one knee. "That...was...surprise...ing...ly...painful," she gasped, climbing back to her feet. She stood, braced with her knees apart, and waved him on. "Again."

His boot lifted her up again. She dropped down to both knees, and for several minutes she said nothing. Shifting slowly to get to her feet, she remarked, "Now...ugh, whoo...I can add that, ugh, to my resume." She coughed, trying to catch her breath. "You will report that to the colonel? That I took two?"

Shard grimaced. "I'm not telling him shit. Why the fuck would he care about whether or not I kick you in the junk?"

She staggered to her feet. "He said I needed two to be considered for promotion."

"That's fuckshit!" Shard retorted. "I've kicked Smiley here a lot of times, and he's not up for promotion."

Smiley spoke up. "Thirteen in one session, that he did."

Both Shard and Splinthrax glanced down at Smiley thinking thirteen sounded like a lot before Splinthrax went on, "Yes, Smiley, but you're a fucking idiot who got trapped in his own pants and needed six Thugs to rescue him."

"The knot!" Smiley cried, the memory flashing back. "The knot was…"

Shard cut him off with a quick kick to the crotch, then looked back up at Splinthrax, holding up three fingers. "And how much is this?"

Dismay flowed across Splinthrax's face as she realized that she might not have reached the level of 'two.' "Razor stubble?"

Nodding, confident the answer wasn't razor stubble, Shard put his hand down. "Now that I have your fucking attention, we can go over the plan a-fucking-gain." Shard grabbed Splinthrax's arm and faced her down the road. "Just up there are the main doors of the fortress. You'll go, armed with the torches, up to the front door and make a lot of noise. Keep your shields up. The Dwarf guards are all whacked on their own crazy juice, so a bunch of flaming torches in the dark will look like a battalion. You'll also have half of the Trolls with you. They'll be picking Dwarves off the walls and add to the confusion. This will force the Dwarves to call all their troops up to the wall. You'll have to keep a tight leash on your thugs. If the Dwarves start dropping big things, pull back, but keep waving the torches, understand?"

She nodded weakly. "What about mages?"

Shard's monobrow laid flat over his eyes. "Have you ever heard of a Dwarven Mage?"

Splinthrax winced. "Fuck do I know?" she retorted. "It's a completely legitimate question."

Growling, Shard conceded, "There are no Dwarven mages because Dwarves are like a magical suck hole. It takes a fuck load of magic to affect them, let alone try to cast something." Shard waved his hand toward the fort. "It's a fort stuck in the middle of fucking nowhere. The Humans aren't coming out here because they're too busy fighting us, and the Elves aren't coming out here because they fucking hate the Dwarves. Look, this is just that simple. You run up, wave your torches, and confuse the shit out of them."

She blinked and wiped the rain from her face. "Again, Captain, we're running into this fire and water thing."

"I thought you said you didn't want to get kicked in the junk again?" Shard growled.

Splinthrax's lips curled up over her tusks as they tightened shut and she crossed her legs.

Shard nodded as he turned to Smiley. "You're in charge of the Bug Heads."

Throughout the world, there was little more fearsome than a Goblin charging an enemy shield wall with a keg of Black Dirt That Blows Stuff Up strapped to his back. Known as Tech Lieutenants, they ordinarily had good, shiny armor, allowing a Goblin to withstand arrows and spears long enough to reach the enemy front line and explode, but Shard was out of good armor and Goblins willing to volunteer to blow up. Fortunately, Princess Hiroki had bestowed upon them a case of her used underwear, and the Goblins lined up for the honor of wearing her favor, which came with a free barrel of Black Dirt That Blows Stuff Up. With their princess' underwear on their heads, the Goblins looked like fierce insects.

Only Goblins had the secret to make Black Dirt That Blows Stuff Up. No one knows which Goblin invented it, or more likely, which Goblin swiped it from a drunk Gnome, but only the Goblins had it, and when they used it, the lamentation often heard from receiving lines was: "Aw, fuck."

"While Splinthrax has the Dwarves distracted," Shard went on, "we move to the rear of the fortress. There, use half of the Bug Heads to blow the outer wall, another half to clear the debris, half to knock down the inner wall, and half in reserve."

Smiley nodded, knowing Shard probably meant four, two, four, and two.

"Once the wall is gone," Shard concluded, "I'll lead the rest of the Thugs in, and the slaughter will begin."

Splinthrax raised her hand.

Shard's monobrow hung low over his eyes. "You have a question, Lieutenant?"

She pointed to her mouth.

Sighing, Shard nodded. "Just ask your fucking question!"

"It's pouring rain, Captain!" she exclaimed, exasperated. "You're not going to get a spark, let alone light a torch or a cask of Black Dirt That Blows Stuff Up!"

Before Shard could speak, a growling hiss like the dry fart from a chaffed butt sounded, echoed through the dark forest, and paralyzed the Goblins with fear. Peeling from the shadows, a tall, boney figure stepped forward quickly with jerky, pained movements. Hooded in torn, filthy robes, the spindly creature, shrieking and howling, charged at Splinthrax, who could only tremble in terror.

"Fie-are will burn in what-terrrr!" The creature's voice ripped into Splinthrax. "My magic good good! My magic strong strong!"

Her knees quivering, Splinthrax stood her ground, defiantly glaring at the witch's silver-masked face. "Captain Shard?" Her eyes glanced back. "Please call off your witch, sir!"

The witch leaned down and peered into Splinthrax's eyes. "Glrrrrr." Her voice grated.

Splinthrax turned her head to avoid the witch's plume of putrid breath. "Ugh! Is she…is she smelling me?"

"Ahhhhh am breathing your ssssssssoul soul!"

"Not my soul!" Splinthrax cried, her resolve weakening. "I need that! Give it back!"

"Alright, Daf-Nee!" Shard barked. "Quit scaring everyone. Give her back her soul."

Daf-Nee whipped around, hissing at Shard. "Never!"

Shard's monobrow lowered, matching her glare. "I don't have fucking time for this. Give her the torches and her soul!"

Grumbling, Daf-Nee rose to her full, towering height and waved her pale, skeletal hand at Splinthrax. "I hope you enjoy joy your ssssssssoul assss much much as I did."

Splinthrax clutched at her armor to see if she could feel her soul returning. "Thank you, mistress!"

Daf-Nee waved dismissively, then called behind her. "Addiko! You bring bring now!"

A Goblin struggling with a heavy sack filled with sticks stepped up. "Private Class First Addiko reorder as porting, sir!" She punched herself in the head in a salute, then staggered from the blow. "Wait, uh…" She shook off the blow and popped to attention. "Class Private Addiko reporting first as ordered." She saluted again, and her knees gave out from the punch to her head.

"Just stop, Addiko," Shard interrupted her. "Give the torches to the lieutenant."

Addiko blinked, focusing on Splinthrax. "Here are the torches, sir! Uh, ma'am, sirma'am!"

Daf-Nee grabbed Addiko's arm to stop the Goblin from saluting again, then reached into the Goblin's sack and pulled out a stick. Daf-Nee held it up. It burst into flame, and the light reflected off her hammered silver mask.

Splinthrax gaped. "She ignited the torch with just her eyes!"

Daf-Nee turned and brandished the torch at Splinthrax. She shoved it into the Goblin's hand. "You burn burn!" Her voice was a torrent of broken glass.

"Burn?" a Goblin spoke up excitedly.

Daf-Nee turned and let out a dragon's roar that sounded like an ogre gargling with blood-stained razors and salt, forcing all the Goblins to cower.

Splinthrax, holding the burning torch and sack, turned to Shard. "Permission to distribute the torches, sir?" She saluted, hitting herself in the head with the torch, and ran off into the darkness before Shard could speak.

Ribsplitter-Jones, unfazed by Daf-Nee's theatrics, shouted at the Goblins to prepare for the attack. Happy to avoid Daf-Nee, the Thugs quickly fell into battle formation.

Daf-Nee coughed, clearing her throat. "By the Glowing Mother's cooking spoon," she said, her voice now as gentle as a horse's bridle chimes, "that is rough on the throat."

Shard scoffed. "Well, serves you right for scaring the fuck outta my Thugs." Shard looked around. "Where did Smiley go?"

"He's cowering behind you." Daf-Nee motioned with a tilt of her head.

"What?" Shard looked down. "Smiley! It's Daf-Nee! You know her!"

Smiley shook his head quickly. "That I do, sir!" His voice trembled. "But I was hoping to keep my soul. I wanted to use it tomorrow, that I did."

Daf-Nee snickered, shaking her head. "You know, Whig, this whole plan of stealing rum makes no sense."

Shard winced at hearing his nickname. "It makes perfect sense," he said as he watched Splinthrax distribute the waterproof torches. "If we threaten the Dwarven rum supply, the Dwarven army will be forced to fall back to protect it. Without the support of the Dwarven troops, the Humans will be forced to retreat, giving Field Marshall Ribsplitter breathing room to organize a defense."

"Yes, Whig..." Daf-Nee nodded, conceding, "but it's Bark-Bite's plan."

Shard pursed his lips as he took in her words. "Bark-Bite will fuck me over less than anyone else."

The Witch stiffed, her body like a bundle of sticks. "Yes, Whig, but he *will* fuck you over."

"So?"

Daf-Nee sagged. "Okay, as long as we all agree this is fuck-wit plan."

"I don't give a fuck-wit about this fuck-wit plan," Shard grunted, pulling on his helmet. "All I want is to fuck shit up, and this—" he pointed to the Dwarven fortress now lit by the torches of the approaching Queer Purple Fucks Company, "—is fucking shit up."

"Okay, Whig." Daf-Nee's voice was gentle. "Promise me one thing?"

"What?"

"Be careful?"

Shard's eyes thinned from beneath his monobrow. "Fuck you, you fucking skank whore, and the fuck skank whore next to you and her mother. I fucking hate you, and fuck you again." He charged her, almost crashing into her frail body. Peering up, his eyes flared red with anger. "By Chorlic's third infected ball, I will kill you!"

Through her mask, Shard could see her eye sparkle with delight. "No you won't! You can't think of a way horrible enough to kill me!" She pirouetted, giggling.

Feeling his teeth threatening to shatter from the force of his fury, Shard turned away, bellowing. "Sergeant Major! Move them out!"

The Black Dragon Company, Shard's Chosen Thugs, began to march.

They moved without delicacy, grunting a cadence to keep step as their thick, calloused feet slapped in the mud as one. Their sergeants filed them into a single line and carefully led them along the narrowing precipice. Lightning flashed white and brought the trail into blinding view for a fleeting instant. The terrible light seared the Goblins' vision, which could see through the darkness like it was day, blinding them. Only the clear shout from their sergeants kept them from marching off the cliff.

The plan, at best, was reckless. The Dwarf Wolf Claw Clan, like every Dwarf clan, had built their fortress to be unassailable. They used the thickest stone, its grain homogenous and free of seams and fissures, pulled from the deepest quarries, and fitted together with perfect engineering, every joist a design marvel. Added to this was basic strategy. The fortress faced south. The parapets had a wide and open view of the long, winding road leading to the thick, black oak doors. Assailing this meant enduring the killing rain of crossbow fire and somehow smashing down doors stronger than steel. The attacker would then face a hall filled with murder holes. Withstanding the barbed spears, ballista bolts, and fermented urine, the attacker would face yet another set of reinforced doors. While it had never been done, an attacker making his way through all that would then be faced with the Dwarf army's greatest defense.

The Dwarven shield wall.

Nothing delighted a Dwarf more than watching an enemy throw themselves against their walls and die. The Dwarven shield wall was legendary throughout the world. They traded mobility for indefatigability. Once formed into their shield wall, they were as any wall, assuming the wall was unbreakable.

Attacking a Dwarven shield wall was certain death.

Dwarf armor was forged in the heat at the center of the Earth, and their ungainly axes sharpened against dragon hide. Dwarves standing in ranks, shields touching, eyes sharp and alert, were as impregnable as the stoutest wall. Only two Goblin commanders in recorded history had broken a Dwarven shield wall. The first was Goblin General Arthric Knight-Chaos, in command of the Black Tsunami Division. He encountered Dwarf Lieutenant Stefen Stonefoot's Garnet Vein Company in the valley of Rile's Crags. Fifty-five Dwarves stood their ground, their beady eyes peering over their shields. Their ranks ran from valley wall to valley wall and stood four ranks deep. Unable to flank, General Knight-Chaos lined up fifteen thousand Goblins in column formation and drove them into the Dwarven lines.

Wave after wave of Goblins crashed into the immobile Dwarven shield wall. The first rank stood with both hands clutching their shields and hoisting them up, while the second rank stood behind them, holding up the first rank. The third rank with their spears did the killing, while the fourth rank resupplied the third rank whenever a spear broke.

The Goblins, their mouths filled with terrifying war cries, crashed into the unmoving Dwarf lines. Again and again the Goblins slammed into the Dwarf lines until Goblin bodies began to pile up. Like a storm-driven ocean wave, Goblins splashed up and over the Dwarven shields as the thugs behind pushed the thugs ahead. As Goblins stumbled over the heads of the Dwarves, the Dwarves and their keen, thick short blades thrust up, killing and killing and killing. More Goblins clambered forward, their bodies being shoved along by the thugs behind them into the killing Dwarf blades.

General Knight-Chaos sent each Goblin battalion into the gap as a long, continuous train until the Dwarves literally drowned in Goblin blood.

The second Goblin commander to ever drive his Thugs into a Dwarven shield wall and claim victory was Captain Wiggletooth Shard of the Black Dragon Company.

Now Shard was being tested again.

Shard, with his big man-sword in hand, scanned the walls above. The precarious trail, rain slick and crumbling, lined the edge of the Dwarven walls. A single misstep, and a thug would plummet to his death.

Shard had to get his Thugs moving. His heart pounding, he charged ahead, eyeing the path. Lightning flared, blinding him. With his big sword in one hand, he placed his free hand on the stone and made his way, feeling ahead with his hard-soled feet. "Give me the rope!" he ordered.

The rough reed braided rope scratched his cheeks as he clamped it in his teeth. He moved forward quickly, too quickly, his toes clawing the mud for traction, dragging the rope along with one hand touching the wall, the other clutching his steel man-sword.

Lightning flashed again, and he felt the tingle of electricity in his palm. Shard leapt, covering the last few feet to solid ground. There he quickly lashed the rope to a tree and waved at Smiley. "Now!" he shouted over the howling wind. "Send over the Bug Heads!"

Clambering desperately, with massive kegs nearly as big as themselves strapped to their backs, the Bug Heads clung to Shard's rope as they made their way along the dwindling, crumbling trail.

Goblin after Goblin followed. Some slipped completely and dangled for several seconds from the rope before scrambling for footing. As each one crossed, Shard shoved them roughly into line, organizing them for the assault. He waited for the Trolls to cross, their ungainly bodies skipping across the wall as easily as crossing the ground, before he ordered the Bug Heads to the ready.

Scanning the tall walls, Shard noted they were clear, meaning the watch had taken Splinthrax's distraction and had run to reinforce the South walls. While it took far too long to get his Thugs across, the plan was working.

"Daf-Nee!" Shard barked. "Where in Caralog's Pimple Covered Ass are you?"

"Right here, Whig," she said calmly from behind.

Shard nearly leapt out of his skin. "Fuck! Do you have to do that?"

She touched the chin of her mask, thinking. "Yes, I do."

Grumbling, Shard dismissed it. "Get ready to light the Bug Heads."

"I do have a question, Whig."

"I don't have fucking time for stupid questions!" Shard barked angrily.

"But really, this is a good question," she persisted. "When the Dwarves hear the first wall blow up, won't they come running to reinforce this wall?" She pointed up. "A handful of Dwarves with crossbows will rip your Thugs to cabbage poop."

Shard growled, not liking to explain his plans. "No, they won't. They will assume the explosions are to distract them from the main attack to the south. The smaller, second explosion will confirm that. When the third knocks down the inner wall, it will be too late, and the Black Dragon will be in their shorts."

Daf-Nee scoffed. "Oh, I can already tell you what you'll find in their shorts, Whig, and it certainly isn't anything to go to war over."

"Light the first set of Bug Heads!" Shard ordered.

"But not all the Thugs are over on this side!"

"Ribsplitter-Jones will bring them over. We have to start this now!"

Shrugging, Daf-Nee accepted. "Well, don't come crying to me when he gacks you for leaving him out of Dwarf killing."

"I swear by my mother's scabby knees I will never come crying to you, skanky slut fuck."

Daf-Nee clutched at the sweep of her robe. "My knees aren't scabby!"

"Light the fucking Bug Heads!"

Huffing, Daf-Nee snapped her fingers, and the fuse for four Bug Heads ignited.

"Run!" Shard bellowed. "Now! For her Highness Hiroki, fulfill your prime directive!"

As all of the Bug Heads lurched forward, Shard tripped up the second set, thus stopping the remaining unlit Bug Heads from running forward. "Take cover!" he shouted, and turned his back to the wall, clamping his hands over his ears.

Seeing their commander duck, the Black Dragon Company followed his example.

Four Bug Heads charged forward and slapped their bodies against the wall. With their faces upturned, they recited, "Her magnificent Highness Princess Hiroki Spinecrack sends her regar…"

Lightning flashed, and the Bug Heads vanished in a clap of thunder, leaving a gaping hole in the side of the Dwarven fort.

Dwarves did not build their forts to be challenged. They built them to instill the idea in anyone looking at them that attacking them was rather stupid. The exterior wall was perfectly fitted stone that needed no mortar or cement. Behind that wall was several feet of dirt and gravel, or in the case of the Wolf Claw Clan, broken ceramic rum bottles. Beyond that was the inner wall of more fitted stone.

Shoving the next group forward as Daf-Nee snapped their fuses alight, Shard sent the next two in. Desperately they charged up the rubble, their feet cutting open on the spilling pile of broken rum bottles. The Thugs leaned forward, using their hands for traction, and ignored the trails of blood.

The explosion showered the Goblins in ceramic dust.

The third wave of Bug Heads entered the hole, the crushed rubble now a perfect ramp.

With his hands over his ears, Shard watched the blast erupt from the hole like a cannon. "Now, you fucks! Go!" he roared, holding his big sword aloft. "Gunny Glenkar! Take point!"

A stout Goblin moved forward, brandishing a blade-spear, waving Goblins on. "Come on, you Thugs! Shields to the front! Dru, goddess of death, is watching! Let's give her a show!" Lining up four Goblins with shields, Glenkar shoved them into the hole and followed them. More Goblins charged in, following his example. First Sergeant Shiro corralled them into groups to keep them from bunching up.

"E'rats!" Ribsplitter-Jones called from across the way. "Ya fug! Ya fuggin' started wi' out me!"

Shard looked back distractedly. "Get the Thugs across! There'll be plenty of Dwarf killing for you!"

"E'rats, fuggin' bedder be." The sergeant major grunted, then barked at his Thugs, "E'rats! Move this shit along! The fuggin' killing's begun!"

With his monobrow hanging low over his red flared eyes, Captain Wiggletooth Shard bellowed his war cry. He ran madly, human sword aloft, up the ramp of shifting, broken rum bottles. His Thugs, driven to wild fury, followed their captain and, their eyes red with Goblin rage, overtook him, knocked him down, and trampled him.

The rough hand of his sergeant major grabbed the back of his armor and hauled him up. "E'rats! Wot the fug ares you doing napping like this!"

Brushing broken pottery from his face, Shard screamed. "Fucks ran me over!"

"Serves you right." Ribsplitter-Jones grunted. "E'rats! Trying to get in killin' wif out yer sergeant. Nots right! Nots right!" He shoved Shard forward into the hole. "Yer a useless fugtwat!"

Hearing steel ring against shields, Shard lurched forward. Spilling out of the hole, Shard saw it led to a courtyard, and Dwarves spilled in from side streets and alleys. They quickly tried to link up into shield walls, while Gunny Glenkar sent Goblin teams to keep them from doing just that.

Shard roared, screaming at his Thugs to follow, and dove head-long into a Dwarf line loosely turning to face him. With both hands on his sword, the grip wet and sticky with rain, Shard slashed forward, the biting edge cutting into a Dwarf helmet with a spittle of sparks. Reposting, the Dwarf snapped his sword at Shard's ducking head, only to feel the horrible white flash of Ribsplitter-Jones' massive, double-bladed axe cut into his arm, whacking it off. Dwarf blood misted in the air, and the Goblins went mad. They drove into the fray, cutting and smashing and biting and spitting, and the Dwarves could only fall beneath the press and struggle to link shields.

Shard stepped back and sucked in a breath with a snort. He glanced over his shoulder. "Stalix! Go!"

From behind, a Goblin corporal nodded, thumbing her scarlet, mischievous, rain-soaked hair from her eyes. Her bottom lip curled in determination and anger. Defiance flashed in her black eyes before she slipped her hood up and vanished into a dark alley. Light on her feet and born with a compass in her head, she moved easily through the unfamiliar maze of buildings to the main gates, only pausing to let Dwarf reinforcements by. Once clear, she slipped into the gate guard's blind spot as she eyed the walls above. The guards up on the walls were focused on the light show from the Queer Purple Fucks, leaving her free to roam.

Stalix moved quickly, her Orkish blades flashing left, then right, leaving the two gate guards awkwardly reaching back to clamp down on the bleeding, gaping holes where their kidneys had been. With them distracted, Corporal Stalix eyed the locks, mildly surprised they were far less complicated than Shard had guessed. She pulled back a lever to free the bulwark and counterbalance and let the portcullis rise. She then crouched down and shouldered the bar up, letting it drop to the ground. She put her back to the door and heaved, pushing them open, letting them block most of the murder holes, and giving her free access to the outer doors.

As she pushed the main doors open, she barely ducked out of the way of the jagged edge of Lieutenant Splinthrax's murderous axe crashing down. Stalix flattened herself against the wall and let the Queer Purple Fucks charge through, with Splinthrax in the lead. The Dwarves from the wall above, their eyes wide with fear and their lips tight with determination, clambered down and plowed into the wave of Goblins. Splinthrax's terrible axe whistled in the air and rended a Dwarf shield. The backstroke of her double-headed axe whacked off one of her Thugs' ears before sweeping wildly forward and denting a Dwarf helmet.

Stalix sighed and looked up into the rain, letting it wash her face as she sought divine intervention. Knowing none was coming, she drew her blades and entered the battle. She slipped behind the Dwarves and deftly cut where the Dwarf armor was the lightest.

The hamstring.

Stumbling and staggering, their faces wrapped in horror and surprise, the Dwarves began to fall to Splinthrax's wicked axe. Their numbers dwindling, the Dwarves retreated.

Incensed, Lieutenant Splinthrax moved forward, her axe inflicting injury to Dwarf and Goblin alike. With her teeth locked and her eyes round and wild, Splinthrax drove her axe forward, only to spark back against Stalix's blades.

The corporal glared at the lieutenant from beneath her crossed blades. "Shard is waiting for you!" she hissed.

Lieutenant Christina 'That Bitch with the Fucking Axe' Splinthrax focused on the corporal, then reared back and drove her axe down.

Stalix felt her teeth rattle as she blocked the blow. "Captain's orders! Don't make me go back to the sergeant major to tell him you've ignored your orders," Stalix hissed.

Splinthrax paused, her face wrestling with defiance and bloodlust. "But, but there are Dwarves…" She pointed with her axe. "Right there!"

Stalix shook her head dismissively. "Stragglers. Shard needs you to crush the flank of the main body and prevent them from forming a shield wall. If they form a wall, we're all dead!"

Growling, Splinthrax barked at her thugs, "Affix codpieces!"

Moving as one, the Queer Purple Fucks Company strapped their dildos on.

Hoisting her axe, Splinthrax bellowed her charge, "Let's fuck 'em up!"

Stalix grabbed the lieutenant's arm and turned her in the right direction, then watched the Queer Purple Fucks Company charge down a side street. She eyed the remaining Dwarves who had formed a little shield wall, enough to hold off an army. She punched herself in the head saluting them, then backed into a shadow.

At the main battle, Shard leapt over a fallen Dwarf and crashed into the fight again, swinging his man-sword with abandon. The Dwarves were still scattered, but not as confused as Shard had hoped. Crushed in the press of bodies, Shard was slammed face to face with a Dwarf, and a braided beard filled with three days of crumbs rubbed his nose.

Unable to move his arms in the crowd, Shard reared his head back and drove it forward, not realizing his opponent had done the same. The two helmeted heads collided, sending lightning flashing across their eyes. In a break, Shard staggered back, shaking his head to clear it. He realized with growing horror he and his Thugs were very, very, fucked.

The Dwarf Wolf Claw Clan, known throughout the world as distillers of the finest rum, were stone cold sober.

Despite Shard's best efforts, the Dwarves were fighting back. They were not spiraled-eyed or spooked on their own hallucinogenic rum. With every strike, every block, they slipped an inch, a half inch, closer to one another. If two shields touched, it instantly became the center, and other Dwarves struggled to join. Shard plunged back in, driving his big man-sword high into their shields, distracting them, as Ribsplitter-Jones' blood-soaked axe slid down the back edge of their shields and cut deep.

Still the Dwarves closed ranks.

The Queer Purple Fucks arrived, their hand-carved codpieces of Goblinwood wet and shiny with rain and glistening in the flashing torch light as they ran out of a side street in a ragged line. The Dwarves, their eyes fixed on the wave of giant dildos charging in like drunken rhinos, turned, breaking open the line.

"Counterattack!" Shard screamed.

"Counterattack!" his Thugs screamed.

The Black Dragon Company launched forward. Their weary limbs blazed anew, their weapons light in their hands. Shard leapt up and brought his sword down with a horrible, two-handed strike. He felt it bite into chainmail, cutting through and biting deep into meat. Shard kicked the Dwarf off his sword and just kept swinging, giving no thought to defense. A stupid, wild grin crawled across his face as he hacked again and again as he shouted over the clamoring din. "Mayhem! Mayhem! May…"

A white streak clanged against his sword, knocking him from his euphoria. More flashes of goose feather fletching appeared, thudding arrows into his Thugs.

Elven arrows.

Confusion filled Shard's eyes. Elves? In a Dwarven fort? The concept was unthinkable. The Dwarves found the Elves too flighty and annoying, while the Elves found the Dwarves incapable of any fashion sense. The idea of them being holed up together in a fort was simply impossible.

Shard's Trolls went to work, flinging their deadly rocks and forcing the Elves under cover, but the damage had been done. The Goblins fell back in confusion, crashing into each other, while the Dwarves quickly moved into formation, forming pockets of broken shield walls. Shard screamed at his Thugs, his orders repeated by his sergeants. The Goblins surged forward to fill the spaces and keep the Dwarves apart.

Blazing balls of angry, blue magic flared up and exploded in the Goblin lines. Shard was knocked back, ass over head, by the blast. Scrambling to find his feet, Shard, his monobrow bent in despair, watched as his worst nightmare walked forward.

A mage.

A human mage in a Dwarf fort was like a fish in the desert, yet there he stood in the middle of the Dwarven pack, his eyes beaming blue light and his hands upraised, flashing blue tendrils from his fingers that arced over the Dwarf heads and into the Goblin lines, caving in their shields.

Shard stepped back, his eyes searching for an idea. "Daf-Nee!" he screamed.

"What, Whig?" she said, kneeling beside him.

"You fucking cum dumpster! Do something!"

She pulled up her sleeve, showing him the stump where her hand had been. "Oh, my widdle Whiggy-poo, when you Goblins cut off my hand, you took my magic. All I have are parlor tricks, Whig." She motioned to the mage, who was tossing balls of magic like grenades as the Dwarves cheered him on. "I could have turned that limp dick into a pile of clacker roaches, turned his bones into splinters and watched him squirm on the floor, but now? I couldn't hurt his feelings. Look at him." She sniffed contemptuously. "The showoff! He's not even good! Getting killed by that cunt-twaddle is beneath me."

Shard turned. The Dwarves were in line, row after row. They were tucked into a corner neatly, shuffling slightly to dress their formation of perfect defense. The mage was putting on a show, tossing up magic that exploded over the Goblins' heads and sent down deadly shafts of light that ripped through their armor and into their flesh.

The muddy ground was quickly turning black with Goblin blood.

"Dress lines!" Shard shouted. "Dress lines! Shields to the front!" Shard glanced to the back wall. He could see the outline of Squiff, the Troll leader. Although the Troll was camouflaged, the splash of the unending rain gave him away. Shard waved to get his attention, then turned back to Daf-Nee. "Get ready!"

She held her arms open, showing her hand was empty. "Get ready for what, Whig? Death by that idiot?"

"You keep saying how much smarter you are, now prove it. Get ready to do what you do best. Be annoying!" Shard searched his Thugs and spotted Stalix's hood dashing through. He then spotted Smiley. "Smiley! I need Bug Heads!"

Dwarves in formation, Elven archers, and a mage.

It was indeed time for Mayhem.

"Daf-Nee!" Shard called. "Now!" He then shouted to his Thugs, "Down!"

Shard's witch rose to her full height, a foot taller than the Goblins around her, and let out a paralyzing screech that drowned out the din of battle. The Dwarves, stalwart in their wall, cringed in their socks while the mage paused his magic barrage and watched curiously.

Holding a torch over her head, Daf-Nee's harsh voice cried in the Elven tongue, "Watch my magic, death death!"

The torch exploded in a brilliant white flash that left dancing spots on the back of every retina that watched, leaving the Dwarves blinking to clear their vision, and the mage confounded as to what the heck just happened. They were all unharmed! Insipid Goblin magic! The mage glanced down at the Dwarves, motioning to the Goblins with a tilt of his head, as a smile creased his face and a chuckle escaped his lips. His eyes glowed blue as he turned to face the Goblins, unaware of the rock sailing smoothly at his head.

The mage blinked as a flash of pink magic sprang up before him and saved him from the rock aimed at the space between his eyes. The mage looked, uncertain what had hit his magic shield, before he realized what had happened. They threw a rock at him! A rock!

The mage pointed and laughed mockingly at the Goblins, waving at the Dwarves to join in. Fake magic and rocks! The mage guffawed, and slowly the Dwarves lowered their discipline and began to giggle, and then laugh.

The body of a dead Elf, blood streaming from a Troll rock to the temple, crashed on their heads, and their laughing quickly stopped. A second Elf slid from his vantage point, a rock still wedged deep in his forehead, and landed on the Dwarf formation.

One Elf slumped and hung slickly from a window as the fourth and final Elf sniper stood in his tower window, his eyes upturned as if to see the rock lodged deep in his head. His bow slipped from his cooling fingers and clacked on the courtyard tile below.

The mage roared furiously as his eyes burned with hot blue magic. His hands were only spheres of growling magic, crackling and sparkling. More power began to build as licks of lightning fell from the sky. The mage screamed, and the sky cracked loud with thunder.

The mage paused, his face slowly growing slack. He blinked, and his eyes cooled, and the light faded from his hands. As rain dripped down his slicked-back hair, he reached back distractedly and patted his robes. When he withdrew his hand, it was covered with bright red blood. He looked at it, watching the rain wash it clean. He looked up, his face emotionless, and pointed at a Goblin running away, her hood flying back and releasing her wild, red hair.

What the mage said before he died Shard didn't understand, but he guessed it was something to the effect of, "That Goblin nicked my kidneys!"

"Now, Smiley!" Shard commanded, and the last Bug Heads sprang forward with their giant kegs of Black Dirt That Blows Stuff Up strapped to their backs, the fuses lit. The Goblins quickly and desperately parted ranks to let them through. The Bug Heads ran forward bent at almost a ninety-degree angle, their eyes round and wide, and their fists in tight little balls. Air wheezed in their lungs.

Sneering, Shard watched the Dwarves' squinty little eyes bulge as their greatest fear chuffed toward then.

The first Dwarf rank dropped to one knee, the edge of their shields thrust into the ground as the second rank reached over the first, locking bottom edge with the first rank's top edge. Rank after rank linked shields until they were all a giant turtle shell.

The Bug Heads stopped at the front rank, unsure what to do. They grabbed the shields and tried to pry them open. That failing, they began to climb up as the last of their fuses burned away.

"Down!" Shard bellowed at his troops.

"Her Royal Highness Princess Hiroki Spinecrack," the Bug Heads began, "sends…"

They vanished in a horrific explosion.

Shard listened as the sound of rocks and debris raining down began to quiet, leaving only the sound of the rain. Rising, Shard snorted, fanning away the lingering smoke as his sergeants ordered his troops to recover.

"Fuckers," Shard mumbled. "Sergeant Major! Organize parties to search for the booze and make sure the little fuckers don't drink any. I want the booze found and secured before we move to the rape phase." Shard tried to peer through the smoke to see the carnage of the Dwarf formation. "Although I doubt there will be much left to rape."

Someone from the Queer Purple Fucks spoke up, "Rape?"

Daf-Nee appeared at his elbow, startling him. "Whig? Before you send your Thugs off to have their fun, there's something you ought to know."

Shard let out a rumbling, hissing sigh. "What the fuck now?"

Daf-Nee pointed with her stump.

Grunting, Shard looked to where she pointed.

A playful snippet of wind dragged back the dirty grey curtain of smoke to reveal the Dwarves, still in turtle formation, except now there were two black scorch marks where the Bug Heads had detonated.

The Goblin Sergeants shouted at their Thugs to form up their ranks and lines.

On silent cue, the Dwarves recovered, forming back into their shield wall.

The rain hissed against the pavement as the Dwarves and Goblins stared at each other.

"Fuck," Shard whispered, looking for an idea.

"E'rats!" Sergeant Major Ribsplitter-Jones barked. "Gives the word! We'll takes 'em by the bullocks!"

"Keep formation!" Shard ordered. "Stand your ground! First Thug who steps forward I will fucking gack myself!"

"E'rats!"

"Stand fast!" Shard screamed. His tusks flashed as his eyes darted around.

"Shard!" Splinthrax pleaded. "Say the word and the Queer Purple Fucks will begin the rape phase!"

Shard didn't respond right away, only shaking his head as he looked at the east wall.

"Fuck, Captain!" Splinthrax shouted. "What are you looking at!" She pointed with her axe. "The Dwarves are there!" She grimaced, her eyes hard. "Queer Purple Fucks, if the Black Dragon Company is afraid, we will make the attack!" She brandished her axe. "Prepare to fuck them up!"

"Stand your ground!" Shard barked, not even looking or caring what they did.

Splinthrax reeled. "But fucking why?"

"The rum," he said quietly.

The east wall, from edge to edge and fifteen feet high, was a set of wide board shelves filled with row after row of clay pots. Each pot was three feet tall and two feet in diameter, with a fat cork plugged tight and sealed with wax. As Shard walked over to it, he could feel the Dwarves become incensed. He paused, looked back to them, then slid closer to the rum.

Their eyes hardened.

Shard had imagined the rum to be hidden in a secret vault, but what was more secure than a Dwarven fort? It was stacked on shelves in the courtyard!

Shifting casually, Shard drew his man-sword. He motioned at the wall of rum, but the Dwarves, apart from casting spears with their eyes, didn't move. Shard nodded, then smiled.

Then struck.

He hammered the cask with his pommel and leapt nimbly out of the way as a tidal wave of rum splashed on the ground. He could hear the Dwarf commanders order their soldiers to stand fast and hold formation.

Ribsplitter-Jones' wide head swiveled around. "What the fug?" His brows lifted. "What the fug are you doing? The rum!"

"I thought you wanted to kill Dwarves," Shard said casually, smashing another cask, this time feeling it splash against his legs. Goblins in the rear broke ranks and dashed over, dropping to their hands and knees to lick the rum-soaked floor.

The Dwarves howled! They shifted anxiously and motioned to step forward, only to be reined in by their sergeants.

Shard smashed another and another, and more Goblins ran over, shoving their faces into the broken pots to drink their fill of the amazing rum. Shard turned, watching the crazed eyes of the Dwarves ready to break rank, raised his sword, and smashed another cask.

Sand rushed against his shins.

Shard stood for several seconds, unsure what had happened. He looked up to the Dwarves. They were looking around idly, some nonchalantly whistling.

A thug dropped down at Shard's feet and started licking the sand. His face twisted up from the bitter taste, but he kept licking.

Shard kicked him away.

Soaking up with rain, Shard stared mindlessly at the spilling black sand.

The Black Dirt That Blows Stuff Up.

Mayhem, Bark-Bite had said. Mayhem.

Only the Goblins had the secret to making the Black Dirt That Blows Stuff Up, yet there it was, ringed around Shard's ankles. Bark-Bite hadn't sent him to steal rum, but to threaten their supply of Black Dirt That Blows Stuff Up. If the Humans and their ability to make everything bigger and better got their hands on the Black Dirt That Blows Stuff Up, the Goblin Nation was finished.

Shard nodded to himself.

Mayhem indeed.

"Fall back," he whispered.

"Wha?" Ribsplitter-Jones responded, peering over to his captain. "Whaddaya mean falls the fug back?"

"Mayhem," Shard said.

Ribsplitter looked down at the Black Dirt That Blows Stuff Up, then at Shard standing in it. "E'rats, ya crazed fugger." He looked back to First Sergeant Shiro. "Rear ranks." He motioned to the hole they had blasted into the wall.

Nodding, Shard repeated. "Mayhem."

Daf-Nee slid over to him. "Whig, honey, what are you doing?" she asked gently as Goblins slipped quietly by.

"Mayhem," he said and waved over one of the Queer Purple Fucks. "I'll take that torch. The rest of you, fuck off."

"Whig," Daf-Nee said carefully. "Whig, this is not a good idea."

"Fuck you, it's a great idea. They're making the Black Dirt That Blows Stuff Up." Shard's black eyes turned and searched hers. "You know what this means. With this, the Humans will roll over our last defenses, and you know they won't stop there, not the Humans. They'll come in ships to Bratanich, the Goblin home nation, and destroy us all." Shard glared at the Dwarves, who stared back at him. "Bark-Bite didn't send me for fucking rum. He sent me here to prove the Humans have the secret to our greatest weapon. He sent me here for Mayhem." Shard laughed breathlessly. "Mayhem he will get."

She nodded in agreement. "Whig, baby, sweetheart, I don't like this idea. Have Smiley do this. Have Addiko do this. Addiko would *love* to do this."

"Fuck off, skank whore."

Splinthrax stomped over to him. "What the fuck are you doing? We're leaving?"

Shard motioned with his head. "You're leaving."

"No, I'm not!" She brandished her axe. "I've got Dwarves to fuck!"

Sighing, Shard called out, "First Sergeant?"

First Sergeant Shiro stopped, turned, and punched Splinthrax in the face.

The Goblin lieutenant stumbled back into the arms of her company. They pushed her back to her feet. "Wow! Fuck! Where am I?" She focused on one of her Thugs. "You'll tell the colonel, right? You'll tell him I took two?"

The Goblin nodded as he led her away.

Daf-Nee nodded, then looked back at Shard. "I, um, Whig, I think I'm having some sort of, uh, what, um, emotion, right now. I can't leave you to do this. I don't like this plan."

"You mentioned that earlier," Shard grumbled, then motioned with his head toward the exit. "Fuck off."

"No, no no no, Whig," she began to plead. "I can't watch this plan."

Smiley stepped over. "Everyone is confused about the plan, that we are."

"E'rats!" Ribsplitter-Jones barked, grabbing everyone's attention. "Et's fugging simple ya little fug! He's standing knee deep in Black

Dirt That Blows Stuff Up with a lit torch, with the fuggen Dwarves right the fug over theres."

Daf-Nee leaned close to Smiley, all pretense of her hissing voice gone. "Yes, Smiley, and Whig needs someone to take his place." Her voice grew coy. "Someone brave, who wants to be a captain."

"Shut up, skank whore," Shard grunted. He motioned with his head. "Sergeant Major, get her out of here."

"Whig," Daf-Nee cautioned, "don't make me use my mommy voice!"

"It would be a fucking first," Shard mumbled.

"And a little late," Ribsplitter-Jones said as he pushed his shoulder into Daf-Nee's stomach and picked her up. Ignoring her shrieks, pleas, and threats, Ribsplitter-Jones punched himself in the head with a salute. "E'rats, ya fugging fug." His eyes softened. "Yer a fugging fug."

Shard waved him casually away. "Fuck you. I don't need your approval, and I suddenly realize I fucking hate you. Not nearly as much as the *fshquart* on your shoulder, but you certainly list on my hate chart."

"Language, Whig!" Daf-Nee shouted.

"Fuck off!" Shard retorted, then ordered, "Sergeant Major! Get the Thugs out of here!" As the sergeant major turned away, Shard motioned Smiley over. "I need to know something." Shard had been watching the Dwarves, reading the confusion in their eyes. "Is this two?" He glanced at Smiley. "Is this breaking Dwarves in formation two?"

Smiley's ever-present smile dimmed. "Well, when you took out that formation during the Jimenez campaign, that was twice."

"So wait, that's more than one, right?"

"That it is. This's thrice."

Shard blinked as he looked back toward the Dwarves. "Fuck, Smiley, is that more or less?"

"More, Captain."

Nodding, Shard looked to his second in command. "You'll tell the colonel, right? That I did it thrice?"

"Oh, of course!" Smiley exclaimed. "Um, on an unrelated note…"

"You may not have my captain's baldric."

"Ah, well. Unrelated, that it is." He nodded. He turned to follow the line of Goblins, then stopped and looked back. "Aren't you coming?"

"No, Smiley," Shard said, his eyes locked on the Dwarven formation before him.

"Okay," Smiley said slowly. "Um, I'm still not getting it, that I am, but I'm feeling that moment when you kick me in the nads is quickly approaching, and I'm thinking, I'll just wait for you outside, that I will."

"You'll find the sergeant major, fall all the Thugs in, and watch the show."

Smiley brightened. "Oh! Wonderful! For a moment I thought you were going to blow yourself up, that I did!"

"Get out, Smiley."

Smiley turned and left.

Captain Wiggletooth Shard of the Black Dragon Company stood before the Dwarf Wolf Claw Clan. Each time the Dwarves looked as if they would move, Shard brandished the blazing torch, making them flinch. With a wall of Black Dirt That Blows Stuff up in an enclosed courtyard, shield wall or not, their destruction was guaranteed.

As the rain began to pound, Shard could hear the shouts of his sergeants dim in the distance, getting his Thugs to safety.

He smiled.

Captain Wiggletooth Shard would present himself to Dru, goddess of Death, with not one, but thrice Dwarven shield walls in tow, shortening his walk on the Long Bridge of Fo.

Shard knew one sentence in Human, Dwarf, Elf, and Gnome. The sentence only made sense at one specific moment.

Holding the torch aloft, his heart pounded against his ribs. Shard screamed in the Dwarven tongue, "Tell Dru, goddess of Death, Wiggletooth Shard sends her another empty-handed soul!"

Shard plunged the torch down into the Black Dirt That Blows Stuff Up.

The Dwarves stacked shields over shields into a turtle in a desperate attempt to withstand the incredible blast.

The rain splashed against the cobblestone.

Shard didn't realize his eyes were closed until he opened them. The torch was burning, hissing in the muddy black sand at his feet, cooking it into a thick, oily plume of dark grey smoke…but nothing more. Quickly Shard stabbed the torch into the Black Dirt That Blows Stuff Up, slowly remembering something about fire and water.

Black Dirt That Blows Stuff Up did not work in the rain.

Shard looked up.

The Dwarves slowly recovered from their turtle formation, and with growing smiles, their stained teeth showing, they began to move forward, their ranks parting. They were more than enough to deal with one Goblin, formation or not.

Shard watched them approach, frantically stabbing his ever-burning torch into the wet Black Dirt That Blows Stuff Up. With his monobrow sagged over his eyes in defeat, Shard looked up.

The rum.

Mayhem.

Shard stood as a crazy smile crept across his lips.

The Dwarves paused as uncertainty flashed in their eyes, their formation instinctively closing.

With a casual toss, Shard sent the burning torch into the swelling puddle of rum.

Blue fire, dark and all but invisible, blazed madly, swelling and climbing everything it touched. Within seconds it burst into bright yellow fire, scaling the wall of shelves that housed the casks of rum and Black Dirt That Blows Stuff Up.

Shard smashed another cask, spilling more rum, and the Dwarves burst forward, smacking the flames with their shields in the desperate attempt to stop the growing conflagration. Some dropped to their knees, splashing rainwater with their hands.

They were the proud Dwarven Wolf Claw Clan, and their magnificent rum was on fire.

Sergeant Major Whoretwang Ribsplitter-Jones bellowed furiously as he drove his Goblins on across the narrow purchase to safe ground beyond. With distraught, saddened eyes he watched his shadow throw itself to the ground as the sky behind lit up in brilliant gold. Explosion after explosion filled the air, the sound crashing louder than the thunder.

He dropped forward, shielding Daf-Nee with his body, as the Fortress of the Wolf Claw Clan exploded in a flash of hellfire.

Slowly, as the night returned, Ribsplitter-Jones climbed to his feet. "E'rats!" he shouted. "Smiley, ya fug! Order yer fugs into formation!"

Brushing mud from his face, Smiley called back, "Sergeant Major! Fall the Thugs in!"

Ribsplitter-Jones roared. "E'rats! Ya fugs! You heard yer lieutenant! Fugging fall in! Sergeants, I needs a count!"

Still draped over his shoulder, Daf-Nee cried, "Whig! My darling little Whig!"

Hearing her, Smiley's face bent in as much of a frown as it could manage. "I'm sorry, that I am, more than anyone, but Wiggletooth Shard, my best friend in the world, is dead, that he is." He cuffed a tear. "Blown up crushing a Dwarf formation, that he did. That's thrice, that it is. Now I am the captain of the Black Dragon Company, that I am."

Daf-Nee, regarded him. "I'm sorry, but what I meant to say was, 'There he is, somehow alive, my darling little Whig.'"

Smiley turned back. "That makes no sense." He pointed to the bright glow of the fortress. "The fortress has blown up with him in it, that is…" He voice trailed off into a high-pitched whine as he clutched his nuts and fell over.

As steam rose from his paulderons, Shard eyed the group. "I need that count, Sergeant Major." He then motioned with a nod. "And you can put the *fshquart* down."

"Whig!" Daf-Nee cried. "My darling! Let me hug you!"

"I will fucking stab you," he hissed.

"Well, I need to hug someone," she said, climbing to her feet. "Addiko! Get over here!"

A Goblin stepped forward. "Private First Class Addiko reporting as…" Daf-Nee threw her long arms around the Goblin and hugged her. "Oh, uh, this is nice."

Climbing to his feet, Smiley tried to shake his testicle back into his scrotum. "I'm actually happy to see you, that I am." He looked up, his smile returning. "How did you survive?"

Shard looked back to the burning fort with a sneer. "I set the rum on fire. The Dwarves shoved me out of the way to try to stop the fire. I took that opportunity to tactically relocate to an advantageous position of counterattack."

"You set the rum on fire?" Smiley sounded scandalous. "The rum? On fire?" He looked around helplessly. "The rum!"

He looked back at Smiley. "Mayhem, Smiley. Mayhem."

* * * * *

Dexter Herron Bio

Lieutenant Dexter Herron (Ret.) was born and raised in Brooklyn, New York. He began writing his first stories on an Underwood typewriter salvaged from a World War Two submarine on sheaves of deceased (natural causes) treant. Updating to the high tech computer, The Commodore 64, he wrote his first novel, Knight of Chaos, a sword and sorcery adventure. His next work, Shard's Thugs, a hilarious Goblin adventure, was written on something more modern.

Joining the Marines, he served in North Africa, Japan, and Eastern Europe. After his enlistment, he finished his college degree in Criminology. Dexter Herron served the people of Mystic Connecticut as a Police Lieutenant until his retirement.

He is married, has 1.5 cats, and lives in a beautiful home nicked named 'The Shire' by all who visit. When he isn't writing, he tinkers with his 1974 Volkswagen Super Beetle named 'Gen.' He is a member of the Society for Creative Anachronism as a Master of Arms. He is an Eagle Scout. His favorite authors are Kurt Vonnegut Jr., Terry Pratchett, J.R.R. Tolkien, Bernard Cornwell, and Frank Miller.

His novels, Shard's Thugs and Knight of Chaos, are available where books are sold. His new works, Law of Shadows, and The Gunslinger and the Mage, will be released in the near future.

# # # # #

Horse's Heart by Sarah A. Hoyt

Horse and Bull save us from night everlasting and ice eternal.

From ice, night, and nothingness, Horse was spun, and Horse's hooves ignited the stars. From the fire in Horse's heart, Bull was born, and in the plenitude of his might, Bull gored Horse. From Horse's blood, gods were created; from Horse's life, gods drew their power, and in the fullness of time, the gods killed Bull. From Bull's blood, men were born, and from Bull's spirit, fyhis was given them.

Life from death. Death from life. The goddesses of each are twins, never parted.

The stranger came into Denre on a windy, wintry afternoon, the dark grey clouds above rent and driven by an angry wind. The sun that now and then pierced through had a drowned quality that made the scene look like something misremembered, something lost in the mists of time and never fully captured in painting or poem or ballad.

The city, as he saw it from the beach, standing next to the pounding grey-green waves, had that quality too: the steep-roofed buildings overtopping the stone wall bleached by encroaching salt.

As he looked, for a moment, the sun gilded the roof of the Lord's house, and a smile twisted the man's lips in something not at all denoting pleasure. "Denre, beloved of Horse," he said, as though reciting something learned in childhood. "Sweet Denre by the sea."

Where he stood, he could have chosen to take the gently curving way from the beach up to the city's main gates, the way taken by merchants and visitors who arrived by sea. He looked at it a long while, but then continued, instead, by the seashore, his bare feet digging into the cold, wet sand.

To be fair, he did not look like the kind of man who should enter a city—no matter how prosperous—by the main gate. Though he held his sandals in his hand, they were the kind any fisherman might wear. And though a cloak draped around his head and shoulders, falling in negligent folds to his ankles, it was a dark and dingy garment, tattered at the bottom in a way that denoted much wear or hard times.

Had anyone been watching, they might have been struck by the fact that, though he moved like an old man, his face—now and then semi-uncovered by the wind—was that of a young man, either in his thirties, or in his twenties, if he'd lived a hard life.

He stopped where there were marks of boats that had rested on the sand and been pushed out to sea, and shaded his eyes with his free hand, looking out at the water as though wondering who'd take sailboats out in such weather.

Then he continued walking, 'til he came to the rough steps carved up the side of the cliff. They'd been there from time immemorial and had once admitted menials to the confines of Denre House. Since the fall of the family, they were used for peddlers and low-status visitors to enter the city, without going via the main gates and inviting questions about their business and why they were there.

Judging by his clothing and the labored, slow way the man climbed, it was entirely possible he was there to become a beggar. Which meant that had any inhabitant seen him, they'd likely have laughed and said good luck finding a stray crumb of bread in Denre these days.

But there was no one at all on the beach, or the stairs, or even keeping token guard on the arched opening in the walls above.

So he walked up the steps unmolested. When he was halfway up, rain erupted out of nowhere, wind driven, lashing him and soaking his wrap.

* * *

The Temple of Horse had seen better days. It had once been the centerpiece of the city of Denre, back when the House of Denre had been second in the kingdom of Areva, its lord important and revered, and the town itself a center of trade with Susapeta.

A vast building of stone covered with a facing of marble, it boasted a colonnaded portico, which led to a sacrificial chamber, also covered in marble, and ornamented in polished brass. The altar was vast, circular, up a set of steps.

None of it had collapsed, and there was nothing at all a casual visitor could have pointed at to indicate disrepair or neglect; it was more like the people who were supposed to shine the brasses and scrub the marble had done so carelessly. The braziers burning around the altar must have been fed with inferior fuel, as their flames wavered and flickered, more blue than bright.

The two priests and one acolyte laboring at the altar also looked like they'd seen better days. The men were too gaunt, their hair white, and the boy was too thin, looking nervy, his black hair caught back in a straggly ponytail, his tunic much mended and seeming in dire need of a wash.

As for the colt lying on the altar, two problems would strike anyone familiar with the rites of Horse. The first was that the animal wasn't flawless, but a scrawny creature, looking like it had some disease of the skin. And the second was that they had drugged the animal. This was obvious by the way it lay sideways on the marble altar, unable even to lift its head, though it attempted to several times.

Even so, they had tied its forelegs and back legs with sturdy ropes, and the older man, the principal prince of Horse, Akakis, kept saying "mind the legs" to the acolyte as, his own hands trembling, he poured the sweet wine over the stone blade.

A poor sacrifice, and he knew it, too, this wild colt, caught outside the city without its dam. It would probably have died anyway, without being dragged to the temple for sacrifice.

The year had been too wet, too cold, the harvest too late, and the wild grasses, too, upon which the wild horses fed had barely started to sprout when they had died, yellowing on the field, and turning rank and spongy. The wild horses were starving, and either the mare had abandoned her foal to save her own life, or the colt was one of twins, abandoned as it couldn't be supported in such a cold year.

It mattered not. Akakis knew only that the foal had life. Uncertain, vacillating life, like the sacred fire in the bronze receptacles, but life nevertheless, and much needed to bolster the power of his failing fyhis. *Their* failing fyhis, he corrected. They must make sure all their fyhis were fed, before the battle that was to come.

He closed his eyes, trying to still the trembling in his arms and hands, as the hunger of his symbiont communicated itself along his arms, demanding, craving food.

Go too long without feeding, and the fyhis started feeding on the host, creating wraiths. Which was part of the reason they were in the fix they were. All those noblemen cast down, exiled, pushed away from any chance to feed their fyhis. All the men that the mad king had sent from their lands—

He didn't want to think of them, though they'd been sighted by the patrols of boatmen sailing too close to the coast, trying to spy the oncoming threat. Kyrva…No, he wouldn't say of Denre, not even in his own thoughts. Kyrva might be the old lord's son, but he'd been left behind, raised as one of the urchins of the village by his old nursemaid. And he was an invaluable scout, fearless. *Possessed of a laughing demon,* his nursemaid and adoptive mother said, but it was no demon. It was simply that he was much what the old lord had been before the king's edicts. He was also, probably, should the new king restore the rights of the dispossessed, the lord of Denre. The oldest boy, Telbar, had been sold into slavery, and though they'd sent scouts the length of Areva, they'd never found him. There was a good chance he was dead. A slave that harbored fyhis was a liability for the host.

The other boy—Akakis opened his eyes briefly to look at the acolyte and whispered, "Teryon, mind the legs."

He recalled the message again that Kyrva…not of Denre…had sent, loud and clear, mind to mind, an extravagant waste of fyhis power in these lean times, *There is an army of wraiths descending on Denre. They're being sent forth by the Susapetans to destroy us. To take us, so they can take the land with no battle.*

An army of wraiths. If it were an army of mortal men, they'd fight with spears. Even if they had scant warriors, and the fishermen had been too hard-pressed fishing to make do on the walls. But an army of wraiths must be fought with fyhis. He lifted his knife even higher, and said quickly, "May Horse accept the life, and return it."

The knife of polished obsidian flashed in the insufficient light and slashed at the Horse's throat. The animal made a week sound, not quite a whinny, and then—

With his fyhis sight, Akakis could see the uncertain light of the colt's life-force flare above the body, then break free. And he could feel his own fyhis in its normal form, like a tiger made of blue light, reach for it with claw and tooth. He was just telling himself that he must share, he must let the other two—

His hesitation and control delayed his fyhis a few seconds. Which was a few seconds too much. A famished fyhis leapt on the altar, his form visible only to those who also bore fyhis symbionts, but since those were all the three present, there was a scream of consternation from the two priests and devotee as the lean, vacillating fyhis reached with sharp claws for the life….and took it.

For a second, for just a second, Akakis raised the knife, bristling with anger, and traced the pale link of light between the fyhis and his symbiont.

He'd have sworn they were alone in the temple, he and his brother priest Myriar, and the boy Teryon. But now he saw there was a man well at the back, knitting himself with the shadow of the wall. A man almost-ragged, dressed as a beggar or a supplicant.

Akakis' voice trembled with frustration and hunger—and where they'd find another horse to sacrifice, he didn't know—as he said, "You, the stranger! You, fyhis thief! Who are you, and by what right do you steal that which is Horse's?"

The man had collected the fyhis to himself. The beast was now invisible, but there was something like an outline around the stranger, enough to see that, despite his clothes, he was well built. And as he stepped forward—though anyone who had seen him earlier would be surprised at the sureness of his step—there was something familiar to his movement.

He pulled down the hood of his cloak, revealing dark, wavy hair pulled back, and the eyes he lifted to the priest were dark, intense blue and almond-shaped, a distinctive shape he was used to seeing in the tapestries and frescoes slowly moldering in the house of the Denre lords.

Of course, it meant nothing. That hair and those eyes which were so distinctive of the house of Denre had been passed, over the three thousand years of the family's hold on the region, to many a by-blow. You could see them in many a vendor in the market stalls on trade day, which explained why they'd managed to hide Kyrva so neatly, of course.

But all the same, Akakis' voice had a less accusatory tone as he repeated, "Who are you?"

The man cleared his throat, and the first two words came out hoarse, as though he'd been unused to speaking, "I am," he said. And then his voice gathered strength, as he added, "Telbar of the house of Denre, the house of Horse. None are more entitled to the fyhis force than I."

At this, Teryon made a strangled sound and spun around. And in that minute, Akakis, who was ready to ask for proof, to demand that the man show a sign of his ancestry, of his legitimacy, and that he was in fact the lost heir, was caught by the similarity in the two faces: Teryon, barely fourteen, downy hair just coming in on lip and chin, and this man, mature and fully formed, his face tanned by the elements. But the nose was the same, and the lips, and the eyes that dropped at the corner.

The sad Denre eyes, grieving for Horse himself.

Akakis was suddenly shaking with something more than his fyhis' hunger. He still didn't know where they'd find a way to feed himself or the boy or Myriar, not to mention Kyrva. As the only Fyhis-bearing men in Denre, they must be fed, so they could defend the city.

"My fyhis was barely restrained from devouring me. I thank you for the life," Telbar said evenly.

Caught between ancestral respect and confusion, Akakis bowed, quickly, almost reluctantly, but disciplined his voice to say, "I am glad that we have—I'm glad you've not become a wraith, but we are facing an army of wraiths headed this way. And we have no one to combat them, except...except you, and I don't think..."

"I know," Telbar said.

"But, but…milord, you are proscribed. You are denied entry to the city. All of your name were barred from Denre by King Dracar, and I—none of us…our feeding your fyhis, though unintended, is a crime against Areva and its kings."

Those very blue eyes looked back at him unperturbed; the urbane voice said once more, "I know." And then with a flickering look at Teryon, who looked as though he'd been poleaxed and remained, mouth partly open, staring, "And yet, you have my brother, and you have not turned him out."

The priest opened his mouth, intending to claim he didn't know who the youth who was his acolyte might have been or what his parentage, but the stranger chuckled, a deep chuckle in his throat. "Do not worry. Dracar is deposed in Areva. His nephew Tuoranel reigns in his place, and he's my comrade at arms. It is by his order that I am here, to resume my house and my family, and leadership of Denre. I am here to hold the frontier against Susapeta, and against the wraiths."

"Well!" the priest said. "And how do we know—"

In that moment, the stranger's mind touched his, impelled by their fyhis. In his mind, clear as day, he saw a youth, not a stripling, but probably not twenty yet, standing in front of the gilded throne of Areva and giving clear orders for "Telbar, Lord of Denre" to have this and to hold that, and to "guard our border."

The vision was so clear, the priest almost bowed to the crown-bearing, brown-haired figure. In fact, as his liege-lord's power withdrew, he was still wide eyed, holding his breath, struggling to bring himself under control. When he managed words, it was to say, "Milord, I don't know if you realize what you are saying. Of all the men and women of Areva, all those who were fyhis bearing, your uncles, your great uncles, your cousins, were expelled with your father. If their bodies live still, they are likely part of that army of wraiths bearing down on us. There are only the three of us, and you, milord, and…and Lord Kyrva." He saw the man smile at the name. "I do not know how we can hold the wraiths back, much less the Susapetans when they come."

The man smiled. For a moment there was in his expression something of Kyrva's laughing demon, but also something of his father, Lord Euridir of Denre as he was, a haughty lifting of the eyebrows, a certainty in the eyes. "You know very well how to solve all this, Akakis. And you must do it."

"Milord! It will be no use without the ring."

But the man moved his hand from under the fold of his cloak and held it up, showing the darkened gold circlet and the blood red stone on it. It was a ruby, Akakis supposed. Or at least had always supposed before, but the legends called it the blood of Horse and said that when Horse had taken human form to sire his son, the first Lord of Denre, he'd left the ring with his concubine to give to the boy.

That was as it might be. Before these disturbed times, Akakis, though he believed in Horse as a metaphor, and knew, of course, that the fyhis—which was Horse's gift to mankind—allowed those who bore it to perform miracles, from teleportation to communication mind-to-mind, from shielding to causing explosions, had always thought all that talk of gods coming down to mingle with mortal women and of the House of Denre being descended from the god of life himself was all very well, and no doubt worked as propaganda for

Denre. But really. It couldn't be believed by any rational man, could it?

Now he wasn't so sure. But he was sure of one thing. "The ring was on your father's finger when he was dragged out of the town by the king's forces, after your lady mother was…after she was killed." He remembered what had happened before the killing, and the screaming of the beautiful, noble lady before they'd given her mercy. Teryon remembered nothing, and Kyrva might or might not remember, but this man had been twelve. He must have heard and known what it meant.

If he did, he gave no sign. He looked, perhaps, a little colder, a little more distant. "My father gave me the ring," he said.

And at that moment, Akakis realized that boys of twelve sold as slaves into the court of Areva probably knew all too well what such screams meant. He had heard of what went on in Areva, and that was before the king had decided to consolidate his power over the land and destroy all the old houses. And then what the man had said reached him, and he said, almost weak with relief, "Lord Euridir lives? He is—"

Telbar shook his head. "No. Lord Euridir does *not* live. He is, as you surmised, a wraith."

A moment of unease and confusion, and Akakis said, "Milord, are you saying that your father's wraith…"

"Yes, that is precisely what I am saying. Now, will you give it to me or not?"

Akakis hesitated. Teryon, who'd been silent 'til then, said, in a voice that was more breath than words, "Sir, sir, we must—"

Akakis could sense in Teryon that if he were not to accede, Teryon would. Not that he blamed him. Sure, they had raised the boy as though he had been a foundling, left at the temple, but someone had told him the truth. Denre was a small town and had been a fiefdom of the same family from the beginning. Or close to the beginning. *Before the stars were fully ignited, Denre was Horse's.*

Still, he wasn't sure. If the ring had come from the wraith, what was this man? No fyhis-bearer could come too close to a wraith and not have his own fyhis devoured by the soulless man, becoming a wraith like him.

"I was one," Telbar said. His voice sounded almost hollow, distant, as though he were trying to remember something in the distant past, something that didn't quite make sense.

"One?"

"A wraith," he said, "but when the ring was given me, I..." He passed a hand across his forehead. "My fyhis recovered. I don't know how. I just know it recovered, and then I found my way here, ahead of them. They—they ask only mercy. They wish to be defeated. If we can do it."

"If I give you Horse?"

Telbar laughed. It was a strange sound, because he did not look at all amused or pleased. "Even with Horse," he said, "it will be difficult. The—it will be difficult. There are many of them. Which is why you must give me Horse now. Right away. Because it's not just fyhis that must be fed. What I've seen of Denre tells me its people are starving. The battle will take everything we have. *Everything.* And we have only a few hours."

Akakis blinked as though wakening. There was that. In a few hours, the wraiths would be here. And as things stood, no one would survive in the town. It would be ten thousand souls destroyed, devoured. Those who had no fyhis would be corpses, and those who had fyhis would become more wraiths, to join the wandering army and attack the next town, and the next, as Susapeta swept behind them, their lords well protected by their own fyhis shield. They would take it all, 'til Areva itself was taken, and every last one of the subjects of the once-proud Arevan Confederation destroyed.

What did it matter if he gave the sacred pendant to this man, who was probably Telbar of Denre, but who might not be sane—because what man would claim to have been a wraith and have returned from that place that was worse than death unscathed?—to attempt to set things to right before the attack.

What was the worst he could do to the people of Denre? Kill them? Make them wraiths? Well, that was going to happen anyway.

Akakis turned, faint with hunger, shaking with the hunger of his fyhis.

In time immemorial—the legend said—when Horse himself had given the mother of his child the ring ornamented with his blood, he'd given the temple he'd established in Denre the carved medallion of his likeness.

The ring passed to the oldest son of the house, usually named Telbar. But the blessing of the temple was necessary for the son to become the true lord of Denre. And only the true lord of Denre could command the seas and the land here around, and ensure the nets were full, and that the trees bore fruit. And that wild horses of the right kind were available for the sacrifice.

He looked at what remained of the poor abandoned colt and almost absently stroked its matted head.

Then he stepped away, around the altar. The pendant of Horse always returned to the temple when the lord died or lost his power. It was something he'd always thought was a long-set spell created by some old priest's fyhis.

Now he went to the place where the pendant had been, these sixteen years, in a niche in the wall, protected by a heavy stone lid, which took the fyhis of the principal priest of Horse to open.

His fyhis was so weakened that for a moment Akakis thought he'd not make it. Then he reached with hands, as well as with fyhis, one assisting the other, and the box slid open.

The pendant was ancient, very ancient, of ivory turned almost golden with age. And for its age, it was carved with immense care and exactness, a depiction of Horse's head, the mane flying, the eyes, suggested in carving, seeming alive. It hung upon a leather cord.

Holding it in his cupped hands, Akakis walked back. He did bow when extending it.

And in the next minute, he had to catch his breath and remind himself that there were no miracles.

As Telbar of Denre took the pendant and tied the thin leather strap around his neck, something like a light flew from ring to pendant, and from pendant to ring, and it seemed to him that Telbar grew stronger, straightened, and that the voice in which he said, "Send men to the North Entrance. There will be horses. Bring them here," sounded like his father's voice when he gave orders.

He sounded more normal as he said, "I don't suppose we can open my house? I need clothes. And I would love a bath."

It was that reassurance of normalcy and humanity that made Akakis fear less for what he had done.

* * *

The house of Denre wasn't a ruin, which had shocked Telbar. It meant that villagers had come in there—covertly, in secret, and frankly at risk of their own lives—while the family was gone and proscribed. But then, the people of Denre had housed and hid his brothers. That he and his sister had been sold into slavery, and all the rest that had happened, couldn't be held against them. He knew how the emissaries of the king had held everyone in fyhis thrall, even the priests and noblemen. There was nothing servants or merchants, farmers or fishermen, no matter how loyal, could have done.

But they'd come back, behind him, as he went from room to room of the abandoned house, avoiding only his mother's room, because he remembered. He'd not seen anything, but he remembered. The rooms would have to be cleaned and set to rights, if they'd not been yet, but not until he married. If he married. If he survived today.

What he'd told Akakis was the truth. The ring and the pendant would allow him to feed his people, both body and fyhis, but he knew the hunger of the wraiths, and how many there were. How many able-bodied men remained in Denre? And how could they fight?

Somehow, without giving any orders, his servants—or perhaps the descendants of his father's servants—had come in, led him to the master's room, filled a bathtub in the adjoining bathing room, laid out a fine, if every day and ornamented tunic, which must have been his father's.

For a moment, for just a moment, Telbar felt tears prickle behind his eyes, realizing that his people had been starving, and yet they'd not looted his house nor sold the possessions of a family they presumed as good as gone. He suspected, should he look for them, all the jewels would still be in the strong house. Devotion like that wasn't rational. But it did move him.

By the time a young man came running into the lord's room, Telbar was dressed, shaved, his hair oiled, his tunic falling gracefully around the sturdy leather belt.

The young man was red-headed and green eyed, and his features reminded Telbar of his sister, Phillida, whom he'd left in the court of Areva. "Kyrva?" he said, half laughing, despite the sting in his eyes. Kyrva had been six, a laughing child, who used to follow him around and imitate everything Telbar did. Now he was a man, sturdy, with overgrown red hair and a beard. But the eyes were the same. He wore a much-mended tunic, folded on the top in such a way that it left the right arm free, in the manner of fishermen. He also wore sturdy sandals, and his calves were white with salt. He and Teryon had been out of Denre with his nurse when the royal troops, all fyhis-bearers, had come. Telbar never knew if they had escaped. 'Til now.

The green eyes looking into his filled with tears, even as the mouth opened in a smile. "Telbar. By Horse's mane. Telbar! We thought you dead."

Telbar smiled. "Sometimes I thought myself dead." He did not add that sometimes he wished he'd been, until he'd been sold to a humble potter and his wife, who'd freed him and raised him as their own, unaware of what had come into their house. And even after, when a raid had killed his foster parents, and he'd found himself in Susapetan hands. It turned out Susapetan princelings didn't treat their slaves better than Arevan courtiers. Only differently. Someday he might tell Kyrva, or he might not. Someday he might tell him how Phillida had found him. How Phillida had conspired with the nephew of the king to depose the tainted regime from the throne of Areva.

But not now. Now he must call food and horses. "Go to the men, the—the fishermen, and tell them put to sea. There will be fish. Then return. I will hold off the sacrifice 'til you do."

In the end, there was not enough space to feed the people—and they looked just as ragged and weak as he had thought—and they'd laid the tables out in the marketplace as fish roasted. And horses, too, once the fyhis had fed on their life force.

He'd not let them serve wine. "No, there will be time for celebration later. Now the wraiths."

* * *

The wraiths were a ragged army, but they were many, and their smell and the sense of their hunger traveled ahead of them like a cloud.

The smell came from their being unwashed. These creatures who had been humans never bathed. They lived on what they could find.

Telbar had seen them fall upon a flock of sheep in a field, while the shepherd ran away.

Telbar shuddered. He did not remember what he'd done, nor who he'd been while among the wraiths. His time hadn't been long, as he'd tracked it afterwards. Only a few days. But he was glad he didn't remember roaming the countryside, his mind empty, his body lost.

He still didn't understand the miracle that had called him back.

He'd woken, like a child wakes in a strange place, surrounded by wraiths, with a large one keeping all others away.

It had taken some effort to remember the face of this wraith as that of the father he'd lost so many years ago. His father's wraith had kept all wraiths away and held something out to him, glistening red in the sullen moonlight: the ring that contained Horse's blood.

On the ramparts, having ordered the doors closed and barricaded with barrels and the remains of the tables, Telbar paced. He wanted to lead a group against the wraiths. No. He wanted to lead a group against the Susapetans who drove them. But though he'd dressed in his father's armor—light sheets of metal with leather sandwiched between, molding to arms and legs and chest and hips—the rest of the men were poorly protected. And they were even more poorly trained.

Kyrva, he thought, had some idea of how to fight, and Teryon might have. Their father's erstwhile master of arms, now a humble shepherd, had nonetheless seen that the sons of the lord had some training.

But it was still not enough. And besides, Telbar bore the ring and the pendant of Horse. Perhaps they would fall to Kyrva, if Telbar died, but he couldn't be sure. After all, the king had a choice as to the ring, and the priests of Horse as to the pendant.

Though one or the other might incline to Kyrva, with Areva in turmoil and invaded, who could tell? And only the lord in possession of the two could command the wild horses, and only he could—at least at times—call the fish to these increasingly frigid shores.

Barred from fighting, though carrying a sword against any invader who might get in, Telbar had armed his people, but more importantly, he, Kyrva, Teryon, and the remaining priests of Horse had built a blue wall of energy with their recently fed fyhis. The wraiths could not penetrate it. Though as Susapeta pushed behind, they had to go somewhere.

At first, they milled between the two living walls of power, not moving; then little by little, they started…disappearing.

On the walls, Telbar felt Kyrva come up behind him. "What is happening?" he asked, wild-eyed. "What is happening to the wraiths?"

"I don't know," Telbar said. "I think it's Father."

"Our Father?"

"Yes, he is a wraith, but an unusual one. I'd fallen—I cannot explain it to you, but I'd become one of them. And then I met Father. He retains his memory, though he's a wraith. Might have been the ring that kept him, all that time…He lifted his hand. He gave it to me, and with it, my fyhis returned to me, and I was whole. I walked here…" He paused. "I don't know what he's doing, but I think it is him. See the figure that moves? I think that's him."

"It was so long ago. I barely remember. Telbar, why did the king of Areva…how…?"

222 | KENNEDY & HOWELL

"Human sacrifice. It gives power such as even horses don't give. They were gorging on it. The noblemen tried to rebel, but...they were put down by the superior human-fed fyhis of the king and his courtiers. Our father and others were sent to exile, barred from feeding their fyhis 'til they became wraiths."

"But Tuoranel of Areva managed to rebel? I heard he's the new king."

"It's a complicated story. One Phillida will tell you if we win, when we go to Areva. Which I think we must do, because I believe Tuora means to marry her."

"Oh." Kyrva paused. "If we win? Look, the wraiths are vanishing."

"Yes, but behind them comes the Susapetan army. How long do you think we can survive in here, without being able to send out the boats for fish?"

"Oh."

Kyrva watched as the wraiths disappeared. The Susapetan army was behind them. They'd meet shield to shield, and even from a distance, Telbar could tell, and knew Kyrva could tell, that the Susapetan shield was stronger. "I don't even know," Telbar said, "that we can hold off their shield. They might break through and slaughter us all."

"Do they also use human sacrifice?"

"I don't believe so. At least I never saw it when—" He stopped, as that was neither the time nor the place. "But there are just too many of them."

The roar of the Susapetans was now audible, deafeningly loud, louder than the sound of the sea.

"Telba!" Kyrva said, calling Telbar by his childhood nickname. "I have an idea."

Telbar looked. Kyrva's eyes danced with mirth. "We have some goats." And impatiently, to Telbar's blank look, "I can rig a pole and lanterns to their horns. I say the goats, because we don't have that many cows, and also it would be harder to take them down the steps to the beach."

"Why would you take the goats to the beach?"

"We shall take the goats out now, before the sun rises. In the dark, it will look like some of us—perhaps the most important among us—are escaping. If you can thin the shield a little, to appear like the fyhis-bearers are leaving? The Susapetans can take the path up the cliff and lay siege to the city. Or, if they think all left behind will be defenseless if they—"

"Go to the beach and capture the fyhis-bearers, and those who might be of use to the king of Areva, and command ransoms? They will take the path around instead. It doesn't matter, they'll think they can always extend, and bar us, too. And they'll be on the beach, and defenseless."

"Yes."

"But Kyrva, can you return?"

"Oh, I'll return."

"Not as a wraith?"

The green eyes laughed at him. "I'll do my best, my lord Denre."

And he'd left, calling to him some of the fisher boys, his foster brothers.

Moments later, the goats moved down, the lights on their horns making a bright spectacle on the sand, approaching the boats.

The Susapetan shield broke, as their fyhis-bearers rushed to the beach to capture the hostages.

And while the best and bravest of the fighters, led by Teryon, who showed his age was nothing to his bravery, went the other way from the high side, separating them from their army and laying into them in the darkness with stave and lance and sword, and whatever implement the locals could lay hands to, Telbar and Akakis and the other priest joined their fyhis.

It was difficult work, and unpleasant, to send the fyhis out as a killing power, a ravening beast of energy that burned everything in its path.

There were screams of men and horses 'til the field was a vast abattoir, a place of bones and horror.

The smell of their death rose to the sky, and it would be so easy, Telbar thought, so easy to avail yourself of their lifeforce. And he wondered if that was how the former king of Areva had fallen, after a battle.

But then he heard in his mind as Kyrva called, "Telbar, Telbar, help!"

There was frantic urgency in the call.

He followed the message blindly, forgetting his temptation. And yet in the following of the request, there was another temptation, another thing he should not be doing. The lord of Denre should not throw himself into the fight and risk dying. He should not...

Before he could help himself, he was running down the steps as he had when he was a boy, the son of the house, running down the steps to see the fishermen pull in the catch, or, on rare occasions, his father return from Areva, sitting very straight on a much better boat, his cloak pulled around his broad shoulders against the wind from the sea.

There was a trick to running down the use-polished, fine sand-covered steps.

Impossible not to slip, but there was a way of catching the slip before it became disastrous, and righting yourself, then slipping again, then catching yourself once more, so that you arrived at the beach with a slide upon the sand, and then righted yourself there, too.

Falling into the instinctive rhythm, Telbar had the fleeting thought that he must look like a child running to play.

But on the beach below, the smell of blood hit him, coppery and sharp.

Men moved around in the semi-darkness, upon which the light of the goats' lanterns served only to cast horrendous shadows.

The party of Denre was victorious, that was easy to see. He recognized the profiles of Teryon and his companions, fighting, seemingly unarmed, while the foes being slashed and falling wore the blunt helmets the Susapetans favored.

Teryon must have used his fyhis to disguise them until it was too late and fallen upon the Susapetans before they were detected.

A frantic look around, and then he recognized Kyrva's silhouette, out by the boats. There, by the light of an errant lantern on the horns of a bleating goat, Kyrva fought two opponents.

One of them would be Kyrva's size and probably his age, but the other was a giant of a man, with pale hair illuminated by moonlight.

That glimpse sent a chill into Telbar's blood. In a moment, he saw his adoptive parents' home blazing, taking what remained of them and their positions, while he was chained at the back of a slave hunter's train.

This...man, the Susapetan prince Salahan, had come deep into Arevan territory, with an armed escort, and taken peasants and potters, mothers and maidens. He'd chained them together and made them walk, over frozen ground and slick, to the slave market in Susaper.

Telbar? Telbar he'd kept for himself, amused at the idea of a slave with fyhis. He'd kept Telbar's fyhis starved, and for a crumb, made him beg and perform. He'd made Telbar serve at table, and clean the stables, and anything that occurred to him. Fortunately, he lacked the imagination and the inclinations of the Arevans, but making one perform for the necessary bite of the life energy to keep from turning a wraith was the same, no matter what the performance was.

For three years Telbar had served, before finding the opportunity and despair to run into the night. To risk becoming a wraith.

And now here stood the man who'd made the lord of Denre behave like a slave. And he was threatening Kyrva.

Telbar might have tried to scream the princeling's name, but what came out was an incoherent scream of rage.

Salahan turned, nonetheless, leaving Kyrva still fully occupied in fighting the younger opponent, but maybe, Telbar thought, with that part of his mind that could still think, this would allow him to win free.

For a moment Salahan looked surprised, then when Telbar lifted the sword to strike, he stepped into form, interposing his shield with the figure of the lion upon it.

Telbar's sword rang upon the shield like a bell tolling.

And then Salahan laughed. "Why, if it isn't the potter's brat," he said. "The slave boy." Salahan made a swipe with his sword at Telbar, a lazy one, probably thinking him wholly untrained. Telbar was not a novice, but he was out of practice. In his ramblings, it had been long since anyone had brought to mind the careful lessons his father had taught him.

He was a second too late in parrying, but he did parry, cursing under his breath that he had not provided himself with a shield such as Salahan wore.

"So you stole armor and got some sword lessons." Salahan grinned.

Telbar wanted to tell him that he was born to this, and that at least he, Telbar of Denre, had never gone after defenseless young men already being attacked by someone else. For that matter, he'd also not killed peasants, or raided their simple houses, or taken their offspring captive.

What he said instead was a word, the single word that rose to his tongue of Susapetan, "Derir." *Coward*, just that, spit out like a curse. And *coward* served.

In the moment of uttering the word, and knowing what it meant—in the moment between roar of rage and calming—he realized that if he had continued charging in that insensate, irate way, he would have been killed. Instead, he had made Salahan angry.

The Susapetan roared like a charging bull and came at Telbar.

Once, in Susaper, he'd put Telbar in a field with a wild bull, and given Telbar only a dagger, telling him that if he wanted to feed his fyhis, he'd have to do it the hard way.

There had been guests, other Susapetans, dressed in silks, resplendent with gold jewelry, sipping wine from jeweled goblets around the low stone wall that separated the space where the bull was kept from them.

Telbar had gone in. And for a while, all he did was dodge the bull, while the spectators applauded and laughed. He had been sure, too, that they were applauding the bull.

Until the bull had charged him and, desperate, Telbar had suddenly ducked low while raising his dagger-bearing arm.

Now, as Salahan charged, Telbar shifted his weight to his back foot, giving the impression that he was going to run. Salahan was an experienced fighter. He must have noticed the movement without even realizing it.

He leapt toward Telbar, sword lifted to split the skull of the Denran.

Only Telbar was not there. He ducked and came up beneath the lion shield, his sword aimed.

Partly his movement, and partly the descending of Salahan's body as his jump ended, impaled the prince of Susapeta upon the heavy sword.

The moment seemed to last forever: Salahan's eyes widening in shocked surprise. His sword arm flaying out one final time and missing Telbar, or mostly missing him. And the sudden, hot spurt of blood coating Telbar's inherited armor.

It must have been only a second, perhaps less, because Telbar pulled his sword free and jumped aside before the heavy body of the giant from Susapeta fell on the sand.

Around him, the other fights seemed to have ended. He looked around, searching for Kyrva. The Susapetan who had attacked Kyrva lay dead between Telbar and where Kyrva had been. But it was hard to see. There was sweat running into Telbar's eyes, and the goats moved around, making the scene seem to change, even when it did not.

In the play of light and shadow, he was sure the place Kyrva had been was empty, and he knew fear for his brother.

And then...by the boats he saw two silhouettes, barely visible, dark against the darker night. Kyrva. And the wraith that had once been the lord of Denre.

Clutching his sword, Telbar ran through the melee on the beach, absently striking at a Susapetan who slashed at him, running to the place of quiet near the boats where Kyrva and his father faced each other.

As he approached, the creature who had been lord of Denre turned to face him. It was a horrible sight to behold, caked with the dirt of years, his eyes vacant, his mouth moving soundlessly.

"He came to me," Kyrva said, in a rush. "He tried to touch me."

Telbar grasped his sword, but something in him said not to strike. Not yet. Perhaps it was a whisper from the ruby on his finger, the pendant on his breast. But he thought the thing needed reassurance. It needed peace.

"We've saved Denre, Father. It is safe. And I'm its lord."

For a moment, nothing happened. Then the lips stopped moving, and the blind eyes turned to him. Wraiths could not speak, but there was such pleading in what had once been the noble face of Lord Euridir of Denre, such a request.

Telbar lifted his bloodied sword and swept it in a simple arc.

There was a sound like a sigh. The head and the body of Euridir of Denre fell to the foaming waves at the ocean's edge. Slowly, slowly, they dissolved and disappeared.

Above, a song of victory had broken out, and someone had lit a bonfire.

Teryon was up the stairs, leading his victorious party back home. They'd gotten the lanterns from the goats, which were climbing the steps on the cliff with them, and there was a festive air to their blood-spattered tunics. He turned toward Kyrva and Telbar and shouted, "May we have wine now, my Lord?"

Tired and half laughing, though he felt tears salty and cold on his face, Telbar shouted back, "You can have what you very well please!"

And then he looked up at his city, lit by fire, rescued by sword. "Sweet Denre by the sea," he said. "The city of Horse." It was a prayer.

* * * * *

Sarah A. Hoyt Bio

Sarah A. Hoyt was born in Portugal and lives in Colorado. Along the way she's published over 32 books (around there anyway. She keeps forgetting some every time she counts) she admits to and a round dozen she doesn't. She also managed to raise two sons, and a countless number of cats. When not writing at speed, she does furniture refinishing or reads history. She was a finalist for the Mythopoeic award with her first book, and has won the Prometheus and the Dragon. To learn more about Sarah and read samples of her work, visit http://sarahahoyt.com.

# # # # #

Island of Bones by William Alan Webb

A Sharp Steel & High Adventure Story

There was a time when heroes carved their own destinies with a mighty sword and a reckless soul. When bravery bested bravado, and fortune favored the bold. Exotic lands teemed with wondrous beasts, and sorcerers laid blasphemous spells. And in those far off days, legendary folk trod the glory road of sharp steel and high adventure.

Chapter 1

*S*ea Scamp rode the storm heavy, laden as she was with supplies for the long voyage to Corland. Many crates and amphorae had shifted, which made her unstable as towering waves slammed her narrow prow. Captain Boren shouted orders to the crewmen working the sails, fighting to keep the delicate balance between having enough sail out to keep them plunging bow first into the waves, and too much, which risked capsizing. Fortunately, the integrity of the hull was never in question, since she was built from rare twokewood, harder than tempered steel, but lighter than other suitable woods.

Boren turned at a scream to see a man in the rigging falling backward into the water. Lurching to the rail, he searched the foaming water for any sign of the lost man, to no avail. Whirling back, he took stock of his ship. Four of his senses were useless. Lightning illuminated the darkness only in brief flashes; otherwise, he was blind. All he could smell or taste was the ocean's brine, and the winds and waves drowned out all other sounds.

But he didn't need any of that to know how *Sea Scamp* fared in the storm. He could *feel* her response through his boots, and by the touch of his fingers on her rails.

Salt spray hung in the air. Water pouring down his forehead blurred his vision. Wiping his eyes for the thousandth time since the storm hit, in the glow from a lightning bolt, he spied the first mate, Kessin, with his arms wrapped around the main mast. Boren timed the boat's broach of the next wave and threw himself toward the center of the deck. He caught the mast and leaned close enough for Kessin to hear him over the howling winds.

"She's riding low and unstable; how much water have we shipped?"

"A foot last time I checked, Captain."

Boren shook his head. "She's too sluggish for just a foot of water. Check the bilge, and be quick."

Kessin's face tensed, and his fear was obvious. No sailor wanted to enter a hold with loose cargo flying around during a storm. It invited serious injury, or even death. But worse was disobeying a direct order from a captain like Boren, so Kessin nodded, as Boren knew he would. He returned sooner than expected, but now it wasn't simple fear that showed in widened eyes, it was terror. Boren knew what he would say before he said it.

"The bilge is full, Captain. It's overflowing into the bottom hold."

Damn! "We can't use the pumps in this storm." Boren had captained many ships through many storms, but never one this bad or this long. If it lasted much longer and the ship took on much more water, she'd sink for sure. There seemed like only one choice left to make.

"Bring me the priest!"

Kessin disappeared down the stairs leading below the fantail, where the ship's passengers rode out the storm in their cabin. Winds howled in Boren's ears, and it seemed hours until Boric Ravensperch staggered onto the deck in Kessin's grip. The priest of Vasta's usually pasty skin looked bone white when illuminated by lightning flashing across the night sky.

"I don't believe in gods, but the boat can't take much more of this. Prevail on your goddess to abate the winds!" demanded Boren.

"Are we going to sink?"

"Perhaps, but if the storm grows worse, we will certainly capsize…either way, you'll end up a shark's dinner!"

"Have we no other choice?"

"None that I can see! Isn't Vasta Goddess of the Winds?"

"This storm doesn't feel natural, Captain! There's something else at work here—"

"We've nothing to lose by trying."

Still yelling to be heard over the noise of the storm, Ravensperch wiped water from his face. "I'll do what I can."

While Ravensperch wasn't a frail man, neither was he stout. But after facing down a demon during the fight that sent them in hasty flight from Toran, his courage had never been in question. Fighting their way forward against the wind, Kessin lashed him to the foremast as Ravensperch braced his back against the wood. Boren watched his arms spread in supplication. Twice enormous waves broke over the bow, completely obscuring Ravensperch in black water, and both times he rose from his knees to continue his prayer.

It lasted for more than an hour. The sodden priest never wavered in shouting his words at the sky, and slowly, as if grudgingly granting her devoted acolyte's prayer, the storm winds died down. They remained strong, and dark clouds still boiled overhead, making sextant readings impossible, but *Sea Scamp* rode easier. Striding through puddles of seawater on the main deck, Boren braced Ravensperch's shoulders.

"You still have your goddess's favor!" he said, no longer having to shout. "Perhaps I am wrong about the gods."

"Gods are capricious, Captain. Vasta may have saved us from one peril only so we can face a greater one. There was resistance to my prayers like I have never felt before. Mark my words, something brought that storm upon us for its own ends. I feel my goddess may have aided simply to thwart the plans of another power."

Ignoring the warning, Boren laughed, releasing all of the pent-up tension from battling the cyclone. "I don't care why she did it! I'm grateful to you and Vasta. Should I decide to worship gods again, I shall let you train me in the ways of your goddess!"

* * *

Alden Havenwulf stared at the cabin ceiling three feet over his nose, breathing deeply and willing his stomach to stop roiling. Dexter Reedman, bent nearly double because of his seven-foot frame, snored in a bunk across the cabin as if lying under a summer moon in a peaceful glen. The Disdanese were a fisher folk who lived at sea for months. The tossing about from the storm was to him like his mother rocking his cradle. Alden's sister Arika and brother Zugon both slept the sleep of the drugged. Badly wounded during the previous week's fight at Sumbarrah Bey's castle in Fiakama, Captain Boren had given them both sleeping potions he kept on board for just such an emergency. He had offered one to Alden, who had declined. He regretted that now.

After being slammed against the bulkhead beside his bed for the better part of a day, it was blessed relief when *Sea Scamp* came to a more even keel. Even so, he couldn't sleep and stumbled up to the main deck, where the sea air revived him.

"I hope you still have your breakfast," Boren said upon seeing him in a flash of lightning. "The larder has to last for weeks yet, so there's no extra to replace it."

Alden ignored him. "Were we blown off course?"

"There's no doubt of that…the only question is how far. We won't know until the sky clears and the navigator can read the stars. But I think it's not a lie to say that I've never sailed these waters before."

"Is that dangerous?"

"Undoubtedly. The Shining Sea has many shoals, and we are in a strong current taking us into unknown waters."

A particularly bright lightning bolt lit the ship at that instant. Boren started to say more, but further words were cut off by the lookout's cry from high atop the main mast.

"Land ahead!"

Boren's attitude instantly changed back to that of an alert watchdog. "Where away?"

"Close aboard, one point to starboard! We're heading for rocks!"

"Hard aport!" the captain called to the helmsman on the fantail. Even in near total darkness, he bounded up the steps like it was bright daylight until he stood beside the ship's wheel. Alden followed him. From the fantail's higher vantage point, Boren intermittently saw shapes like jagged gray teeth through the crashing surf some three hundred yards ahead.

Cupping hands around his mouth, the captain yelled orders to his crew. "Brake the mainsail! Helmsman, feather the boat! Kessin, unship the bilge pumps. Be quick!"

The helmsman immediately threw the wheel hard to starboard as crewmen worked the ropes. Boren leaned over the side to read the ship's momentum in the ship's wake, and pointed at the helmsman to indicate when to spin the wheel back to port. A galley or man-o-war could not have responded fast enough to avoid crashing into the rocks, but *Sea Scamp* was built to do things other ships couldn't, even with her bilges full. Under Boren's leadership, the boat came around until it struck only a glancing blow against one outlying boulder. With the oars shipped, the rock's rough surface barely scratched the twokewood side.

Alden stood with arms crossed during the maneuvers, knowing there was nothing he could do to help. On land he had no equal in a fight, but handling a boat was not his forte.

"I know just enough about ships to know that was brilliant handling, Captain," he said.

Boren shook his head. "T'was not my doing. We handled the mainsail faster than ever before...faster than should be possible. Had we not done that, we would have hit the rocks bow on. Kessin, who is that man on the mainsheet line? I don't recognize him."

Still dripping water from waves breaking over the rails, Kessin turned, studied the man a moment, and shrugged. "I don't know Captain! But I'll find out."

"No need," Alden said. "That's not a man."

In the darkness even Alden's superior eyesight couldn't make out details on Boren's face, but he could hear the fear in the man's voice.

"It was that *thing*?"

"If you mean Setvan? Aye, Captain, it was the Icthonian."

"I fear him," Boren said.

"As well you should."

* * * * *

Chapter 2

The rocks around the island all had a conical shape, and were formed of a porous stone. Luminescent foam glowed greenish-blue where it met the rocks. Between them, Alden saw angular shapes that could only be the ruins of ships, while beyond them a beach rose up to a ridgeline with regular slopes on either side. As the storm abated, so did the lightning, making details impossible to pick out. Alden only saw a sharp crest rising from a forward slope, which then disappeared into ground fog in a gentle upward arc. Scrub grasses and sea oats grew in clumps here and there.

Sea Scamp was on the lee side of the storm now, and Boren assembled his passengers on the fantail. Alden stood to his right, behind the helmsman. He wore no armor, but did have his sword and dagger belt, with its lone remaining knife out of the dozen he'd started with. Ravensperch leaned against the starboard rail, arms folded, beside Dexter and his enormous axe.

The last of them, Setvan, projected the illusion of a wiry, gray-bearded crew member. His natural form, that of a massive, eight-foot tall half-man, half-bear, was too unnerving to the crew. They still thought of him as a were-creature, as did most men, although Icthonians weren't shape-shifters. What they did was project the illusion of being anyone, or anything, they wanted. To humans, they were what they chose to be. The only ones not fooled by their illusions were those of the Ancient Races, like the Corlandish, with whom they had once been allies.

"How are your siblings?" Boren asked Alden.

"Still sleeping. They aren't even aware there was a storm. You have my thanks, Captain."

"Our load shifted during the storm," Boren said without further preamble. "We also took on a lot of water. Together they have disrupted the boat's trim more than I would like. First we must pump the bilges—"

"Do you use force pumps?" Dexter said.

Boren nodded. "Aye, and the bilges are overflowing. We also have some damage I'd like to assess and, since it would be foolish to blindly sail south without taking sextant readings, I mean to put in at this island until the weather clears…"

"What are you not telling us?" Alden said.

"This place appears on none of my charts. It looks uninhabited…" He lifted his eyes to Setvan. "But we all know that looks can deceive us. We've already seen wreckage, and unless I miss my guess, we'll see more when day breaks. My crew lost our best bowman overboard during the storm, and while some of the others might be good archers, they're not warriors. You *are*, and we need to know if there are islanders who may not want us here."

"You want us to go ashore," Alden said. It was not a question.

Boren nodded. "We *need* you to. If something happens to *Sea Scamp*, none of us are getting home."

"He has a point," Ravensperch said.

"I'd do anything to get off this boat for a while. What say you, Dexter?"

"I grew up on boats, so being on the water is more natural to me than on land—"

"Like a whale?" Ravensperch said. He couldn't resist using the nickname he'd given the giant redhead the first time they'd met.

Dexter ignored him. "But I'll go, if nothing else, to keep Alden safe."

"I don't think I need you for that," Alden said, eyes narrowed.

"As has been proven wrong in the past few weeks."

"That's not how I remember it." Alden turned to Boren. "We'll explore inland to verify nothing threatens us. I'll admit these waters have an ominous feel to them."

"Good. It should be daylight soon. Even with the low clouds, we should be able to see well enough to effect repairs."

"How long will you need?"

"I should think several hours at the least. When *Sea Scamp* is again ready for sea, I'll blow the foghorn." Boren turned and pointed at the place Setvan's illusion of being a crew member had been standing, except now it was gone. "Where did he go?"

"I don't know," Alden said, "and I think that's the point. You won't know if he's among your crew or not, so it would probably be a bad idea to leave without us."

* * *

The winds remained out of the southwest, keeping *Sea Scamp* on the lee side of the island. Sharp rocks continued to ring the beach for a mile on the north side. The ominous feeling grew in Alden's gut as the regularity of their placement, and uniformity of size and shape, made it ever clearer they were unnatural in origin. The entire bow of a merchant galley lay wedged between two of them, with the rest of the ship long gone.

A few miles down the north coast, a cliff soared sheer and more than one hundred feet high, its face riddled with cavities and cracks. Even in the darkness, Alden could tell that the stone was a light gray color, mottled here and there with darker patches. Once again he felt like his brain was trying to warn him of something, but he couldn't understand what.

The cliff curved away, ending abruptly at a beach like the one they had already passed, protected by the same strange standing stones. At its top they could see that the escarpment was also curved, or maybe round. Two perfect and identical arches opened in the rock, like gateways thirty feet wide and fifty tall. Nine smaller holes ringed the stone above the two arches at regular intervals.

A shiver ran down Alden's neck as his brain recognized the shape before his conscious mind did…it was carved in the shape of a skull—but not a *human* skull—something far more monstrous.

"What do you make of that?" he said to Ravensperch, who leaned on the rail beside him. The priest's vision had the same limitations as all non-Corlandish did, so nearly a minute passed before he answered, his voiced now tinged with horror.

"Ulucht…"

"That thing behind your altar, in the Temple of Vasta?"

Ravensperch nodded and responded in Alden's native tongue, Corlandish, not the common language of Irsu they had been speaking. "Yes. The Toranese God of Dreams. Those rocks are the Teeth of Ulucht, which he uses to feast on nightmares! This is an evil place, and we must leave without making landfall!"

"I care only about Junt," Alden said, "not some Toranese abomination. Let him do his worst."

Dexter leaned close to Ravensperch. "He keeps you laughing, doesn't he?"

But Ravensperch's eyes were wide, and his voice shrill. "You know not what you say, Alden! Junt is not the only god you should fear."

"I *fear* no god. I have fought the Queen of Death and Darkness and bested her."

"That's not how I remember it," Dexter said.

"She is a demigod, not a goddess. Nor does Ulucht rule the underworld; his dominion is the world of dreams. Every time you sleep, you enter his realm."

"All the same, if he shows up, I'll kill him as I did Ullu. I've stood up to the fires of Hell, and I'll not let some dream demon best me."

With that he climbed down the stairs to don what remained of his armor.

"That's still not what happened!" Dexter called after him.

* * *

Despite Ravensperch's protests, Captain Boren steered *Sea Scamp* through one of the arches. Near absolute darkness inside made navigating the cavernous interior treacherous. Every noise echoed from the ceiling high overhead, and everyone spoke in low voices without being told. At the far end, a lighter area indicated where the overhead dome sloped down and ended ten feet above the shoreline. Without the protective rocks to keep her away from the beach, *Sea Scamp* gently grounded on rocky sand.

Alden leapt off the bow onto firm soil, rapier at the ready in his left hand. Dexter climbed down more slowly, clutching his massive axe. Both men now wore armor. Alden wore greaves, gauntlets, vambraces, and a breastplate, with supple leather pants and boots, while Dexter's protection was a coat of ring mail over a simple cotton shirt, and pants and boots similar to Alden's. Last over the side was Ravensperch, whom the crew lowered by a rope.

"I don't understand why I had to come," the priest said. "This is blade work."

Alden nodded to the sheath on Ravenperch's belt. "And you carry a knife."

"He's right," Dexter said. "A knife's a blade."

Ravensperch answered him with a puckered scowl.

The sky had begun to lighten with imminent dawn. As they spread out, things skittered away underfoot which Alden first judged to be crabs. Yet the tingling feeling on the back of his neck that warned him of danger, the instinct that had saved his life countless times, caused him to drop into a crouch. Like a striking snake, his hand shot out, and he caught a tiny crab. Squinting, he inspected it as best he could in the darkness until it stung his finger. He dropped it and then crunched it under his boot, waving his finger as pain burned the tip.

"What happened?" Ravensperch asked.

"It stung me."

An oppressive feeling of being watched made him pause to listen for any strange sounds riding the wind. Finally, hearing nothing, he motioned them to move ahead.

"Be cautious," he said.

"Who made you our leader?" Dexter said after moving up beside his friend.

"The smartest one always leads."

"Then as leader, I delegate you to go first."

In the growing light, details of the island began to emerge from the darkness. Boulder-strewn fields rose at a gentle angle toward the spine of a ridge. Between the huge stones, the soil was covered in white and gray rocks, some sharp, some concave. They crunched underfoot. Moss grew here and there, and sparse grasses, but mostly the island appeared barren of life.

"Strange...there are no birds," Ravensperch said. "No life at all beside those crabs."

"*If* they were crabs," answered Alden. Like most pure-blooded Corlandish, limited now to the royal bloodlines, his eyesight was superb.

"Meaning what?" said Dexter.

"They had heads sticking out from the front of their shells, on long necks, and their claws looked more like hands."

"You're as daft as your sister."

"It's a good thing you didn't say that when my sister was here."

"I saved her life; she wouldn't hurt me. But that doesn't stop you from being daft."

"I know what I saw."

Alden dropped into a squat again to study the strange rocks, now that pre-dawn light brought the world back into focus. Another rain squall started, and drops splattered around him as he held up a smooth, oval stone. Turning it over, he nearly dropped it in shock. It wasn't a rock at all. It was a skull the size of his fist, a smaller version of the cliff face they had just sailed through. Two empty eye sockets stared back at him. There was no place for a nose such as humans had, but instead there were nine holes arrayed over the eyes in a crescent formation. Only the upper jaw remained of an elongated mouth below the eyes, filled with arrowhead-shaped teeth reminiscent of the stones ringing the island.

Standing, he passed the skull to Ravensperch. The priest's already pale countenance lost what little color it had upon realizing what it was he held.

"Ulucht…" he said, breathless.

Dexter bent down and picked up something, holding it in his palm for the others to see. It was a claw, except instead of two pincers like on a normal crab, there were five, arranged in the shape of a human hand. Nor was it a shell, but was formed of thin bone, hollow in the center as if it once had marrow.

"That's big enough to hurt," Dexter said.

Alden pointed a finger and swept it from beach to ridge. "They're everywhere, thousands of them."

"What are they?"

Both men turned to Ravensperch. The priest stared at the claw, transfixed, for a long moment.

When he spoke, his voice carried a grim undertone. "Ulucht is a Toranese deity. His home is said to be in the World of Dreams, accessible through a pit somewhere in the Shining Sea. I never believed those stories, or thought of him as having a physical form before, but now…"

"But this skull resembles him?" Dexter asked, no longer joking.

Ravensperch nodded. "His touch is said to burn like acid. If those things have tentacles like his…"

"You had his mask hanging behind the altar in the Temple of Vasta," Alden said, "but you didn't believe he was real?"

"I didn't say he wasn't *real*," Ravensperch corrected. "I said that I didn't know he could take physical form. And I'll gladly accept donations for performing rituals for gods other than Vasta, who isn't even Toranese. I would perform the proper rituals for Junt if I knew them, or you didn't. Ulucht is a powerful deity on Toran, and many folk curry his favor."

"People who can pay," Alden said.

"Of course," Ravensperch said, as if that was too obvious to need mentioning.

Dexter's entire attitude changed. The corners of his wide blue eyes were usually crinkled in a smile or laugh, but now those eyes squinted into the twilight world of dawn as it filtered through the dark storm clouds. He pointed to the left and made a sweeping motion until he aimed to the far right.

"Those crab things are gathering. There are a lot of them."

Indistinct in the shadows, Alden nevertheless saw a mass of the cat-sized crabs enclosing them in a semi-circle. The closest of them were no more than fifty feet away, near enough to see they numbered in the thousands.

"If I didn't know better," Alden said, "I'd guess they were gathering for an attack."

"Do you know better?" asked Ravensperch.

"No."

"Then why don't I use the boat's foredeck to better give you warning?" Ravensperch said.

"I wouldn't wager that those things can't climb," Dexter said. "If you did, you'd likely lose."

"You think they could invade the ship?"

"I don't know…I've never heard of crabs attacking people, but then I've never seen crabs like this before, either."

"Then what do we do?" Ravensperch said in a rising voice. "If those things want a fight, you can't possibly kill them all."

Alden rubbed the bridge of his nose, as he often did when thinking through a problem. "Whatever is going on here is beyond my ken. To answer your question, if they desire our deaths, they would likely overwhelm us and the crew, kill Arika and Zugon where they lie, and feast on our flesh. But if we lead them away from the ship, they might follow."

He pointed at the ridge, where, through a light fog, they saw a large structure atop the ridgeline no more than half a mile away. The roof curved upward at each end. Sharp stones ringed it like a fortress wall.

"That looks like a temple," Ravensperch blurted.

"All the more reason to leave it alone," Dexter said. "I've had my fill of gods and demons. And I'm not too keen on the idea of putting more distance between us and the ship, either. She's seaworthy enough to sail in an emergency."

"Captain Boren says she's not."

"Captain Boren is an old woman."

"I vote for setting sail without delay," Ravensperch said.

Dexter nodded. "As do I."

The priest pointed at the giant redhead with his thumb. "When I agree with the whale, you know it must be the right thing to do. The captain will see reason."

"I'll make certain of it," Dexter said.

"Excellent," Alden said. "We're all agreed, then! We'll lead the crabs away from the ship to allow Captain Boren time to make repairs." He then stalked up the field of bones without saying another word.

"I hate it when he does that," Dexter said, hefting his axe over his shoulder and striding after his friend. With a longing glance backward at *Sea Scamp*, Ravensperch shook his head and followed them.

* * * * *

Chapter 3

The mass of crabs followed them as they trudged toward the ridge top, filling in between the trio and *Sea Scamp*, but keeping a distance of fifty feet. Alden didn't need to look back to know the crabs trailed them instead of threatening the ship. He didn't allow himself to think about *why* they did it, he was only concerned with drawing them away from his brother and sister.

"We're going to have to fight through them to get back," Alden muttered.

"I've eaten a lot of crabs in my life," Dexter said, "but I've never battled them."

"Today's your chance."

The angle of the slope increased. Larger boulders had rolled down from above and collected in a crease, forcing them to climb over several when no path could be found around the rocks. The crabs had no such problems and skittered up and over them like ants. Once beyond this natural barrier, the large stones thinned out as they climbed.

"Have we gone far enough?" Dexter said. "I reckon it's been an hour since we left the ship, and some of the crabs appear to have gotten bigger."

Alden nodded. "Not appeared to; larger ones have joined them. I've seen several the size of a dog."

"So we turn back?"

Low clouds seemed to hang just above the ridge, although it was no more than five hundred feet high at its peak. Just at that moment a shaft of sunlight broke through. As if to entice them further, the light glinted from what appeared to be a roof of solid gold.

Dexter gaped as golden light lit the ridgetop surrounding the temple. "Forget what I said, let's go on." He didn't wait for agreement before stepping off.

But Ravensperch stamped his foot. "This is madness! Something's luring us, Alden. It wants us on top of that ridge."

"I don't doubt that you're right, Boric. But you couldn't drag Dexter away from all that gold."

"*If* it's gold!"

"Go ahead and stop him, then."

Cupping hands around his mouth, Ravensperch called after the towering Disdan, "Come back, Whale, it's a trap. You're being lured to your death!"

Dexter turned and cocked his head as if Ravensperch spoke a language he didn't understand. His expression was one Alden had seen often enough, wide-eyed greed. He abruptly whirled and headed for the ridgetop with very long, very fast strides.

"Whale! Damn you!"

He didn't even slow down. Hands on hips, Ravensperch scowled at Alden. "I'm not going up there, Alden. We need to return to the ship, now!"

"I have no doubt that you're correct." Alden broke into a trot to catch up with the fast-moving Disdan.

"That's the wrong direction!" Ravensperch called after him.

The crabs scurried after them, moving closer than ever, and barely out of range of a sword thrust. Having no other choice, Ravensperch trotted in Alden's wake.

"We're walking into a trap," he said, huffing between words.

"You've said that."

"I wanted to make certain you heard me."

"I did."

When they got within one hundred feet of the temple, the morning had brightened enough for Alden to spot the first birds they'd seen on the island. Dozens of them perched along the roof and on the stones guarding the building. The size of hawks, they were black with red crests and sharp, hooked beaks. Eyes like onyx watched the three men approach.

Dexter walked straight for a gap in the stones, axe over his shoulder as if strolling along a quiet forest path. Ravensperch paused long enough to inspect the birds, but realized the crabs were at his heels and hurried to catch up with Alden, whose pace never slowed.

"Carrion birds only live where there's carrion," he muttered. "I'm thinking we're on the day's menu."

Alden shook his head. "By the time the crabs are done with us, there won't be anything left for the birds."

Now, with daylight increasing by the minute, and the clouds overhead showing signs of breaking up, they saw another heap of bones outside the standing stones circling the temple. These looked familiar, not like those of the strange crabs. Alden bent down and picked up a human skull, with fractures on both sides and holes in the dome.

"Something crushed this," he said, "and ate the brain."

Ravensperch began to tremble, as if spasms afflicted his entire body. He pressed his fists into the sides of his head and closed his eyes. When he spoke, the words came out in breathless rasps. "Ulucht does that...to all who enter the realm of nightmare...but here?"

The priest licked his lips, clearly terrified, and pointed at the mass of crabs almost within a hand's reach. Their claws opened and snapped shut as if they were already feasting on the humans' flesh. "I didn't believe the texts when they spoke of the Samtoth, the Servants of Ulucht, creatures that his malice has corrupted into horrible versions of himself. But I now see with my own eyes that the ancients knew whereof they wrote."

"Samtoths?"

"Yes, but Samtoth is also plural."

"It's likely they mean us harm…"

"They exist for no other purpose."

Alden rubbed his forehead and then the bridge of his nose. "As my father used to say when we children tried to lie our way out of some violation of the family rules, 'I've heard this tale before.'"

The Corlandishman called out to Dexter, who was about to pass through the opening in the stones. The Samtoth had moved again, creating a narrow corridor for them to join their towering companion.

"Dexter, for Junt's sake, hold! Do not go in there!"

Sunlight struck Dexter's hair, illuminating the wild mane in shades of red against the shadows inside the building. He waved Alden's words away with one hand and passed through the gap into the inner temple complex.

* * *

Captain Boren jabbed with a short spear to keep the rats away from an amphora of spilled wheat, while three crewmen scooped the kernels back into the container. A series of prisms in the deck above brought natural light into the hold, which greatly speeded their work. A pile of dead and wounded rats lay to one side, to later be skinned and thrown into the cook pot.

It wouldn't be the first time the crew of *Sea Scamp* had eaten vermin during a long voyage, and he doubted it would be the last. Kessin, the first mate, found him pushing a twitching rat off the head of the spear onto the pile.

"The sprit was cracked right enough, just like you said. The other spars are sound, but we've got a lot of torn sail. I've got four o' the lads stichin' 'em up now."

"What of the hull? I felt her shudder at least once. It felt like we struck a rock."

"I've walked the hull from bow to stern. She's intact, Captain."

"Have you checked the outer hull?"

Kessin turned away and licked his lips. "None of the lads will enter the water…it's them damned crabs, they's unnatural, Captain. They scare the boys somethin' fierce."

With a vicious kick, Boren sent the still moving rat flying into the bulkhead. He could feel the veins pulsing at his temples, and his broad forehead felt hot.

"Crabs?" he bellowed. "My crew is afraid of some *crabs*? Would they rather sink during the next storm? Get somebody in the water, Kessin, or I'll find a first mate who can!"

* * *

Despite the mass of Samtoth close on every side, Alden approached the gap in the stones cautiously and with rapier drawn. Rusted hinges driven into the rock on either side held shards of rotted wood, making clear there had once been a gate. The intact skeleton of a man lay twisted like he'd been caught from behind while fleeing. Hair still clung to bits of skin on the skull, the entire back of which was missing. Strips of clothing and leather-soled boots were those of a mariner.

They passed the dead man and finally got a good look at the temple itself. It was an open-air design, massive columns holding up an angled roof with upturned eaves characteristic of the Toranese. The building looked to be about fifty feet wide by ninety long, with the roof soaring thirty feet overhead. A simple altar of crimson granite, with flecks as white as bone, lay on the far side of a circular pit. Behind the altar was a titanic statue wrought in the same stone. The hideous visage of the now familiar nine-tentacled god, Ulucht, sat atop a long, thick neck of corded muscle. In turn, the neck protruded from the body of a crab. Ten-foot-long tentacles ringed the face above huge eyes like those of a squid, and it held the dagger-toothed maw of an eel. Its claws were the same five-fingered ones as on the Samtoth that now drove them forward into the temple proper. It stood nearly twenty-five feet tall from the ground to the top of its head.

Aside from the golden roof and gold-plated columns, morning sunlight glinted from piles of precious gemstones and artifacts of gold and silver scattered over the temple floor like fallen leaves in late autumn. Coins, lockets, brooches, rings, chalices, swords with jeweled handles, ceremonial daggers, chains, and ornate armor lay heaped about. Alden found Dexter kneeling near the pit, axe beside him, scooping up glinting objects and stuffing them into a small rucksack on his belt.

"Alden, we're rich again! This is even better than the Star of Nhoje!"

No, Alden thought, *it's not*. The Star of Nhoje had been a fabled diamond the size of a man's fist, with a perfect star-shaped ruby embedded in its center. Except the ruby wasn't a ruby, it was a demon, and the diamond was its prison. Kings had lost kingdoms for it. Now it was lost forever, after Ravensperch had released the demon during the battle in Fiakama, where Zugon had lost his right hand, and Arika had been wounded.

Still, despite being largely unmoved by wealth, Alden understood the lure of the jewels and the gold. Dexter craved them as one who'd grown up poor would, while Alden saw them as a means to an end. To break away from his father's family and establish his own house would require great treasure. So he'd taken two steps to join Dexter before halting. He felt the pull of something unnatural, something compelling him to scoop up whatever he wanted, but like seeing through Setvan's illusions, he saw the thoughts for the lies they were. The gods and sorceries of Men had less effect on those of the Ancient Races, and he asked himself, *Where did so much wealth come from, if not from men lured into the same trap?*

As if something had read his mind and realized the lure wouldn't work, the first man-sized Samtoth crawled out of the pit.

* * *

Boren leaned over the railing next to Kessin, watching the two men swimming under the hull to inspect for damage.

"Who's down there?"

"Rut and Donlon. They was the only ones not terrified by the crabs." Kessin nodded toward shore, where a small group of the strange creatures stood immobile, watching.

Boren nodded. "They're both good men; I trust them." He raised his voice and looked over his shoulder, knowing the rest of the crew was trying to eavesdrop. "Which is more than I can say for the rest of you cowards!"

To a man they slunk away to find other duties. Boren raised his eyebrows and stared after them, then glanced toward shore. The crabs were gone.

* * *

Dexter knelt only twenty feet from the pit when the first of the man-sized Samtoth appeared. Whatever spell the lure of gold had cast on him was broken by the sight of eight such abominations. He growled in frustration, put the axe on his right shoulder, and spread his legs into a fighting stance.

The axe was an artifact of Elder Days. A four-foot haft of yellowish iron-oak supported a double-sided head, with one side being a huge, curved blade ending in double concavities on the bottom. Each toe of the blade ended in hooks to front and back. The other side of the head also had hooks and cutting edges, and a foot-long, leaf-shaped blade extended from the pommel. The metal of the head and the blade was similar to Corlandish steel, which is harder, lighter, and less brittle than the best iron-based steel. The whole measured nearly six feet long, and weighed fifteen pounds, far too much for a normal man to use in combat. Dexter Reedman was not only very tall, his own weight topped three hundred pounds, and none of it was fat.

Without needing to speak, Alden and Dexter moved to stand back to back, as they had so many times before. Ravensperch drew a knife and nervously eyed the smaller Samtoth that feinted in and out toward them. He kicked one of the little Samtoth as it tried to nip his ankle, catching it flush on the toe of his boot. The thing flew backward and rolled. When it tried to stand, it fell sideways, with several legs broken. The instant they spotted the weakness, ten of its fellows rushed in and tore away chunks with their hand-like claws, shoving the flesh into their huge mouths. Within seconds they'd stripped away half of its shell and were gorging on the internal organs.

Alden watched it happen, now understanding all the bones and all the treasure. Storm-tossed mariners put in on the island to ride out foul weather, or were driven into the rocks. No doubt the storms were of Ulucht's making. Once ashore, the immeasurable wealth of the temple drew them like flies, where they were systematically butchered and eaten.

And then, as one, the Samtoth attacked.

Dexter swung the axe downward in a whistling arc and swept away a dozen of the cat-sized ones, scattering them like chaff. With the backswing, he sliced off the claw of one of the large ones that had reached for his head. Many of the surviving Samtoth descended on their dead and wounded fellows, devouring them without hesitation.

Alden's left arm moved like a piston, faster than the fastest snake, skewering four of the creatures, one after the other. Drawing his last throwing knife, he flung it at the nearest of the man-sized Samtoth. It tumbled beneath the outstretched tentacles and penetrated the neck up to its hilt. With a strangled cry the thing stumbled backward until its legs collapsed, leaving it thrashing on the treasure-strewn floor. Precious jewels flew in all directions. Two of the Samtoth fought over the remains.

The sequence of events became a blur in Alden's mind, as they always did in the heat of battle. His superior reflexes took over, and he moved without conscious thought, a condition his father described as the dance of death. He thrust, stabbed, and kicked, while the sharp claws of the Samtoth left his ankles and shins bleeding into his boots. One of them jumped onto his leg, but before it could take out a chunk of flesh, he snatched it by a claw and flung it into the pit.

The smaller Samtoth retreated as two of the big ones moved forward, one on each side. Alden thrust toward the neck of the one on the left. His sword got through cleanly, but struck its shell instead of its neck. In return, a tentacle slapped his face and left red welts where the suckers touched flesh.

"Junt!" he cursed. There was nowhere to retreat, since Dexter's back touched his, and with the two large Samtoth both grasping for him, Alden decided on a desperate tactic. He crouched, sprang forward toward the one on the left as it claws snapped shut above him, and aimed the point of his sword at the base of the thing's neck. This time the sharp steel found flesh. Dark red blood gushed onto Alden's fist. But even before the Samtoth's brain realized it was dying, he leapt toward the other one.

It was still reacting to his attack on the other one, turning on six legs and swinging its claws. By sheer bad luck, one of them smashed into Alden's jaw and knocked him sideways. Red sparkles filled his vision, and his jaw ached, but there was no time for that. Thrusting through the kaleidoscope of colors blinding him, the sword penetrated one of the Samtoth's legs. He jerked the rapier free and stabbed at another one. The Samtoth lost its balance and tottered to one side, limping away from the fight.

Some of the smaller Samtoth took advantage to attack while he was down. Using his arm, he swept them away and pushed back to his feet. His face burned where it had been grabbed by the tentacles.

Dexter, meanwhile, swung the huge axe back and forth like a farmer scything grain. Judging by their twitching corpses, several of the large Samtoth had tried to dart forward after the axe head passed them, only to be cut to pieces on the backswing. Blood and gore coated the giant man from head to toe, and Alden couldn't tell how much of it was Dexter's and how much Samtoth. As for Ravensperch, he bled from a score of gouges, but still held his knife, now clotted with blood.

For a moment the attacking Samtoth moved back, while others gorged themselves on the dead. Only three of the biggest ones still posed a threat.

"*Now* can we go back to the ship?" Ravensperch yelled, his voice shrill.

"I think we'd better," Alden replied. "Dexter, let's leave while we can!"

But Dexter had already started picking out diamonds and emeralds from the slurry of crab guts and blood on the floor.

Having no more patience, Alden grabbed him by the shoulder and jerked. "We need to get back to the ship…now!"

"And leave all of this?" He swept his hand to indicate the immeasurable wealth covering the temple floor.

"You can't spend gold when you're dead!"

"I can try!"

Alden went to say something else, but it was too late. At a loud *crack*, they all turned to see the enormous statue of Ulucht behind the altar rise out of its squat. The tentacles began waving, and the black eyes opened. Slit pupils searched the temple before they found and focused on the three intruders.

* * * * *

Chapter 4

Boren heard the screams before he heard Kessin calling for him. He'd been inspecting repairs to the main sail on the starboard quarter and crossed to broad on the port bow, where Kessin directed several bowmen where to shoot.

"What's happened?" he demanded.

"Rut got dragged under," Kessin said, pointing to a swirl of bubbles in the red-stained water. "We tried to pull up Donlon, but when we got him out of the water, his legs were covered by crabs. They were ripping him apart, and he fell backward, and now we can't see him."

One of the archers loosed an arrow, which hit home and transfixed a crab the size of a rat. Splashes marked the place where other crabs attacked the body.

"Do we up anchor and sail, Captain?"

Boren wanted to say 'yes,' and almost did, but he'd given his word...and then there was the thing called Setvan. He could appear to be anyone, even Kessin, but behind the illusion was a thing out of nightmare. Boren had felt the razor-sharp points of its claws on his neck back in Custacrak, and feared it even more than he did the crabs. If he needed an excuse, he had a good one.

"No! We wait for Alden's return. All hands on deck and armed. Archers to the rigging. Make ready to sail, and to repel those things if they try to come aboard."

"Aye, sir," Kessin said, giving him a doubtful glance.

"And First Mate...blow the horn!"

"Aye, sir!"

* * *

There was no time to stand and gawk at the sight of the statue coming to life. Dexter held his axe at the ready. Ulucht himself, or his simulacrum, circled round the pit. Alden moved beside him, rapier at inside left guard. As for Ravensperch, he tore a strip from his undershirt to bind a wound on his right forearm.

"This thing is beyond us, Alden," Ravensperch said. "We must flee, and we must flee *now!*"

"Valor holds the line," Alden replied. "So I've been taught from childhood. If it trods the ground, it can be killed."

"You're mad!"

"Wait 'til you've been around him longer," Dexter said, bringing the axe back in preparation for another swing. "He knows more platitudes than anyone I've ever met."

Alden ignored Dexter. "We must buy them more time to ready the ship."

As if in answer, the distant call of a horn echoed over the island. Ulucht's head tilted upward at the sound and, with speed that belied its bulk, skittered forward at the speed of a fast horse. The whipping tentacles surprised Alden. They wrapped around his legs and lifted him off his feet, upside down and high off the floor.

Through vision going red, Alden saw a huge mouth beneath him, open and filled with sharp teeth a foot long. Desperately he ran his blade through a tentacle, to no apparent effect. He hacked at the tough flesh, but again, Ulucht seemed not to notice. But arrayed as they were above the thing's eyes, the tentacles had to lower him past the huge orbs as it prepared to crush him between the deadly teeth, and that was his chance.

In his peripheral vision he saw Dexter bring the axe down on the monster's shell, followed by a loud *crunch* as the blade shattered its external armor. As it roared in pain, Alden swung back and forth until his blade came close to one of the great eyes. Stretching, he swung the tip, and felt the satisfying resistance of something thick and gelatinous giving way to his steel.

Ulucht thrashed in pain and dropped him headfirst, but Alden had been on the outward swing, so instead of landing in its mouth, he glanced off the lower jaw, and hit the ground. Woozy, he got up on hands and knees in time to see one of the cat-sized Samtoth rushing forward. It grabbed for his right forearm, but got only the vambrace, so Alden raised that arm and slammed the Samtoth hard into the ground. It let go and staggered away on three broken legs.

"Back!" he yelled, pushing up to his feet. He didn't see one of the last man-sized Samtoth charging him. With a swipe of its right claw, it meant to disembowel him, and would have if not for his breastplate. It was pure Corlandish steel. The last piece of the full suit of plate armor forged by the legendary smith Destor Ironhand. The would-be fatal thrust instead scraped along the impenetrable metal without injuring him, and before the crab could recover, Alden thrust the rapier into the soft tissue under its arm. Screeching in pain, it skittered backward. Together the three men fell back, fighting, as Samtoth of all sizes charged forward.

Ulucht made chittering noises that Alden knew had to be commands, but sounded like *skree, skree*. Despite their terrible losses, the Samtoth surged forward again.

* * *

Kessin used a short paddle to knock a crab back into the water. "Captain, they's coming over the rail!"

Boren used a four-foot-long section from the broken bowsprit like a club to smash a crab the size of his head into paste. The shattered husk slid back off the rail into the water. Still holding the paddle, Kessin limped toward him with blood running down his right cheek.

"We've gotta sail, Captain."

"No, not until they return."

"I hate to say's it, but they ain't makin' it back." He pointed halfway up the slope, where Alden and Dexter fought, nearly obscured inside a maelstrom of dust kicked up by the fighting, with only flashes of steel to show they were still alive. Then a gust cleared the air, and they gaped at the colossal monstrosity towering over the battle...Ulucht.

"Mother of Demerus," Boren whispered. As he watched, the tentacles of the giant crab reached out for Dexter. He froze in place and could only stare at a nightmare come to life.

In his peripheral vision, he saw one of his crewmen leap off the bow and run up the beach toward the three men, but two crabs had climbed the side and gotten onto the deck, and Boren spun as claws dug into his pants. The trance was broken, and monster or no monster, he had to defend his ship. He couldn't worry about Alden's fate when that of *Sea Scamp* hung in the balance, but as much as he now wanted to, he couldn't leave without risking being torn apart by Setvan. Or so he told himself.

* * *

The surviving Samtoth had again retreated, but Alden now felt certain they were being directed by Ulucht as a general commands his army. He could even see they were reorganizing.

They'd fought more than halfway to the ship, but fatigue and blood loss were taking their toll. "Let us be away before they come back," said Alden.

"It won't be long," Ravensperch added.

Despite his friend's immense strength, swinging a fifteen-pound axe would eventually wear down even the strongest man, especially with dozens of wounds leeching his stamina. Alden heard it in his voice when he answered.

"You go, I'll be along."

"You'll be swallowed. We've killed many, but they still number more than we can count."

Dexter laughed. "What are the words your Corlandish Army lives by?"

"Valor holds the line."

"It does, and it will. Go, I'll be right behind you."

Before Alden could say anything else, Ravensperch interrupted them. Weary, he pointed at the Samtoth. "Thank Vasta I don't have to hear any more of that sentimental rubbish...here they come again!"

The instant Alden raised his sword, all pain and fatigue vanished as the fire of battle rushed through his veins. Only this time he could see the onslaught was coordinated, with all Samtoth rushing in at the same time, and from all directions, including Ulucht. Without a miracle, it would be the final fight.

One of Ulucht's two injured legs once again bore weight, so it moved much faster than Dexter anticipated. From his angle to Dexter's left, Alden could see what Ulucht intended, but his cry of warning died on his lips as the last of the man-sized Samtoth slammed bodily into him, knocking him to the ground, where its tentacles wrapped around his body. His arms were pinned as the Samtoth settled on his chest. His skin burned where the suckers touched the flesh of his arms above his vambraces, and on his neck above the breastplate. It felt like being prodded with a white-hot knife. Saliva from the thing's mouth drooled on his face as it opened wide to crush his head.

Driven by pain and the panic of imminent death, Alden's superior strength loosened the creature's hold long enough to roll over and get his knees beneath him. Then it jumped onto his back, and the tentacles wrapped around his face. Screaming in pain, Alden straightened, holding the Samtoth's entire weight on his knees, turned around his rapier and, as he felt teeth digging into his scalp, plunged the blade deep into its brain.

The Samtoth instantly went limp, and Alden shrugged it off. That's when he noticed Ravensperch lying on his back, fighting with one of the last cat-sized Samtoth. He ran it through, killing the thing.

With a momentary respite, Alden felt like glowing embers had been thrown onto his forehead and cheeks. Blood trickled into his eyes. A fast wipe on a shirt sleeve only helped for a second, but it was long enough to see the towering Ulucht whip its head from right to left, slinging all nine tentacles like thick whips that lifted Dexter off his feet and threw him ten feet backward. He lay still some fifty feet away from Alden. Ulucht moved forward like a scorpion.

Alden forced his legs to move and took one step to aid Dexter, but then felt things crawling up his legs. Dozens of small crabs the size of his fist scaled his greaves and pants. Using his fists, he crushed several, and knocked the rest off, but when he turned back to Dexter, Ulucht had gripped his friend in both claws and lifted him halfway to its maw. He hung limp in the claw, either unconscious or dead.

Alden was too late.

Then, from his right, a huge, dark bulk raced into view. Although dwarfed by the god, its muscular form was that of an enormous bear. Foot-long talons, which Alden knew to have an edge sharper than a sword, flashed upward toward the Ulucht's left claw. With a loud snapping sound, the newcomer's claws sliced through hard shell like it was linen.

Setvan had joined the fight.

Reeling backward under the assault, Ulucht's remaining pincers let go of Dexter as it turned to face this new threat. Alden only caught glimpses of its eyes under the tangle of tentacles, but he could have sworn he saw fear in them.

Tentacles frantically reached for the Icthonian, as did its claw, but Setvan moved with a speed that amazed even Alden. Setvan jumped *under* the idol, whose stomach was fully ten feet off the ground. Raising his arm straight up, Setvan ran his claws through the soft shell of its underbelly, slicing four deep troughs from under its neck to its tail. Blood and greenish gore poured from the wounds.

Ulucht flopped on its legs, thrashing the ground in agony. Alden felt the vibrations through the soles of his boots like earthquakes.

But gods are not so easily defeated.

Even as Ulucht stepped back and away from the new attacker, four tentacles whipped into Setvan's body like a charging bull. He staggered backward, stunned, and three more tentacles wrapped around his torso.

Setvan bellowed in pain, a terrible sound that reminded Alden of the dying Yetondi he'd killed so long before, part human and part beast. He knew the agony of those suckers, as only the fire of battle had allowed him to ignore the pain of his face and arms. As he watched, Setvan's claws dug into the tentacles over and over again, as Ulucht shook him like a lizard with a rat.

The Samtoth had momentarily retreated again, and the thought flashed through his brain that without Ulucht to guide them, their attacks would cease. Claws reached for the Icthonian, and he fought back, but without help, Alden knew Setvan would die, and after him, the rest of them would be next.

A rapier would have no effect against such a thing, so, gulping a deep breath, he dashed between Ulucht's legs for the spot where Dexter's axe lay. It was too heavy for him to wield for long, yet it was the only weapon that might work. Foul-smelling ichor dripped on him as he ran under the ruptured belly. He dove to avoid a grasping claw, rolled several times, and wound up next to the axe. Grasping it, his hand coated in blood, dirt, and sweat, the wood slipped in his grasp. There was no time to swing before the claw reached down from above to snatch him off the ground, so he reversed the weapon and thrust up with the blade on the bottom of the haft.

The force of Ulucht's downward thrust impaled his claw on the blade. A keening wail escaped the horrible mouth. When Ulucht ripped the claw free, the blade caught in the shell, and Alden couldn't hold it. He let go before the upside head tore into his hands. Ulucht shook the weapon free, and it landed ten paces to Alden's left. As he ran to pick it back up, he spotted Ravensperch standing with arms outstretched, face tilted toward the sky.

* * *

Some part of Ravensperch's mind sensed the Samtoth crawling back toward him, but he couldn't be distracted now, regardless of what else happened. He tilted his head as far back as it would go and closed his eyes. He shouted to be heard over the clamor of battle.

"Great Vasta, your unworthy servant begs your help against a power whose very presence in this world defames the glory of your name! If you aid us in our just cause, I will build a temple for you the like of which this world has never seen! I will elevate you in the minds of men and sing your praises for all the remainder of my days, if only you save us from the clutches of one who does not belong in this world, *your* world, fouling the very air you give us to breathe!"

Something stung his ankle. Ravensperch used that to fuel his prayer. "As sacrifice to you, mighty Vasta, I offer up my pain and beg you to accept this sacrifice as proof of my words!"

A roaring sound sprang up on his right. Tilting his head, Ravensperch saw a swirling wind rotating further down the beach, a vortex that spun faster and faster. Rocks swept upward into the cloud of debris, small at first, but as the winds grew strong, boulders began to rise. The top of the funnel likewise climbed into the scudding clouds overhead, drawing more and more power from the sky. And then, as Ravensperch watched, the tornado moved toward Ulucht.

* * * * *

Chapter 5

The instant Alden saw the winds spring up, he knew what it meant. Grabbing the axe, he sprinted toward Ulucht. Freeing Setvan wasn't even a conscious thought. His mind was too overwhelmed with pain, enemies, and the presence of a blasphemous crab-god to do anything except react. He only knew that in seconds his friend would die unless he could free him. As he ran, a desperate plan came to him.

Ulucht held his injured right claw high overhead, presumably to protect it from further injury. With one leg broken, another injured, and the left claw also damaged, he still had most of his tentacles, which were deadly enough in their own right. Alden saw two of them reaching for him and raised the axe as high overhead as possible.

The tentacles wrapped around his torso and squeezed. Like a constrictor snake, he felt the air forced out of his lungs. His ears pounded as his heartbeat raced, trying to force blood through veins squeezed shut by the pressure. But his arms remained free, and as the god raised him off the ground, he swung the axe downward with all of his remaining strength.

Steel sliced through the tough skin as if it was parchment, severing the tips of both tentacles. Alden fell and landed on his back. Although groggy, he pushed to his knees and unwrapped the now dead tentacles from his body. Once again pushing himself upright, he felt the axe pulled from his grasp, and peered into Dexter's blood-drenched face.

"My turn now," he said.

Using only one hand, Dexter threw the huge weapon like a throwing axe. It tumbled through the air and smashed into Ulucht's carapace below the neck. Shrieking in agony, Ulucht released Setvan and used its eight remaining tentacles to pull the axe free and throw it back at Dexter. It missed badly, and Dexter retrieved it.

Setvan hit the ground and rolled, bleeding from more than a dozen places where the suckers had penetrated fur to reach flesh. On hands and knees, he half-crawled, half-walked to Alden and Dexter's side. They were joined by Ravensperch. And while they had badly injured the enormous body of the god, Ulucht was anything but beaten. They all sensed he was about to charge, even as smaller Samtoth stung and clawed them.

Then the roar of the tornado drowned out everything else. The funnel swept toward them at ever-increasing speed. Rocks pounded against Ulucht's shell, and the giant crab turned away to shield his eyes. Boulders struck him, and they all heard a loud *crack*! With the god caught in the center of the vortex, Alden realized this might be their last chance to escape.

"Run!" he said. "Make for the ship!"

Dexter and Ravensperch followed with no argument. But Setvan held back. When Alden noticed, he stopped and yelled over the wind.

"Come on, this is our chance!"

"Fear not, Alden, I'll be along. Tell the captain to ready his archers!"

Alden had been in too many battles to argue further.

* * *

Boren was standing on the fo'c'sle, near the newly replaced bowsprit, when he spotted Alden, Dexter and Ravensperch running for the boat. He'd been too busy fighting for his ship to watch much of what had occurred on shore, but after the incredible happenings of the day, the sight of a god-come-to-life inside a swirling tornado didn't shock him.

"Archers!" he heard Alden screaming. "Gather your archers!"

Kessin had come up beside them and saw their passengers running over the stony ground.

"The ship's ready, Captain; we can push off at your word."

A knot of crewmen stood by awaiting orders on the main deck, close to the fo'c'sle. Many bore wounds, and all were eager to be away from such a cursed island.

"Archers to the fo'c'sle!"

"Sir?"

"Have you lost your hearing, First Mate? Get the archers up here now!"

"But...sir, the men don't like these passengers being on board for so long. We're smugglers, not corsairs, or a transport. Some think they're bad luck. Now's our chance to leave them."

Boren grabbed him by the throat and drew him close. "Are you disobeying my orders?" Boren's eyes widened in fury, and he turned to face the rest of his crew. "Does any man among you question my orders? *Sea Scamp* is my ship! I am her master! Any mutinous dog who challenges my orders can step forward now, and let's find out who lives and who dies!"

They all shrank back as if being whipped. The first mate, Kessin, held up his hands as if to ward off a blow to the face.

"Whatever you say, Captain!" He whirled and barked orders. Within seconds, seven archers had gathered on the forecastle.

"If that thing comes close," Boren said, pointing at Ulucht, "kill it! Shoot for the eyes!"

"I can't see any eyes, Captain," said one of the men.

"Aim for the neck, aim for anything except the shell!"

"Aye, sir!" several yelled in unison.

They all nocked arrows and waited.

* * *

Other crewmen threw ropes over the bow. Five small Samtoth got to them before the humans did, and snapped their claws as Alden reached for the rope. Using the pommel of his sword, he crushed one, and knocked the others off. Using his blade and boots, he kept the Samtoth away as Dexter scrambled up to the deck and pulled Ravensperch after him. Alden then followed. As he climbed, something stung the back of neck and pulled at his hair. Once aboard ship, Dexter plucked off the Samtoth and smashed it into the deck.

"Where's Setvan?" Alden said.

Dexter pointed at the beach. Fifty feet from the ship, Setvan had turned to face his pursuer, Ulucht. Both were much the worse for battle, and although Setvan's matted fur showed his numerous wounds, the god had fared even worse. The tornado had dissipated, but its effects were plain to see. Ulucht's shell had cracked in many places, only two fingers of his left claw still worked, four tentacles remained usable, and he tilted sideways on two broken legs. The eye Alden had stabbed leaked a milky fluid that mixed with green-tinged blood leaking from the ghastly wound under his neck, where the axe had struck. Gore leaked from his underside. A mortal creature would have died by now, yet still the god came on, apparently intent on destroying those who had wrecked his lair.

With a last effort, Ulucht heaved his bulk as if to crush the Icthonian by sheer weight. Setvan raised his claws to inflict whatever damage he could before death took him, and then the first flight of arrows arced from *Sea Scamp*'s fo'c'sle. Four struck his carapace and bounced off, while another embedded in a tentacle, doing no serious harm. But one flew between the tentacles and struck his good eye, while another drove into his neck. As Ulucht hesitated at this new threat, Setvan drove his claws upward into the wound beneath his neck, in the same spot as the arrow.

The god staggered back as more arrows rained on him. Seeing his chance, Setvan turned and loped toward the ship, in obvious pain. Once there, he leapt, caught the rail, and pulled his huge body onto the deck with one hand. The minute Ulucht backed away, the Samtoth assaulting *Sea Scamp* vanished back into the water.

"All hands aboard!" Kessin yelled.

"Cast off!" commanded Boren. "Archers, maintain your fire; all other rowers, man your oars. Get us out of here."

Even as the ship slipped beyond arrow range, they all stared to see if Ulucht would follow them out to sea. Crabs were, after all, creatures of the deep.

Only Ravensperch wasn't worried. "He's the God of the Dream Realm," the priest said, "not of the sea. Ermo would not be pleased at having his kingdom invaded by another god."

Only once *Sea Scamp*'s prow slipped past the archway in the cliff face did they begin to relax. That's when Boren first noticed the condition of his passengers.

"Take them below," he said. "Have the physician tend them, and administer potions to help them sleep. Then set a guard on their cabin. Kessin, I'm giving you the responsibility to keep them safe."

"No need for a guard," said Setvan. Even though he now appeared as nothing more than an average-sized crewman, Boren could feel the heat from his bulk. "I'll see to that."

The captain shook his head. "Thank you, but no. *Sea Scamp* is my ship, and my passengers will be safe on my ship, won't they, Kessin?"

"Aye, Captain," the first mate said, looking down.

"Very well then, carry on."

"Once you've seen to their needs, have the navigator take readings at the first opportunity and advise me on course corrections."

"What course once we've cleared the island?"

"South by southwest." Now that he'd chastised his first mate, Boren clapped him on the shoulder. "We're going somewhere you've never been before, Kessin."

"Where would that be, Captain?"

Boren winked. "Beyond the beyond."

* * * * *

Epilogue

"Is it...always like this?" Ravensperch asked. Like Alden, he was splattered with blood and bits of red shell that were stuck to his clothes. Welts covered every inch of exposed skin.

Alden had been on countless battlefields in his short life, and knew what the priest meant. He nodded slowly, once again wiping blood from his eyes. The bodies of hundreds of crabs littered the slope, some still moving, most smashed beyond recognition.

"Always."

Dexter leaned over a tub of fresh water, now turned red as he washed blood from his face. Most of it wasn't his.

"Did you notice the black birds?" he asked, his voice dragging with fatigue.

The purpose of the black birds had become known within minutes of the battle ending. They landed among the crab corpses and began a feast that would likely go on for days.

"I'm thinking they were expecting human flesh," Setvan said.

"Or perhaps Icthonian," Alden said. "Either way, both are off the menu, at least for today. They'll have to settle for crab."

"I could eat two dozen crabs right now," Dexter muttered. He managed a wan smile. "Or better yet, lobsters."

"I doubt they taste like the crabs you're used to," Setvan answered.

"No matter how bad they taste, it's nothing a bowl of melted butter wouldn't fix." Dexter chuckled at his own joke, but then winced. Alden knew the feeling; even breathing deeply hurt.

Ravensperch had the last word. "I wonder if they had the same thought about us."

* * * * *

William Alan Webb Bio

As a West Tennessee native raised in the 60s and 70s, and born into a family with a long tradition of military service, it should be no surprise that the three chief influences on Bill's life have been military history, science fiction and fantasy and the natural world. In 1972 he won the Tennessee State High School Dual Chess Championship, and spent every waking moment playing board games, role-playing games, and naval miniatures. College featured dual concentrations in History and English. Everything after that is anti-climax, except for wife, kids, published books and all that kind of stuff.

Website: www.thelastbrigade.com

Facebook page:

https://www.facebook.com/keepyouupallnightbooks

\# \# \# \# \#

Goddess's Tears by Cedar Sanderson

I t was another day of flowers, blood, and tears. Soleh looked down at her hands, then slowly opened them and let the axe fall. It landed on the patch of Goddess's Tears blooming out of season, and a spatter of blood from her ruined hands followed it.

She had wrought havoc, and now could feel nothing, nothing at all. With an effort, she lifted her head to look at the ruins of her home. The body of her last son, wrapped in white linen, lay in the one unscathed room. She turned and mechanically walked toward the stables, her eyes wide and unseeing in the darkness of the world around her.

She hadn't seen the blow that took her brother's head, or the ones it must have taken to fell her mother and father as they rode into the ambush to buy their children time. The blow that had struck Soleh senseless from her saddle had left her with no memories but that of flowers, blood, and tears for weeks afterward. It wasn't until she was brought here, to what would become her home for long years, that she had begun to remember. Memory had been no comfort, when he had used her as a sadistic political tool, raising her from slave girl to Goddess-blessed wife.

Soleh had known he bore no love for her, or even kindness, although he liked that people said it of him. He simply desired to further shame the family who had called him a bastard and tolerated him only because the king dictated it. She was a thorn in their side.

He drove many thorns into them as time passed, and the wounds festered. Soleh had done her best to live as the Goddess commanded, until she could no longer bear it. In the dark she swore vengeance upon her child's soul. She would heal no more. She would finally lay claim to her heritage of betrayal and bloodshed. The last fragment of her mother's seal called to her since she had been unable to save her son from the fever she herself had brought home from nursing the villagers.

Soleh closed her hand around the broken bit of glass, concealing its glow. The darkness was complete, and the grasp of death withheld itself from her soul.

The hands that had wrought such havoc to the house were no delicate lady's fingers. They bore the calluses of rough work, and she blessed the perverse quirk in her husband that allowed her no servants. It was her hands that scoured the stone floors of their home. Her hands that split the wood and laid the fires, and that work had preserved the solid muscles of the girl who had been trained to fight, building on them until she was grown into a woman of great strength.

Soleh had always been careful to conceal her abilities. Her children would have suffered if she were not willing to take the brunt of his anger. Her neighbors would have shunned her entirely if they did not pity her.

But today she had lifted the axe and brought the butt of it around to smash into the apparently solid stone, and the way the mortar buckled would have sent the market-ladies fluttering in fear. Soleh had bared her teeth in a caricature of a smile as she had laid open her husband's deepest secret. She had worked into the night, knowing he was a full day's ride away in the Capital, and she had not sent word of their tiny son's illness. There had been no time.

"I must go," she whispered, her voice hoarse and broken.

When dawn broke, she had crossed the border already, and she never looked back. Around her, the select string of horses tugged at their lines. Relentlessly she kept them on the trail and their noses pointed ever northward.

* * *

The men rode into the courtyard through the shattered gate. The burned stables still smoked gently in the cool morning air. Arden, lord of Belcastle, held his hand high, and the hoof beats and creak of saddles stopped, leaving only the faint jingle of tack as nervous horses shifted restlessly under his men.

"Bergen, Tor, with me," he said finally, after a slow survey of the wreck of his half-brother's home. He dismounted stiffly. *I'm too old to be indulging in heroics*, he thought ruefully as he rubbed his left knee for a moment before starting toward the broken door.

But no one was here, that was easy to see and hear. An eerie silence hung over the house. There had been no lights nor signs of life since they had ridden through the village a half hour before. His brother had chosen an oddly isolated location for his manor house.

The front door had been completely shattered, and lay across the threshold, making it difficult to enter. They stepped through the broken wood carefully—and into chaos. No fires lit the house. Still they saw feathers, cloth, and blood everywhere.

Arden swore under his breath, then spoke loud enough to be heard, "Raiders have been here."

"No raiders did that." Bergen pointed at the gaping hole. Candles guttered inside the room hidden behind what had looked like a seamless wall, and with their dying lights, they revealed the horror of his brother's true nature.

"Gods." Arden whispered as he took in the foul altar. "What manner of treachery is this?"

"My lord!" One of the men appeared from a corridor, then shrank back as he saw the demonic visage hanging over the stained altar, candles lit in its eyes, and wax running down the cheeks of the dark god.

Arden turned away from the scene, his face ashen. "What is it?"

The man was pressed against the wall, his eyes fixed on the formerly hidden room. "There is a dead child..."

With an oath, Arden pushed past him. He strode down the hall in pitch darkness, until he came to the small chamber where the crib stood. The tiny body still lay there, lit by a sunbeam from the window. He walked up to it and looked down, pity in his eyes.

"Lord?" One of the men asked behind him. "Was this...Did the child...?"

"Not as a sacrifice. By illness or chance," Arden answered, then turned. "This place reeks of wrongness. I do not think there were any raiders, at least not in search of the ordinary things."

He gestured at the room surrounding them. "This is untouched."

"Surely this is servant's quarters, sire?" The man looked around the humble area in confusion.

Bergen spoke from behind him, and the man jumped. They were all spooked. "This is where his wife lived. They had no servants."

Arden nodded. Only a few knew that, and he had never slept under his brother's roof. His skin crawled, and he offered up a brief prayer at knowing he had not been in the same place as that altar for longer than necessary. The duration of a meal, served by her own hands…He met Bergen's eyes. "Have you found her?"

The armsman shook his head. "No."

* * *

Soleh came to the end of the world on the evening of the fifth day. The trail had been fading for some time, and she had begun to release the horses, one at a time.

Her head swam with hunger and pain, and she no longer cared what became of them, any of them. She swayed in the saddle and stared down the cliff. Below her, only shadows. Above, stars were beginning to glimmer in the velvet night.

She slid off the horse and loosed the saddle. The mare looked around in mild curiosity as Soleh smacked her on the rump. She wandered off, dropped her head, and cropped at the dusty grass, then moved back in the direction they had come from, looking for greener browse. Soleh stood alone on the edge of the precipice, feeling the breeze on her face.

Her mother's talisman had brought her here, along with the dim memory of her mother telling her to go to the end of the world and ask for weapons in direst need. *In the name of the clan Froststalker,* her mother's voice whispered on the wind. Soleh held out her arms, feeling the coolness penetrate her clothing. The wind gusted up the cliff, and she leaned into it. The ground shifted at her feet, and she looked down. The edge of the cliff crumbled beneath her toes. She threw herself backward, but it was too late.

Soleh twisted as she fell, clutching for anything solid, and landed on an incline with bruising force. She didn't dare let go of the rocks she gripped. She lay there, panting with terror, for long moments until she was certain the ground had stopped moving. Her pendant of broken glass, knotted into a leather cord, lay next to her face. It glimmered to life, and she stared at it blindly.

Slowly Soleh sat up, her body wracked with pain. Every breath she took sent thrusts of hot agony searing into her lungs. She shook her head to clear her mind and looked around. Above her, the broken earth was reft, leaving her prostrate on stone steps that clung to the edge of the cliff. Long ago they had doubtless been hidden in a cave, but time had eroded it into the void. All that remained was the cavity that had swallowed her.

Soleh realized she could not go up again. The landslide had taken the steps above her head away, and the only way was down. Painfully, she began to descend. Cautious, shaking, fearing that at any movement the rest of the ancient stair would give way, she crept spider-like downward. Step by step, time stretched, and she was never certain, afterward, how long she descended. The stairs plunged toward the heart of the earth. The walls closed over her head, becoming a tunnel. She dared not stand and walk, for the steps oozed a noisome slime, and even on her hands and knees, she slipped from time to time.

Eventually the stairs ceased to be, and she sat on the earth floor of a tunnel in the pitch dark, wondering what to do next. The sliver of glass around her neck flared from a dim glow into brightness, and it illumined her surroundings well enough to walk. Legs trembling,

Soleh held the talisman on the palm of her hand, high over her head to keep it from blinding her.

The light revealed three ways branching off the small circular room at the foot of the stairs. The walls were tall and straight, and had been crafted of laid stones so close-matched, no mortar interrupted their seams. The halls that led away were utterly black and dark, with no distinguishing marks to separate them. Twice the woman's boot-clad feet stumbled around the room, pausing at the stairs each time.

The stairs led nowhere, but the halls seemed to be an unsolvable enigma. The light in her hand flickered, and she wept uncontrollably at the thought of being alone in the dark until her heart finally stopped of hunger, thirst, or fear. The tears painted trails through the filth on her cheeks, but she walked around a third time, and this time she saw the pattern in the light's fluctuations. Not that it was fading, but that it brightened when she faced one direction, dimmed in another. She plunged into the darkness of the hall it favored.

* * *

The night had been miserable, with a storm blowing relentlessly over his men and himself until they had come to him requesting he break off their pursuit. "Surely a mere woman is dead already."

Arden had fixed his eyes on the man who said this to him. "She is not an ordinary woman."

"She led your brother into witchcraft and to commune with demons," another said hoarsely, with a wet cough to punctuate his declaration.

Bergen shook his head, raindrops glistening in his dark beard. "He's done that himself. I dunno I'd defend her, but that abomination…" He trailed off, then leaned out of the tent door to spit.

Arden nodded. "We ride on in the morning." He held up a hand to quell the protests. "Only until noon, then we turn back. I don't think you are wrong about the effects of this storm, should she have found no shelter."

His group found the end of the world well before midday. The storm, having passed during the night, had left in its wake a peculiarly bright blue sky with the sun beaming down cheerfully. No one grumbled, but Arden stood on the new cliffside, staring out over the valley, and wondered if she had jumped, or if the landslide had borne her to her death. He shivered, imagining the feeling of being sucked into the maw of cold, wet earth and bruising stones before death came to ease that pain.

Bergen came up behind him. "All the horses are accounted for, sir. She can't have gone far on foot, less'n she grew wings." He looked down the face of the cliff.

"Still, she could have walked…"

Bergen shook his head emphatically. "All her gear, what there was of it, is over there." He hooked his thumb over his shoulder. "There's no cover. Tent an' her blanket's sopping wet."

"Oh." Arden looked down at the mist hovering like clouds below his feet. The spill of black earth from the landslide vanished into it. Even if she was lying down there, they'd never see her. "Round up the animals; we will take them back, at least."

Bergen grunted and turned away. The edge made him nervous. "Never was sure why we wanted to take her back, anyway."

"We thought raiders had taken her." Arden knew he sounded a bit stilted, but appearances...

Bergen snorted derisively. He didn't stop walking, though, so Arden let it drop.

* * *

Far, far beneath their feet, Soleh became aware she no longer walked through a vaulted hallway. The walls had fallen away from the talisman's pool of green light. She stopped and turned all the way around, but other than the ground under her feet, the darkness was a soft veil draped over her globe of illumination. Soleh crouched and could see a floor of intricate mosaic in patterns that writhed before her eyes. She blinked, but still they seemed to move, entwining around one another. She settled on her haunches and looked upward, deciding that her current state of fasting was causing the floor's weirdness.

She closed her fingers around the crystal piece, covering the light. Her fingers glowed oddly, lit green through her red blood. The light solved only a small part of her problems, and she would still die if she did not find food and drink. In the gathered dark, Soleh slowed her breathing and opened her ears to listen carefully. Faintly she heard a soft drip, then another. She opened her hand and let the light blaze out again. Licking her cracked lips, she walked in the direction of the water.

There was nothing to see, only the floor and the darkness, for many steps. The floor felt dry and level, but she didn't look at it. The mosaic made her head ache.

When she put her foot down and heard the splash, it startled her. She froze in place, then looked down at her feet. One of them was immersed in inky blackness. She picked it up, and the water slid off it with reluctance. Crouching, she held her light close to it and could see the scattered reflection off ripples into the distance. Oddly, one reflection seemed to stay still a few feet away from her. Soleh closed her hand around the sliver, shutting off her light, and the pinprick of light did not go away. Instead, it grew larger, as though it were drawing nearer to her.

Alarmed, she stepped back quickly. Still, the light came rushing onward at a great speed. She took another step, and fell, though she was sure the ground had been smooth and level behind her. Scuttling backward, she huddled on the ground, unable to tear her eyes from the soft green brilliance that now filled the inky pool with radiance. The surface of the water began to bulge, as though what rose from the unfathomable depths was huge. Soleh caught a sobbing breath in her throat, her hand clasping the sliver of glassy crystal tightly to her heart. Terror held her an icy captive, and she could not have moved even if she wanted to at that moment.

The water boiled up with a great roar. She threw a hand up in front of her face to shield her eyes from the dazzling brilliance that erupted from the pool.

With a sound like thunder, a voice echoed from unseen walls all around her, "Who comes?"

Soleh pressed her eyes shut with her fingers, not daring to look. She could hear the water splashing, then settling into tiny waves that made a soft susurrus, but reassuringly without footsteps. Eventually, there was no motion at all. She moved her hand, and through her eyelids she saw no glow, so she ventured to open her eyes. Before her in the center of the pool an enormous creature stood, shrouded in darkness. Its glowing green eyes fixed on her.

"Daughter, how came thou to me?" it asked gently. Nothing moved—no part of it looked like a mouth—but the voice rang from walls around her in every direction.

Soleh, shaking, held out her hand with the sliver on it. "This…this brought me," she said, her voice hoarse with disuse and thirst.

"How came the crystal to you, child?"

She crouched at the edge of the pool. "It was the only thing of my mother's that remained after her death. My whole family died that day. I was taken from there and sold as a slave; even my clothes were stripped from me. Only this, in my hand, was I able to hide and save."

"Name yourself." The unmoving presence had no emotion in its echoing voice. Soleh straightened and pulled herself to her feet, standing erect in the face of the dark being.

"I am named Soleh Froststalker, daughter of Istregeld and Kotan." Soleh took a deep breath and continued calmly, "My mother bid me, in extremis, to follow a guiding light unto the end of the earth, and there to lay claim to my clan's weapons."

"What would you do with these weapons, Froststalker woman?"

Soleh shuddered. "I would have a vengeance." She heard the harshness in her voice and did not care. She was dying, but to have a chance…

"What price would you pay for the weapons and your revenge?"

She took a step forward into the water of the pool. She wasn't sure when she had drawn closer to the liquid, or if it had come to her. The cool of it soothed her burning skin. "I would pay with my life."

"Yes." The voice reverberated for a long moment, and Soleh felt the water rise up her ankles. She said nothing. Waiting. Watching the glow in the eyes grow brighter until they almost illuminated the strange planes of the being who spoke to her at the end of the world.

"Swim to me, child." The voice was softer. "Come hither and be fed, be healed, be at ease."

Soleh shuddered as the water lapped her knees. "Will I be given the weapons of my people?"

"You have no idea what form they take. You know not the price that must be extracted to carry them."

"It matters not. I must have them," she insisted, as the water swirled to her waist.

"Then you shall. Come."

Soleh took a last breath and then dove into the water, kicking off toward the creature swiftly. The water closed over her head. She swam for all she was worth. She came to the surface for a gulp of air, blinked the heavy water from her lashes, then reached out with tired arms to continue.

Her clothing dragged at her limbs and pulled her down. She kicked off her boots with difficulty. The rags of her clothing came apart with desperate fingers pulling at it, and she kept kicking toward the surface again.

Her head broke the plane of the water and air with a great gasp. She could swim no longer. Staying afloat taxed the last of her strength.

A bare whisper of sound broke through her frantic efforts. "Will you pay?"

"Yes!" she gasped. Her head went under, and she gulped the thick water as she tried to keep from breathing it. She coughed, then inhaled as she realized she had air again. "I will pay."

"The price is not your life, child."

Soleh sobbed as she felt a thick, solid presence twine around her. "I have paid with my body already, but if you will…"

The light from the crystal hanging around her neck, the sole remaining scrap of her garments, showed her the broad, black head of the creature tenderly supporting her exhausted body. Yellow eyes with slivers of black pupils met hers with an unblinking regard.

"Your body is a mere tool. No, the price for the weapons and your heart's desire is your death."

"No!" Soleh screamed and struggled. She plunged beneath the ink-dark water that was more than water once again. Choking, she came again to the surface with the aid of the huge snake cradling her. "I must not die yet," she whispered to it, her cheek resting against its blunt nose. "I must…"

"No." The voice was back to thunder, echoes ringing in her very bones. "*Not to die*. That is the price, Soleh Froststalker. Your eternal unrest. Your soul shall never know the solace of struggle's end."

The snake undulated and bore her closer to the translucent tower that spoke. Through the loose strands of her hair, Soleh could make out that the water came to mid-chest, if it were modeled after a man, which it was not. She had no idea how large it actually was.

"I will pay." She felt as though she were broken. Her heart fluttered against the cage of her ribs like a frightened bird. If she said that she wished to die, well, she would die here regardless.

"You will gain your weapons." The creature stooped, or perhaps sank, but the eyes came inexorably closer and closer to her. "Companions will aid your way. The weapons of your clan will come to your hands when they are needed."

Soleh shivered. The eyes were on a level with hers now as she lay in the coils of the great snake. "How…"

"Bha comes."

With hardly a ripple of the dark liquid, *it* was gone, and Soleh found herself with only the snake for company. She looked into its large eyes again, with their dilated pupils, now that the light of the other was gone. "Are you Bha?"

He might have shaken his head, or perhaps not, but when he started to uncoil beneath her, she clung to his neck unconsciously. He pulled her to the edge of the pool. Soleh let her feet touch the bottom and let go of him, but he entwined himself around her, from her leg, around her waist, and then over her shoulder until his wedge-shaped head rested on her breast. She walked out of the water with the glimmer of two eyes in the shadows waiting for them.

When she stepped forward, she held out one hand. "Bha."

The cat paced out of the dark, his coat sleek and blacker than the night. His head reached past Soleh's waist, and he stared into the woman's eyes. Soleh looked back intently and felt a wave of dizziness pass through her. She closed her eyes and shook her head, wondering why she no longer felt hunger, or thirst. She opened her eyes again as she felt the warmth of fur touch her face. She leaned into the greeting, forehead to forehead with the mighty panther.

"I greet thee," she whispered in the tongue of her mother. "I beg of thee…" she stumbled, trying to remember the rest of the words, "companionship," she finished in the language of her husband.

The cat wrapped its body around her, and as she looked down, Soleh startled. The snake was gone, but she was marked with tattoo ink from foot to shoulder in the outline of where it had been, every scale marked with black and gold. She buried her fingers in the warm ruff of Bha and walked with him out of the water, feeling the new strength filling her.

"I'm ready," she told her companion.

* * *

Arden mounted and spoke sharply to one of his men, "No, leave it."

The man shot him a puzzled look, then shrugged and mounted.

Arden watched until they had all turned and rode toward home. Only then did he surrender his vigil and turn after them, leaving the end of the world at his back.

Bergen rode by him. "Lord, I know we dinnae need the money for the horse and gear, but why?"

Arden shrugged. "I don't know. It felt right to leave it here, where…"

"She's dead," Bergen said bluntly. "We spent a day longer than we should hae, searching and watching."

"Aye." Arden twisted around to look one last time at the bank of clouds rising and spilling onto the land from the rift valley. "Still. They can be her memorial."

"A mare?" Bergen shook his head, but he stopped trying to argue with his lord and master. He clicked his tongue at his own gelding and urged him forward to catch up with the men he deemed laggardly.

"Why not?" Arden knew no one would hear him, as softly as he was speaking. "He may be my brother, but even a dog deserved a better master."

They rode out in silence that took hours to lift, with nervous glances around them at the brush lining their path home. Bergen, at the head of the small column, held up his hand wordlessly, and the trained men pulled their horses to a stop immediately. Even well-trained men, however, cannot bring a horse to a halt instantaneously or silently. There was some clattering, the column shrank and widened, and the ambush caught them clustered. The only saving grace was their quick response to the scout's signal. It kept them in a more open forest that allowed some of them to scatter when the forest wildings fell on them like rabid beasts.

Arden watched in horror as the first arrows arced from heavy cover into the men at the lead. Bergen fell or dismounted from his steed, it was difficult to see which, but another man nearer his lord fell with an arrow in his throat. When his body hit the ground, the finality of it jarred Arden into action. He drew his sword and spurred his horse forward over the fallen man.

The attackers were out of their cover now and fighting hand to sword with his men. They carried only knives—long, wickedly sharp, but lacking in reach compared to the steel Arden used. He cut one man across the face, sending him reeling backward. Arden twisted to slash at another, who was pulling a man from his saddle while stabbing him in the guts.

Too late to save him, Arden thought in the instant before his plunging horse bore him onward into a knot of fighting men. Two or three of his own men, unhorsed, struggled with a number of wildmen.

Arden saw that none of them wore proper armor, unlike his men, who at least bore mail shirts. When one of his blows went wild and struck his own man on the shoulder, it merely glanced off, leaving no real harm beyond a bruise. On the wildings, his sword cut through their flesh and bit into their bones.

Before he could think through what was happening, he had broken through to the other side, and had to fight his horse to turn and face battle once more.

The restive mount meant that by the time Arden could pay attention again, the fight was over. Bergen, unhorsed but seemingly unscathed, strode toward a fallen warrior with sword in hand, point down and intent clear.

"Stay!" Arden shouted at him. "Leave the wounded alive!"

Bergen glared at his lord, put his sword to the man's throat, and paused.

Arden nudged his reluctant horse again, urging the beast to move past the gutted man lying on the path, and joined his armsman. Around them, the forest had fallen silent, but for the low moans of the wounded.

Arden slid from his saddle and knelt by the wilding. The man's eyes rolled in panic from Arden's face to the blade that hung a mere hairs-width from his skin.

"Do you understand me?" Arden snarled. He wanted Bergen to complete his bloodthirsty task, but he wanted answers more.

The man's eyes, whites showing all around the deep, dark pupils that had almost eclipsed any iris color, fixed on Arden's face. He worked his lips, but no sound came from them.

"Bergen." Arden didn't take his eyes from the wilding.

"Run him through?" The armsman sounded hoarse.

The wilding shuddered. From the smell, his bladder had released as well. "No. He hears me. Get water."

The steel disappeared from Arden's peripheral vision, but he never broke his gaze from the wilding's inky black, terrified eyes. Bergen returned and thrust a waterskin into Arden's hands. Arden uncapped it and poured some onto the prostrate man's face. He gasped, sputtered, and choked, but never moved. Arden directed the stream onto the man's eyes, and the other closed them tightly.

"Speak. You are dead and washed." Arden's throat was raw, and his voice came out harsh.

Without opening his eyes, the wilding coughed, then spoke softly in a monotone, "I am dead, but washed. What wouldst thou know?"

"The name of the one who set you on us."

The wilding shuddered again, longer and deeper this time than even when he was certain he would be skewered on Bergen's sword.

He's more afraid of the answer than he was of death. Arden cocked his head, considering. "Speak, dead one," he ordered again.

The man groaned, then whispered, "The demon walks on two legs, but he is not a man."

"A name." Arden demanded. He leaned nearer the dying man, hearing the breath rattle in his throat. "You cannot go to join your ancestors until I have the name!"

"They say he is the bastard of Belcastle." The blood that frothed up with a terrible gurgle on the heels of those words put an end to Arden's questions.

"Damn!" Arden leaped to his feet. "Is there another that still lives?"

The silence that came back to him in answer was absolute. His men, their eyes sunken and dark, just stared at him with dead enemies at their feet.

* * *

S oleh lay on her belly under a tangle of vines, hidden from the fray. She had landed in a heap on the hard ground, knocking the breath out of her. By the time she had realized the screaming and clashing of steel had been a battle and not her ringing ears, it was too late for her to decide on flight or fight. She watched and recognized the leader. She had only met him twice, but she had seen good in his eyes. He would lead her to her husband. Her hands twitched, longing for the feel of a weapon and a clear strike at the man who had stolen her children.

"Soon," she whispered, as much to herself as to Bha, who lay at her side like a deep, solid shadow. "They will lead us to him."

The big cat blinked his luminous eyes slowly before turning his head to look at Arden, who stomped toward his horse. He shouted for the group of survivors to leave the enemy lie where they had fallen, to take only their own dead when they rode. Soleh watched as they gathered their small force back up and headed down the trail again.

Soleh wriggled out of her hiding place and stood up, looking down at herself. She had been naked in the tunnel; now she wore a sturdy tunic and buckskin pants. Bha yawned and crawled out, then turned and padded in the opposite direction as the men had taken.

"Bha…" Soleh trotted to catch up with him. The cat was as bad as any cat she'd known for following directions. She stopped when she saw what he headed for. Soleh looked from him to her mare, who grazed at the verge, and then decided she should not question it. The mare remained unsaddled, as she had left it, but had been freshly brushed. The gray lifted her head and pricked her ears, then came to the woman with bright eyes. Soleh pulled the belt she wore from around her waist, grateful it was a doubled sash long enough to make a halter.

Bha settled on his haunches while Soleh mounted. She looked down at him. "I follow them, now."

She wheeled the horse with her knees and urged the reluctant beast through the corpses that lined the trail. Soleh was so occupied with managing her horse that she didn't realize Bha had disappeared until later. Looking around at the thick brush, she shrugged and kept on the trail of her unwitting guides. Bha was a cat. Cats came and went.

Lightly burdened, the mare easily kept pace with the war-weary men. As the sun's light angled and dipped below the treetops, Soleh found it difficult to keep far enough back to remain out of sight. Finally she slid off the mare and continued on foot, leading her mount with a hand on her nose to keep her from calling out to her kin. Soleh smelled the campfires as twilight deepened into gloom, and led her horse off the trail a good distance until she located some browse. Repurposing the sash as a hobble, she settled the horse and left her grazing while she slipped closer to the camp.

She expected a sentry to be alert. Surely a band of men so recently under attack would be wary of another. Soleh slipped into the brush and wriggled underneath branches until she could observe unseen. A man stood outside the light of the fires, facing the way they had come. Had she continued down the trail, she would have been spotted, and the alarm raised instantly. She could not see the other side of camp, due to the rise in the ground. She could hear the murmur of voices, and the scent of rich cooking stew made her stomach growl loudly.

Not wanting to alarm the sentry, she started to work her way back to her horse, until the sound of something big moving in the trees made her freeze. Soleh listened intently, her mouth slightly open to silence the sound of her own breathing. The moon was just beginning to rise. Ragged wisps of clouds passing before its shining face kept the shadows in the forest moving.

The harsh gurgle of something else, more solid than a shadow, turned her head, and she choked as the smell hit her with the force of a blow. Suppressing her stomach's rebellion as it went from hunger to visceral revulsion, Soleh stood stock still. Something instinctual told her that any movement would catch its attention, whatever it was.

As the clouds passed in front of the moon, Soleh saw the massive creature move, passing between her and the distant glow of the fires. Wrong and twisted, it wavered as it moved, as though it were not wholly there. Soleh felt a warmth resting against her chest, and she put her hand up to touch the crystal. It was glowing, she realized, looking down at it. She could see it through the fabric of her tunic. Wrapping one hand around it to eliminate the telltale light, she knew what she had to do.

The soft leather boots, a final gift from her clan's god, carried her over the forest floor almost soundlessly. She pursued the stygian hunter stalking the men at the fires. It flickered as the moon came out, shifting from shadow to shadow, ever closer to the sentry who stood looking in the wrong direction. As it reached the perimeter of the camp, it suddenly took on a stinking solidity. The elusive putrescence of its warped body flooded the entire camp and gave it away, but far too late, as it leapt on the nearest man.

Soleh raced toward it, too slow. It opened slavering jaws wide enough to snatch the man up whole and snap him in half before he even managed a scream.

The men in the camp were awake and shouting, some holding their swords ready. For a breath, the demonic hell-spawned beast only looked at them with too many eyes, too few legs, and a shape that defied description.

Soleh felt a weight against her back, and reached up over her shoulder to feel the hilt of a longsword bound into a scabbard there. The weapon she had been promised. With a shriek she pulled the steel and leapt onto the twisted back of the monstrosity. She plunged the sword into it up to the hilt.

It screamed and reared up. Soleh clung to the hilt of her sword as she lost her footing. The blade tore through the viscid flesh, sending her plummeting toward the ground. She landed on her feet, pulling the sword free of the demon, strands of mucilaginous fluids trailing her steel. She thrust again into its haunches, finally striking spongy bone.

She was not alone in hacking at the terrible thing. Men dodged the raking, long-taloned hands set too low on its body and chopped at what they could reach. One hewed an arm clean off, but the hand still spasmodically tried to grasp anything near it.

Soleh kicked it away and hewed into the demon's other hand with her two-handed sword like she swung a kitchen axe. It screamed and then bent nearly double, trying to bite her. Over her head, Arden's sword squelched as it plunged deeply into the thing. Now the being gurgled and thrashed. The swords rose and fell again and again until it finally lay completely still.

Panting, Soleh looked at Arden over the reeking carcass. She lifted her blade in salute and silently backed away toward the shadows. One of the men made a move to stop her, but Bha was suddenly there, fangs bared. The man stopped dead in his tracks.

Soleh turned and walked away from the camp. Bha, after a moment, paced beside her as she headed toward the hobbled mare. To her surprise, Soleh found her own pack, the one she had lost at the end of the world, lying near the horse.

"You got this for me." She picked up the waterskin and gulped greedily from it. The finest wine could not have tasted better.

Bha twitched just the end of her dark tail, then looked away, up at the moon. The fight with the demon had taken very little time. Soleh shivered and looked at the dark substance that had splashed all her clothing. "I may never be clean again."

* * *

Arden stood over the rotting bulk, shaking. The body was already starting to deliquesce, and he stepped back quickly to keep the black goo from washing over his boots. Bergen appeared at his side, offering him a cloth. Arden took it gratefully, wiping his sword blade clean of the disgusting smears remaining of the demon's blood.

"Was that..." One of the other men skirted around the puddle, nodding his chin at it as he spoke.

"No," Arden snapped. "That was a demon sent after us."

"What about her, then?" Bergen looked at the forest, his eyes scanning restlessly.

"She fought it *with* us," the man who had approached pointed out in a dull tone. "It ate Roric. *Ate* him."

"She did fight with us," said Arden. "That does not make her a friend."

Bergen raised shaggy eyebrows, and Arden met his glance with a glare and a tiny shake of his head. He didn't want the men, in their state, to know who she was. Not after they had declared her dead.

"We need to move camp," Arden said to no one in particular. "We can't stay here tonight."

"Where are we going to be safe again?" the man who was in shock asked. "What else is going to come out of the night at us?"

"Nothing else tonight." Arden thought quickly. "The goddess watches over us. Did she not send her avatar?"

The man gaped at him. Arden gestured at the ooze. "She struck it a blow no mortal woman could have done."

He nodded mutely, accepting it.

Arden gestured at the horses. "Gather up the strays. We will ride as soon as we can break camp."

None of the men protested this decision. The stench turned stomachs, and its rotting corpse, even without the remains of the man it had killed, bore witness that it was not a nightmare. In silence they loaded the pack animals and the macabre burdens they had to bear, then in the darkness they turned toward home.

None of them noticed the lone rider far behind them, guided by her giant cat companion, and pulled onward by internal forces they would not have been able to fathom.

Morning came early. They had come to the edge of civilization again, or at least to the occasional charcoal burner's hut, deserted and eerie in the dim light of dawn. They chose not to stop again after the disastrous first camp, so when the attack broke, they were beyond weary and nearly unable to defend themselves.

They rode out into the meadow. The light, open space had seemed like freedom from the dark unknown shadows of the forest lurking all around them. Horses stepped a little faster, their ears pricking toward the light and promise of clear vision all around. Halfway into the meadow, the great bat-winged demon stooped on them and carried the man suffering from shock off in clutching talons.

Bergen bellowed, "Ride! Ride for the trees!"

Arden watched helplessly as his man shrank into a dot, so high had the creature borne him in the space of a few heartbeats. Then the dot grew larger again. Arden grew sick as he realized the demon had simply dropped the man, dead or alive, to plummet earthward. He shouted with Bergen, urging the tired men back under cover. There were so few remaining. Only eight of the fourteen who had ridden out with him. Men who had trusted his leadership, who knew the dangers of raiders. None of them had anticipated it might have been an elaborate trap.

Arden spurred his horse out into the open meadow to seize the reins of a man who simply sat looking up into the sky, his jaw slack. The lord's sudden appearance seemed to galvanize them into action, and five followed him into the relative safety of the trees. One never moved, staring upward. The falling man struck him from his horse.

Arden could not spare a moment to grasp the horror. He lashed about left and right with the loose ends of his reins, striking men and horses alike to keep them moving deeper into the forest.

Soleh met them there on the trail, her fatigue rolling away from her like a blanket. She reached over her shoulder for the second time, calling on her unseen weapons. This time she grasped a strung bow. With her other hand, she reached without looking into the space near her knee, and drew an arrow from midair. She never even looked at the men, who parted before her as she galloped out into the meadow, drawing her bow. It had been many years since she had ridden thusly, with her mother shouting encouragement and suggestions from the edge of the training fields.

She sent an arrow into the breast of the demon as it swooped overhead, near enough for her to smell the fearful stench familiar from the night before. A single arrow could not possibly have been enough, but with a shrill cry, it crumpled and fell to the ground. Soleh drew the bow with another arrow to send it back to the hell it had come from, when Bergen leaped from his horse and ran to it, sword in hand.

A swift stroke had its head off, and they both watched the corpse spasm for a brief moment. Then it began to steam and rot before their eyes. Bergen turned and walked toward her.

"Lady." He bowed slightly.

Arden rode up behind her, his men lingering in the forest, unwilling or unable to bring themselves back into the open.

"Soleh." He dismounted. "We were certain raiders had taken you."

Soleh looked down at them both. "No." Her voice sounded strange to her own ears. "There were no raiders."

Bergen raised his bushy gray eyebrows. "No? Then what, or who...?"

Soleh laid the bow across her lap. "I did. I wanted to reveal him to those who came after."

"Where did you go?" Arden asked. "At the end of the world, where the cliffs are tallest..." His voice failed him.

"I went to my clan's last refuge." Her throat hurt. Had she been shouting? Soleh couldn't remember for certain. "I went to ask for the strength to take my revenge and to ensure my children were safe."

Arden exchanged a look with Bergen. "The children are with their foster parents, safe, as of the day we left."

"But after that?" She looked across the meadow, away from them. Distantly she could just make out movement over the roll of the land. Someone rode out from the lonely keep that kept watch here at the fringes of civilization. "When he finds what I have done, he will try to make sure we all are silent."

She looked down at Arden, seeing the deep lines in his face. "You were kind to me."

"I was only polite." He remembered the strangeness of that meal in his brother's house. "I should have done more."

She arched her brows. "For a woman? No, I meant for the horse and my pack."

He shrugged, uncomfortable. "I felt it was necessary to leave...something. In remembrance." He didn't want to think about the strange pricking of his soul there at the edge, how small and insignificant he had felt looking down into the clouds and rocks far below.

"It was a help." She stroked the bow. "I must go."

"We can help," Arden urged her. "We can all go to see the children and ensure their safety."

"No. Only I can walk the path set before me. I have paid the price already, but you have not, and you have yet the chance for peace and rest." She lifted the bow and pulled an arrow from no-where. "He comes."

The two men turned and looked over the twisted remains of the bat creature and saw the rider who had approached while they spoke. Soleh's husband, the man who shared a father with Arden, the man who had set hell on their heels to hide his secrets.

Soleh kicked her mare into a canter and rode to meet him.

"Wife!" he shouted when she was close enough to hear. "Put down the bow!"

"I shall not." She nocked the arrow and fired at him.

He put out a hand, and the arrow bounced off it. "Cease. It is useless."

"Never!" She laughed, tipping her head back. "I shall fight you with my every breath, and I shall rejoice in every drop of your blood I shed. Come! Fight me like a man!"

He turned his horse and spurred it cruelly, galloping away from them toward the distant keep. Soleh rode after him, crouching low over her mare's neck, racing him for the gate. When she reached it, she slid from the horse, leaving the bow hanging on the saddle. Now a courtyard of stone walls enclosed them, and a single rough squared tower loomed over them.

"Why should I fight you, woman? I have more power than you have ever dreamed of. I can give you everything you want."

She shook her head. "You have no understanding of what I want. You don't care for me, or my desires. You have power, yes, but from what source?"

He dismounted with a leap and stood before her, a smile on his face. "You know where the power comes from. And you know what I can do with it."

Soleh bared her teeth in something that on another face might have been a grin. "Do you think your foul god has countless pets in his pit to issue them without number?"

The man who had given her children, then taken them from her, sneered. "You will fall under a pile of seething demonic forces, witch. And I shall eat your heart."

She shook her head and reached back over her shoulder. The axe handle fit snugly into her hand, an old, familiar friend. It was not what she had been expecting, but it was yet not a surprise, this gift from her clan's god. She swung and saw his eyes widen in surprise. He hadn't been done talking.

He leaped back and came close to falling, one hand instinctively flung backward to catch himself. The other hand came up and splayed in front of his face.

"Coward," she hissed at him. She could feel a constriction around her chest, and she fought for breath. "Fight. Like. A. Man," she panted, each word an effort.

Suddenly the pressure went away, and Soleh gasped for air. Sparkles swam in her peripheral vision as her heart raced again. The vast head of a snake swayed in and out of the center of her vision, and it took her some time to remember there had been a snake. The snake she had borne on her skin now rippled off her body and coiled, its head weaving in some complicated pattern.

"Witch!" her husband screamed, his hands open and empty. "What familiars have you?"

"Only my companions." Soleh stepped around the snake cautiously, testing the effect it was having on him.

He dropped his hands, finally, and reached for his sword. Soleh felt a surge of satisfaction overtake her as she lifted her axe again.

She caught sight of Bha then, sitting upright behind him, golden eyes calmly fixed on his back, the only movement a flicker of restless black tail.

Soleh realized they were cutting off his connection to magic. With a growl, she leapt at him again. The steel of his blade met the wedge of the axe and snapped, but the force of it jarred her backwards, and she stepped back as he swung again, wildly, with the fragment of his blade.

Soleh dropped to one knee and rolled under his arm, coming up slightly behind him, closer to Bha. Her eyes widened as he didn't turn toward her, but swung yet again, his sword shard gouging into the mouth and neck of her snake companion. The snake writhed, great coils looping around its enemy in its death throes. Soleh ran forward with a shriek, raising her axe high over her head as she prepared to strike him a final blow.

With a death's head grin, he calmly stepped out of the weakening coils and met her with his elbow crooked in front of him. Her steel met an invisible shield and skittered off it with a tooth-aching squeal.

"Now who will run?" he cooed. In his other hand he still held the broken sword, and he stood up straight, taking another step toward her. "Run, *wife*." His voice changed, taking on a harsh tone that rang like metal in her ears.

"I stand," she gasped. Her knee ached from her fall earlier, and her chest heaved with her efforts. She lifted the axe again.

He swung his seemingly empty arm at her, and she parried the unseen magic with her oak haft and steel head. The impact rocked both of them, but he recovered sooner than she expected, and brought his broken sword over the shield and onto her head. Soleh never saw the pommel coming, and fell, half-senseless, at his feet.

His cruel laughter echoed over her as she clenched her fingers on the stones, grasping without feel. Her axe lay behind him, fallen from numbed hands that now burned like fire. She lifted her head and saw the broken head of the snake. Then she saw the black silken paws of Bha moving slowly around her husband, circling nearer.

The man spun around, sword dangling from his hand, which seemed to have lost some usefulness.

Soleh swayed as she managed to get to her knees, slowly, painfully. She could not reach her axe. It lay in front of him now.

She tried to reach over her shoulder for another weapon, but her arm would not bend in that direction. She whimpered in pain and tried to push it with her other hand, but it would not obey her.

Bha fenced in his own way with the magician. He darted forward, biting at the shield, then danced back out of his reach as he attempted to stab him with his short steel shard. Soleh shuddered. Bha bared his fangs in a taunt, then whirled, scraping the stones with his claws as he ran toward the wall.

Her husband laughed, then turned back to finish Soleh.

Soleh knelt at his feet. Her face was turned upward, and her tears of pain and frustration streaked her bloody, filthy cheeks.

"I shall not die," she whispered.

"Pathetic." He lifted the sword over his head, blade ready to fall.

"*You* shall." She pulled her working hand free from where she had hidden the fang of her companion. The fang that Bha had sent sliding over the stones to her when the big cat had turned tail and run. The fang dripped with venom that slid blue over Soleh's fingers. Then she stabbed her husband in the groin with all her remaining strength, and it ran red with his blood.

He screamed, and the sword fell with a clatter as he sank to his knees, clutching the fang with both hands. For an instant no longer than a heartbeat, they were face to face. With wide eyes and foam already erupting from his mouth, he fought for a strangled breath.

"Justice," she breathed as she swung what was left of his sword and took head from body.

Leaning on the blade, she levered herself to her feet and looked down at what was left of him, lying partly on the body of her clan god's avatar. She raised her heavy head and looked for Bha.

The big cat walked through the gate coolly, Arden on her heels. His mouth dropped open as he took in the scene.

"Bear witness," Soleh croaked. Bha paced forward, leaving the man in her wake, and came to Soleh. Lightly, he leaped upward to put his paws on Soleh's shoulders, then touched his nose to the woman's forehead. His tears dropped down onto Soleh's cheeks. Soleh drew another breath, feeling the coolness of the inky water again.

"What foul magic is this?" Arden asked hoarsely.

"Ask him." Soleh gestured at the body near her feet. She reached for and sheathed the axe. "Get a full accounting from him of the manner in which he has gained his living. Of the slaves whose souls fed his master, who then showered him with money, power, and influence on the king."

Arden felt his jaw drop. "You speak treason."

"I speak truth." She rubbed a hand across her face, smearing the blood droplets there. "I speak what should have been said long ago, but I lacked the strength."

"This cannot be known," Arden muttered, looking down at the ruin of the man who had advised the king. "It could tear apart the kingdom and topple the peace of the lands."

"It *must* be known." She headed for the open gate to look for her horse. Bha met her on padded feet. He growled at Arden, and it was this that sparked the man's reaction. The sleeplessness, the fear, the gnawing terror of the demonic attacks, all of them flooded over him, and he drew his sword.

"You cannot tell of this!" Arden shouted, and swung.

Soleh tucked and rolled, and came up holding her own sword. Their blades crossed with a clash that drew sparks, but while he pushed, she yielded not an inch. Their eyes met over the locked swords.

"Surrender." His voice was a harsh croak. "Surrender, and we shall seek out your lost ones. This cannot be spoken of."

She shook her head, and he marveled that she seemed effortless in her resistance against him. "I can have no peace. You have not asked me what price I paid that I might fight him. I cannot *die*, Arden of Belcastle."

He took a step back, lowering his weapon. She stood still, hers still raised against him. "You are...You have a powerful geas on you."

She nodded. "I do. I bear it for their sake, those who are passed beyond the silvery waters, and those who yet remain."

Arden braced the point of his blade in the earth, heedless of the damage he did it. He leaned on the hilt heavily, exhausted suddenly. "I shall die someday, alone, as I was born in body." He looked back up at her glowing eyes. "But I shall be hopeful and rejoicing in spirit."

She lifted her blade to her forehead in a silent salute, and then was gone, running alongside her shadowy companion with swift and silent feet.

He stood there for a long time, staring at the patch of Goddess's Tears blooming between the stones at his feet. Blood drops peppered their delicate, white petals.

* * * * *

Cedar Sanderson Bio

Cedar Sanderson was born a military brat and spent her childhood moving to new duty stations. Her formative years after her father left the Air Force were spent being home-schooled on the Alaskan frontier. Growing up without television, or even electricity, made her into an avid reader. Having finished college in Ohio to secure a BS in Forensic Science and Investigation, she is now a chemist, while running a household, an art and design business, and writing novels on the side with occasional forays into coloring books and children's stories.

She has written more short stories than she can keep track of, and the recent publication of *Possum Creek Massacre* makes her eighth novel in print. She also has a blog with over a decade of essays, recipes, and artwork for you to explore should you so desire at http://www.cedarwrites.com.

# # # # #

Hold the Line by Kevin Steverson & Tyler Ackerman

Chapter One

The Empire of Minth
Western Border

Ahorn blew. The sound rose from the center. The same three notes were taken up by others up and down the line, using the instruments made from the curved horn of a great fish. Several times a year, fleets based off the eastern coast of Minth hunted them. The fishermen were free to profit from the delicate flesh and the large scales of the huge fish, but the Emperor claimed the horns for his forces.

Noryen looked over at those with him and said, "They come. We might as well ride up and join the lines. We're not doing much good back here."

Suzanne reached up with both hands and pulled her long blond hair up into a pony tail. She held it with one hand and took the strip of leather out of her mouth. She wrapped it around several times and tied it off. She tilted her head from side to side, stretching her neck.

"Yeah," she said, "There's no scouting to be done when the enemy is right in front of us."

Brind looked over and up to the other four already in their saddles. "Let me get this strap tightened first. I almost rolled in the last skirmish."

"I saw that." Calnate grinned. He winked at Torbit. "Don't think I wasn't to mention it later over a mug or two."

Brind shook his head, his beard sweeping back and forth across his chest. "By the time you finished telling the story, I would have been hanging on underneath my horse, both boots in the air at his flanks."

"It would make for a better story," Torbit said. "I swear I saw your horse's back feet hopping as he tried to avoid your cloak."

"You saw it too?" Calnate said, looking over at his cousin. "I feared the poor animal would break a leg on his big head. I truly felt for the beast. Such a fine bloodline, too."

"Yeah," Torbit agreed. "Perhaps you should no longer ride him. You could run alongside us. I mean, Orcs don't ride and they cover plenty of ground, or so they say."

"He's nigh as big as an Orc," Calnate mentioned. "Poor horse."

Brind laughed. "Wide in the shoulders does not equal the height of an Orc. Though, I will admit, I'll not skip a meal. To do other would make me as skinny as you are, which now that I think on it, being able to hide behind a young pine tree has served you well in scouting."

"Hey!" Calnate exclaimed. "That's uncalled for. I wasn't insulting you. I was merely showing concern for the horse." He winked at Torbit again.

Noryen turned his fidgeting horse around and patted her neck, settling her. He grinned along with the others. "Get it tight and mount up. I'm sure the knight commander has a place in the line for us."

"We always wait on one of you three," Suzanne said with a crooked smile of her own. "Oh, and if any of you ever think to joke on my size, you'll sleep with the fish in the nearest pond." Her smile broke into a full-fledged tooth-showing grin.

Wide eyed, Torbit said, "Leave it to Suzy to make me rather face the horde then sleep around the campfire knowing I might have said the wrong thing about her needing a new saddle one day. I mean, saddles can be outgrown, you know."

"Young ones do it all the time," agreed Brind, with a serious look. He swung up into his saddle and shifted slightly to get his boot in the other stirrup.

Noryen looked at Suzanne and raised his hands in mock surrender. Her mouth was open in question and the expression on her face was one of disbelief. She narrowed her eyes and slowly reached into the pouch on her belt. The other three men spurred their horses and tried to get away fast enough to avoid the stones she carried for her hunting sling. It wasn't fast enough, two of the stones she threw hit Brind in the back of his hardened leather helmet as he followed the other two, laughing as hard as they were.

"I'm not a young one," Suzanne shouted as she chased them. "I'm twenty two years old. And that's just how many knots I'll put on the lot of you!"

Noryen reached down and patted the side of his horse's neck and said, "You see what I have to work with, girl? Remind me to not set my bowl of mush down in the morning. I'm sure theirs will be full of sea salt, as soon as they take their eyes off of it." He urged her forward to catch up with the rest of his scout squad.

* * * * *

Chapter Two

They rode through the tree line past the cooling fires, tents, and shelters to the back of a massive formation of foot soldiers. Five hundred wide and twenty deep, there were ten thousand of them on the left flank. Beyond them, covering the end of the line, four companies of cavalry nearly four hundred in number, stirred. Their horses were restless as they anticipated the upcoming battle. All were Minth-bred warhorses, the envy of every knight and cavalry soldier on the entire planet of Kerr. Not as large as draft horses, which would be too slow in battle, a Minth horse was still larger and stronger than the typical riding horse, with exceptional intelligence.

The five scouts turned north and rode past the group of foot soldiers. Several men and women of the last rank turned and watched them go with the occasional wave. Most of those who saw them knew they were part of the Emperor's Own. If the greens and browns of their leather and cloaks didn't give them away as scouts, the horses they rode did. They were not as muscular as a warhorse, but the obvious speed the beasts could attain showed in their stature.

"There," Noryen said, "the knight commander and his captains are between the formations of foot soldiers."

"I see him," Suzanne said as she rode up beside him. She glanced back at the other three nodding. The fun and games among the friends was forgotten now.

"Do you think he wants us with him?" asked Calnate.

"The last time we were sent to the far side," observed Torbit. "But now, with the addition of Duke Jorna's cavalry, there are more horses over there than we just passed."

"We'll see," Noryen answered. "To be honest, I don't mind being surrounded by the archers."

The five rode to the center of the line and met one of the knight commander's squires. He was riding a warhorse bearing the red and yellow colors of the knight commander's duchy on the tunic covering his chain mail armor. On his shoulders were the black coverings indicating his rank as a squire. He had the head piece of his mail pulled up covering his dark hair.

"Sergeant Noryen," he said raising a hand in greeting. "I was told to watch for you. Sir Maytok said you would be along once you heard the 'be ready' signal." He spun his big horse around as it kept dancing, trying to return to the front of the formation where several of the other squires and knights were.

"Lord Marlan," Noryen replied, in greeting, "he knows us well. Where does he want us? It's not as if there is any scouting to be done. The horde is in front of us."

"With him," answered the squire. "And why do you insist on calling me Lord?' Marlan asked with a shake of his head. He grinned at the scout. "As a squire, my family is of no import until I become a knight. My training holds precedence. Then I will go back and play the politics and do what I can to improve the lands my father will give me."

"I'm afraid it's not to change, my lord," Noryen said. "Unless you order it so," he added.

"I'd not give orders, unless they were absolutely necessary," the young man said. "It makes the ones necessary seem to carry less weight."

"That one shows the makings of a fine leader," Brind said to no one in particular. He said it low enough the squire would not hear.

"Aye," agreed Torbit. "I'd follow him now, and it's not for his skill with the sword, either."

"As would I," Calnate added. "But, it does help knowing what the man can do in a fight. I've never seen the like."

As they rode towards the knight commander, Noryen looked beyond the forward row, across the wide plain. There, on the far side of the field, less than a bowshot in front of the canyons separating the Minth Empire and the Western Borderlands, was the largest horde he had ever seen. The numbers had grown since they pushed them back nearly to the edge of where they had emerged from a month ago. The effort had cost many lives. Funeral pyres still burned along with several villages and towns behind the Minth forces.

Goblins. Tens of thousands of Goblins. For some reason, the four-foot-tall creatures had come down from their mountain lairs through the canyons between the two nations. They boiled up out of the gullies and draws, massed together, and moved east into the western part of Minth. Twice they had been forced back.

Something or someone was pushing them on. Driving them into the flat lands. For whatever reason, they chose to invade the more populated of the two. Perhaps it was the other side of the Western Borderlands, Orcanth, deciding it for them. The Orcs would not tolerate Goblin lairs bordering their tribal lands.

Noryen's thoughts were interrupted when he heard his name called. "Sergeant Noryen," the knight commander said. "Join us."

"Yes, my lord," Noryen answered. He dismounted and handed his reins to a page. The girl looked to be fourteen or fifteen and wore sword and chainmail, and she had a small shield strapped to her back. Unsure whose daughter she was, Noryen nodded politely and thanked her.

"My lord," Noryen said as he walked up to the two standing several feet in front of the forces. He acknowledged the mage in dark blue robes standing beside Sir Maytok. "Mage Anelia." She smiled and pushed a strand of red hair out of her face.

"Sergeant Noryen, the man I wanted to speak to," Sir Maytok said. "We think this is the last of the horde, as no more have joined them this morning. There is something I would like you to observe and give me your opinion of. Mage Anelia will show you in her far seeing glass. Give her a moment to cast the spell again. I will refrain from explaining what I see. I would like to know if you come to the same conclusion."

The mage held a round piece of glass in one hand. She held the other over it and began to speak a language Noryen did not know, nor would he have reason to ever learn. He had not been born with the gift.

* * * * *

Chapter Three

Mage Anelia handed the piece of glass to Noryen. "Hold it to your eye and look through it," she explained.

Noryen held it to his eye and quickly pulled it away. His first view through it was disorientating. He rubbed his eye and slowly put the glass in front of it again. Once he knew it was similar to the view tubes ship captains used, designed to allow one to see farther, he was more prepared.

As the leader of a squad of scouts, he carried a smaller version of those, but his only gave him the illusion of being half again as close to what he was looking at. The larger ones, used on ships, were too big for a scout to carry and keep from being damaged. They were also extremely expensive to purchase from the clan of Gnomes who made them. Being in the Emperor's Own had its advantages but coin of that amount wasn't available unless it helped to earn a profit.

The view he now had was many times closer than his own. It was as if he was standing within the enemy's formation. He scanned to the left and right, taking note of the weapons the Goblins used. Nearly all had short swords of various designs. Some were hooked, others serrated, while still others extended from their hilts at odd angles. The ones on the flanks of the mass held spears. He also realized several groups were carrying short bows made from horns. It looked to be from the long-horned mountain goats living in the mountain ranges above the Goblin lairs.

He looked farther back in the mass of creatures and saw what the knight commander wished him to observe. There, in the back and standing well over twelve feet tall was an Ogre. The Ogre appeared to be yelling at several of the Goblins. All three flinched every time the Ogre emphasized its point with hand gestures towards the forces of Minth.

Noryen studied the Ogre. The creature wore a combination of hardened leather and fur. Noryen noticed the glint of pieces of metal affixed to the armor. Beside it, standing on its own, a huge studded club had its business end embedded in the ground with the handle up.

As he observed the scene behind the horde, he saw two more Ogres come up out of the draw leading to the canyons behind them. Both of these Ogres wore furs embellished with skulls of various animals. One wore a fur hat fixed with the antlers of a huge deer or moose. When the Ogre turned to look back into the canyon, he was sure it was a moose.

"Shaman," Noryen said while still looking through the piece of glass. "My lord, they are being driven by the Ogres. Two of them are shamans."

"That is what I surmised," Sir Maytok concurred. "Mage Anelia finds it hard to believe Ogres can use magic. I know you witnessed one several years ago, so I wanted you to see them firsthand."

Noryen took his eye from the glass, looked at the mage, and said, "The one I witnessed years ago killed dozens with blue lightning coming from a small skull she held. I was the only one of the scouts to survive. My sergeant and the rest of my squad died that night. The Ogre, which we determined was a she after we finally killed her, was dressed similarly as these two with bones and skulls."

"Blue lightning?" Mage Anelia asked. "Are you certain it was blue?"

"I'll never forget it," Noryen said. "It lit up the night."

"It was not magic, my lord," the mage said, relieved. "The presence of blue means it was a prayer spell, granted by whatever demon the Ogres worship. They will not be able to counter my magic. On the other hand, I cannot counter theirs. Perhaps you should call Brother Nathon and several of his church forward from the wounded camp."

"Excellent idea," the knight commander said. He turned to Squire Marlan. "Ask Brother Nathon if he and several of his fellow clerics will come forward. Ensure he knows of the importance of haste. The horde may surge towards us at any moment."

"At once, sir," the squire said. He wheeled his horse around and left at a gallop. The ranks of archers behind them parted to let him through.

Sir Maytok spoke while Noryen continued to scan the horde. He said, "When they attack, we will finally be rid of them. I believe we can defeat them now because we have the extra cavalry to shore up the right flank. I have received word a contingent from the Mountain Kingdom marches to join us. They will arrive tomorrow after the noon meal if they march through the night. They are traveling the main road, so they are moving as quickly as possible."

"Times like this, I wish the Dwarves rode horses to battle," Noryen said, "or ponies."

"I as well," agreed the knight commander. "Still, the speed of their forced march is impressive. If the horde waits until tomorrow to come forward one last time, we will take the field easily. The addition of five thousand will tilt the scales in our favor."

"I am afraid they won't wait, my lord," Noryen said. He handed the glass back to the mage, its spell worn off. "The shamans are walking towards their flanks. I think they intend to disrupt the cavalry. Trust me when I tell you, the lightning striking among the horses will do just that, my lord."

* * * * *

Chapter Four

S quire Marlan returned a quarter of an hourglass later. With him on a small wagon were two men and a woman. All three wore robes the light blue color of seawater, indicating the order of Saint Minokath, Lord of the Sea. A page rushed to hold the horses while the clerics climbed down from the wagon designed to move injured from the battlefield quickly.

"Sir Maytok," Brother Nathon said, "the young lord says you have need of me."

"I do," confirmed the knight commander. "The horde are led by Ogres. Two of them wear the garb of shamans. They move towards the flanks of their lines now. Sergeant Noryen says they have the ability to cast prayer spells of lightning. You can imagine what it will do to cavalry."

"I can indeed," the cleric said. He turned to Noryen. "My son, I am not questioning you. To lead a squad of the Emperor's Own Scouts, you know your business. Can you tell me if the lightening comes from their hands or from an object?"

Noryen answered. "The one I witnessed held a small skull in her hand. The bolts came from it."

"Transference," Brother Nathon said. The two clerics with him nodded in agreement.

"Can it be countered?" Sir Maytok asked. "Without the cavalry to shore up both ends, some of the horde may swing around and roll up one side."

One of the knights, standing nearby, dismissed the idea with a wave of his hand and said, "Impossible, my lord. Goblins do not possess the discipline to perform a maneuver like that. They are at best, a mob pointed in a direction."

The knight commander turned to answer the challenge to his leadership. The knight he faced had been difficult to work with, much less command. It was never anything outright insubordinate, but it often toed the line.

Before he could speak, his squire spoke up defending him. "Sir Bolnaire, you would do well to remember to whom you speak. Sir Maytok has been chosen to lead the Emperor's forces. You would also do well to remember the military history I'm sure you were taught. Less than fifty years ago, a horde swept across below the Grand Lake and did exactly that. It was two months before the forces could be mustered to drive them back into their mountains."

Noryen raised an eyebrow but stayed silent. Sir Bolnaire turned a shade of red but lowered his head slightly and said, "Yes, my lord." The squire did not correct him on the title. The knight stepped back.

Brother Nathon, oblivious to the power play among the officers, said, "They cannot be countered as some mages may do to others casting magic spells. It does not work with prayer spells."

The cleric smiled at his friend, Anelia, both having spent considerable time in the emperor's castle. He continued. "What we can do is use the very laws of nature our Creator, in His infinite wisdom, has placed upon Kerr."

The two clerics spoke out at hearing this. One quoted, "in infinite wisdom." The other spoke part of a passage from the Book of the One, as well, "All is of the Creator's design, from the deities to dust."

Brother Nathon explained. "Lightning is a powerful thing, destroying what it touches. At times it destroys that which it does not directly touch by traveling across the water. It has happened on ships, ponds, and on rain-soaked surfaces. It is one of the many wonders of Kerr, having have been observed, but never explained. Simply put, lightning travels across water. The skulls transfer it to where they are pointed. If we can manage to wet the skull and the shaman's hand it is possible to divert the path of the lightning back to the Ogre."

"I don't like where this is going," Suzanne whispered to Brind.

Brind wrinkled his nose as if he smelled something unpleasant. "I smell a mission for those with the swiftest horses." He swung a leg over his horse, and stepped down out of the stirrup to work on the offending strap of his saddle.

Calnate and Torbit both dismounted and moved to help him, one holding the horse by the bridle, the other at the saddle. Suzanne watched them, holding the reins of their mounts, content to wait on the guidance of Noryen instead of continuing to listen to the officer's discussions.

* * * * *

Chapter Five

"Here is the plan," Noryen explained. "Suzanne, take Calnate and Torbit and ride for the left flank near the hills. The knight commander has loaned us one of his squires for this mission. I will ride for the right with Brind and Lord Marlan. His horse is exceptionally well bred and is near as fast as ours, despite its warhorse size."

"Are we really to try and hit the Ogre with earthen mugs of water?" Suzanne asked. "Won't it spill as we ride or when we throw them?"

Marlan spoke up. "The clerics are preparing several for each of us now. A thin piece of oiled leather is being tied around the rim of each. It should hold until we need them."

Brind laughed and said, "As many rocks as you throw at us, Suzy, you should hit him right in his hand with the mug."

"Riding for an Ogre," Calnate said, "around the edge of a Goblin horde." He shook his head. "Madness! That's what it is, and we are fools for attempting it." He paused, grinned, and said, "I get first shot at it! I claim first!"

"Not if I beat you to the throw," Torbit countered.

Sergeant Noryen looked at the squire and shrugged. He had no excuse for his squad. They were a tight group and most of the time they tended to relieve stress with fun and competition among themselves. Even if they had never attempted something before, they would find a way to challenge each other to be better at it.

Shortly, the three clerics brought cloth bags with mugs of water in each. The sound of them bumping against each other made Noryen flinch. He accepted his and put his arm and head through the strap. It hung at an angle at his chest, easily available as he rode. The others did the same.

"The mugs contain holy seawater," Brother Nathon explained. "I prayed and was blessed by Saint Minokath, who granted a prayer spell. Once it covers something it will become four times the amount in the mug and not dry up as normal water. It will take nearly twice as long."

"How long will the prayer spell last?" Suzanne asked. She glanced at the other three scouts with a slight smile.

"If the water is not used in two turns of an hour glass, the blessing will fade," the cleric explained. "Why do you ask, daughter? Surely you will be within striking distance by then."

"She wants to keep one to use on one of us later," Torbit answered. "She needs prayer, Brother. Lots of prayer. She torments us with her jokes and unwarranted attacks when we least expect it. We three are innocent men, subject to her cruel sense of humor."

Brind elbowed Calnate and said, "She may be beyond help. Pray for us instead, Brother, for we suffer greatly."

Brother Nathon gave the pretty blond a sideways look, but said nothing. He walked over to the wagon and climbed up with the other two. As they rode back towards the rear area, he glanced again at the scout, unsure if she was as innocent as she looked.

The look on Suzanne's face was enough to cause the squire to look wide eyed at Sergeant Noryen and ask, "What just happened?"

Before Noryen could answer, Suzanne said, in a sweet voice. "Think nothing of it, my lord. It was only the three of them ensuring snakes in their bedrolls some night in the near future, or perhaps a bit of rotted log infested with biting ants."

Torbit and Calnate rode after her with Calnate desperately calling out, "Suzy! It wasn't me! It was them; *they* lied to the Brother! Suzy! You know I hate snakes!"

* * *

An hour later, Noryen led Brind and Marlan through the trees, careful to stay out of sight. They skirted the edge of the open fields as they made their way well ahead their own lines. In the distance he heard the horns again. Five notes. The horde was surging forward, and the Human line was moving to meet them.

The three of them eased their mounts to the edge of the trees. Noryen glanced over at the squire to ensure the cloak they gave him kept most of the bright colors of his mail and tunic from being obvious. They were not completely concealed, as they were mounted, but at least the flashes of bright colors would not be seen by the moving horde in front of them.

As the breeze blew their way, Brind settled his horse, held a hand over his nose, and said, "That's one smell I'll never get used to."

"Aye," agreed Squire Marlan, "it turns the stomach."

The last of the spear-wielding unit passed them more than a bowshot away. The sound of their yelling and growling reached the three men easily. The Ogre was among the last of them, occasionally kicking stragglers or swiping at them with a huge bone club. Their eyes were on the line of Humans coming to meet the rest of the horde towards the center of the field. The cavalry they expected to hit them held back for the time being.

Noryen looked at the others and nodded. He edged his horse past the last of the trees and tapped his horse with both heels. He tapped again harder and leaned forward, rising up slightly in his stir-rups. His well-trained horse broke into a hard gallop. Followed by the others, he veered towards the back of the horde, aiming for the Ogre. The sounds of battle across the field nearly drowned out the sounds of the three horse's hooves striking the ground.

As they got closer, one of the Goblins glanced their way and let out a shriek, pointing at them with his spear. Several others joined in, causing the Ogre to look their way. By this time all three of them had a mug in their hand but were not close enough to hope to hit it. With a bellow, the Ogre turned towards them, club held high.

Several Goblins hurled their spears. Noryen was easily able to veer out of the path of them as they wobbled in flight. They were not made for throwing. In the last few skirmishes, the Goblins had held them to use against mounted men above them, often going after the mount first to disrupt the charge. With only three horses and riders bearing down on them, the Goblins wanted to bring the men down so they could swarm them with numbers.

Brind was the first to hurl his mug. It sailed ahead and landed near the Ogre, breaking against a small misshaped shield of one of the Goblins. True to Brother Nathon's word, the amount of water splashing up and covering several Goblins near it was much more than the mug held. Brind reached for another and threw it, missing again.

The Ogre hesitated, not understanding what was hurled his way. Two more mugs came sailing in. Both missed. The Ogre grabbed a soaked Goblin, picked it up and sniffed. Satisfied it wasn't oil, it threw the Goblin to the ground and took large strides towards the incoming riders. Several Goblins followed.

The three pulled on their reins and veered away before any of the spears could hit them, and before they came within striking distance of the club. Once at a safe distance, they turned back, stopping their horses. Brind, out of mugs, had his bow off his shoulder, and he shot an arrow. It hit the Ogre in its shoulder, enraging it even more. Marlan threw his last mug. It landed at the Ogre's feet, splashing its legs.

Noryen, with the last mug, hurled it as hard as he could, hoping it flew straight and didn't hit low. The mug struck the Ogre in its chest, soaking its furs and leather. The Ogre stopped, and with a huge hand wiped his chest. It looked at its hand, smelled it one more time to be sure it wasn't some type of oil, and reached to its belt. The hand came up holding the skull of an animal, canines evident on it.

With a wicked grin, the monster spoke several words in its own language. The skull glowed blue, and lightning surged from it. The lightning engulfed its hand and ran back up the screaming shaman's arm. As the lightning enveloped the Ogre's head and upper body, the huge beast dropped to its knees, fell to its side, and lay kicking. Several Goblins standing in the wet grass near it spasmed and fell, their bodies rigid as they jerked. Others ran screaming back towards the others. It didn't take long for all of the ones who turned with the Ogre to flee after the moving mass of the rest of the horde.

The skull lay shattered next to the stirring shaman's blackened hand. Squire Marlan jumped from his horse, drew his sword, and with two hands brought the blade down on its neck. It took three blows to remove the huge head. Leaving it with the body, he quickly mounted again, and they rode hard down the edge of the trees back towards the waiting cavalry.

* * * * *

Chapter Six

As the cavalry charged, Noryen and Brind followed the squire on the edge of the formation, and they rode into the mass of Goblins. As scouts, they didn't ride trained warhorses, but they held their own with their longswords and used their horses' agility to dart in and away from groups of Goblins.

Brind cried out in anger when his leg was cut but continued to fight with renewed vigor. Warhorses and their riders fought the four-foot creatures all around them in a controlled chaos. Noryen was amazed at the young lord's ability to strike the Goblins, cutting through spears and killing them, while his horse reared and stomped, seemingly fighting on its own.

Many of the men and women around them had their mounts killed or injured beyond riding. On foot, they fought on in groups of twos and threes as they attempted to keep from being overrun. Eventually they were able to push the spear unit into the rest of the horde, away from the edge of the battlefield. It was at great cost, but the fear of the horde swinging around the flank was over. The battle continued to rage across the width of the field.

Like most large battles, the lines ebbed and flowed. The horde gained ground, only to lose it. On the far side, the foot soldiers pushed the creatures back a bow shot, only to have the Goblins surge back, urged on by several clan leaders screaming and killing some of their own to get their point across.

In the middle of the field, both sides emptied quivers before they clashed. The knight commander, several of his officers, their squires, and few pages deemed ready to fight on horse were the only mounted ones there. As such, they had been the targets of several flights at the onset.

The first couple of flights were pushed away from the commander and those with him, using gusts of wind conjured by Mage Anelia. Once the Goblins reached them, she stood her ground and began casting other spells, killing Goblins by the scores with balls of flames and burning darts which flew from her fingers. Those mounted near her fought on until there was only two remaining on horseback.

After what seemed like an eternity to those fighting for their lives, the Goblin clans began pulling back, flowing around the remaining Ogre as he screamed at them to fight. His huge club sent several flying as he swept it in front of him. The rout increased as more turned and fled. The knight commander, slumping on his horse, instructed the nearest signal soldier to sound the regroup. He knew his forces were too exhausted to pursue across the field.

Leaving the cavalry with a quarter of their starting numbers, Noryen led Brind and Marlan back to the center and the knight commander. Noryen looked across the battlefield, littered with dead and wounded, and shook his head. Both sides had taken devastating losses. The Humans were better fighters, with far superior weapons and shields, but the Goblins made up for it in sheer numbers. He hoped they continued running, down into the canyons, back to where they came from.

Men and women dragged the wounded towards the rear, to the clerics, herbalists, and camp followers. Fires burned with pots of water and herbs as they were treated. Wagons rolled out into the battle area and more wounded were loaded. For some, mercy was given. Any Goblin found alive was put down. Moving among them, young teenage boys and girls collected arrows to bring back to the remaining archers. The other weapons would wait, because the Goblins stopped this side of the canyons.

Noryen and his companions arrived at the command tent to find Sir Maytok being treated. His thigh was cut to the bone, and he had lost a lot of blood. The page beside him, her tunic covered in blood and gore, had a concerned look. His face was pale as he looked up at his squire with a grimace. Brother Nathon placed a hand on the soaked bandage and prayed. There was a blue glow under his palm, and the knight commander lay back, relief on his face, his pain eased.

Brother Nathon turned to the squire. "My lord, Sir Maytok will live. The wound is closed. I can do nothing for his loss of blood. It will be days before he can mount a horse safely. I must go; there are others in need."

"Go, Brother," Marlan said. "Save as many as you can."

The cleric stopped when he noticed the bandage on Brind's thigh. Brind waved him on. "It's not bad, Brother; I can still walk, and I can fight."

Brother Nathon held the flap of the tent open, looking out. He stepped to the side to allow Suzanne, Calnate, and Torbit entry before he left. The three of them showed obvious signs of battle. A handful of hair had escaped Suzanne's pony tail, Calnate had a bandage wrapped around his left forearm, and Torbit's armor was missing pieces of the strips of hardened leather. All had the blood of the creatures on them.

"There you are," Noryen said. The relief was evident in his voice. "Which of you hit the shaman with a mug?"

Suzanne looked at her squad mates before answering. When she turned back to Noryen the look on her face was a mix of disbelief and disgust. She said, "None of them hit."

From the bed, Sir Maytok asked, "Did it wreak havoc among the cavalry? How did they fair?"

"My lord, the unit took many losses, but not from the Ogre and her lightning," Suzanne said quickly. "The losses were from the slimy little beasts and their spears before we killed the lot of them."

"It was the same for our flank," Marlan said with a knowing nod. "The numbers of them were too much."

"Wait," Brind asked. "If you didn't hit with the mugs, how did you keep the lightning from hitting among the horses?"

"We had to dismount," Suzanne explained, "because we would be seen to early. We left our horses in a small draw behind a hill. We stayed low below the waist-high grasses and got as close as we dared. The shaman was behind the Goblins. Well behind. We rose up and each threw a mug, missing the Ogre. Some splashed her feet but no more. She turned towards us as we came out of the tall grasses. We threw again but they landed beyond her, as she was coming fast. I dropped my next mug in my haste, breaking it, and drew my sword. She swung her club, barely missing Calnate as he dove away, breaking his last in the process."

Noryen looked over at Calnate and noticed he was still wet. Suzanne continued, "I blocked the swing at me, and it jarred my teeth. It didn't cause me to drop my sword, but it was close—if I hadn't had a two-handed grip, I would have. It was then I saw the last mug we had go sailing past the shaman. Calnate had his sword out and both of us tried to get close enough to strike, but she had long arms and the bone club. Up close we could see bits of steel had been pounded into it and sharpened. It was a standoff, but then she reached to her waist and pulled the skull from its tie. She held it out, but Torbit fired an arrow that hit her in the forearm."

Calnate added, "She dropped the skull, and I kicked away from her."

"So she wasn't able to use it," surmised Noryen.

"Not exactly," Suzanne answered. "It landed near Torbit, and we kept fighting. Once he told us he wet it, we backed away towards the high grasses as we fought. When she found the skull, she grabbed it, held it out, and spoke. The lightning engulfed her hand, she dropped to her knees, and her whole body shook. It knocked the fur hat and antlers off her head. When the lightening faded, she slumped to the ground. She didn't move so I made sure she was dead."

"Well done," Squire Marlan said. He paused a moment, then he turned back and asked, "How did he wet it?"

Suzanne's face turned the deepest shade of red Noryen had ever seen. His eyes widened at what he heard next.

"My lord," Suzanne stammered. "He, it…"

"Hey!" Torbit exclaimed. "My back was turned while I did it. I do have some manners, you know. What else was I going to do? My water bag was hanging on my saddle on the other side of the hill."

Even Knight Commander Maytok laughed from his bed.

* * * * *

Chapter Seven

Early the next morning, Noryen and his scouts were eating when the sound of three notes sent them running to the commander's tent. The horde was stirring across the field again.

Inside the tent, Sir Maytok was sitting up in his bed. Mage Anelia sat on a stool on the other side of him. His face was still pale, and his hands shook slightly as he sipped from a small mug. Other than Squire Marlan and the knight commander's page, a man and a woman were in the tent, in the typical leather of archers, as well as a young, red-eyed nobleman in chainmail. Noryen didn't know the man.

"Sergeant Noryen," Squire Marlan said, 'will you ask your scouts to step inside? I realize it will be crowded but it is necessary."

When Noryen returned with his scouts, the squire was near the knight commander in whispered conversation. Sir Maytok reached up and put a hand on the young lord's arm. His squire nodded once and clasped the bedridden man's forearm. Squire Marlan left the tent and returned minutes later with a leather backpack. He put it beside the knight commander.

Everyone in the tent remained silent while the squire was gone.

Sir Maytok finally said, "The Goblins' numbers have grown again through the night. They have not the numbers they had yesterday, but they still greatly outnumber the forces we have able to fight."

He paused a moment, looking around, and then continued, "All of my knights and captains are dead or cannot fight due to their wounds. All of them. Young Lord Jonth was the under-captain of the cavalry on our right flank. He will take command of what is left of the unit."

He indicated the two in leather standing beside each other. "These two sergeants will command the remaining archers. I have ordered some to go onto the battle field and retrieve bows from the dead. There are men and women yet capable of shooting at an angle from behind us. They cannot enter the field due to their wounds but they will help at the onset."

The knight commander shifted as he tried to get comfortable. "We must have a leader on the field of battle, one the forces believe in. They are tired, they are hurt, and they are scared. It is only natural, as they know we are gravely outnumbered. Oh, they will fight to the last man and woman, I have no doubt. But...but with someone to rally them, they may yet win the day."

"If we don't hold out until the Dwarves arrive all is lost. They will catch them on the road where they can't form up and slaughter them. The horde will sweep across western Minth, destroying villages and towns, and the numbers killed will be beyond comprehension. By the time the Emperor can gather more forces it may be years, if ever, that the empire is free of them."

He looked up at Squire Marlan and said, "It is time. Not now because we are short of leaders, but because you have earned it. These past two years, you have accomplished every task I have given you. You have grown as a man and a leader. Kneel, Squire Marlan."

Squire Marlan knelt beside the bed. With shaking hands, Sir Maytok reached over and unbuttoned the two black patches indicating the rank of squire from his shoulders. He placed them on the bed and held his hand out. His page handed him his sword.

Using both hands, as it was nearly too heavy for the weakened man, he placed it on one shoulder and then the other, saying, "I dub thee Sir Marlan, Knight of the Minth Empire. Rise Sir Marlan."

Sir Marlan rose and turned to the knight commander. Sir Maytok laid his sword beside him, reached for the pack, and fumbled it open. He pulled out a tunic and handed it to Sir Marlan.

The new knight unfastened his sword belt and handed it to the page. "Will you hold this for me, Page Kalissa?"

"Certainly, sir," Kalissa answered, taking the belt and sword.

Sir Marlan pulled off his tunic of Sir Maytok's colors and put his own on. It had the colors of the Emperor himself—Sir Marlan's father. Noryen nodded in appreciation. The page handed his belt and weapon back to him and he strapped them on. Sir Marlan reached into the pack and pulled out another tunic.

Prince Marlan, turned back to the knight commander and asked, "Maytok, if you will?"

"Yes, my lord," the knight commander answered, "and thank you for this."

Sir Maytok held a hand out toward his page. She stepped over and took her father's hand. There was a question in her eyes.

"Kalissa," he said, "you have been an exceptional page. Never once did you attempt to use your family name and connections while performing your duties. I knew when it became time for you to become a squire, it would have to be to another knight for training. Even though there has been none, I cannot show the slightest appearance of favoritism to my daughter."

He continued, "I thought it would be some time before I had to let you go, but the time is now. You have shown wisdom beyond your years in dealing with others as you treat the soldiers with respect, regardless of their stature. You have shown talent on your horse, on the practice field, and now in battle.'

"Others much older than you did not survive yesterday. It was due to your ability with sword and shield. You stood fighting over Mage Anelia when she became too exhausted to cast another spell."

Prince Marlan added, "It was not without notice by many."

"Thank you," Mage Anelia said, standing briefly. She was still tired, but the sincerity in her thanks was clearly evident. Her eyes glistened as she smiled at the young woman.

Using her hand, her father turned her towards Prince Marlan.

"Page Kalissa," the prince said, "I am offering you the position of Squire to me personally, and as a member of the Emperor's Own. Will you accept?"

The young woman straightened and said, "I will, my lord."

"Your sword?" Prince Marlan asked and held out a hand. He offered the tunic in the other.

Kalissa took off her sword and then her tunic. Her chain mail showed several places where she had been struck; there were undoubtedly bruises under her shirt and britches beneath the mail. She put on the new tunic; it matched the prince's but was a little long. Once she put her sword belt back on, she slid her dagger from its sheath and cut some the bottom of the tunic off to ensure she could move properly.

Realizing she hadn't asked permission to cut the garment, she looked up quickly at her knight, the expression on her face apologetic. The grin she received let her know it was something the prince himself would have done in her place. He reached over and buttoned the black patches on her shoulders.

Those in the tent broke into applause for the two promoted. Brind whistled appreciatively, much to Suzanne's embarrassment. Noryen laughed at her.

Prince Marlan turned to Lord Jonth and said, "These two sergeants will lead on the field of battle today. I am aware you are now a Duke. My condolences on your family's loss. For the empire, I acknowledge your accession, but time is short and you have estates in your duchy in need of ownership. Both of the previous owners perished with no heirs. What say you?"

"I am now the Duke," Lord Jonth agreed as the realization hit him. He pursed his lips, remembering the day before. "My father and brother fought well yesterday; they will be remembered. You are correct, Prince Marlan. I must think of my duchy and my soldiers."

The young duke asked the two archers by name to kneel and dubbed them as an estate lord and lady in his duchy. The scouts started to applaud, but Prince Marlan held up a hand to stop them. They looked around, puzzled.

"When all the new estate lords and ladies have been announced we will applaud again," he explained. "I will ask the five of you to kneel at once, for we must get to our forces and prepare for the upcoming battle."

* * * * *

Chapter Eight

Outside of the tent, Prince Marlan turned to the scouts and said, "Lord Brind, with your wound, I think it's best we keep you mounted as much as possible. Take command of the cavalry on the other flank. You will have several sergeants with experience. They will help you. The soldiers need to see an officer fighting among them."

He turned to Calnate and Torbit. "You two will lead the foot soldiers on our left. There are two units. One of you take the far side, the other the near."

"Lady Suzanne," he said, "take the unit of foot soldiers on the right nearest the cavalry. Lord Noryen will lead the unit closer."

He looked at each of them in turn, holding their eyes for a moment. "The soldiers need officers. They have to know someone is there to make decisions and to fight with them. They need leaders. I have seen how you jest among yourselves, but I know, from the past and recently of your abilities. I know you each would die for the other without hesitation. This is what your soldiers need to see…to know you would do the same for them. Go, and know you have my trust."

* * *

An hour later, the forces of Minth were formed on the edge of the battlefield as the Goblins stirred across the way. Prince Marlan sat atop his warhorse, Mage Anelia beside him on Suzanne's horse. The Mage glanced down at her small spell book, to reassure herself, reached over and put her hand on the prince's throat, and spoke in the ancient language of mage-speak.

Satisfied her spell worked, she nodded at him and rode back behind the archers. As fatigued as she was, her spells would be limited and so she would cast what she was able from behind the lines.

Prince Marlan rode out more than a bowshot and wheeled his horse to face the Minth forces. When he spoke, his voice carried plainly to everyone, including those in the rear at the camps tending to the wounded, and to the wounded, themselves. Behind him, the remaining Ogre and his horde could not hear him, not that they understood the language of Humans, anyway.

"Men and women of Minth. You come from across the Empire. From the seas on the far side, to the lands near us, and everywhere in between. Today...today we fight for those still there. For your families, your mothers, fathers, brothers, and sisters. We fight for our children. For those you have and for those you wish for one day."

Once he knew he had been seen by all those on the edge of the field, he slowly rode towards his forces and continued as every Human listened intently. "We must fight as there will be no sunrise tomorrow if we do not prevail. Even if we do, there will be no sunrise for some, but there will be for your families. This horde will not destroy everything in its path."

Behind him, with a clamor, the Goblin horde surged forward. He ignored them as he walked his horse back towards his forces. As he rode closer, more and more of the soldiers could tell it was Prince Marlan in the colors of the empire. Shouts of his name rippled up and down the line. He pulled his horse up, a stone's throw out front and dismounted. He slapped his horse's rump, and it ran towards the rear between the archers and foot soldiers.

Squire Kalissa walked out to join him. She held her shield and her sword by her side. She faced the enemy and raised them to the ready.

Prince Marlan tuned and faced the horde as well, his hands on his hips.

There was silence among the Minth Forces, and their prince observed the nightmare coming towards them. Prince Marlan drew his long sword, gripped it with two hands, and held it ready above one shoulder, his elbows up.

He spoke and every Human ear heard his words. "They come, but they will go no farther. We will. Hold. The. Line."

The thousands of men and women behind him cheered as one, the noise loud enough that the Goblins heard it, causing them to slow for a moment until their clan leaders and the huge Ogre striding behind them urged them forward.

* * *

For Noryen, the battle was a blur. He moved forward once the archers finished with flight after flight of arrows, along with the occasional fireball that landed among the advancing horde. The sound of battle rang around him as he fought desperately. His long sword flashed as he killed Goblin after Goblin and parried against short swords, spears, and small warped axes. Inspired, his soldiers fought like possessed men and women all around him. Many of them fell.

It was the same, up and down the line, as his scouts urged their troops forward into the onslaught. The sound and smell of battle overpowered the senses until each was in a world of their own against the nearest Goblins. In a desperate fight to survive, it was kill or be killed. There was no other option. The horde pushed but could not move the forces of Minth as the battle raged on, each side taking losses.

Near noon, the numbers of Goblins began to tell, and foot by foot, the lines moved back towards the tree line and the wounded. Noryen heard a cheer from the wounded as five thousand Dwarves trotted past them onto the field of battle and spread left and right, their hammers and picks flashing in the sunlight as they joined and pushed the horde back. The army from the Mountain Kingdom bordering the southern border of Minth had arrived, and the tide was turned.

As most of the Goblins died across the battlefield, many were piled around Prince Marlan and his squire as they cut through the horde. The vile creatures still living split and moved away from the two of them, leaving a path for the Ogre to reach them. He strode up, confident he would crush the leader of the Humans. His horde was finished, but he would kill this one, at least.

Slowly the clash of steel on iron diminished until there was only the sound of the wounded and horses. All turned towards the center of the field. Some of those on the far sides moved towards the center, herding the muttering Goblins as they went. Many helped the wounded while others watched.

Without pausing, the huge Ogre stepped forward and swung his studded club. It dug deep where Prince Marlan had been standing. The prince danced to the side, his sword flashed, and he cut the Ogre's arm. The Ogre kicked out and dealt a glancing blow with a huge boot, spinning the prince away. The dance was on as they fought; the Ogre towered over the Human, yet he was unable to match Prince Marlan's speed. It stretched on, neither with a true advantage.

Occasionally a Goblin or three would dart in, thinking to help the Ogre, but Squire Kalissa was quick to dispatch them with her sword or the occasional blow with the edge of her shield. She moved around the two, fighting a dance of her own, until the Goblins nearby realized it was sure death to attempt it.

Finally, the Ogre tired, and Prince Marlan dealt a crippling cut to the back of one knee. The Ogre fell and did not have a chance to recover before a series of strikes ended the fight. At once, the forces of Minth turned on the creatures and ended their threat permanently. The beasts were not thinking beings in the sense they deserved quarter, and so none was given. Even one left alive would attack, given the slightest opportunity.

The day ended with everyone helping tend to the wounded. Wounds were bound in the field, mercy was given when needed, and others were carted off in wagons. All five scouts survived with minor wounds and were able to help. Brind brought some of the cavalry and their horses to aid. Prince Marlan and Squire Kalissa made more trips than they could count, carrying Humans and Dwarves to the rear to the Human and Dwarven clerics, herbalists, and healers.

* * * * *

Chapter Nine

Three months later...

The Emperor of Minth pushed his plate away, and servants scrambled to move it for him, and each of them were unsurprised as the most powerful man in the empire thanked them for it with a smile. He, like his son, took no one for granted.

He continued explaining to his son, "I have instructed Duke Jonth to ensure his new estate owners are allowed to combine their estates. He was unaware they were betrothed when he made them nobility. They will own the corner of his duchy and the kingdom bordering the sea."

The Emperor turned to his right and asked, "Anelia, what will you do now?"

"I think I will go to Gar-Noth, to the new Halls of Magic being built," Mage Anelia said. "The idea of a center for the learning of magic is intriguing."

He looked up and down the table at his guests, then turned to his son and asked, "What will you do with your kingdom?"

The Emperor of Minth had announced, at this dinner, he was giving Western Minth to his son to rule as he saw fit. In a grand ceremony planned the next week, he would step down and become only a king. The empire was too vast to rule and protect for one man. It was time to make it smaller, and offering his son a large portion was an easy decision.

The people of the western part of the empire knew of the Prince's deeds during the invasion of the horde. The story didn't take long to circulate among the entire empire, but those in the west were the ones in the path of the horde, and it resonated more with them. Along with the prince, his officers were spoken of everywhere, as well.

"It will not be a kingdom, father," answered Prince Marlan, surprising everyone.

"What will you do?" his father asked again. He was genuinely curious. He knew his son was no fool, so whatever was planned would be interesting.

Prince Marlan looked at each of the former scouts and said, "I will divide it into six equal baronies. I will take the one bordering Minth. Lord Noryen will take the one bordering the canyons. Lady Suzanne, Lord Calnate, Lord Brind, and Lord Torbit will have the others."

There was silence in the hall. He continued. "I will not rule over them. We will be equals. I believe it will be called the Baronies West."

* * * * *

Kevin Steverson Bio

Kevin Steverson is a retired veteran of the U.S. Army. He is a published songwriter as well as an author. He lives in the northeast Georgia foothills where he continues to refuse to shave ever again. Trim…maybe. Shave…never! When he is not on the road as a Tour Manager he can be found at home writing in one fashion or another.

* * * * *

Follow Kevin Online

Website: www.kevinsteverson.com

Instagram: kevin.steverson

Facebook: https://www.facebook.com/kevin.steverson.9

Twitter: @CallMeCatHead

* * * * *

Tyler Ackerman Bio

Tyler Ackerman is a singer/songwriter and an international touring artist. He is one half of the duo Cypress Spring. He lives in Ohio, where he and Melissa are raising their two boys. A fan of the fantasy genre, his first foray into writing stories as opposed to songs is a collaboration with the novel Burnt.

# # # # #

What's in a Name
by Rob Howell

The horse reared, and its hooves flashed before he could dodge away. They hammered into him, ripping open his neck and chest. He reached up to stanch the blood, but it just flowed through his fingers. He saw death and knew none would remember his name.

That thought saddened him, but then—

I don't remember my name!

He fought against the terror. Raised every weapon he could muster against it. It defeated him easily. He sank into its darkness.

Then voices battered his ears, waking him and filling his head with pain. At first, all he could do was catch his breath and stop his heart from racing. Only then could he recognize the voices and understand their words.

"There's nothing wrong with the foal," said Bedarth, *liffrea* and counselor to the cyning. "Nothing wrong with his hooves or any bones. His teeth are fine. Nothing's causing him pain."

"Then he's just a foul-tempered brute," replied Cynric, second of that name, son of Alfred, and Cyning of Middlemarch.

"Yes." Bedarth chuckled. "Have you decided on his name yet?"

"No. Every time we try something, he just kicks or bites."

"Every creature should have a name," said Bedarth.

He's right.

"He'll pick his name soon enough."

"When the World Tree decides."

"Yes." Cynric sighed. "What has the World Tree decided about Edward?"

He means me! I'm Edward, son of Aethelred.

A wave of nausea and pain followed his joy. He leaned over the side of his pallet and did all he could to avoid retching. After several hard swallows, he held it back. Now only the headache remained. He sat up, which brought another wave of nausea. He was ready for it, though, and after a moment it subsided. He opened his eyes. The candles in the room, dim though they were, took their turn to attack his senses. His eyes would not quite focus on anything.

"He's not ready yet," said Bedarth.

"It's been a full sixday."

Six days since what?

"Yes," replied Bedarth. "But he's still not ready, and it may be many more days. Head injuries are tricky."

"You're a *liffrea*. Use your magic," the cyning snapped.

"Life-lord or not, head injuries are *tricky*."

Cynric muttered softly.

"He's no danger to you now," said Bedarth.

"When will he be?"

"He may never be. He's an honorable man."

"That's what makes him dangerous to me."

"He has a greater duty, though he knows it not yet."

Despite another wave of nausea, Edward rose and opened the door. He shielded his eyes from the brighter light in the other room. "What's this greater duty?"

The two men turned to him.

The taller smiled. "Why, to serve the World Tree. As you have always done."

"That's no answer, Bedarth," Edward snapped.

"But it is the truth."

Edward turned to Cynric. "Why would I ever be a danger to you? I have always served you and your son according to my sworn oaths."

Cynric glanced at Bedarth, who shook his head slightly. The cyning cocked his head sadly at Edward. "Because you are indeed an honorable man, as was your father, and your father's father."

"Where is Penwulf?" Edward demanded. "I must go to his side."

Bedarth turned toward a pot of mulled cider by the fire. He took a mug from the mantle and reached for the ladle.

"Stop that and tell me," Edward snapped.

Bedarth ignored him and filled the mug. "Here, my boy."

"What is going on?"

"Some Imperial cinnamon just arrived. You'll like this, my boy." He held out the mug again.

With little grace, Edward took the mug. "But—"

"Sit down, relax, and drink. While you're doing so, I'll do the same, and then I'll answer your questions."

"No! Tell me where Penwulf is. I'll not relax until I know where to find my oath-sworn lord."

Bedarth considered.

"Enough," stated Cynric. "I'll go get your answer."

He soon returned, followed by his armsmaster, Hlodowic. The grizzled man's crutch thumped along the wooden floor. In his other hand, he held a sack. Without looking at Edward, he dumped its contents on a table.

Edward's mind swirled as he recognized the helm given to him by his father on the day Edward swore to be Penwulf's man. Without thinking, he lifted his left arm as if using a shield to defend against a blow aimed at his head...

* * *

A sword glanced off the iron edge of Edward's raised shield. He pulled the shield down to deflect the spear aimed at his thegn-brother Theodoric's ribs and brought his sword over his head to block the next strike. With the recoil of the impact, he flipped his wrist over and drove the blade through Ivarr's cheekplate and into his jaw.

He would have spared a sad thought that Ivarr would never bore him with talk of women again, but Dagmar stepped into the gap. He slashed again, more to keep her off-balance than with any hope of harm. She pressed in close enough that Edward punched her face with his shield boss.

She staggered back. He stepped in, slashed left to cut the tip off the spear aimed at Theodoric, and then right to force Dagmar back again. That step put him next to Leofric, but the man didn't notice as he started another thrust at Theodoric. Edward slashed through Leofric's chain hauberk.

I told Leofric his single-minded focus would kill him someday.

The regret disappeared when Edward saw Hlodowic's axe rising and striking out of the corner of his eye.

"Shift over, Theodoric! Ware Hlodowic's axe!"

Edward felt Theodoric move, and he followed to cover his back.

But Theodoric was too slow, no matter that Hlodowic could only wield his axe with one hand, using the other for his crutch. The armsmaster slid his axe past Theodoric's guard, ripping a long gash into hauberk and chest. Theodoric crumpled to the ground.

Wolf take him! Edward jumped over and slashed at Hlodowic's crutch. Hlodowic nimbly shifted it out of place and struck back. Edward's shield shook at the crash.

Then Penwulf was there, stabbing past Edward's shield with his spear. One of his thrusts grazed just past Hlodowic, who shifted ever so slightly out of the way. Edward tried to follow up but leaned back instead at Hlodowic's return strike.

Edward twitched enough to slide a slashing blade that he had not consciously seen past his head. He looked left to his father, who had led the right side of Cynric's line.

"Penwulf, get out of here! I think the left has collapsed!" Edward shouted to his lord.

Penwulf replied with another thrust at Hlodowic, which the armsmaster blocked easily.

I will make them regret training me, he thought. With the precise footwork demanded by Hlodowic and swift strikes taught by his father from the moment he could lift a blade, he slew two more close friends, and wounded others.

He snapped his blade at Hlodowic's cheek, and the older man shifted his axe handle over to block it. Edward's sword struck the iron-reinforced shaft. He sent its keen edge at Hlodowic again, with the same result, but simultaneously sliding his shield back to his left to block the thrust his father aimed at his ribs.

Then he twisted his body and chopped down at his father. To Edward's surprise—later, he would guess his father was tired from the long battle—the blow ripped through his father's neck at the shoulder.

His father's face filled with pain, and he collapsed, dying at Edward's feet. His blood slid along the water-pattern of the sword he had also presented Edward on his oathday.

Edward's eyes locked on the crimson tendrils, but he had no time for that, nor for the memories filling his mind. He attacked Hlodowic again, but the armsmaster anticipated the strike and blocked it contemptuously.

However, the left wing had, indeed, collapsed, and his father had been merely the harbinger of their doom. Edward slashed and moved and blocked and thrust until his world exploded with a ringing strike from Hlodowic's axe from an angle Edward never expected.

The last thing he saw was his father smiling at him with lifeless eyes.

* * *

Edward opened his eyes and fell to his knees. The cup of cider slid from his hand to crash on the floor, leaving a shard-filled puddle. He stared at the remains of his helm. Hlodowic's axe had sundered its heavy bronze boar crest and left a sharp indentation from left to right across the steel top plates.

"The smith who made your helm learned well from Weyland," grunted Hlodowic. "Penwulf's smith paid less attention."

Edward looked up at the other two.

"Yes, my boy," said Bedarth, "Penwulf died on top of you."

"I slew him with the return swing after I felled you," said Hlodowic.

Edward looked at his hands. "Then I am foresworn…"

"You're not foresworn," snapped Bedarth.

"I am." His eyes hardened. "Unless…"

"I shall make no mistake this time if you feel you must strike at my lord," growled Hlodowic.

"If you slay me, then I would not be dishonored." Edward rose.

"Your oath to the World Tree would be foresworn if you strike at Cynric now," said Bedarth.

Edward snarled at the *liffrea*, "I swore no oath to the World Tree."

"But you did, my boy. Every time you prayed to it, you reaffirmed that oath. Have you not long accepted that your time will come when *it* deems your branch has grown, and not when *you* wish it? If you tell me you have not, then I know you are truly foresworn."

"But—"

"You are not yet healed." All three turned to look at Cynric. "That is your task, Bedarth. I don't argue Edward's point. You shall give him his health that he may fulfill all of the debts he believes he owes." He turned to Hlodowic. "As for you, his father served me well, and he served my son well. If the World Tree demands it, I shall face him myself and gladly pay whatever price she demands of me."

"And where will he stay? I'll not have him in the armsmen's hall!" snapped Hlodowic.

"He'll stay here," said Bedarth.

"Leeching off the cyning, no doubt."

"He'll do chores for me. He'll earn his keep." Bedarth smiled. "I would not dream to tell you how you keep the armsmen's hall. That is between you, your lord, and the World Tree. But at the same time, this is *my* domain, and I will keep it as I choose."

Hlodowic glowered.

"Yes, you will," agreed Cynric. "But I have not yet asked you, Edward. You may choose to leave. I will give you food, a horse, and all that you need."

Edward blinked. "I…" He cleared his throat. "If Bedarth will heal me, I will stay and do those tasks he requires." He spoke to the floor. "When I am healthy, though, I *will* fulfill my oath."

"Excellent." Bedarth smiled again.

"Then it is agreed." Cynric started to leave, but turned back. "And Hlodowic, you shall train him as you did before. You will tell us both when he is ready. Truly ready. I will have your oath upon this."

"That I swear." With hard eyes never leaving Edward, Hlodowic growled, "This also I swear. He shall not survive the slaying of you, should that come to pass."

* * *

Edward enjoyed the weight of armor and weapons, even if the new helm felt wrong, and his feet seemed to have forgotten all the years of training. He was out of balance with every swing. A small part was the sword, which was not the sword his father gave him. No one had told him of its fate, and he had not yet asked.

The bigger part, though, was lack of practice. He stumbled around the field, eagerly pursued by Ealdwine, nephew to Cynric and son of one of Middlemarch's most prominent ealdormen. He filled every blow at Edward with scorn and hate, landing more than a few on Edward's heavy scale armor.

Whatever bruises his ribs earned would be nothing compared to the spike each impact sent through his head.

"Hold!" snapped Hlodowic.

The youth swung once more with his blunted blade. Edward's tired arm was too slow to lift his shield to completely block it. The blade glanced off the shield's edge and then off the top of his helm.

Edward fell to his knees to catch his breath from the pain.

Hlodowic stomped over, grabbing Ealdwine by the front of his armor. "When I say 'hold,' you will damn well hold, or I will see to it you never spend another moment on my practice field."

The youth started to protest. "But I—"

"I don't care, Ealdwine. I don't care what son of Loki stands before you or who your father is. You will do what I say on this field. Understand?"

Ealdwine started to protest again, but stopped at Edward's laugh.

"Do it, boy. Test Hlodowic. I did, and you see where I am."

"Keep to yourself, kinslayer."

"Keep quiet, both of you," snarled Hlodowic. He turned on Edward. "And what in One-Eye's name was that? Did my axe rob you of all the training we gave you?"

Edward rose, still panting.

"Well?" demanded the armsmaster. "You going to argue with me, too?"

"No. You're right, I lost all focus."

"You will *not* embarrass your father by doing that again, or I'll make sure you *can't* ever swing a sword again."

"Then I'd better try again."

Edward still felt off, but after the next round of sparring, it was Ealdwine stumbling away, ears ringing.

* * *

Two days later Edward removed his helm, gasping for breath. Sweat dropped from his brow. He looked up to see Hlodowic glaring at him.

Edward sighed. "Still wretched, I know. I can't keep my shield up, and I'm winded far too quickly. Then my footwork gets messy, meaning I can't swing a sword right."

Hlodowic's glare lessened not, but he said, "Only the gods would take the blow I gave you without harm lasting many days."

Edward's eyes widened. "Thank you."

"Hmmph." Hlodowic turned to leave.

"Hlodowic?"

"What?"

"Show me what you did."

The armsmaster glared at him. Eventually he said, "I felled a kinslayer."

"Yes, you did. I think about that every day." Edward looked at his hands, before turning his gaze back on the armsmaster. "But you did something strange to hit me, and I couldn't block it."

"You blocked many blows that day. At least four of Cynric's men were aiming for you at the end."

Edward shrugged. "Yes, but I don't think I could've blocked your blow if it had just been you and me. It was...different."

Hlodowic considered. "It's no great secret, I suppose. I've had over two decades since I lost my leg. I've been fighting with that axe in one hand ever since."

"Show me," commanded Edward.

Hlodowic lifted his axe and sent it dancing.

"Right there."

The armsmaster stopped, holding the axe extended, perfectly still and stable despite its weight. Then he nodded. "Yes, that twist. Oddly, it's something I could never do when I had two hands. I only figured it out when I learned how to fight with only one. More like using a sword than an axe, though with longer reach."

"The gods give as they take away."

Hlodowic stared at Edward for a long moment, then finally nodded. "Get cleaned up. You're a mess, and it would not do for you to irritate Bedarth. And make sure to oil that armor."

"Yes, armsmaster."

* * *

Edward stopped short when he reached the practice field. His sister Aethelflaed awaited him, fully armed and armored.

"Aethelflaed—"

"Hlodowic said I'm not allowed to kill you yet, but I *will* make you hurt," she snarled. Edward barely had time to raise his shield.

Worse than the impact of her blows was the way she moved. He knew it matched his own. Their father had trained them both, after all.

She maneuvered him around the field, striking at the open targets their father had taught would appear. Even knowing they were coming, he could only block some of them.

He jumped back as a slash swept right at his groin.

She took advantage of his lack of balance to hammer him in the helm.

He reeled back, eyes swirling, forcing back the familiar nausea.

She chased him, sword snapping at any available target.

He frantically retreated in a circle, mostly deflecting her blows.

Mostly.

Suddenly she took a breath, and Edward seized the chance to regain his balance.

He started throwing the same patterns, but he kept his distance and used his longer arms to keep her from closing the range. He circled sometimes to the right, sometimes the left, eluding her advance.

Finally, his temper flared. He stepped into her next charge, bashing his shield into hers, driving her steel shield edge ripping through her cheek. He followed with a hammer blow at her now exposed sword arm, and a sharp *crack* sliced through the crisp morning air.

"Hold!" Hlodowic yelled.

Edward dropped sword and shield and knelt next to his sister. "Aethelflaed, I'm so sorry."

"May the Great Wolf feed on your heart," she hissed.

"May the Great Wolf feed on you both." Hlodowic slammed the butt of his axe onto a pavestone. "Edward, take your sister to Bedarth."

"I can go myself," she snarled.

"And carry your arms? Or do you propose to leave them sitting in the grass?" He helped her up. "Do as I say, lass."

Edward put his training arms back on the rack and returned. She almost hissed at him when he picked up her sword and shield.

Neither said anything as they walked to Bedarth's house.

The *liffrea* looked up when they entered. "Aethelflaed..." Then he took in the way she held her arm and the expression on Edward's face. "Sit here," he commanded.

As she complied, he turned to Edward. "Go get my bag. Idiot!" Aethelflaed hissed.

The old man turned his glare to her. "As if I don't know you're the one who started all of this. Plain as the sky's gem that you convinced Hlodowic to let you spar this morning, before we knew you were here. I've no doubt you surprised him. Then you attacked him until he lost his temper." He glanced back and forth at the two. Both avoided the *liffrea*'s eyes.

Edward brought the bag over.

Bedarth pulled item after item from the bag, laying each next to him, muttering, "I wonder if it's possible some Loki-spawn stole your parents' true children and replaced them with you. Neither of them would've been dumb enough for this sort of folly, yet here you both are, as stupid as Loki with mistletoe!"

Then he put his hands on her arm, closed his eyes, and focused. Sweat beaded his brow. Then he drew a long, shuddering breath.

"It's a clean break. You'll not have infection, and I've started the bone knitting back together, but it'll still be weeks before I want you wielding a sword again."

She glared at Edward and struck her cruelest blow. "At least he didn't kill *me*."

* * *

Several dozen mail-clad warriors turned to face Edward as he entered the meadhall.

He stopped. Usually at this time of morning, the hall held only a few people, but not on this day.

Aethelflaed was one, her right arm in a splint, the other holding a short spear. The others stood and stared with cold, hard eyes. None unsheathed a sword or grabbed one of the many spears leaning against the oak-timber wall, but all seemed ready to do so at a moment's notice.

Edward turned away. When he reached the far door leading to the practice field, he glanced back. The warriors, who all remained dear to him, stood ready to follow with grim, hateful looks on their faces. He left.

Outside, he shivered at the bite in the autumn morning air as he made his way down to the field, followed by the warriors.

Cynric stood on the field, footprints clearly marked in the frosted dew on the grass. He wore his lamellar armor and his boar-crested helm. His breath fogged in the cold, clear air. He had his shield slung along his back, a sword at his side, and another sword, sheathed, in his hands.

"Hlodowic says you're ready," said the cyning. He held out the sheathed sword.

Edward shook his head. "I don't know."

"You're better than you were last time I trained you." Hlodowic stomped out. He, too, wore armor, his axe crooked over his shoulder. "You're ready," he snarled. He grabbed the handle of his axe. "As am I."

"Here's your sword." Cynric held out the sheathed blade, belt wrapped around it.

"I'm not worthy of that blade."

Cynric held it out again. "If you're going to slay me, it should be with the steel your father, my thegn, gave you."

"The World Tree would approve, if it thought such a deed should be done," said a voice from behind Edward. He turned around to see Bedarth standing next to the warriors. The *liffrea* grimaced. "Though I don't believe She does."

"I need to fulfill my oath to Penwulf."

"You *did*, lad. You fulfilled it. You fell before he died."

"And yet I still live, and he does not."

"But—"

"Be done with it, Bedarth," said Cynric. "I said it before and I'll say it again. I agree with Edward. That he was not at fault, that he did all he could and then some, that his father died with a smile on his face, none of that changes the fact that he swore to die before my son, and he did not."

Edward nodded, face grim and set.

"Your *faithless* son," snapped Hlodowic.

"Penwulf's failings are his to answer before the Victory-Judge. Woden alone will decide his fate. Edward's oath, though, brooks no argument. He swore to serve Penwulf, and he did, just as his father swore to serve me. Do you think Aethelred wanted to fight against Edward? He did not, but he never shirked his duty. His son is the same sort."

Cynric held out the sword once more. "So I stand here, offering the steel your oaths earned you, once as a youth, and now again as a man."

Edward took the scabbard and unsheathed the blade, staring at the water-patterned steel. Someone had cared for it in the sixdays since the battle, as it bore the iridescent sheen of oil, and a keen edge. He put the blade back in the scabbard and belted it around his waist.

Bedarth opened his mouth again, but halted at the look on Cynric's face. "Fools," he muttered.

Hlodowic said nothing, but lifted his axe off his shoulder.

"Pick the shield that suits you, Edward." Cynric gestured at a line of round, oaken shields lining the field. "Whatever happens, there is much to be done today. The measures must be set before the milling, and we must start training the new foals. It would be well to get this business completed." With that, he buckled his helm and slid his shield around to the front.

Edward went to the line of shields. He picked one painted in blue and yellow quarters. Stepping out on the field, he drew his sword. It felt right in his hand.

Cynric tapped the metal edge of his shield twice with his sword. "Begin."

The two circled each other. Cynric stepped in, but merely lifted his shoulder in a feint before stepping back out of range.

Edward's breathing settled, and this time he advanced. Cynric blocked Edward's strike at his head with the shield's edge and blocked his next strike with his sword.

They circled again, then stepped forward at the same time. The shock of their colliding shields prevented either from following with an effective shot, but Cynric continued to press. He pushed Edward's shield clear, and Edward jumped out of range.

Cynric laughed. "I've not forgotten everything your father taught me."

Edward charged in, bashing with his shield and swinging a long, complex series of blows. Cynric blocked them all, with the exception of two, where Edward's quickness forced him to withdraw out of range.

Eventually, Edward stepped back, breathing heavily, covering his retreat with his shield.

Fool! You still don't have the same stamina you once had.

But the shock of the cyning's steel on his shield did not follow. Instead the cyning stood apart, waiting.

Edward suddenly realized Cynric had not swung a single blow in the exchange. Nor at any time before. He had simply defended himself. Muttering rose from the warriors behind him.

"Do you wish to die?" Edward snapped.

"Not at all."

"Then fight!" Edward stepped in, again pressing hard. Again, Cynric blocked and eluded, refusing to strike back.

"What are you thinking?" asked Edward after the flurry.

"You swore an oath, and you think you have to slay me to fulfill it. I, too, swore oaths."

"Then why do you not fight?"

"My oaths do not include slaying you."

"Even your oath to the World Tree?" demanded Edward.

"Especially to Her."

"Why? I can't slay myself, so you shouldn't be able to just allow me to kill you."

"Have you given me a scratch yet?"

"No, but—"

"I will defend myself. Nor do I doubt the risk. But just as you feel you must strike at me, I feel I cannot strike back."

"But—" Tears streamed from his eyes. "I can't. Not like this."

Cynric sheathed his sword and moved next to Edward. "Can't what?"

"I can't just cut you down." He looked at the cyning, sword at his side.

The cyning shook his head.

"Please," begged Edward.

"I will not strike against you. You served my son honorably, as your father served me. My oaths demand that I reward you, not slay you."

His sword slipped from his hand. He fell to his knees next to it. "What am I to do? How can I ever regain my honor?"

Bedarth knelt next to him. "You'll do whatever the World Tree asks of you."

"What could she want of a kin-slaying oath-breaker like myself?"

"I don't know; she hasn't told me. I do know that she has something else for you to do. Something other than throwing yourself on Cynric's sword or Hlodowic's axe."

"I—" Edward looked up to see his sister regarding him, not with hate, but with clear eyes reflecting hard thoughts. "Now I have wasted my father's death."

"Wasted? I think not. I went to your father on the eve of the battle. I offered him a chance to lead the rear guard. He almost punched me. " Cynric laughed. "I should have known not to insult him. He would have killed you and trusted the wisdom of the Victory-Judge, and I am sure he tried to do just that."

The cyning squatted next to Edward. "But I think he is in Valhalla now, regaling everyone with the skill of his son." He glanced to Aethleflaed. "Of both his children. He awaits you there."

"Better hurry before he drinks all One-Eye's mead," said Hlodowic.

Edward shook his head. "It is all so simple for you."

Cynric and Bedarth shared a look.

"Come, Edward," said the *liffrea*. "Let's get you cleaned up. The cyning has much to do."

When they reached his house, Bedarth hurried inside. "Close the door, swiftly. These cold mornings sink to my bones. There's some mulled cider on the fire. Fill my cup while I tidy up."

Edward said nothing, but slowly did as he was bid.

"Go get me water so I can warm it for a bath." He held out a pair of buckets.

Edward completed the task in silence. By midday, he had cleaned himself, his clothes, and his weapons. His sword had taken the longest, for he kept staring at the swirling pattern.

After lunch, Bedarth stacked a pile of large books in front of him. "It's probably past time for me to begin your studies."

Edward narrowed his eyes. "What studies?"

"What will you do with the rest of your life?"

"I hadn't thought of it."

"I have."

"And what have you decided."

"Would Cynric accept your oath?"

"What? Uh…"

"The answer is yes. He trusts and values you, as he showed on the field. He knows you counselled Penwulf against his chosen course, but stood by his side nonetheless."

"That matters not."

"Not at all. Cynric would gladly accept your oath, but he can't. Few others of his warband would accept you. You saw that as well."

"As they should not."

"No other lord in the Seven Kingdoms would accept your oath. They don't know you as Cynric does, and they would wonder. All they would know is that you raised your sword against him, and in so doing slew your father. Some will think you are nithing."

"I am."

"Cynric does not believe so. Nor does Hlodowic."

"Very well. No lord will have me. Then what else is there?"

"Do you want to leave the Seven Kingdoms? There are places you could go. There are lords in Periaslavl who would both value and trust your sword arm. Any captain from the Western Isles would accept you on their ship. Your skills are worthy enough to earn a place in Makhaira's Imperial Guard. And there are places farther to the east where you could go."

"I don't know." Edward hesitated. "I've lived by my sword since my father put a blade in my hand. Look where it's gotten me."

"It is more than you realize, lad."

"Be that as it may, I don't want to serve a lord who would accept a warrior without honor."

"I agree. Even so, I do not think your time as a warrior is complete, though it is not all you will be."

"You have ideas."

"Yes." Bedarth sipped from his cup. "I can train you to be more than a swordsman, though I will insist you continue to train with Hlodowic."

"What would you teach me?"

"Languages. History. The world. Anything that crosses my mind."

"What must I do?"

"The first thing you must do is to look at everything. Look and feel and listen and smell and taste. Then, when you have seen all there is to see, you must look again."

"That makes no sense."

"It will, lad. It will." Bedarth pushed a book in front of Edward. "We will start with this poem."

By the end of it, Edward was sobbing.

"Almost as if the poet wrote it about you, isn't it?" asked Bedarth.

Edward nodded.

"'Alas for the byrnied warrior. Alas for the bright cup. Alas for the honor-hopes of kinsmen.' So clear how the poet said it." Bedarth sighed. "It is our hope of honor that we have lost greatest of all. Penwulf's treason hurt everyone, even if he was defeated. Even if his death will ultimately, I suspect, prove better for Middlemarch than had he succeeded Cynric. He never learned patience. He never learned to look once, much less look again, and our people suffered because of it."

"What do you mean?"

"On the face of it, he was correct. He was the heir, and the title of Mearcweard was his by right."

"Yes."

"Then why did Cynric not give him that title?"

Edward sighed. "Bestowing the title brings with it its own power."

"Exactly, and more than you know. It brings with it not simply the right to muster the fyrd along the marches. The title itself has Line magic intertwined with it."

"It's magical on its own? How?"

"That's a lesson for another day, though I will teach you all I know about how magic works. But you must know it follows its own rules. Penwulf never looked again at what that meant."

"What is the title's magic?"

"It gives courage and pride to the warriors following it. However, each day after it's bestowed, that power lessens. Eventually it becomes simply another title, until it is withdrawn and bestowed upon another at their time of need."

"I knew there was more to it. Penwulf scorned every suggestion to wait and let Cynric give him the title in good time."

"His greed and jealousy were all the more because he knew of the magic. I was there several times when Cynric explained his reasons. But Cynric's rule has been wise, and even those across the marches appreciated him."

"Meaning there hasn't been a need for a marchwarden."

"Exactly, yet Penwulf's desire to possess that magic grew every day." Bedarth sighed. "He was always fascinated by magic."

"I wish he'd been some sort of kurios. Had he possessed some magical talent—"

"He would have still broken faith at some point, I think. These histories—" Bedarth waved at the books and codices, "—are littered with souls such as Penwulf. Rare are their successes."

Edward looked at the poem before him. "'Alas for the honor-hopes of kinsmen.'" He looked up, tears trailing down his face. "Alas for the honor-hope of *this* kinsman."

Bedarth wrapped his arm around the younger man and held him while he wept.

* * *

"What a strange word."

"Ofereode," said Bedarth with a chuckle.

"I've read everything I can in Sevenish and never seen it anywhere else."

"Over-went?"

"Yes." Bedarth shrugged. "This poem was ancient when someone finally wrote it down. Given the context, most people say the line basically means, 'That went away, so may this as well.'"

"The poet's name is 'dear one?'"

"Deor, yes, so he says. Interestingly, though, in older dialects 'deor' can also mean 'ferocious' or 'bold as a wild beast.'"

"How in One-Eye's name did a word come to mean both 'dear' and 'ferocious?'"

"You'll have to ask Woden when you get to Valhalla." Bedarth laughed.

The door opened abruptly, and they spun to see Ealdwine, gasping for breath.

He blurted, "Bedarth. Need you. Corral."

"Someone hurt?"

Ealdwine nodded.

"Badly?"

The youth nodded again.

Bedarth rose and pointed at a pouch hanging on a hook and two large cases. "Edward, bring those."

They hurried to the corral to see a wall formed in two ranks, shields in front, and spears pointing from behind them at a tall, young, chestnut horse pawing, snorting, and circling around. A rope dangled around his neck. Periodically he jumped in to snap a hoof off a shield before darting away.

Behind the shield wall, a crumpled figure lay screaming in the dirt at Cynric's feet.

Bedarth rushed forward. "Get out of my way. All of you except the cyning, go find something to do." He knelt at the man's side. "Edward, put the cases there, then hand me the pouch."

Edward complied.

"What happened?" asked Bedarth.

"Loki-damned brute not only threw him, but stomped all over him before we could drive him back." Cynric sighed. "Such a shame.

I had high hopes of that horse. His sire and dam are two of my favorites."

"Oh, he's *that* horse. Why weren't you more careful?" demanded the *liffrea*.

"We were." Cynric sighed again. "At least, we thought we were."

Edward locked eyes with the horse, who whinnied and kicked out again. "He is impressive."

"The dam was the fiercest battle-steed I've ever seen. The sire was meaner, though not as good in a battle. No help but to kill this one, though. He's thrown every rider we've tried on him."

Slowly a broad smile grew on Edward's face. He picked up a stick from the side of the corral.

Bedarth looked up. "Where are you going, boy?"

"To see if I can save that horse. If I can ride him, then he'll live."

"You swore an oath to the World Tree not to throw your life away!"

"Look and look again, Bedarth."

The *liffrea*'s eyes narrowed. "What's that supposed to mean?"

"The World Tree demands I face every battle with honor. It demands I defend my kinfolk and live up to my oaths. You yourself told me that. If I let him die without trying to save him, I would break my oath as much if not more than killing myself." Edward looked at his fingers. "Besides…"

"Besides?"

"The World Tree wants this fight. For both of us."

The *liffrea* stared into his eyes and then shook his head. "It's always annoying when a pupil actually pays attention to my lessons." He turned back to the man on the ground.

Edward looked at the cyning. "What about you?"

"I don't want either of you dead, and I think that's most likely." Cynric grimaced. "But at least this way there's a chance. May Wyrd and the World Tree bless you."

With a laugh, Edward stepped up to the shield wall. "Let me through," he commanded.

Startled, the ranks opened a path.

At the front of the line, Edward stopped and stared at the horse for a moment.

The great beast stared back, challenge and pride in his eyes. Then he reared, striking at Edward with both hooves, but he was ready. He skipped to the right and rapped the horse across the nose with his stick.

The horse snapped back.

Fortunately Edward was already jumping away, and the teeth only ripped through his sleeve.

Well, that didn't work. No real surprise, as I'm sure every other trainer tried the same thing.

He stepped in again with the stick raised, but when the horse turned to snap at him, Edward dodged the teeth to reach for the horse's mane. The horse turned far quicker than a creature that size should have managed, forcing Edward back with raised hooves.

Edward rolled under the hooves and grabbed the rope as he came to his feet. The horse reared and twisted, yanking it out of his hands.

Edward dove to the ground just as a hind hoof punched the air where he had been. He tumbled desperately to the other side of the horse, giving himself enough time to regain his footing.

The moment he did so, he swung the stick at the horse's nose. Though it hit, once more it did little but irritate the horse. Bright teeth snapped at him.

He stepped to the side, grabbed its mane, and tried to jump on its back.

But the horse would have none of it. As Edward started his jump, he twisted and flung him to the side.

Edward dusted himself off as they circled each other.

Going to have to tire him out.

He could not contain his joyful laugh as the horse dared him to come closer. The horse whinnied in response, and the two advanced again.

This time Edward dodged to the left, snapping the stick on the horse's nose. He ducked the expected bite and grabbed his mane, again making as if to jump on its back. When the twist came, though, he held on and moved with it.

The horse rolled. Edward let go and stumbled hastily out of the way. He started to step back in, but the horse heaved up and snapped out his front hooves again.

The circled warriors cried out. Hooves flashed past his chin, and he felt the wind of their passage.

But they passed with no mark on him.

He circled. *Be patient, idiot!*

The horse pranced to match him.

He feinted in, and the horse reared, but Edward bounced back.

Again he feinted. Again the horse raised his hooves. Again Edward stepped back.

The third time was no feint. He struck the horse's nose again, intending to step past the teeth again, but the horse slashed with his hooves instead. One hoof cut across his thigh, spraying blood across the shields hemming them in.

Edward barely noticed, grabbing the rope. Again he was ready when the horse tried to fling him away. He rolled under the horse, pulling the rope with him. It ran along the horse's belly, taut against its flesh, striping his flank with a long welt.

The horse screamed and twisted to cow-kick at him. Startled, Edward jumped left, away from the right rear hoof, but the left hoof clipped his side and knocked him breathless across the corral.

Fortunately he landed in front of the shield wall. The spearmen brandished their weapons to cover him.

He noticed the blood trickling down his leg. The he touched his side, wincing.

Cracked a rib, I'd guess.

But he laughed again as he rose. The horse, mouth flecked with foam, whinnied back, just as he had done before. Then he trotted back, giving Edward room to advance.

He's enjoying this as much as I am!

"Stay here, you idiot."

He turned back to see Aethelflaed, spear held in one hand, braced on her hip.

"I can't let him die."

"He's just a horse. A great horse, but just a horse."

Edward cocked his head at her. "He's a horse worthy of our father."

"You—" She snorted. "Loki take you, that he is. Doesn't quite have father's temper, though."

"Especially when we irritated mother."

Aethelflaed smiled, tears in her eyes. "I'd rather tame this beast with my broken arm than face father the day you destroyed her flower garden."

"It was an accident!"

"Go see if the horse believes you. Father surely didn't."

Edward laughed and turned back.

The horse pawed at the ground, clearly impatient.

He advanced at a crouch, stick in his left hand. He circled to the left, and the horse pranced around to keep him from the welt on his flank. Then he snapped his forehooves out again.

Edward dodged, again to the left, but this time it was the horse who had anticipated his foe's movement. He turned and launched a hind hoof at where he expected Edward to be.

But Edward rolled under the hoof to get in close, and he snapped the stick along the rope welt.

The horse screamed and bit down.

This time, the bite connected, ripping a chunk from Edward's left shoulder.

Edward yelled and stepped back. Both horse and man heaved for breath, but neither paused. They rushed at each other again.

The horse's forelimb caught Edward's arm and spun him around. He struck at the welt again, earning another scream from the horse. He struck again, getting the same reward.

However, he'd stayed in one place for too long. A hoof struck his left arm solidly, breaking a bone. Edward yowled in pain as he staggered back into the corral's fence. He ducked under a fencepost to shield himself from the next striking hoof, then grabbed the stick and swung as hard as he could at the horse's muzzle.

He missed, hitting far higher than he intended, and the horse backed off, blinking one great eye. Edward stumbled back out of hoof range.

The horse charged forward, this time to trample rather than strike. Edward lunged to his left, blocking the hooves as best he could with the stick. In the swirling press, he slammed the stick on a forelimb. The horse screamed again and both stepped back.

Edward gasped for breath, holding his arm. The horse lifted his lip and whinnied, his flanks heaving. Edward circled, and instead of prancing to face him, the horse simply turned in place, favoring the forelimb.

Maybe now he's tired. Maybe he's ready. He snorted. *I hope he's ready.*

He slid the stick into his belt and stepped forward slowly. The horse matched him.

Yes! He's going to—

The horse snapped at his right arm, too fast for Edward to react. The teeth clamped onto him and he yelled in pain.

The horse released him and then waved his head, teeth bared, flecks of foam flying as they flashed in the sun.

But Edward didn't move. Instead he stared at his right arm.

The Wolf's bite would not have hurt less, yet there's no blood.

The teeth snapped at his nose. He brushed them away. The horse whinnied and then bit on his right shoulder. Again, hard enough to hurt, but clearly not to wound.

He reached up to stroke the horse's muzzle. The teeth flashed again, but not to bite. More than anything, the horse seemed to be making sure Edward would remember them.

"I know, lad. You've got teeth and you're willing to use them."

The horse shook his head and whinnied.

"I've got to ride you, or they'll kill you."

The horse whinnied again. He bit at Edward's shoulder again.

Just a nibble.

Edward looked into the horse's eyes.

"Well, lad, I guess the time has come for to cast the final throw." With that, Edward grabbed the horse's mane, and using all the strength that remained in his legs, jumped up. In his fatigue and pain, he could not quite swing his leg all the way across the horse's back, but the horse made a weird hop and almost flung Edward into his seat.

Edward sat up, eyes filled with wonder. He patted the horse's neck. "Back and forth a couple of times. Let's show them you're actually letting me ride you." He pulled the mane slightly to the right, and the horse turned. It limped along the fence.

"Back to the other side, lad. Then we'll see if Bedarth can help both of us. Don't be surprised if he calls you an idiot, too."

The horse whinnied, but accepted his suggestion to turn around and come back along the fence.

Edward patted his neck again. "Are you going to bite them if they come to groom you?"

The horse whinnied and bared his teeth.

"Are you going to draw blood?"

The horse snuffled.

"Very well." Edward laughed. "I'll tell them to watch their fingers. Give them a sporting chance." He slid off the horse's back, staggering a bit as he landed. The horse leaned in to support him.

Bedarth stomped up, followed by Cynric, who was shaking his head.

"Done having fun? Idiots!" Bedarth peered at the horse's eye.

"Told you," Edward said to the horse. The horse whinnied.

The *liffrea* concentrated for a moment. "His eye will be fine, you just missed it. I've stopped any infection, but it'll be sore for a while."

The horse bit softly on Bedarth's shoulder.

"You great fool." The *liffrea* stroked the horse's muzzle.

"He'll let anyone groom him now, assuming they do a good job," Edward said to the cyning, "but they'd best watch his teeth."

Cynric snorted. "I don't think that'll be something the lads will forget." He waved some forward. "You heard Edward?"

They nodded.

"I also don't think just anyone can ride him." The cyning looked at Edward. "I promised you a horse when you leave. I believe the choice has been made."

The horse nickered and nibbled at Edward's right shoulder.

"Thank you."

"You'll train him, though. And you'll train him to be the battle-steed of legend I hoped for."

"That I will." Suddenly tears filled Edward's eyes, and he hugged the beast. "I swear it as long as folk kindle fire, ships sail, child calls to mother, the sun shines, and as long as the falcon flies the long spring day with a fair wind behind him on wings outspread."

Startled, Bedarth looked at Edward. Then a great, broad smile spread across his face. "In that case, you'd better give him a name."

"You never named him?"

Cynric snorted. "We've never found one that suited, except for Loki-son."

Edward thought for a moment, then smiled at Bedarth. "I guess One-Eye knew all along I would someday need a word that meant both 'dear one' and 'ferocious.'"

* * * * *

Rob Howell Bio

Rob Howell is the creator of the Shijuren fantasy setting (www.shijuren.org) and an author in the Four Horsemen Universe (www.mercenaryguild.org). He writes primarily medieval fantasy, space opera, military science fiction, and alternate history.

He is a reformed medieval academic, a former IT professional, and a retired soda jerk.

His parents discovered quickly books were the only way to keep Rob quiet. He latched onto the Hardy Boys series first and then anything he could reach. Without books, it's unlikely all three would have survived.

His latest release in Shijuren is *Where Now the Rider*, the third in the Edward series of swords and sorcery mysteries. The next release in that world is *None Call Me Mother*, the conclusion to the epic fantasy trilogy *The Kreisens*.

You can find him online at: www.robhowell.org and his blog at www.robhowell.org/blog.

# # # # #

The Errand by
Jon R. Osborne
A Milesian Accords Tale

"**O**din tests us," Geirr complained as they tramped through the thinning fog. "No captives, little loot, and now we run to our boat with our tails between our legs."

"Bite your tongue," Helgri snapped. They had numbered a dozen when they attacked a nearby village. "An Ulsterman dogs us, not the wrath of a god."

"This man hunts us like deer. We've lost half our number to his traps and arrows," Geirr retorted. "I say the gods sent him to vex us."

"You test my patience, Geirr. The beach lays ahead," Helgri said.

"The other warbands—" A meaty *thunk* interrupted Geirr.

* * *

As soon as Nechtan released the arrow, he grabbed another. His target clutched at the shaft buried halfway into his chest, gurgling blood. The Northman gave a strangled cry and collapsed.

"Down," the leader hissed, yanking his shield off his back as he hunkered low. Only one of his fellows followed suit and turned to

385

face the trail behind them. One man drew his sword, while the other two unlimbered their bows.

Nechtan let fly at one of the archers. They posed a potential threat. Unlike his meticulous first shot, this arrow flew a hair off target, impaling the man's arm as opposed to felling him. It reduced the threat he presented, but he might live.

"There! On the hill!" the other archer pointed in Nechtan's direction. He should have nocked an arrow. Nechtan scooped up the other arrow he had leant against the tree. He aimed at the pointing man, ready to duck behind the tree should the northerner remember his own bow. Despite the hasty shot, the arrow flew true.

The swordsman, drawn by his fellow's voice, turned and stepped into the line of fire. He lacked chainmail, worn by the highest warriors among the raiders, so Nechtan's arrow pierced the padded tunic easily. The swordsman spun and dropped.

The archer drew back his own arrow. Nechtan had no doubt the raider's arrow could reach him, even firing up hill. Nechtan rolled behind the tree as the arrow whistled by. He yanked an arrow from his quiver and stepped from the opposite side of the tree, in a race to see who could nock and fire the fastest.

Nechtan won. His rushed shot flew high, striking the archer in the helmet. The arrow caromed off into the brush, but the impact spoiled the northerner's aim, and his projectile disappeared into the sky.

The leader pulled out an odd object Nechtan had never seen. It resembled a bow affixed to the end of a plank. The leader lay the strange thing on the upper rim of his shield, but didn't reach for the bow string.

Nechtan dismissed him as a distraction. The northern archer already had an arrow, but Nechtan didn't give him time to nock it.

Nechtan's target tried to sidestep, so the sinking arrow buried itself in his hip instead of his groin.

Nechtan heard a loud twang and a wooden clack. Something sliced across his thigh—a stubby arrow protruded from his breeches. As Nechtan jerked in pain, his foot slipped in the wet grass. He scrambled for purchase as the turf broke away in clods. His descent gained speed on the muddy bluff, and Nechtan flailed for a handhold as he crashed through the brush above the trail.

The impact knocked the wind out of Nechtan, and he'd lost his bow. He shoved himself off the soil in time to see the Northmen's leader's shield. It slammed into him, cracking against his skull, and he saw stars.

"No," the leader said as Nechtan's vision tunneled. "Take him to the boat." The world faded to black.

* * *

Nechtan awoke to the stench of salt, piss, and tar. He lurched, and water sprayed his face. His stomach threatened to add vomit to the bouquet of odors. He cracked his eyes open. A sail billowed above him.

"Helgri, your slave is awake," a voice shouted in the northern speech.

Nechtan sat up despite the pounding in his head. A length of rope bound his arms, chafing his wrists. He could separate his hands by no more than a foot. He sat in a raider's ship. Three dozen men manned oars along the sides of the boat. With some satisfaction, Nechtan noted several vacant seats along the oars.

He wasn't the only captive. A dozen women and girls huddled in the bottom of the ship next to a pile of spoils, but Nechtan recognized none of them. The Northmen had raided multiple villages, then. Nechtan returned his gaze to the rowers. A few weren't Northmen, and one wore a monk's robes.

Someone seized Nechtan's tunic and hauled him to his feet. "What should I call you, slave?" the leader growled in his native speech. Nechtan bit his tongue. No need to reveal he understood their language. Helgri turned to another Northman. "Give him some water and put him at an oar."

The water was tepid and salty, but Nechtan gulped it as though it was the finest ale. Another Northman shoved him to an empty bench and stuck an oar in his hands. "Row!"

Rebellion would gain nothing besides a beating, assuming they didn't pitch him in the sea, so Nechtan rowed. He put in enough effort to avoid attention, but no more than his fellow oarsmen. He needed to harbor his strength.

A sharp, barking cry echoed across the water, answered by another. Past the length of his oar, Nechtan spied rocky shores shrouded in haze.

"Seals," one of the northerners muttered. "Watch for rocks!" he called to the man keeping watch over the prow.

Helgri stomped to the man. "Is there a problem?"

The other northerner spat. "The land to the east is full of bad omens and foul spirits. We should veer north and west to follow the coast of Ywst. We can harbor in Stjornavagr for the night."

Nechtan recognized the name of the Northman settlement. Many raiders used it as a waystation between their homelands and the targets of their raids. Could he escape there? If he did, how would he get home? Perhaps he would remain—the hunting would be plentiful.

A splash caught his attention. Seals broke the surface outside the sweep of the oars, barking at the intruders. The northerners ignored the beasts or smacked the water with their oars. Luckily for the seals, the Northmen couldn't hunt them in the open water. Even if they killed a seal, how would they retrieve it?

Helgri hefted his strange bow on a plank. He jerked back the bowstring, and it caught on the wood, though Nechtan could not divine how from his view. The northern leader laid a short arrow in front of the string. He pointed the weapon out to sea, sighting over the top of the plank. Nechtan followed the Northman's aim—a seal bobbed among the waves, watching the men in the boat.

Nechtan dug his oar into the water and held it below the waves with all his might. The ship lurched as Helgri squeezed a lever on the underside of his weapon. With a loud twang, the arrow whistled into the sea. The seal barked once and disappeared.

Nechtan raised his oar, but not before Helgri noticed. The northern leader seized Nechtan's tunic and yanked him to his feet. "You did that on purpose!"

Helgri hurled Nechtan against the gunwale and loomed over him. If Nechtan's hands were free, he could send Helgri overboard, and the Northman's chain armor would drag him under.

"Maybe I should send you into the sea?" Helgri snarled. He reached for Nechtan again.

Nechtan looped the rope between his hands around Helgri's wrist and yanked him forward. Both men stumbled against the edge of the boat, and Helgri realized his danger. The Northerner fumbled for his dagger with his offhand. Behind him, the other raiders yelled and cheered.

Nechtan braced his foot against the rowing bench and shoved. Helgri dropped his dagger to catch hold of the gunwale. The knife bounced off the oar and splashed into the water. Movement from the sea caught Nechtan's attention. A woman with large brown eyes gazed at him from the ocean. She clung to an oar with one hand and lunged from the water. She snagged Helgri's trapped wrist and hauled both men overboard.

The sea smothered the din of the bellowing Northmen. A weight on Nechtan's arms dragged him further below the surface—Helgri and his iron mail. The Northman thrashed as Nechtan tried to disentangle them, so Nechtan kicked at Helgri. His foot connected with something solid, and Helgri stilled long enough for Nechtan to unloop the rope.

Before Nechtan could swim for the surface, Helgri seized his ankle. Nechtan's lungs burned. The northern raider would drag them both to their deaths. Nechtan drove his free foot down three times before he dislocated Helgri's thumb.

Colorful spots bloomed in Nechtan's vision. How far to the surface? His bound wrists hindered him. He didn't have time to find the knots by touch. Darkness replaced the swirling colors. Something brushed against him, and lips pressed upon his own.

* * *

Nechtan coughed and spat out seawater. It marked the second time today he'd awoken somewhere strange. He rose to his elbows; the rope connecting his wrists had split or been cut. He surveyed the rocky beach. There was no sign of Helgri, nor the woman who'd yanked them off the boat. Had she kissed him and dragged him ashore?

Nechtan coughed and spat briny phlegm as he stood on unsteady legs. Legends of faeries who took the form of seals sprang to mind. A decade ago, or was it three, Nechtan would have crossed himself at the mere thought. He'd since learned legends and gods were far more complicated than the local monk from his childhood had let on.

Nechtan scanned further inland. Brilliant green fields rose toward a ridge to the west, and another curved ridge rose to the east. A stream trickled onto the beach from the north. Nechtan's hatred for water transformed to a burning thirst. He staggered to the stream and followed it inland to a pool below a shallow waterfall.

The water was cool and fresh, but Nechtan resisted the urge to guzzle from the stream. He splashed away the salt from his face and hair, then once he worked the knots free from his wrist, he washed where the hemp had rubbed his skin raw.

The stinging subsided, and he examined the chaffed bands around his wrists. Once he cleaned them off, they faded from angry red to pink. He debated making camp here at the pool. He had no equipment—the raiders had stripped him of his gear, supplies, and weapons. If he could find dry wood, he could make a fire.

He peered toward the sea. The ridges formed a bowl, open at the south to the sea. If he built a fire here, it could be spotted from a boat. He'd at least want to put the ridge between him and the ocean. He wrapped the pieces of hemp around his belt and climbed above the waterfall.

A small loch below the eastern ridge fed the stream, so Nechtan hiked around its western edge. The azure water of the loch rivaled the verdant hue of the grass and shrubs. Had his near-death experience heightened his senses? A slope rose to a slight dip in the ridge; a walkable pass inland. As Nechtan trudged up the rise, he spotted a stag at the crest. The beast sported a majestic rack of antlers and watched Nechtan, unafraid.

Nechtan paused ten yards away from the stag. He glanced to where his torn tunic exposed part of his chest and the knotwork stag tattoo adorning it. "I suppose my father sent you."

The beast snorted, turned, and walked east. Nechtan fell into step alongside the stag.

"Did he send the selkie as well?" Nechtan asked, but the creature gave no answer. He peered back over his shoulder, and rolling hills had replaced the ridge. Ahead, a path cut through a pine forest and led toward low mountains. After a few minutes following the stag, the trees to the right thinned to reveal a stone and timber fortification. The fortress squatted on a flat top hill.

"I guess that's our destination," Nechtan muttered. The stag was gone.

Nechtan picked his way up the hill through the trees. Halfway along the slope, he found a well-used track. Nechtan followed the pathway uphill. Armed men and women watched him from the wall, but they did not raise bows or brandish spears. Granted, unarmed and bedraggled, he wouldn't appear threatening.

Wherever he was, Nechtan could still smell the sea. To the south he spied an inlet, and beyond it, open water. The trackway began at the fort's timber gate and curved in the direction of the inlet.

"Where in the name of God am I?" Nechtan muttered as he stood before the closed gate. Should he beat on it with his fist? The guards had watched him approach.

The gate inched open with a wooden groan. Beyond the entrance stood a woman, tall and regal. The afternoon sun set her burnished copper hair ablaze, and she studied Nechtan with sea-green eyes. Nechtan instinctively bowed.

"Greetings, Nechtan, son of Carweth. Do you know who I am?" Her accent marked her as hailing from south of Nechtan's Ulster, perhaps Connacht or Meath. What was she doing in Alba? Perhaps she'd been wed to an Alban noble.

"I'm afraid you have me at a disadvantage, Milady." Nechtan noted the woman held a spear at her side, and a sword hung from her belt.

"I am Scathach."

"I am honored, Lady Scathach," Nechtan bowed again. The woman regarded him as though she expected him to say more. "I apologize for showing up at your gate, but I escaped a Northman raiding ship and washed up...I'm sorry. How do you know who I am?"

"I am Scathach, and this is my domain," the woman replied with a slight smile, as though it would explain everything. When Nechtan's expression remained blank, she added, "Have you not heard the tale of Cu Chulainn?"

"What lad hasn't, but it was long ago. Are you saying you're descended from the Scathach in the tales?" Nechtan asked, careful to not let his tone grow incredulous. He didn't want to offend her, especially if he could avoid sleeping out on the bare ground come nightfall.

Scathach sighed. "I *am* the Scathach of legend, and this is Dunos Scaith, my holdfast. When you washed ashore, I felt it, and sent your father's totem to bring you here."

"Why? How?" Nechtan hastily added, "Not to seem ungrateful."

"We are in the Glaswold, in my domain. I brought you here because I have an errand to see if you are worthy."

Glaswold? Perhaps it was a Dalriada kingdom. "Worthy of what?"

"Learning from me, of course." She made it sound as obvious as the sun rising in the east. She swept her hand across the yard of the fortress. "These men and women serve here in exchange for tutelage in the art of war."

"You want me to be a guard?" It would beat being cold and hungry, but guarding a hilltop sounded monotonous. Nechtan hadn't seen any other signs of habitation since he came ashore.

"I've heard of your exploits in Ulster and north of Dublin. Your talent would be wasted standing around with a spear, son of

Carweth. I know what your father is, and his gifts to you," Scathach stated. "First, I have a task for you."

He hadn't agreed to anything yet, but Nechtan held his tongue. Instead, he asked, "What is this errand?"

"Norsemen entered my domain and captured my daughter, Uathach. Even now, they spirit her toward their ship on the other side of the island. You must track them and return her to me." Scathach's face remained impassive as she waited for Nechtan's response.

"I love hunting those fair-haired bastards, but I don't even have a knife," Nechtan said. *How can she be so calm? Why haven't any of the guards standing around been dispatched?*

A guard stepped forward, bearing weapons and a sturdy leather bag. "Take these weapons—a bow, arrows, a sword, and a knife," Scathach said as she counted the items off on her fingers. "The bag contains a blanket, food, and a few sundries you may find useful."

Nechtan collected the gear, taking a moment to examine one of the arrows. A sharp iron-bladed head topped the shaft. "How many are going with me?" Nechtan asked as he situated the gear. He resisted the urge to dig out the food despite the growling of his stomach.

"None. I need a tracker who can take them unaware. Regardless of their skill in sword and spear, my guards would slow you and give you away," Scathach replied. "Once you cross into the Dunwold, time will be of the essence."

"Dunwold? Is that a neighboring kingdom?" Nechtan didn't know the lay of this island. Back home, he knew every stream and every village.

"No. The Dunwold refers to the World of Man, whereas we call the otherworld the Glaswold." Scathach reached into the folds of her dress and drew out an arrow with crimson fletching. "Right now, an hour passing in the Dunwold takes seven hours here."

Nechtan tried to wrap his head around the idea. He'd heard tales of faerie lands where spending a day there could mean a year in the mortal world. A week here meant a day there. "So I can scamper ahead of them, return to the Dunworld, er...Dunwold, and beat them to their ship."

"Not quite so easily. The crossing points are limited—a discussion for another time—so you must overtake them through deftness," Scathach said. She held out the red-fletched arrow. "Take this arrow. You may need it."

One more arrow for the quiver. Nechtan noted the arrow had a sharp bronze point instead of an iron blade. If he was reduced to firing a practice arrow, he might as well use harsh curses. Still, he tucked the arrow away. "Where did your people lose the trail?"

"The raiders took her from a pool east of here, at the base of a waterfall. You'll find a collection of pools and waterfalls where streams join the river." Scathach gestured east. Nechtan peered through the open gate and spotted the tell-tale crease in the trees. "I know their ship waits across the island to the northeast, but no more. Ravens make for poor guides in such matters."

"Right. I'll be off to kill some Northmen." Nechtan paused. "How did they get here—to the Glaswold?"

"From the pools, you'll see a small peak jutting from the ground before the proper mountains behind it. Circle this peak three times in the direction of the sun, and you'll cross the ford between worlds," Scathach said.

"That's it? Walk around a pointy hill three times?" Nechtan had expected something more dramatic, with druids and standing stones.

"A powerful geas protects my daughter as long as she remains on the island. Once they take her from its shores, they can...do what evil men do. Good hunting," Scathach pronounced, as though it were a blessing. Perhaps coming from her, it was.

Nechtan nodded and set off. The gate creaked shut behind him, closing with a thud as he descended the hill. The sun had scarcely moved by the time he backtracked the river to the pools. Streams tumbled down stony beds into those pools. At the highest pool, he found a spear. It wasn't as grand as Scathach's, but ornate knotwork carvings decorated the shaft.

Nechtan brought the weapon along. He didn't favor the spear, but if he found an opportunity to free Uathach, he could arm her. The peak Scathach spoke of jutted from the nearby valley floor, a stone pyramid with a crack running down its face.

Three times around proved more challenging than Nechtan had expected. A ridge formed a spine behind the peak, requiring Nechtan to climb or double the length of each circuit. On the third trip around the peak, Nechtan gazed west. He could see the hill, but no fort dominated its crest.

Nechtan gauged how much sun remained. Once it grew dark, tracking his quarry would prove impossible. If they'd beached their ship northeast, the mountains limited their potential routes. Nechtan hastened along the edge of the vale, confident he could find the trail at the northern lip of the valley.

A game trail along the bank of a pond bore fruit. Boot marks and holes left by spear butts marred the mud. Nechtan traced the footprints along the path. Short strides—they were in no hurry, or their captive slowed them. A smaller print marked her presence. An adult, or close enough, so Nechtan knew what awaited her once her captors spirited her beyond the reach of her mother's curse.

Nechtan scanned the horizon. An inlet was visible two miles away, but the trail led more northerly, toward a copse of pine. A hill to the east of the trees stood clear. He could circumvent the woods and have the high ground in case they broke to the east.

Gnawing on a chunk of smoked ham from the bag, Nechtan jogged toward the hill. He paused where the path crossed a larger trackway. Passing wagons and horses had worn the east-west track, and some of the traffic broadened the path north. The stony ground clung to its secrets, but Nechtan spotted a familiar circular indentation in a muddy patch. The raiders had steered north through the woods.

Nechtan muttered a prayer of thanks that the hill sloped gently as he paralleled the woods. He was losing light. Would they stop for the night? Traipsing about in the dark would be folly. At the next brook trickling down the hillside, Nechtan headed for the trees.

He paused in the streambed to rub mud on his cheeks and forehead, so his skin wouldn't shine like the moon over open water.

It didn't take long for him to find the trackway through the trees. He checked the muddy patch created by the stream crossing the pathway, but he spotted no prints or marks from a spear butt.

Nechtan dug through his bag, taking a quick inventory. He unwound the rope and formed a plan. After all, a good hunter relied on more than his bow.

* * *

Baggi's bones ached with weariness. A full day's march, and for what? A wench none of them could touch for fear of their manhood shriveling off. Runi had cast stones and confirmed the woman's claim. To defile her on the island invited the wrath of her gods—they would wither everything between the offending man's legs.

Baggi spat. Svaldr had insisted on this mad quest with no loot. The short, stocky Godhi who advised Svaldr hadn't even come on this fool's errand. He remained safely back in Foresvik, swilling mead and feasting. At least the foolish wench lacked any guards—though Baggi could do with spilling a bit of blood now.

Something at the edge of the path caught Baggi's attention. He and Gunnar preceded the rest, as though anyone on this island of fishermen and sheepherders would put up a fight. A spear stuck out of the ground, jammed point down into the turf. It wasn't gold or silver, but the polished haft gleamed in the fading light.

Baggi reached for the spear. *Crack!* Something yanked his foot skyward. Baggi dropped his own spear and grabbed for the one impaled in the ground. It popped free of the dirt without slowing his arch. The last thing Baggi saw was a pine tree.

* * *

Baggi's shriek preceded a sickening crunch, and his spear clattered to the dirt. Gunnar shucked his shield from his back and clutched his spear, waiting for an enemy to emerge from the pine trees flanking the path.

Svaldr strode forward unafraid and demanded, "What happened?"

Gunnar shrugged behind his shield. "I don't know, Svaldr. One moment Baggi walked beside me, another a troll yanked him into the forest."

"A troll?" Svaldr spat and glared into the trees. "Do you see any trolls?"

"Of course not," Gunnar replied. "It's why they are so dangerous. They blend into the forest until they snatch you and crush you."

"You spend too much time drinking with the storytellers," Svaldr said. "This isn't the work of a troll. I'd wager we're dealing with a Loki-cursed trickster who laid a snare. Come on. We can reach the boat in a few hours."

"Where's Ketill?" Runi cried from the rear of the group. "He was here a minute ago."

Gunnar reached inside his tunic for the metal cross dangling from his neck. Svaldr might still cling to the old gods, but Gunnar was hedging his bets. If the old gods wouldn't save him from angry trolls, maybe the new god would.

* * *

Nechtan lowered the body to the pine needle–covered ground.

Two down, four to go.

Two of the Northmen flanked Uathach, holding her by the arms. Nechtan could only see her auburn tresses, but she stood almost as tall as the men around her.

Is she a warrior like her mother?

He slunk deeper into the trees to get ahead of the Northmen while they dithered in worry.

* * *

"That is Baggi's shield," Gunnar hissed.

Ingmar peered into the woods. "We should release the woman. We've angered the trolls and wights by stealing her."

"Why have we stopped?" Svaldr demanded.

"It's Baggi's shield." Gunnar pointed to the round red and white shield propped up in the middle of the path. "At best it's a warning, and at worst it's a trap."

"I am surrounded by fools and old women," Svaldr snarled. He strode forward and kicked the shield. A snap preceded a wooden creak as a branch whipped into the pathway. Gunnar spotted an arrow lashed to the end of the branch before it slammed into Svaldr's chest.

As they gaped at Svaldr's prone form, a bowstring twanged, and an arrow whistled. Ingmar clutched at his throat, where a shaft with brown fletching protruded.

Another arrow buried its bladed head in Runi's shield. The attackers lurked in the trees to their right. Gunnar hunkered behind his own shield, hoping the enemy didn't flank both sides of the path.

"We should forget the woman and make for the boat," Gunnar said.

Svaldr coughed from the ground. "We will not abandon my prize." He rolled to his feet and pushed himself upright. The shattered shaft of the arrow protruded from his mail shirt. Svaldr extricated the arrowhead and cast it onto the ground. "Let's not give this trickster any more time to prepare surprises for us. Once we are free of the trees, he will have to face us on open ground."

* * *

Nechtan didn't waste time looting the corpse, save for enough arrows to fill his quiver. Their leader was correct—once the Northmen cleared the forest, Nechtan would lose his advantage. The raiders passed inviting campsites, so they intended to march for their ship.

Nechtan debated tailing them and picking them off. The trail through the woods twisted with the land and trees, so he could get close to them, but it also meant they could charge him before he could drop more than one.

He knelt and examined the discarded arrowhead. It had punched through the raider's armor as planned, but no blood stained the blades. Fibers caught behind the head when the leader had yanked it out meant the point had penetrated his clothes as well. Nechtan tucked away the arrowhead. With the sun setting, he didn't have time to build any more traps.

That didn't mean he was out of tricks.

* * *

Gunnar glanced over his shoulder, nearly tripping on a root. Had he heard something, or was his mind playing tricks? Svaldr walked in front, followed by Runi, guiding the woman. That left Gunnar to bring up the rear and dwell on Ketill and Ingmar.

The trees thinned ahead, and Gunnar spotted a familiar hill. The inlet was a mile farther along the path. They could reach the beach in twilight. Agmund and Toki would keep a fire burning on the beach to guide them. If only this were a proper raid, instead of the few warriors Svaldr had paid for this mad quest. Even a troll would not trouble a proper warband.

The jangle of metal and creak of leather caught Gunnar's ear. He scanned the woods behind them. Ketill jogged among the thinning trees, hurrying to catch up to them.

Perhaps he's bested our stalker?

"Ketill!" Gunnar shouted, waving. Too late, he spotted the bow behind Ketill's shield.

* * *

Nechtan let the shield slip from his grasp. With the fool Northman shouting at him, the others would figure out Nechtan wasn't their missing comrade. Nechtan's clumsy first shot grazed the Northman's side, sparking off the mail.

Free of the shield, Nechtan nocked another arrow while the raider gaped at him. Nechtan's shot beat the rising shield, sinking in below the man's collarbone. The northerner stumbled back. The leader seized Uathach by the arm and barked an order at the remaining raider.

The man charged behind his shield, leaning forward as he ran to expose as little as possible. Nechtan fired an arrow into the Northman's leg, above the knee. The man bellowed in pain, and his step faltered, but he kept coming. He hefted his spear as he limped toward Nechtan.

Nechtan put an arrow through the man's unarmored spear arm. The bladed head jutted out one side, the fletched end out the other. To the warrior's credit, he clung to his spear. With a sweep of his wounded arm, the northerner snapped the arrowhead off against his shield.

With a roar, the northerner lunged the remaining few yards. Nechtan tossed aside his bow and yanked his sword free of its sheath. He regretted discarding the shield, as his opponent thrust the spearhead for Nechtan's heart.

Nechtan twisted aside to his left. The northerner attempted to arrest his trajectory, but Nechtan jabbed his sword into the man's flank below his spear arm. The blade sank between ribs, and blood frothed from the wound. The northerner stumbled to his knees and dropped his spear.

The leader, Svaldr, left Nechtan no time to savor his victory. He had drawn his sword and closed the distance. Hate smoldered in Svaldr's eyes, but he did not make a reckless charge. "I will slay you, trickster, and I will leave this accursed island with my treasure. Once we're at sea and free of the curse, I will plunder her."

"We'll see about that. You started with half a dozen, and now you stand alone," Nechtan retorted. "I'm no trickster. I'm a hunter, and I prey on Northmen."

If Nechtan's use of the northern tongue surprised Svaldr, he hid it. "I am Svaldr Iron-Skinned, little huntsman. You've bitten off more than you can chew."

Svaldr stepped in, shield ready and sword high. Nechtan tossed his sword to his left hand and jabbed under Svaldr's raised blade. The point punched into the mail shirt and stopped. Svaldr's counter-stroke forced Nechtan into an awkward parry as he backpedaled.

"A good try, huntsman, but your blade cannot harm me." Svaldr grinned wickedly. "A shame the same can't be said for you." The northern leader launched a flurry of slashes, pressing Nechtan back. Nechtan flicked the tip of his sword across Svaldr's unarmored fore-arm.

Svaldr laughed. "I'm sorry, were you expecting blood? Maybe you hoped I would drop my weapon?" He laughed again and re-newed his attacks.

Nechtan parried and dodged. Svaldr blocked the few jabs and cuts Nechtan slipped in with his shield. Nechtan's arm ached from each reverberating blow when their blades met. On the next clash of steel, Nechtan punched Svaldr in the mouth. The Northman's eyes widened as he blinked tears of pain.

Svaldr spat blood and half a tooth. "You misbegotten son of a—"

Nechtan swept his heel behind Svaldr's boot and shoved. The northerner tumbled back, unable to arrest his fall without releasing his weapon or shield. Nechtan drove his sword into the fallen man's belly, only to strike stone below the mail shirt. With a reverse stroke, he swiped it across Svaldr's unarmored knee. The blade cleanly sliced open the Northman's breeches, but left the skin unmarred.

Svaldr lashed out with his sword, but his clumsy swing from his back meant the difference between a deep cut and the blade cleaving Nechtan's leg.

"At least one of us feels the sting of steel," Svaldr snarled and rolled forward to a crouched position. Keeping his shield ready, he stood. "I'll give you credit, huntsman. It's a rare man who can bring me any pain. Perhaps you'll ascend to Valhalla after I kill you."

Svaldr rained a brutal storm of blows at Nechtan. Nechtan ducked and dodged as many as possible, and parried when he couldn't. A slash to the elbow of Svaldr's shield arm did nothing but trim the sleeve of his tunic. It cost Nechtan a cut on his shoulder when he didn't spin away fast enough.

Nechtan's boot brushed the discarded shield. Ducking Svaldr's next swing, Nechtan grabbed the shield off the ground. He didn't have much experience fighting with a shield, but his sword seemed next to useless. He parried Svaldr's next blow and drove his shield into Svaldr's. Svaldr's shield jerked up and struck him in the cheek. Svaldr snarled, and the wooden edge of the shield left a welt. Nechtan sidestepped a thrust, slipping away from the strike and driving his shield edge-first into Svaldr's back. The Northman howled in rage. Steel couldn't hurt him, but flesh and wood struck true.

Nechtan gave ground under another torrent of slashes. He watched Svaldr's swings and the dip of the shield each time Svaldr pressed forward. The next step, Nechtan slammed his shield edge-ward for Svaldr's throat.

Laugh that off!

Svaldr interposed his shield, leaving Nechtan off balance.

Fool!

Svaldr had tricked him this time. Svaldr's sword clashed with Nechtan's blade, and he wrenched the smaller weapon from Nechtan's grasp. Svaldr's counterstroke struck Nechtan in the side of the head. Nechtan staggered backward off the path and tumbled into a trickling streambed.

* * *

Svaldr gazed into the dusk-shadowed gully. The huntsman sprawled in the stream, unmoving. Mud-slick stones lined the steep slope—a difficult and time-consuming climb. Svaldr spat blood and turned away. The woman remained where he had left her. She must realize there was nowhere for her to run.

Svaldr took her by the elbow. "Come. Let us see if you put up a struggle when your curse no longer wards you."

Within minutes, Svaldr could make out the dark shape of the boat on the beach. Two of his men hunched over a small fire but rose with weapons in hand as soon as Svaldr's boots crunched on the rocky beach.

"Where are the others?" Agmund asked.

"This beauty had one persistent guardian who dogged us halfway across the island," Svaldr replied. "Make ready to cast off. I want to enjoy my prize."

* * *

Nechtan awoke in running water with his head ringing. He sat up and eased off the helmet. The ragged metal of the rent left by Svaldr's sword scraped his skin. How long had he been out? Judging by the sky, it couldn't have been more than a couple of minutes. He'd lost his sword in the fall but didn't want to waste precious time searching for it.

How long until Svaldr reaches his ship?

Nechtan scrambled up the side of the gully, his sliced leg burning with the effort. His bow lay where he'd dropped it. He grabbed it and one of the Northmen's swords. The blade wouldn't penetrate whatever enchantment guarded Svaldr, but Nechtan couldn't parry barehanded.

As he adjusted his gear, Nechtan spotted the red fletching among the drab greys and browns in his quiver. It would be one shot.

Nechtan set off at a jog, resisting the urge to stop and puke. He'd have time later—he hoped.

He spotted Svaldr and Uathach standing next to a campfire while Svaldr growled orders to two more Northmen.

Splendid.

As much as Nechtan enjoyed killing the raiders, he'd had his fill for the day. Two more obstacles between him and Svaldr.

At least the boat was small. Given the number of northern corpses Nechtan had left behind, there couldn't be many more left. Unfortunately, that meant they would be quicker to put it to sea. Already one of the men moved to lug the wood and stone anchor off the beach.

Nechtan drew an arrow, but had to discard the cracked shaft. The next one proved intact. Nechtan nocked it and drew as he stalked toward the beach. The other man tossed down a pair of oars to help lever the boat into the water. Nechtan was out of time.

The first arrow whistled behind Svaldr's head, away from Uathach. The second one struck him in the shoulder and dangled from the chainmail when it didn't pierce his flesh.

"Huntsman, you should have accepted the gift the gods gave you when the helmet kept your brains inside your skull." Svaldr unsheathed his sword, but didn't bother unlimbering his shield. "Agmund, you and Toki get my prize on the boat. I'll deal with this nuisance once and for all."

Nechtan drew back another arrow. He aimed past the crimson fletching as Svaldr stalked toward him. At ten yards away, Nechtan let the arrow fly. The bronze tip buried in Svaldr's throat with a meaty *thwock.*

Svaldr's eyes narrowed, and he grabbed for the shaft. Nechtan charged the Northman, bowling him over onto the rocky ground. Svaldr's sword skittered across the stones. As he flailed for the weapon, Nechtan seized the wrist of the hand clutching the bronze-pointed shaft and shoved with both hands. The sharp bronze tip gouged open the side of Svaldr's neck, and blood sprayed past his hand.

"You…" Blood bubbled from Svaldr's lips with a last rasp, and he ceased struggling.

Nechtan rolled off Svaldr. He debated finding a large stone to cave in Svaldr's head for good measure, but at least two Northmen remained. One of them appeared at the prow of the boat, screaming and impaled on a spear. His arms windmilled as he fell from the boat onto the beach. The impact drove the spear the rest of the way through his body.

A strangled cry sounded from within the boat. Nechtan ran to the side of the craft. The other man slumped against the gunwale, clutching at the rope wrapped around his neck. The rope jerked, accompanied by a crunch, and the raider went still.

Uathach hefted the dead man by the rope and tossed him over-board. She eyed Nechtan. "Did you *try* to wait until the last minute?"

"Were you ever in any danger?" Nechtan asked. He clumsily climbed into the boat, exhaustion and the day's injuries taking their toll. When he faltered, Uathach grabbed him by the tunic and hauled him the rest of the way in. "You could have killed them any time you wanted."

Uathach shrugged. "It wasn't my challenge. It was your trial."

"Your mother allowed Northmen to kidnap you in order to *test* me?" Nechtan peered over the bow to check that Svaldr hadn't risen from the brink of death to stab him in the back.

"Everything with my mother is a test," Uathach replied. "If you hadn't happened along, she may have charged other warriors with the task."

Svaldr hadn't budged. Nechtan sat on the foredeck. "Why me?"

"Why do so many heroes ask that question?" Uathach uncovered an oilcloth-covered chest and rummaged within. "At least they brought us provisions. We can camp here."

"You didn't answer my question," Nechtan noted.

Uathach sighed. "Your father is an aos sidhe, one of the so-called fair folk. He's placed well enough in one of the courts to bend the right ears so word would reach my mother. For someone with little formal training, your exploits impressed her. Morrigan's ravens brought word of your capture, so mother sent the selkie to fetch you to the Glaswold."

"How did the Northmen know how to enter the otherworld?" Nechtan asked. He rooted in his bag for what remained of the provisions Scathach had given him. The soggy hardtack had smooshed into the soaked blanket.

"A bitter dwarf told them. There's some cheese and salted fish." Uathach tossed a bundle from the chest onto the deck. She produced a bottle from behind her back. "Pour this on your wounds to clean them. It wouldn't do for you to die of infection before you even begin your training."

The clear liquid bubbled where it met an open wound and burned like red-hot iron. Nechtan clenched his teeth, not wanting to appear weak in front of Uathach. She handed him strips of clean linen to bandage his wounds. Did she have a bag hidden under her cloak?

After a meager dinner, followed by mead from the boat's provisions, fatigue weighed heavy on Nechtan's limbs. The hard planks of the boat would make a better bed than the stony beach. Nechtan yawned.

Uathach unrolled a large, thick wool blanket from the chest. She unpinned her cloak. "Come here. This blanket won't provide much padding, but it will have to do."

Nechtan blushed. "I'll be fine. I've slept rougher than this."

"I won't offer twice, huntsman. Join me in the blanket. Despite your disheveled state, I find you appealing enough. Killing those two fools only stoked my pent-up frustration."

Nechtan eased onto the blanket. "What about the curse?"

"You mean the one claiming any man who takes me on this island will have his manhood wither and his jewels rot off?" Uathach smirked.

Nechtan didn't find it funny. "Well, yes."

"For one, you aren't 'taking' anything." Uathach knelt on the blanket and kissed him. "For the other, the curse affects one specific lout. When the rumor spread the curse would strike any man who forced himself upon me, I saw no reason to correct the misconception."

A new surge of strength banished any thoughts of weariness and sleep. "Is this some sort of reward?"

"Don't be ridiculous," Uathach whispered in his ear. "Think of it as another test, huntsman."

* * * * *

Jon R. Osborne Bio

Jon R. Osborne is a veteran gamemaster and journalism major turned science fiction and fantasy author. The second book in the Jon's The Milesian Accords modern fantasy trilogy, "A Tempered Warrior", was a 2018 Dragon Awards finalist for Best Fantasy Novel. Jon is also a core author in the military science fiction Four Horseman Universe, where he was first published in 2017.

Jon resides in Indianapolis, where he plays role-playing games, writes science fiction and fantasy, and lives the nerd life. You can find out more at http://jonrosborne.com and at https://www.facebook.com/jonrosborne.

# # # # #

No Trade for Nice Guys
by D.J. Butler

"Look," Indrajit Twang said, "this isn't hard. You can tell us where you got the necklace. We know it was a black-market dealer of some kind, someone willing to sell stolen goods, and that's who *we're* looking for. We don't care about you. Our *patron* doesn't care about you."

"Patron?" Fibulous Mosk, the pottery merchant, was pale green, nearly spherical, and sweating. The fingers of all four of his hands, sixteen digits in total, drummed on his countertop.

"Yes, our patron." Indrajit took a large red vase from the shelves and hefted it. Imitation astrological Bonean glyphs were painted around the vase's mouth in gold to add class, but the color of the glazing clearly said the work was local. He swung the vase experimentally, as if considering how he might smash it on the floor. Indrajit's partner Fix joined in the implied threat, hoisting a pair of red clay jugs by their handles. "Did you think we were here on our own? What, just looking for a little stolen jewelry?"

Mosk shrugged. "I don't know you guys."

"You haven't heard of us? The Protagonists? We're a famous jobber company. We're the terror of risk-merchants and joint-stock promoters throughout the Paper Sook."

The merchant shrugged again, helpless.

"Anyway," Indrajit continued, "we *are*, and our patron is looking for the thief who stole this necklace. Our patron spotted the jewelry at a ball of some kind, around your wife's lovely green neck." In actuality, the necklace had been spotted by Grit Wopal, the Yifft who was the head of the Lord Chamberlain's Ears, and to whom Indrajit and Fix reported. And also, in even more actuality, Mosk's wife didn't have a neck. Indrajit had no idea how she wore the necklace, which he and Fix had retrieved from her wardrobe. "To track our way back to the thief, we need to find the vendor. So just tell us where you bought it, and we'll have no more trouble."

Fix flashed the jewelry to remind the merchant and sharpen his wits.

Mosk hissed, the upturned cups that sprouted from his head like grass on a picnic field trembling. "What did you do with my wife?"

"Nothing," Indrajit said.

"But you're going to hurt her if I don't turn over my…jeweler? You stole her necklace to show me you could hurt my family if you want to?"

Fix met Indrajit's gaze and squinted. He could do that, even standing to Indrajit's side, because Indrajit's eyes were set so far back on the sides of his skull, Fix sometimes teased him he was descended from a fish.

Fix shook his head, a subtle warning to his friend.

"We're not going to hurt your wife," Indrajit said.

The green shopkeeper's eyes narrowed. "Nice guys, is it? Yours is no trade for nice guys."

Fix smashed a jug against the countertop, sending baked clay shards flying in all directions.

"Okay, okay!" The merchant waved his hands in surrender to avert any more destruction. "I'll tell you!"

Fix raised the second jug over his head, and Indrajit set the necklace on the countertop. "We're listening," Indrajit said.

Mosk cocked his head at Fix. "Does he *ever* talk, then?"

"He talks more when you get to know him," Indrajit said. "It isn't an improvement."

"Do I get the necklace back?" Mosk licked his lips. In contrast to the pale green of his skin, his tongue was a bright crimson.

"If the information pans out—" Indrajit started to say.

"No," Fix said. Indrajit's partner was shorter than he was, but broad-shouldered and stocky. The high-pitched, soft voice that came out of him still surprised Indrajit, though they'd been partners now for weeks. Feminine though the voice could sound, it was still forceful. "We keep the necklace."

"No?" Mosk was disappointed, and the thin blue ridges over his eyes rose up and wrinkled together. Then they coalesced into a stony glare of resolve. "In that case, I can't see that I have any reason to help you."

"Sure you do," Indrajit said, thinking fast. He had planned to give the man back the necklace, provided his information proved to be accurate. "You'll help us *because* we're the good guys."

Mosk shook his head. "If I help you, then my source gets angry with me."

"Maybe," Indrajit shrugged, "but you know we'll play nice with your jeweler, just like we're being nice with you."

"That doesn't guarantee my source will forgive me."

"True," Indrajit agreed, "but if we have to go back to our patron and report failure, he'll be angry."

"Our patron is Orem Thrush," Fix said. "The lord chamberlain."

"Thrush?" Fibulous Mosk grew visibly paler.

"Orem Thrush," Fix said again. "The beast with a hundred faces, who walks unseen among the people of Kish because he can take any face he wants."

That wasn't completely accurate, but there was truth in it. Thrush's face could metamorphose into masks resembling the faces of those around him. Indrajit wasn't really sure whether Thrush consciously controlled the phenomenon, but it allowed the lord chamberlain to move about Kish anonymously. It also gave rise to extravagant rumors.

"He'll probably kill us," Indrajit said. "And then he'll send some other jobbers to catch the thief. And those guys will be better armed, more numerous, and probably really mean. You know, typical short-tunic bruisers. And just like *we* found you and your wife, *they'll* find you and your wife."

"They'll beat the information out of you," Fix said. "Or out of her."

"And your jeweler will meet them, and be really unhappy."

Fix nodded solemnly. "We're gentle. We're your best option."

"We really are." Indrajit recovered the necklace and slid it into the pocket of his kilt. "So save everyone the trouble, won't you? Just tell us who sold you the necklace."

"Was it in the Spill?" Fix suggested. "In the Alley of Ten Thousand Eyes?" The street he named was a narrow avenue that was home to a dozen jewelers. It was located near the Paper Sook, where Indrajit and Fix spent much of their time, because the presence of so much money meant the area crawled with armed guards, and crime was rare.

Or anyway, some crimes, like robbery and burglary, were rare.

Fibulous Mosk shuddered. "It's in the Dregs."

Indrajit frowned. "I don't know a jeweler in the Dregs. Do you?"

"There are no jewelers in the Dregs," Fix said. "Pickpockets, lepers, burglars, madmen, whores, beggars, cut-throats, sell-swords—"

"*Cheap* swell-swords," Indrajit said.

Fix nodded. "…smugglers, kidnappers, arsonists, poisoners, and drug addicts, yes. But no jewelers."

"My source isn't a jeweler," Mosk said. "It's a fence. I…needed to impress my wife. Buying goods that were…previously owned—"

"*Stolen*," Fix said.

"…was the only way I could afford what she wanted."

"That makes more sense," Indrajit said. "A fence would be right at home in the Dregs."

"Why are you calling your fence 'it?'" Fix asked.

"Because I don't know whether my source is a man or a woman. And no one else does, either. Its name is Jaxter Boom."

"Jaxter Boom," Fix said. "The Puppeteer."

"Whoa." Indrajit shook his head. "A jeweler, I believe. A fence, that makes sense. But puppets?"

"They call Boom the Puppeteer because it controls so many other fences," Mosk said, "as well as smugglers and thieves. The Puppeteer is a gangster, a crime lord."

"My kind of people," Indrajit lied. "Well, then, tell us how to find this Puppeteer, and we're on our way."

The green drained right out of Mosk, leaving him looking nearly white.

"Come on." Indrajit tapped his thumb against the pommel of his leaf-bladed broadsword, Vacho. "Give us the streets, and our business here is done. You never have to see us again—or at least not until you commit risk-merchantry fraud, or swindle your investors."

Fix was looking intently at the pottery merchant.

Fibulous Mosk trembled.

"One last time," Indrajit began, swelling his voice up to trumpet level.

"No need," Fix said. "I know where the Puppeteer lives."

"Really?" Indrajit felt caught off-balance. "They can't have taught you that at the ashrama, as one of your ten thousand useless pieces of knowledge." Fix had been plucked from the street as a child and raised to become a priest of Salish-Bozar the White, god of useless knowledge. He'd walked away from the priesthood for a woman, who in turned had married someone else.

Mosk shook so violently, he knocked his ledger from his countertop.

"You forget that I'm *from* here," Fix said. "I was a street urchin for years before I was ever a devotee of Salish-Bozar. Everyone knows the lair of the Puppeteer. That was a useful piece of information, especially for any kid who ever aspired to be a thief."

"Lair, that's good. We should call our offices a 'lair.'" Indrajit looked back at the shopkeeper, who was melting into the corner, the gnarled ridges on his face softened and gone flat. "We're done here, then?"

Fix nodded. "We're done. And you, Mosk," he added, his voice tightening into a high-pitched snarl, "don't you *dare* warn the Puppeteer that we're coming."

Indrajit and Fix exited onto the street. Outside, the summer sun baked the cobblestones of the Lee even through the thick, wet swaddling of summer haze. Indrajit followed Fix as the shorter man turned right, downhill, and then ducked into a large cloth merchant's tent just down the street and across from the potter's shop.

"I'm glad you caught on," Fix whispered, as the two men turned to look back at Mosk's shop. "I was worried you were going to push him too far and make him snap."

"*I'm* worried you played that last line a little too hard." Indrajit sniffed. "You can tell a *child* not to do exactly the thing that you want it to do, but a grown man?"

"I had to plant the thought in his head," Fix said. "It will work, and it will work quickly. He'll send his shop boy any minute."

A third person intruded into their conversation; the shop's clerk was tall and thin, with luminous circles under her eyes and dry, scaly skin. An orange tail whisked the cobblestones behind her. She smiled. "Can I show you gentlemen any fabric?"

Fix grunted.

"Yes." Indrajit sighed. "Bring me a bolt of your cheapest, coarsest cloth. Burlap, if you have it. I mean really, the worst you have."

The clerk sniffed. "We don't carry cheap cloth here. Perhaps you'd prefer to shop in the Caravanserai."

"Your least elegant, then," Indrajit said. "Whatever no one else is buying." He pressed two bits into the clerk's hand; she sniffed but didn't return the money, then she disappeared into the deeper chambers of the tent.

"You're a prodigal," Fix said, "a spendthrift."

"I know what a prodigal is."

"You didn't have to give her money."

Indrajit kept his eyes pinned on the door. "We might be gone before she gets back, and I don't want to ruin her day."

"You didn't want to ruin Mosk's day, either, so you were going to let him keep the lord chamberlain's stolen necklace."

"Which the lord chamberlain doesn't care that much about, because *he's* willing to let *us* keep it."

"Let me rephrase myself. You were willing to give away the biggest part of the payment Orem Thrush promised us—three-quarters of our reward, if I'm any judge of jewelry at all—for finding this thief."

"Which we're only entitled to if we actually bring back the thief. Alive. Thrush really emphasized the *alive* part." Indrajit shuddered, thinking of the beating he'd received the first time he'd entered the presence of Orem Thrush. "To be tortured, presumably."

"Think about what you're saying. You were willing to spend money we haven't actually earned yet, and might not earn at all."

Indrajit sighed. "Now you're going to tell me we have a business to run and expenses to cover."

"I'm glad to see I don't have to." Fix snorted. "Mosk isn't entirely wrong when he says this is no trade for nice guys."

"He's right about that," Indrajit said. "This is a trade for *heroes*."

The clerk returned with a bolt of cloth. It was undyed linen, and Indrajit wasted only moments fingering it. "Fifteen cubits," he said to the clerk. "One ten-cubit length, and one five-cubit."

The clerk cut the lengths of fabric, named a price, and Indrajit handed over the coins.

"You could have bargained," Fix said. "Now you've got two lengths of cheap fabric that was surprisingly costly."

"False." Indrajit tossed the ten-cubit length to his partner. "Now *you* have a toga, and *I* have a cloak. Assuming they taught you to tie a toga at the ashrama."

At that moment, Fibulous Mosk himself scurried out the front door of his shop and turned uphill, toward the Crown, the finest quarter of Kish, and the one that lay within its walls about the top of the hill upon which Kish sprawled. Through the Crown was the shortest, and the safest, route to the Dregs. The potter had a broad hat on his head, with a scarf swathed around his neck and chin to screen him from the sun, and also to hide his face. Indrajit recognized the merchant by his green forehead and the pale green skin of his four forearms.

Fix quickly folded himself into a toga. He was Kishi, the most common race of man in Kish, so the toga ought to make him essentially invisible, especially in the wealthier quarters of the city. It also nicely hid his hatchet and long knives, and his spear might be mistaken for a walking staff, especially at a distance. Indrajit, on the other hand, was tall, with wide-set eyes, a bony ridge for a nose, and a faint greenish tint to his mahogany skin, so he had a hard time disappearing into a crowd, even in Kish, where half the thousand races of man passed through the streets every day; instead, he wrapped the linen about his head and shoulders as a cloak.

Then they slipped into the street and followed the potter.

The Lee, lying on the landward side of Kish, was sheltered from the brunt of the weather that came in from the sea. On the south-facing slopes of Kish's mound, it got the largest share of heat and light in all seasons. The summer sun hammered upon Indrajit and Fix both, but Fix was a native, and underneath his toga he wore only his kilt, and the hike up into the Crown brought only the faintest trace of a crown of sweat to his brow. Indrajit, who was from cooler and wetter climes, and who now isolated his face from what breeze there was behind a linen hood, was soon panting.

Jobbers in green and gold, wearing the hammer and sword device of the lord farrier, watched the gates. Indrajit ignored them and was ignored in turn, shuffling through the gates a stone's throw behind the four-armed potter.

Chanting came from Indrajit's right as they passed within a few streets of the Sun Seat. Celebrants there would be preparing to receive the procession that marked the longest day of the year and marked one of the two turning points of the city's calendar. The summer procession, like its winter counterpart, was a holdover from the old Imperial days, when Kish had indulged in much more ceremony.

Turning right shortly beyond the Sun Seat, Indrajit and Fix followed the pottery merchant through another gate and into the Dregs.

Several quarters could reasonably vie for the title of 'worst quarter of Kish.' The Dregs did not *smell* the worst—that distinction belonged to either the East or West Flats, where the city's fishers lived and hauled in their catches. The city's worst abuses of power were likely planned in the Crown, and its financial crimes were committed in the Spill. But the Dregs was home to the contagious, the footpads, the poxy, and the murderous. It was the weeping sore of Kish.

"You didn't really live in here as a street urchin," he murmured to his partner.

"I was a homeless beggar child," Fix said. "I slept wherever people wouldn't kick me out. Believe it or not, yes, some of the more welcoming corners I slept in were here."

"Ugh." Indrajit raised his knee to step carefully over a pile of droppings whose species of origin he couldn't even guess at.

Mosk turned and turned again. At each change of direction, Indrajit and Fix rushed to catch up and then carefully watched as the merchant turned down a narrow alley, and then into a tiny plaza, choked by buildings that rose around it and leaned inward as they climbed, leaving a patch of bright sky at the top only a quarter the size of the stained cobblestones below.

Within the plaza, Mosk stood at a broad, unmarked door, talking to a tall figure wearing a black cloak. A drooping mass of flesh like an elephant's trunk descended from the open hood and twitched as Mosk whispered urgently.

Indrajit's long legs took him across the plaza in three quick steps. "Friend Mosk!" he called, letting his hood fall back to reveal his face. Just in case, he kept his hand on Vacho's hilt, concealed under his cloak. "Friend Mosk, thank you!"

Fibulous Mosk wheeled. His scarf fell away from his face, and terror twisted his green features. "But! But!"

Indrajit addressed the cloaked guard. "Our friend Fibulous has such a quick pace, he nearly left us behind. But you'd have looked a little silly, coming into Jaxter Boom's...office...to introduce us to Boom...without us!"

Fix caught up, throwing an arm around the pottery merchant. Indrajit heard the man's knees knock.

The guard shook with slow laughter. Long, shaggy hair hung down around the proboscis, trembling like leaves in the wind. "The Protagonists. You would be Indrajit Twang, and the shorter one is Fiximon Nasoprominentus Fascicular. The scholar."

"Dammit, Twang," Fix snarled. "Stop telling people that's my name."

"It's not my fault your name is so short," Indrajit protested. "It's an undignified name for a literary man."

The guard laughed again. "You've arrived earlier than we expected. My master will be pleased. But you don't need an introduction."

Indrajit felt uneasy. "In that case," he said slowly, "we should probably let our mutual friend go. He has pots to sell."

Fibulous Mosk made a squeaking noise as he escaped, one that might have been intended to communicate relief or gratitude.

The doorman opened the door. Within the hood, two twinkles briefly flashed in Indrajit's direction, hinting at unseen eyes. Indrajit discreetly checked that the necklace was safely stowed in his kilt pocket, smiled at the guard, and stepped through the door. Fix followed.

The steps immediately behind the door descended steeply, each step so narrow it could barely accommodate one of Indrajit's sandaled heels. The ceiling overhead was low, forcing him to stoop.

"Be glad you're not a Grokonk," Fix said.

"The existence of low ceilings is the least of *many* reasons why I am relieved not to be a Grokonk. The choice between being voiceless and sexless is a much more serious drawback."

"I don't know," Fix said. "You would do fine as a voiceless man."

The stairs ended in a high-ceilinged, long chamber with arches opening onto dark passages along both sides. At the far end of the room, two coal-filled braziers gave light, illuminating a glass wall, behind which sloshed dark water. The glass didn't rise all the way to the ceiling, and its depths were dark, suggesting that Indrajit was only seeing the very end of a large tank. To the left and right, two low pedestals stood pressed against the glass. Two young Kishi, a woman and a man, stood on the pedestals. They leaned back against the glass as if they needed the support; their bodies were emaciated, and their eyes vacant.

Indrajit and Fix strode forward. Behind him and to his right, Indrajit heard the steps of the guard with the long nose.

"Surely neither of these wretches can be the famed Jaxter Boom," Indrajit said.

"Boom is coming," Proboscis told them.

Indrajit heard many footfalls. Keeping his facial expression light and cheerful, he turned his head slightly. In his excellent peripheral vision, he saw all the arches exiting the room, as well as the exit to the staircase, filling with armed men. They wore no uniform, and their weapons were irregular, suggesting they weren't a jobber company or any other kind of irregular force—just thugs hired by Jaxter Boom, armed with long knives, short spears, clubs, and axes.

"Good," he said.

With a muted *whoosh* sound, something pressed itself against the glass. For a moment, Indrajit saw only indistinguishable flesh, pink and so pale it was almost white, but then a lashless blue eye opened, pressing itself against the glass. With a soft *splash*, two masses of pink flesh rose above the glass wall, unfurling themselves until Indrajit could see they were tentacles. The tentacles reached forward, each touching the back of the skull of one of the Kishi standing on the pedestals—

And then pushing forward, entering the heads of the Kishi.

The two Kishi straightened their backs, standing up. Energy seemed to fill their frames; their backs straightened, and their vacant eyes lit up, but the light was unnatural and sickly.

"I am Jaxter Boom," the Kishi said. Their voices spoke at the same pitch and in perfect unison, but somehow managed to clash with each other.

Indrajit took a deep breath.

"I assume you are the…person in the tank, and not the people standing on pedestals in front of us," he said.

"Correct," the Kishi answered in unison.

"That must be uncomfortable for *them*," Indrajit said.

"They have neither comfort nor discomfort," the Kishi said together. "They have ceased to be men, and are now simply the Voices of Jaxter Boom."

"You have two for the symmetry?" Indrajit asked. "Or because it lets you shout louder?"

"You have two because they wear out quickly," Fix said softly. "Look at them, they're wasting away. And with two at all times, you won't be left without a Voice. You must keep…spares."

"Correct, Fix of the Protagonists," the Voices said.

Indrajit wanted to know more, out of natural curiosity and because, as Recital Thane, he had yet to compose his additions to the Blaatshi Epic, and this strange race of men was not one that yet appeared in the Epic. Indrajit wanted to know more so that he could construct pointed kennings and compose stock epithets.

In addition, Indrajit was curious how Boom knew their names and expected their arrival.

But he also didn't want to aggravate this crime lord in its own lair.

"A thief sold you this." He held up the necklace so that the lashless eye could gaze directly at it. "We're hunting the thief."

"I have the thief," the Voices said. "She tried to cheat me. If you're seeking justice, be assured that the thief shall receive it."

The thief was a woman. "We've been tasked with bringing the thief back alive," Indrajit said, smiling. "Perhaps you could surrender her to us, and rest easy in the knowledge that the lord chamberlain will have her punished thoroughly enough for the wrongs she has committed against both of you."

There followed a long moment of silence.

"No," the Voices said. "I do not think I shall surrender my prerogative of justice so easily."

What could the thief have done to so irritate this crime lord that it wanted her punished, yet hadn't killed her already?

"We're prepared to pay," Indrajit said.

Fix groaned in disgust.

"How much?" the Voices asked.

"Nothing," Indrajit said, "until we see the thief and can ascertain that she's really the one who robbed the lord chamberlain. And then we're willing to negotiate. Where is she? In some cell? Stretched on the rack? You're not planning on using her as one of your Voices, are you?"

"I'll permit you to see her," the Voices said, "for the price of the necklace."

"We might be willing to pay the necklace," Indrajit said, "if you give her to us first."

"The necklace for a look." The Voices made a horrible rasping noise that might have been laughter.

"What kind of spendthrifts do you take us for?" Indrajit scowled.

"Agreed," Fix said. "The necklace for a look."

Indrajit stared at his partner.

Fix whispered, "I think more is going on here than it appears."

"So it's bad if I spend money, but prudent if you do it?" Indrajit asked.

"In this case, yes."

"Throw the necklace into the tank," the Voices commanded.

"If I'm wrong," Fix continued, "I'll take responsibility for the necklace."

"Don't be an idiot," Indrajit told his partner. "If you're wrong, we tell Grit Wopal we never found the necklace."

He threw the jewelry into the tank. It sank past the staring eye, settling on the bottom, still visible as a dull, brassy glow.

"Bring in the thief," the Voices commanded.

A rustle of voices and padding feet to Indrajit's left ended as a young woman stumbled out into the room. Her hands were tied with a thong, and she wore a simple tunic and skirt, both of silk, which had once been elegant, but were now ragged and filthy. She had an ordinary Kishi complexion and an unremarkable, rather blocky face beneath long black hair. As she glared at Indrajit, something flashed through her eyes.

Hope? Recognition?

Then the woman straightened her back and snarled. There was something familiar about her.

"How about it, then?" Indrajit asked. "Did you steal from the lord chamberlain?"

"The hells with you!" the girl snapped.

"Well, *that* was certainly worth three quarters of our pay," he murmured to Fix.

"Look again," Fix murmured back.

The young woman's face was subtly shifting. Her skin grew darker, and her nose began to bulge up in a bony ridge as her eyes seemed to swim toward her ears.

"Frozen hells," Indrajit said.

"Do you understand what you are seeing here?" the Voices asked.

Indrajit thought furiously. They were vastly outnumbered. Jaxter Boom was not going to surrender his prisoner; he was going to use her to get leverage against the lord chamberlain, and possibly for nefarious purposes.

Certainly for nefarious purposes—what other kind of purpose could such a creature have?

"You'll recall that you once had questions about my people's ancestry," Indrajit said softly.

"I still maintain that you are descended from your goddess," Fix answered.

"Good. I see only one way out by which we are not outnumbered, oh, about twenty to one."

"I'm ready," Fix said.

"Do you *understand*?" the Voices demanded.

Indrajit played dumb just a little longer. He stepped closer to the young woman, who had to be kin to Orem Thrush—a daughter? a niece?—and pretended to examine her as he would a ylakka he was considering purchasing.

He needed to get into position.

And besides, maybe they could still get out without violence.

"She looks poor, more than anything else," Indrajit said. "She's wearing someone else's stolen clothing, obviously, but she can't be a very good thief, because she's worn that to rags and hasn't been able to buy or steal a replacement."

"I'll wear your head for a helmet," the girl said to him, "and make a kilt of your hide."

She certainly sounded like Orem Thrush.

While all eyes were on Indrajit, Fix drifted back, positioning himself close to one of the Voices.

"You have the necklace," Indrajit said to Jaxter Boom. "On top of that, I'll give you ten Imperials to let us take her back to the lord chamberlain for *punishment*." He met the girl's gaze as he spoke, and saw again the flicker of emotion.

"You idiot," the Voices boomed. "How well do you know your master?"

Indrajit shrugged, took a deep breath, and sighed. "I know him well enough to *go!*"

He shouted this last word, and as he shouted it, he grabbed the young woman, wrapped his hands around her hips, and hurled her up and over the glass.

At the same moment, Fix leaped onto the pedestal and stabbed a long knife into one of the tentacles, just beside the Voice's skull.

Men roared and drew weapons. Indrajit kicked over the nearest brazier, sending glowing coals in an arc toward the center of the room, and then grabbed for the second tentacle.

Jaxter Boom yanked both its tentacles back. This had the effect of pulling Fix into the tank, and as the short man hit the water, he was raising his spear over his head with his right hand, preparing to stab. The disappearance of the tentacles also meant that Indrajit missed his grab, grabbing instead the top of the glass and scrabbling to drag himself up and over—

But hands seized his ankles.

Indrajit dragged his upper body closer to the tank, touching the glass with his chin. Dark ichor clouded the water of the tank as Fix stabbed into Jaxter Boom's eye. The two Voices staggered forward into the crowd of criminals, knocking some men down and tripping others. Blows landed on Indrajit's back and legs. He bellowed and shook himself, trying to writhe free. Looking back, he saw the guard with the long nose holding tightly to his right leg. Indrajit lost both sandals, but was also losing his grip on the glass—

The thief grabbed Indrajit by the head. Placing her feet against the glass, she kicked herself back and down, and with the weight of her body, she hauled Indrajit away from the men grabbing him.

Indrajit kicked, landing a blow on Long Nose's face.

Then he splashed into the water just ahead of two sword points. Through the glass, he saw men with spears plowing through the crowd.

"Are we sure there's a way out?" the young woman asked.

"No," Indrajit said. "Take a deep breath!"

She did, and he grabbed the cord that tied her hands together. It made a convenient handle by which to pull her, and Indrajit dove.

Fix's kicking feet ahead of him indicated the path, and Indrajit followed. Thin, wispy clouds of black ichor dissipated as Indrajit swam directly into them, shattering them with his one-armed stroke. He fought his way out of his own burlap cloak, and then through the clinging fabric of Fix's burlap toga.

Fix plunged into darkness and disappeared.

Were they going to die? Had Indrajit made a terrible, final mistake?

For long moments he struggled against black despair as he stroked. The rescued prisoner had taken a breath as directed, and she was cooperating, kicking her feet behind her, but she was doing so awkwardly. She wasn't a great swimmer, and if she started to run out of air, she might panic.

Behind him, Indrajit heard faint splashes. Looking over his shoulder, he saw the heads and shafts of long spears being stabbed into the water. Then he heard a larger splash and saw the first of Jaxter Boom's men plunge into the water.

He focused on the path ahead and saw a glimmer of light. Fix wiggled, a dark silhouette on the right side of Indrajit's frame of vision. Then the light shone down directly on Fix's body, and Indrajit saw his partner stop, look upward, and then swim up toward the light.

Toward air, hopefully. Indrajit's lungs ached.

Four long tentacles reached out from the darkness and grabbed Fix.

Indrajit yelled out of pure instinct, and shouted the last air from his lungs out into the water. Instantly, he felt dizzy, and sank. He was going to die, suffocated or crushed by the same arms that were now drawing Fix out of the light and back into darkness.

His foot touched rock and he felt the young woman thrashing. Bracing himself, he pushed her forward toward the light, and then with his right hand he drew Vacho from its sheath.

Inanely, some part of him wanted to shout a battle cry, like the heroes of the Epic. Vacho was, after all, named after the lightning-sword of Inder, an ancient name of the city's great storm god, Hort. Fortunately Indrajit had mastered his instinct to yell again, and instead lunged through the shaft of light into the darkness, left hand extended and groping, right hand tucked under his shoulder, ready to stab.

To his left, the young woman's feet kicked as she swam up to the light.

Indrajit's fingers found something elastic and smooth, something that tensed as he touched it. His head swam; much more time without air and he would pass out. He closed his hand, found his fingers wrapped around something rope-like, and then pulled himself toward it. In the gloom, he saw Fix, shuddering, a tentacle wrapped around his neck. He saw pale skin, and then an eye.

Indrajit stabbed.

Black ichor jetted from the eye and struck Indrajit in the face.

Darkness. Lights flashed in his vision.

Something hit Indrajit, but he wasn't sure.

What it was.

Warm. He felt.

Warm.

* * *

Air forced its way into Indrajit's lungs, and he coughed. Hands gripped his face. Indrajit spat out water, and the hands shifted, turning him over onto his side. He gagged, coughed again, and then suddenly he was sucking in warm air. His limbs felt numb and leaden.

"See?" He heard Fix's voice say. "He's at least half fish."

His vision returned, and Indrajit struggled through more coughing to sit up. He was sprawled on a stretch of rocks, and the air reeked of salt and decay.

Fix and the young woman they had rescued stood over him.

"I guess Boom must live in the sea," Fix said, looking out at the water.

Indrajit decided he didn't want to know which of the two had breathed air into him. He wobbled, but with Fix's help, he was able to stand up, and then Fix handed him Vacho, hilt first.

"Thanks." Indrajit sheathed his weapon. Sensation was gradually returning to his arms and legs.

"I only ever saw it in the water," the woman said.

"Ouch." Indrajit shook a sharp, stabbing rock out of his foot.

"You guys work for my father," the young woman said.

"You're not a thief." Indrajit took deep breaths, trying to shake a lingering feeling of dizziness.

She shook her head. "My name is Yalka, and that was my necklace. I was kidnapped."

"Boom sold the necklace as a signal," Fix said. "He wanted us to find him and learn he held Yalka, so he could have leverage over Yalka's father."

"I guess your father didn't want to tell anyone his daughter had disappeared," Indrajit said to the girl. "And he sent us because he knew we wouldn't want to kill anyone, even someone we thought was a thief."

Fix shook his head. "He sent us because we're the best." He raised a hand, and in it he held Yalka Thrush's necklace. He held it out toward the girl.

"We'd better get moving," Indrajit said. "By the smells, we're near the East Flats, which means we have a bit of a run to get you home. And some of those fellows might be able to swim."

"Keep the necklace," Yalka Thrush said. "It's a fair trade."

* * * * *

D.J. Butler Bio

D.J. (Dave) Butler has been a lawyer, a consultant, an editor, and a corporate trainer. His novels include *Witchy Eye, Witchy Winter*, and *Witchy Kingdom* from Baen Books, as well as the forthcoming modern fantasy novel, *The Cunning Man*. He also writes for children: the steampunk fantasy adventure tales *The Kidnap Plot, the Giant's Seat*, and *The Library Machine* are published by Knopf. Other novels include *City of the Saints* from WordFire Press.

Dave also organizes writing retreats and anarcho-libertarian writers' events, and travels the country with the Bard's Tower to sell books. He plays guitar and banjo whenever he can, and likes to hang out in Utah with his children.

# # # # #

Fistful of Silver by
Quincy J. Allen

A Guardians of Pelinon Novelette

One

Careful of the black bird perched on his saddle, Rellen guided his black stallion, Shaddeth, through the iron gates of Calamath City. He entered the shadow-filled stone portal stretching thirty feet ahead and felt the chill of winter that still clung to the southern regions of the Pelinon Kingdom. With one hand, Rellen pulled his black woolen cloak tighter around his leather pauldrons and the bandoleer of pouches that crossed his chest. With his other, he held before him a small sphere of obsidian—the Eye of Tuluum—suspended upon a silver chain draped around his neck. His keen gray eyes were fixed upon the dramatic angle of the stone as it leaned forward several inches away from his body, defying gravity.

Shaddeth's hooves, covered by the white feathering at his fetlocks, clopped slowly across cobbled stones, sending heavy echoes ahead and drawing the wary eyes of two city guards in green tunics who stood in the sunlight just beyond the portal. One of them eyed Shaddeth's muscled, chainmail-clad form with an appraising eye, while the other seemed intent upon the dagger-like blaze of white running down the middle of Shaddeth's face. Both guards had stern expressions, as if Rellen—or the horse—were guilty of some crime.

Rellen exited the portal, relishing the warmth of the late afternoon sun, and nodded to the guards, who remained silent as he passed by. Ahead lay a wide-open half-circle of cobbled stones about forty yards across with a fountain at its center, and three streets entering the area. A tall pile of aged firewood lay between the portal and the fountain, and a group of youths added to the pile one log at a time. A dozen or so men and women in the bright southern garments of the region busily hung holly branches and pine wreaths upon the doors and balconies of the shops that faced in toward the fountain. Rellen realized they were preparing for the Winter Solstice Celebration the following night. He'd been on the road for several weeks and had forgotten all about it.

As Rellen passed the fountain, the pendant swung back and dangled freely in his hand. Rellen pulled up short and sighed with frustration.

"That's all you're going to give me?" he asked quietly.

The Eye gave no reply—not that he expected one—so he slipped the stubborn relic beneath his tunic, where the cold obsidian gem chilled his chest. As usual, the Eye had provided only enough information to direct him to where he was supposed to be.

"I guess I'll have to do it the old-fashioned way," he lamented. "As usual."

Turning in his saddle, one hand resting upon the wrapped bundle of books lashed to Shaddeth's withers, he looked to the nearest of the guards.

"Can you direct me to the City Guard Tower?" he asked.

"Aye," the guard replied. "Straight up Barony Road, there." He pointed past the fountain and down the middle street. "Seven blocks and you'll see it on the right. Gray stone walls and a bell tower four stories up."

"My thanks," Rellen replied. Before turning back, he noticed two small, sharp-horned beetles with thick blue carapaces crawling across the bundle of books. He'd been plagued by the creatures since he entered the region. They weren't dangerous, but if you squashed them, their stench was horrible. He flicked them both off his books, adjusted the heavy crossbow dangling from his saddle, and gave Shaddeth's reins a shake that set the warhorse moving once again.

Rellen's eyes drifted across the faces of those preparing for the Solstice, and he noted something strange. The Winter Solstice was a happy time, marking when the days would grow longer and the nights shorter. Calamath was an agrarian city, and he would have assumed these people would be in better spirits. They all seemed subdued—quiet, and almost fearful. Then he saw more city guards, all of them with wary eyes, as if they feared some sort of danger or subterfuge.

Rellen proceeded along Barony Road, the shop fronts rolling by, when a commotion ahead broke the calm.

"Please don't take him!" a woman cried as a guard held her shoulders. "He's done nothing wrong!"

Two more guards stood in the street, one of them holding a set of shackles in his hands.

As Rellen approached, two other guards hauled a big fellow out of what appeared to be a pottery shop. The prisoner had long, wavy red hair and a nose one could plow a field with, but for all his size, and what appeared to a thick frame beneath winter wool, he was no match for the guards. They dragged him into the street.

A number of passersby stared on, but they did not stop, and many hastily disappeared into nearby shops, as if they were fearful they might also be clapped in irons.

"I tell you, I'm innocent!" the man shouted.

"Of course you are," a guard growled. "All you Nissra cultists are innocent."

"You can take it up with the lieutenant," another guard said. "All that stands between you and freedom is a purification rite."

"There's nothing to purify, I tell you." The man struggled in their grasp. "I do not have the taint of evil upon me!"

"Then you've got nothing to fear, do you?" the guard with the chains asked.

"Just go through the rite!" the woman cried. "Do as they say, and everything will be fine."

The man looked to his wife with frightened eyes and slowly relaxed.

Taking a deep breath, he said, "I will, Magdelain. I'll be home soon. I promise."

Rellen didn't slow as he watched a guard shackle the shopkeeper.

One of the guards looked up at him with guarded eyes.

"Move along," he ordered, pointing down the street. "You'll only find trouble here."

Rellen nodded and proceeded up the street with an easy *clip-clop* of Shaddeth's hooves. The street was busy, with people from all walks of life moving about. Most of the shops had a wreath on their door or balcony. He spied three-sconce candelabras in many of the windows, candles burning bright, meant to stave off darkness during the longest night of the year.

He crossed several blocks before spying a bell tower on the righthand side. He made his way to it and guided Shaddeth to a wide area on the near side with several hitching posts. He quickly dismounted and secured Shaddeth's reins to the post nearest a heavy wooden door cut into the side of the stonework guard tower.

Taking a quick inventory of everything secured to his mount, and confident Shaddeth would stomp anyone foolish enough to lay a hand on his belongings, he pulled a small strip of vellum and a charcoal stick from a pouch and scrawled the message, *"Eye led to Calamath. Seeking bounties."* Rolling the vellum up, he held it before the black bird on his saddle, who obediently clamped down on it with its beak. When Rellen stepped back, the bird leapt from the saddle and flew northeast.

Giving a satisfied nod, he moved up to the heavy wooden door, opened it, and stepped inside.

Lanterns hanging on the walls and from a low ceiling lit the interior of the guard tower, a mixture of gray stone and dark timbers. The front double doors to his left were closed, but not barred. A weapons rack full of pikes, heavy spears, and longswords adorned one wall, and there was a large, empty cage on the far side of the room. A desk filled the space to Rellen's right, and beyond the desk was a closed wooden door. Behind the desk sat a sour-looking city guard with dark, curly hair down to his shoulders and piggy eyes of green that narrowed as Rellen stepped up.

"Can I help you?" the guard asked tersely. His eyes rolled from the falchions at Rellen's hips, up along the bandoleer of pouches, and stopped at Rellen's placid countenance.

"I suspect you can," Rellen said easily. "I am Rellen of Corsia, and I wish to check in with the captain of the Guard."

"I'm Lieutenant Stevin Maddock, and nobody sees the captain just by coming in here and asking. He's a busy man, and being from the capital city doesn't amount to a pile of rat shit around here."

Rellen blinked a few times and let a slim, patient smile work its way onto his face.

"Of course it doesn't," he replied calmly. "What does amount to a good deal more is that I'm a bounty hunter come to Calamath to review your board and see what might be of interest to me."

Maddock sneered when he heard the term *bounty hunter*.

"Let me see your writ," he barked, holding out his hand.

"I'm afraid I'll only present that to the captain. It is not only my right, but it's been my experience that starting with the captain has a tendency to alleviate any future... *misunderstandings*."

Maddock blew out an irritated breath.

"We don't need your kind in Calamath," he said bitterly. "You should leave the city."

Rellen smiled broadly. He was accustomed to such treatment, having faced it with some frequency in the smaller baronies he'd visited across the realm.

"Well, Lieutenant Maddock, if it was up to you—or even the Baron, himself—I'd leave forthwith. Unfortunately for you, it's not." He put just a hint of an edge on the last word. "Assuming I don't break any laws, only a magistrate, or King Saren himself, can order me to leave this or any other city. As a member of the Guild, my duty is to check in with the City Guard, which is why I'm here, and I have every right to do so with your captain. Would you please fetch him?"

As Maddock stood, a decidedly bitter look upon his face, the front double doors opened inward with a thud, and two guards led in the red-headed shopkeeper, who was now secured in shackles. They marched him in toward the closed door at the back of the room.

Maddock nodded in satisfaction as they passed by and opened the door.

"Lock that Nissran up with the others." Turning to Rellen, he said, "Alright, bounty hunter, come with me."

Maddock followed the guards and their prisoner, with Rellen in tow. They entered a second room with a large desk on the right where a middle-aged man sat, going through a stack of vellum. His eyes flitted up to the guards, who led their prisoner through an iron door at the back of the room, and then he shifted his gaze to Maddock and Rellen.

"Captain Kellith Hendron," Maddock said stiffly, "this is bounty hunter Rellen of Corsia, here to check in."

"Thank you, Lieutenant. That will be all," Hendron said.

"Yes, sir," Maddock said. With a parting sneer at Rellen, he walked out of the room, leaving the door open behind him.

Rellen stepped up to the desk, reached into a pouch at his waist, and pulled out a folded piece of heavy vellum. He handed it over to the captain.

"Thank you," Hendron said. "It was Rellen, yes?"

"That's correct, Captain."

The captain unfolded and read through the writ. When he got to the bottom, his eyes widened in mild surprise. "This is signed by King Saren himself."

"Yes, sir," Rellen said easily. "I knew him when he was young." The captain raised his eyes expectantly, but Rellen offered no further explanation. "If I may, I'd like to review the board."

Captain Hendron took one last look at the writ, drew in a long breath, and let it out. Folding the vellum, he handed it back. "Of course," he said as Rellen slipped the writ back into its pouch.

Hendron rose and moved around the desk, leading Rellen to the board on the far side of the room. Bounty posters covered it, with most of them depicting rough sketches of criminal faces. Some Rellen recognized as Capital Bounties offered by the king, but others were regional or local in nature, with most of those showing the Seal of Calamath.

Rellen reviewed the board slowly, but nothing caught his attention. He didn't know what he was looking for, but that wasn't unusual. The Eye of Tuluum had led him to Calamath, and his duty as a bounty hunter had brought him to the board.

There was only one thing for him to do now.

He pulled out the Eye and dangled it in front of the board. Moving his hand over each bounty, he watched for any sort of reaction. Suddenly, the Eye slid forward, once again defying gravity. The poster before it didn't have a sketch, or even a description of the criminal. It simply held the name "Ravager," and posted a bounty of five hundred pieces of gold.

Rellen smiled. "Tell me about this one," he said, turning to the captain.

Hendron had been staring at the Eye, mildly surprised at its behavior, but he then shifted his gaze to Rellen.

"The Ravager." Hendron let out a slow breath and went very calm. "The killings started a month ago. We've found twelve bodies inside the city so far, one every two or sometimes three days. Each one was slashed to ribbons with blades, and the killer carved the sigil of Nissra into each forehead."

"Do you suspect that shopkeeper they just brought in?" Rellen said.

Hendron looked surprised. "Not that I'm aware of," he said. "To be perfectly honest, I don't know why they brought that fellow in, although it's possible he's been accused of Nissra involvement. The Nissra cult has been growing steadily for the past six months or so. When we discover them, we perform a purification ritual to purge the taint of Nissra. That was mostly under control, until these murders started."

Rellen knew little about Nissra. What he did know could be summarized in the fact that she was a minor blood goddess in the

Zalliphur pantheon. She had a host of demons at her disposal, and she tasked her minions and followers with seeking the flesh and blood of non-faithful—the more innocent, the better. He also knew that there was little place for such filth in civilized societies. Nissra cults were a plague—one Rellen had never faced—but he knew they needed eradication.

"That's some pendant you have there," Hendron said, changing the subject. "What does it do? Lead you to evil?"

Rellen gave a slight chuckle.

"No," he said wryly. "Nothing so direct. It's a scrying stone of sorts. It leads me to places, sometimes things, but it only works on destinations relevant to me, and it can be fickle. It led me to this city, and it led me to that." He pointed to the bounty poster. "But it won't lead me to people, and therefore, not the Ravager. That I'll have to do the old-fashioned way."

"Where did you get such a thing?" Hendron asked, genuinely curious.

Rellen smiled. "Oh, I picked this up when I was young. It's a long story, one I'm not inclined to tell."

Hendron looked like he was going to press the matter when thudding footsteps filled the outer room, followed by a boy shouting, "My Da is dead! The Ravager got him. Please come help!"

"There it is," Hendron said quietly. "Just a little later than expected."

Rellen turned curious eyes to Hendron as the captain strode into the next room. He followed to find a small, dark-haired lad in threadbare clothing standing before Lieutenant Maddock.

"It's alright, son," Hendron said, stepping up to the boy. "We're here to help."

Lieutenant Maddock's gaze turned from the boy to his captain. "It seems we have another mess to clean up."

"Let the boy lead you to his father," Hendron replied. "Find out what you can, and if the silver is there, bring it back to me immediately." Hendron shook his head. "Gods-be-damned Nissrans," he grumbled in a low voice.

"I'd like to go with them, Captain Hendron," Rellen said. "It seems my pendant has brought me to the right place at the right time."

"We don't need help from a damned bounty hunter," Maddock growled.

Hendron looked hesitant. "I'm not sure that's a good idea. I'd prefer that Maddock go alone. A bounty hunter in the mix could complicate an already tangled affair."

"Respectfully, Captain, my writ gives me the authority to tag along. While I am oath-bound not to interfere with your investigation, I am permitted to observe civil operations in pursuit of a bounty."

Captain Hendron sighed. "Very well," he said, opening his eyes once again. He glanced at Rellen and then turned his gaze to Lieutenant Maddock. "Maybe a fresh set of eyes might help. Take him along."

Rellen hadn't thought it possible, but Maddock's features grew even more sour.

"Yes, Captain," Maddock said.

* * * * *

Two

The boy led Maddock about ten blocks south into the city, with Rellen following on horseback, before guiding them into a maze of alleys that smelled of emptied chamber pots and rotting vegetables. Wooden balconies hung over their path, blocking out much of the waning sunlight and adding more chill to the air. There were dead-end alleys and dilapidated courtyards all along the way, a testament to the more impoverished area of the city they now occupied. Occasionally, a man or woman with nervous eyes would steal a glance over a balcony as the three passed by. Maddock said not a word once they'd left the guard tower, and he seemed to be going out of his way to keep his back to Rellen.

After navigating enough maze for Rellen to worry about minotaurs, they made one final turn and entered a filthy inner courtyard of sorts, where a crowd had gathered, chattering in low hisses and whispers. From Shaddeth's saddle, Rellen saw that the crowd surrounded two teenage boys with angry eyes who stood facing away from each other. The older one, a lad of roughly sixteen years, threatened the crowd with a rusty short sword. The other, perhaps twelve, hefted a cleaver that looked gigantic in his small hands. The two boys stood guard over something that lay between them, and Rellen heard the sobbing cries of a woman nearby. The features and dark hair of the two boys, so very much like the lad who'd led them there, proclaimed their obvious kinship.

Rellen dismounted as the boy led Maddock toward the edge of the crowd.

"Make way!" Maddock shouted.

The nearest peasants turned angry eyes toward the intrusive command, but those same eyes grew wary, even fearful, when they spied Maddock's guard tunic. Those in his path parted quickly, shoving people to get out of his way. The last of the crowd separated, revealing the two boys guarding the horribly ravaged body of a middle-aged man in blood-soaked rough woolen garb. The area was slick with blood, and the victim appeared to have been killed by a thousand cuts. Most of his arms and legs had been exposed, for his killer had chosen to slash through the garments rather than removing them to undertake what Rellen suspected was some sort of sacrifice.

Several of the blue horned beetles crawled along the pavement nearby, but they seemed uninterested in the body or the blood. Rellen made sure not to step on any of them, for he didn't want to experience that stench again. Once had been quite enough.

"I brought them, Dalen," their guide shouted as he ran up to the eldest of the two boys standing guard.

"They killed him," Dalen said, his eyes upturned to Maddock. "They butchered him like an animal!"

"I know, boy," Maddock said tersely. "I have eyes. Now step aside so I can do my job. We'll see justice done yet. I promise."

Dalen hesitated a moment and then moved off, his gaze turning to the slashed husk of his father.

Rellen moved in as well, stepping off to one side so he could get a good look at what had happened.

The body was laid out face up, with arms slightly away from the body, and the palms upward. In the left palm someone had stacked a neat pile of silver coins. Although the coins were pristine, the victim was entirely covered in blood. Rellen had seen worse in his time, but not by much. He bent over to inspect the mark of Nissra clearly carved into the man's forehead. It was a neat circle of exposed white skull, with deep gouges carved into the bone that formed two curves in a V shape topped by a half-circle. And to the right of the mark, a perfect near-half-circle had been cut into the flesh.

"It's just like the others," Maddock said, crouching down on the other side of the body.

"Exactly?" Rellen asked.

Maddock hesitated, and for a moment he had a thoughtful look upon his face.

"Well, that curved line on the forehead is bowed more than the last one..." he finally said. "It's almost a complete half circle now."

"But the others were different?" Rellen focused his attention on the small curve cut into the man's forehead.

"Yes. Each body had a different sized curve or a straight line right there."

"I'm assuming you've gotten rid of the previous bodies?" Rellen asked, hoping to see the other marks.

"Of course. They'd all been carved up the same. We burned each within a few days of discovery."

"Curse the luck," Rellen muttered under his breath.

"Listen, bounty hunter, they were always the same on the arms and legs, and there didn't seem to be any on the torso, except for the last one across the throat."

"I meant no disrespect," Rellen said softly. "It's just that such details can be important to someone with my training. Could you draw those lines and curves in order from memory?" He pulled out a piece of vellum and charcoal.

Maddock gave a curious smile. "Sure...I can't imagine what you'll be able to make of them, though." Maddock took the vellum and charcoal and started making marks.

"You let me worry about that," Rellen replied. "No detail is too small in my line of work."

"Whatever you say."

Crouching, Rellen dipped a finger into the blood on the cobblestones. It was mostly dry, which meant the body had been there most of the day. His instincts told him the murder had happened no more than a few hours before sunrise.

"Tell me, son," Rellen said, rising to face Dalen, "when did you find him?"

"Maybe an hour ago," Dalen replied as tears rolled down his cheeks. "We'd been searching all morning when my brother Shadol found him back here."

"Did anyone touch anything?"

"No, sir," Dalen said. "When the three of us got here, I sent Thukal to get the city guard. The crowd gathered while we waited."

"When did you see your father last?"

A woman with auburn hair, a stained apron, and a neat but faded dress stepped up as she dabbed at the tears on her face with a kerchief.

"He was home last night at nine bells," she said. "He left for a tavern—I don't know which one—and we didn't see him until Dalen found...*this*." Her eyes flicked to her husband's body, and she turned away, her body wracked with sobs. She threaded her way through the crowd toward the perimeter.

Rellen glanced at Maddock, who seemed bored with the whole thing. He had to concede, finding twelve bodies like this deadened ones senses to such carnage, but Maddock's disinterest seemed peculiar. Maybe Maddock was just that surly. Maybe he'd given up trying to figure out who had committed the crimes. Even Rellen had to admit, for a city guard, there wasn't a lot to work with, especially in a city where the Nissra cult was gaining a foothold.

He glanced up and realized the buildings rose on three sides around the small courtyard, and there were no balconies or windows facing inward. It was a perfect place to do what had been done to this man. Normally his screams would have been heard for a great distance, but there were both magical and herbal means of silencing a person when one wanted to do something terrible. Rellen had used such means himself in the past.

"Did anyone hear or see anything?" he asked, looking around the gathered peasants. Maddock gave him another sour look.

Several said, "No," and most of the heads shook in the negative. Many of them held fear in their eyes, so he couldn't be certain if anyone knew anything or not. These people would be fearful of both the Ravager *and* the city guard. They were caught in the middle. He'd seen it before, and he suspected none of them would speak up even if they thought it was safe.

Rellen moved around the body, past Maddock, and crouched over the open palm full of silver coins.

"Curious about the coins," Rellen said. He counted twelve, and they were stacked neatly into a small pyramid. "They all had this?"

Maddock blew out an irritated breath. "The first had one coin, the second two, and so on. I would assume the next body, if there is one, will have thirteen. They were all laid out like this, and they all had the mark of Nissra in their foreheads. There were no tracks leading away from the scene, no bits of hair or paper left behind. Nothing. And nobody ever heard or saw what happened."

Rellen examined the body from head to toe. At the victim's waist, he saw a coin purse, and it appeared to be full.

"So the Ravager didn't rob them, either. Why leave the silver?"

"We don't know, bounty hunter. Why don't *you* figure it out?"

"Where are the rest?"

"Of the coins? The captain has them all in his desk…as evidence. Although I can't imagine what good that will do."

Maddock bent over and retrieved the coins from the victim's hand. He was about to slip them into a pouch at his waist when Rellen stepped up.

"I don't suppose I could exchange a silver for one of those, could I?" he asked.

Maddock glared at him. "This is evidence," he barked. "It all has to go to the captain."

Rellen smiled. "Let me rephrase that." He reached into a pouch and pulled out a silver coin and a gold one. "I'll gladly exchange a silver to replace one of those and add a gold for your trouble. You said yourself that you didn't see how it could be used as evidence." Rellen knew that he was just on the edge of breaking his oath to the law. He could feel a twinge—just a tingle—deep in his guts, but there was nothing explicitly unlawful about him possessing a piece of evidence, so long as he didn't steal it, and all parties were aware of the transaction.

Maddock narrowed his eyes and licked his lips thoughtfully. His eyes shifted back and forth. Rellen could see Maddock's mind working.

"Alright," he finally said. "What harm is there? A fistful of silver is still a fistful of silver." He held out one of the coins and, for a flickering moment, he looked at Rellen as if he were calculating something. Then for the first time, Maddock smiled. "I guess you're not so bad after all."

"I'm glad you think so," Rellen said, taking the coin. He placed the silver and gold into Maddock's hand, nodded his thanks, and knelt down over the body once again. "So what can you tell me about the wounds?"

Maddock sighed. "It's just like the other eleven. Arms and legs slashed to pieces, clothes still on, and blood everywhere. I'd have to say it is peculiar that the slashes seem to be pretty consistently placed, as if each one was put where it belonged."

"So it's probably a ritual…" Rellen said to himself. "Perhaps even magical." He let his eyes move from one slash to the next, looking for a pattern or shape that might hold meaning.

"Look," Maddock said, only a little tersely, "I examined each one as soon as I got to it." He crouched beside Rellen. "I don't know what you think you'll be able to find that I didn't."

"Maybe nothing, but it's worth checking." He glanced at Maddock. "Besides, I may have a few tricks that you don't." He gave the lieutenant a wink and then pulled a bit of deeply black powder from one of the pouches on his bandoleer. He closed his eyes, whispered an incantation in the Arcana language, and sprinkled the powder over the body from waist to chin, letting the last of it fall over the victim's heart.

The powder swirled over the body, slowly at first, gaining speed in tiny black cyclones, and then coalesced into one large sphere about an inch in diameter. The sphere hovered over the victim's chest for a few moments, and then vibrated as it spun on its vertical axis. A few moments later, the sphere divided, splitting into two spheres with one about twice the size of the other. They orbited each other for a few seconds, rejoined once again, and then, with a small flash of light, exploded into a puff of smoke that floated slowly away.

Rellen cocked his head to the side. He'd never seen the spell do that before.

"What are you doing there?" Maddock asked.

"It's a simple incantation meant to reveal how many souls took the victim's life. It coalesces on the lifeforces present at the time of death. And your Ravager appears to be *Ravagers*."

Maddock looked worried. "Are you certain?"

"Fairly so. Although there was something strange…see how the big one split into two?"

"Yes."

"Well, let's just say that's a little out of the ordinary." Rellen didn't know why the spheres would separate and rejoin like they did. Normally there would be a sphere for each participant in the killing. He had no idea what it meant.

"So there were two of them, and not just one," Maddock said. "Hell, the city has more Nissrans every day. What difference does it make? We should just hunt them all down and give them the purification ritual. Problem solved. Can we go now?"

For a moment, he considered calling Maddock out on his disinterest, but then something occurred to him. *What if he's one of the Ravagers? Or part of the cult and protecting the killer?*

He looked back at the body, letting his eyes run over it from head to toe. Something didn't add up. A deep patch of blood soaked the center of the man's woolen tunic, but there weren't any slashes through the material there. Granted, blood covered the clothing, but the concentration on his chest looked out of place somehow.

"Lieutenant," Rellen said, looking up. "You said the marks were the same on the arms, legs, and throat."

"That's right."

"Did you strip them down...look at their chests and backs?"

"No. There weren't any slashes in the fabric like the rest of the body. We burned them just as we found them."

Rellen's eyes drifted back to the blood-soaked tunic. He lifted the victim's garment up from the waist and was surprised to find a small set of sigils carved into the flesh with a narrow blade, just over the heart. He pulled a piece of cloth from a pouch on his belt and wiped away most of the blood that obscured them. He immediately recognized the language of the sigils.

When he looked up, Maddock's eyes were fixed upon the symbols, and his expression was blank.

"Could I have that vellum and charcoal?" Rellen asked, holding out his hand.

Maddock handed them over, and Rellen quickly sketched the sigils.

"What are they?" Maddock asked.

"Sigils. The language is Azjerbahn, and it's used in the dark arts."

"So it's a spell?" Maddock asked.

"I honestly don't know…could be just ritual. Or maybe these Ravagers are completely out of their heads. I may be able to find out, though. Is there a magic school in this city?"

"Yes. It's near the Duke's castle…on the south side, along the main thoroughfare. Do you want me to keep this body?"

"No," Rellen said, rising to his feet. He slipped the charcoal into the pouch he kept it in and folded the vellum. Heading for Shaddeth, he looked over his shoulder. "I think I have what I need."

"What are you going to do now?" Maddock looked slightly confused.

"First, I'm going to find an inn. Then I plan on finding the Ravagers…After that, I'm going to get paid." He smiled. "So where's a good inn?"

"There's one just a couple doors down the street from the magic school, actually," Maddock said, "called the Green Gryphon. My cousin runs it."

"Perfect," Rellen said, pulling himself up into the saddle. "I'll see you around, Lieutenant."

With that, he pulled on the reins and guided Shaddeth back the way they had come, leaving a wake of perplexed faces behind him.

* * * * *

Three

The owner of the Green Gryphon—a spindly man named Mr. Cray—had suspicious eyes, a hawk nose, and tidy linen clothing of forest green. He led Rellen to a door halfway along the second floor of the inn, slid a key into the lock, and pushed the door open with a flourish.

"There she be, sir." Cray pulled the key out and slipped it into Rellen's shirt pocket.

Rellen, having left Shaddeth at the livery stable next door, was burdened with his heavy crossbow, saddlebags, and the bundle of books. He entered a simple room with a bed, dresser, table, small fireplace, and a row of coat-pegs just inside the door. He laid his gear upon the table and followed that with both falchions.

"Thank you, Mr. Cray. This will do nicely." He stepped up to the door, slipped Cray a silver, and smiled. "Now if you'll excuse me, I have some work to do." Without another word, he closed the door on a surprised face, slipped the key from his pocket, and locked the bolt.

Rellen moved to the fireplace, took several split logs from the pile beside it, and set them on the hearth. He placed his hand upon the logs, uttered a quick incantation, and the bottom-most log ignited with a sparking flash.

As the flames quickly spread across the other logs, he made his way to the table. Sitting down in the creaking chair, he pulled out a small sheet of vellum and a piece of charcoal from one of his pouches, and began writing.

"Hunting a killer—or killers—of twelve. Likely related to growing Nissra cult. Magic probably involved. Nothing solid. It could involve constabulary. Send a detachment."

Pulling a black feather from a pouch on his bandoleer, he placed it upon the table, closed his eyes, and gesticulated several times with both of his hands as he uttered a lengthy incantation. He felt the energy coalesce in the space before him and pour into the feather. Soon, the feather glowed an unearthly blue. He spoke the incantation again, focusing his will upon it. When he finished, the feather glowed white and transformed into a crow. The bird came to life, turned its head, and blinked at him several times.

Rellen rolled up the small piece of vellum and let the creature bite down upon it. He then went to the window, opened it onto the main street, and waited as the bird leapt from the table and flew out. It quickly adjusted its course and headed northeast.

With that out of the way, Rellen undid the strap securing the books and set them to the side one by one. When he got to a particularly thick, leather-bound tome entitled the *Lingua Magica*, he set the rest aside and thumbed through it until he came to a section titled "Azjerbahn." Retrieving his sketch of the sigils from the victim's chest, he began the painstaking process of translation.

It took him several hours, but when he was done, he examined what he had produced.

"Bonds cut from seething flesh, tying mother and son, the mother breaks upon fullest night."

He read it again.

And again.

Rellen shook his head. The bloody thing didn't make much sense to him. Did it mean cutting bonds to free something? Was it creating bonds cut from flesh? He was dealing with the Nissra cult, so it really could be either. Who was mother? Who was son? And how could a mother be born?

"Better to sleep on it," he said quietly. Over the years, he'd found that sleeping helped him solve magical mysteries. He could feel fatigue working its way into his body, so he had more than one reason to turn in.

He rose to his feet with one last thing to do. He considered doing what he always did, but something told him that changing his routine might bear fruit.

He turned to the fire, placed his palms together, and pointed his fingers at the flames. He focused his will upon the glowing embers beneath the hearth and picked out two. He uttered a brief incantation of some potency, and as he pulled his hands apart, both embers lifted out and floated through the air toward him, until each hovered above one of his open palms. He focused upon the one above his left hand and spoke another incantation that caused the ember to glow more brightly. When it was white hot, he stretched his hand out toward the window, the ember following obediently, and he blew once upon it. The ember sailed toward the window, impacted upon the glass, and spread across the entire surface with a flash of ruby light. He repeated the same process, this time blowing the ember over his other hand toward the door, where it impacted and spread across the entire surface.

Rellen let out a long, weary breath.

The spells of the day had taken their toll, and with a wash of deep fatigue, he moved over to the bed, grabbing one of his falchions along the way, and lay down upon the bed fully clothed and still in his leather armor. It was an old ritual, and one he was unlikely to abandon.

* * * * *

Four

A loud *WHUFF* of flame followed by a man screaming in agony sent Rellen leaping from the bed, falchion in hand. In the pale glow of the dying fire, he saw a man lying on the floor just inside the open door, writhing in pain and screaming.

The window shattered with another *WHUFF* as a man tumbled through. He immediately fell to the floor and added his screams to the chaos.

A shadow filled the doorway, and Rellen watched a burly man with a short sword tentatively stick his weapon and then his hand through the opening.

"You can come in," Rellen called over the screaming. "The spell is spent. Besides, what would your masters think of such cowardice?"

Rellen's taunt had the desired effect.

The man's pock-marked features turned furious.

"*Infidel*," the last intruder hissed as he charged in. He swung his weapon in a fast, overhand arc Rellen parried easily with a clang of steel on steel. The attacker drew the blade back and sent a fist flying toward Rellen's chin. Rellen leaned back, blocked another slash of the short sword, and then kicked the assailant squarely in the crotch.

The man grunted, doubling over as Rellen side-stepped, raised his blade, and separated the man's head from his shoulders with a wet *THUCK*. Without pausing, Rellen stepped forward and thrust his blade through the throat of the man writhing by the door, silencing him.

Wrenching his falchion free, Rellen turned on the man writhing by the window, although his screams were easing into a pained groan.

Rellen stepped up and unceremoniously kicked the last assailant across the jaw, snapping his head back and forth. His groaning stopped, but his breathing didn't.

"I still have use for you, my friend." Rellen said with satisfaction.

There was a commotion downstairs as footsteps thumped toward the base of the stairs.

Rellen grabbed the unconscious man's collar and hauled him up into the chair. Laying his sword upon the table, he pulled a long leather strap from a pouch on his belt, pulled the man's arms behind his back, and slapped the leather strap around his wrists. Concentrating his will, he made several brief gestures, and the strap slithered like a snake, tightening and tying itself off in a firm knot.

As Rellen stood, heavy feet pounded up the stairs and came to his open door.

Mr. Cray and two burly house thugs with studded clubs came to an immediate halt, staring at the carnage in the room.

"Great gods," the innkeeper blurted.

"It's alright, Mr. Cray," Rellen soothed. "I'm fine." He glanced at the two bodies on the floor. "They aren't, I'm afraid." He gave the innkeeper a satisfied smile. "I did manage to restrain this fellow, however," he said, nodding to the assailant in the chair. Something made him do a double-take, and he stole a glance at the unconscious man. In the weak glow of the embers, it was hard to tell, but there was something familiar about him.

"Who's going to clean up this mess?" Cray demanded. "There's blood everywhere, and it's spreading."

Rellen turned to the perturbed innkeeper.

"Let's talk about that," he offered. He moved to his saddlebag, pulled out five gold coins, and set them on the table. "Would that cover a broken window, someone with a mop, and two funerals?"

Cray's features shifted from angry to larcenous. He stepped up to the table and swept the coins away with a motion so fast Rellen didn't see where they went.

"I believe it would, sir," Cray replied. "Shall I get the city guards?" he asked tentatively. "I can send for my cousin."

Rellen was suddenly wary. Although it was sensible for Cray to consider the guards, there was something in the way he offered that got Rellen to thinking. What if Maddock was at the heart of all this, or at least involved? Had the lieutenant sent Rellen here so Cray could tell the killers where to go?

"I'd rather not," Rellen replied. "At least not yet. I don't know who's involved in all of this, and I'd like to surprise them once I do."

"You're not suggesting my cousin is involved, are you?" Cray asked, shocked.

"Not at all," Rellen soothed. "However, once he knows of this, he or someone else will have to investigate, and that could affect my own efforts." Rellen eyed Cray. "Frankly, I'd like to find whomever is responsible before the city guard does. As a bounty hunter, I don't have to worry about bringing them to the magistrate before killing them."

"I suppose I see your point," Cray replied.

"Infidels!" the prisoner shouted. Rellen, Cray, and the two house thugs turned surprised faces toward the man secured to the chair. "Nissra shall bathe in your blood!"

The man's eyes were full of fury and hatred. He yelped once in pain, his body convulsed into a quivering moment of tension, and he went limp in the chair with a final explosion of breath.

They all stood there, stunned.

"I did not expect that," Rellen said with a good deal of disappointment. He had a few tricks that would have gotten him at least a few straight answers. "Make that *three* funerals," Rellen added sullenly, looking to Cray.

"It'll cost you another gold," Cray replied.

Rellen rolled his eyes and let out his breath slowly. He dipped a finger into his coin purse and pulled out another gold coin. He handed it over, and it disappeared into Cray's pocket as quickly as the others.

Rellen moved over and inspected the corpse, bewildered at how the man could have died. It didn't take him long to find a ring on the man's right index finger with a needle sticking out the side and several drops of blood on his thumb.

He carefully slipped the ring off and discovered the mark of Nissra on either side. He stepped back, an irritated look upon his face, and stared at the man's features. Then it hit him. It was the shop owner who had been arrested the day before.

How is that possible? Rellen thought.

The odds that Maddock or even Captain Hendron were part of this had just gone up. It also meant Rellen unequivocally could not trust Cray.

"Is everything alright?" Cray asked, interrupting Rellen's train of suspicions.

"Hmm?" Rellen looked to the innkeeper. "Oh, yes. Just thinking." Rellen wiped his falchion off on the sleeve of the dead shopkeeper. "Now, if you don't mind, I'd like to change to a room that isn't so…breezy."

"Of course," Cray said. He turned to the house thugs. "Attend to the bodies, and get Hilda to mop up in here." Turning to Rellen, he said, "Collect your things and meet me at the end of the hall. The last room doesn't have any windows."

"I certainly appreciate that," Rellen said as he started collecting his things.

Cray disappeared down the stairs, and Rellen looked forward, hopefully, to sleeping the rest of the night.

* * * * *

Five

R ellen managed several hours of uninterrupted sleep before waking shortly after sunrise. Having placed a minor portal lock spell upon the door of his new room, he left the inn and walked down the street to a large stone building that looked almost as expansive as the baron's keep further along the cobbled way. While the baron's fortress was made of mortared tan blocks, the magic school was a seamless, navy-blue stone that appeared to be cut from a single monolith.

The streets and shops were full of people preparing for the Solstice celebration taking place that night. Even with city guards on every street corner, the people of Calamath seemed to be in better spirits than the day before.

Rellen strode up the long stairs of the school and entered the massive wooden doors, which were standing open. The room beyond was a quarter sphere twenty feet across, and as smooth as glass. A set of banners hung from the curved surface, one above each of four closed doors of black stone. In the center of the chamber an intricate, curving framework of silvery vines four feet high supported a sphere of blue crystal the size of a human head.

Having seen such a device before, at both King Saren's keep and the magic school where he was trained, Rellen stepped up to the stone, leaned in and said, "I am Rellen of Corsia. I wish to speak with the chancellor." And then he whispered, "Aegon sul vas narivum."

Only a handful of people knew the phrase. How and why Rellen did was a closely guarded secret, meant to protect not only him, but the entire kingdom.

A moment later, a small yellow spark drifted out of the sphere and passed beneath a phoenix banner toward a door that was opening silently. Rellen brushed off his armor and strode through the door to find a spiral staircase that went both up and down. The spark drifted upward, and Rellen obediently followed. He made his way up three flights and down a long, sconce-lit hallway to a black stone door. The spark disappeared through it, so Rellen knocked three times.

The door opened silently, exposing a wide room entirely lined with bookshelves jammed to overflowing. Off to one side was a tidy workbench with a wide assortment of arcane tools and paraphernalia, along with several small creatures of bizarre form, each contained in a small glass container. One was insect-like, another mammalian, and the last reptilian in nature. Each had distinctly humanoid faces, and where he would have expected claws or talons, they had what looked very much like tiny human hands.

At the far side of the room was a large desk of dark wood covered with more books. Behind that sat an aged human in green robes, with a bare scalp and a long white beard that disappeared behind the desk. As Rellen entered, the man raised piercing yellow eyes from the large tome in his hands.

Rellen approached slowly and stopped only a few paces from the desk.

"Good morning, *Guardian*," the chancellor said easily. "How may I help a servant of the Crown?"

Rellen nodded. Guardians were sworn servants of King Saren III and acted as eyes, ears, and even fists of his will.

"Good morning, Chancellor," Rellen said, bowing his head slightly. "I have come seeking answers. I hunt the Ravager."

The chancellor raised an eyebrow.

"You may call me Thorril, and if you seek the Ravager, then you seek the bane of this city."

"Indeed," Rellen admitted. "It would seem that Nissra's roots have burrowed deep here."

"Many at the school have grown increasingly concerned with what is happening, but the constabulary has not yet called upon us to lend assistance. In fact, you are the first to come here seeking aid in the matter."

Rellen's brow furrowed. "Does this trouble you?" It certainly troubled him.

"Deeply," Thorril replied, "but you know the law as well as I. We are forbidden from interfering unless specifically asked."

Rellen nodded.

"I would see this Ravager dead or imprisoned as quickly as possible," Thorril said. "What is it you wish to know?"

"As you may be aware, each victim had the sign of Nissra cut into their foreheads." Rellen reached into a pouch and pulled out the sheet with the sigils he'd copied, as well as Maddock's series of curves and lines. He laid it down facing Thorril.

"Each of these curves and lines was associated with the mark of Nissra on the victims' foreheads. I don't know what they signify. The sigils, however, were carved into the chests of at least the latest victim, and I managed to translate it. I believe it means, '*Bonds cut from seething flesh, tying mother and son, the mother breaks upon fullest night.*' Beyond that, I have no idea.

"The sigils are obviously Azjerbahn." Thorril eyed Rellen. "Do you know that language?" There was a hint of suspicion in his voice.

"No, sir," Rellen replied easily. "I travel with a copy of the *Lingua Magica*. It took me hours to sort this out."

Thorril eased a little. "I suspect that phrase is part of a larger portal spell, but that's merely an educated guess. It is likely an attempt to cross the barrier between planes, but which ones or for what purpose is beyond my reckoning without seeing more of the spell. And even then, it might only be known to the caster." The chancellor paused for a moment. He traced his finger along the curves and lines that Maddock had scrawled upon the vellum.

"Wait a minute..." Thorril cocked his head to the side. "Those appear to be..." His brow furrowed. He lifted his spindly frame out from behind the desk and shuffled to a nearby bookshelf. He pulled out a thick tome, opened it, and thumbed through thick pages before stopping. He turned and held out the book. "Look at this."

The page held the first portion of a spell in the Bailian arcane language, and it was meant for drawing power from full moons in order to purify cursed people or items.

"I believe those are moon signs," Thorril said. He stared at Rellen. "This all started about a month ago, yes?"

"That's what they told me," Rellen replied.

"That would have been around the time of the new moon." Thorril stroked his beard. "The solstice celebration tonight coincides with the new moon." He looked deeply concerned. "A new moon on the Solstice is a very rare occurrence. It will be the darkest day, with the darkest moon, in seventy-five years. If I were working with dark magics, that would be a potent day, indeed. And I'd bet a sack full of gold this all started with the last new moon. Was there a pentagram around the bodies?"

Rellen shook his head. "Not around the one I saw. I'll ask the lieutenant I've been working with if there were pentagrams around any of the others."

"Very peculiar." Thorril said. "If they're working with some sort of portal or gate, anything that came through would be unconstrained, which, when dealing with such magic, can be not only dangerous but *lethal*. Any caster worth his salt would know this, which suggests they didn't care. Based upon what you've told me, I suspect they are working with a spell that builds in potency with each iteration, and if I'm any judge, it will culminate with the new moon tonight during the height of the solstice celebration."

"That does make sense," Rellen agreed. "There's something else…" Rellen pulled out the coin he'd gotten from Maddock and presented it to Thorril. "The bodies were laid out with silver coins in their palms. The first victim had one, and each subsequent victim had one more."

Thorril raised an eyebrow.

"Does it mean something?" Rellen asked.

Thorril carefully took the coin and inspected it for a few moments, turning it in his bony fingers.

"It depends." He eyed Rellen for a moment and then focused upon the coin. He whispered something under his breath that Rellen didn't understand and traced his finger around the coin's edge. Holding it up, he turned it left and right as if it were a prism in sunlight. "Silver is a potent metal, with influence and efficacy across most planes. As currency, it can procure assistance from all manner of intra-planar creatures. If it was being used here, it was probably a combination of both spell component and currency. If so, the coins would be linked to one another. The fact that the number of coins increased with each killing lends itself to the notion that they're building up the potency, and if it is a portal spell, nearly anything might be able to come through at this point."

"Could the coins be linked to people?" Rellen asked, wondering if he could use them to track the killers.

"Probably…to those who died, anyway," Thorril replied, handing the coin back, "and that's assuming it was a rite of some sort. *Possibly* to those who performed the rite, although it's unlikely. Such links bind to the spirit that was released, not those who released it. I must confess, however, I'm not well versed in spellcraft involving Azjerbahn."

"Do you know of anyone in Calamath who is?" Rellen asked.

"Not at *this* school," Thorril said defensively. He seemed offended by the mere suggestion. "I don't permit the teaching of the darker magics, and neither did my predecessor."

"That doesn't answer the question," Rellen said quietly.

The chancellor drew in a slow breath and let it out even more slowly, eyeing Rellen. "You're right," he finally said. "It does not."

"So, who?"

"I'll tell you," Thorril said, lowering his voice, "but you must swear as a Guardian that you will not share who gave you this information."

"I so swear it," Rellen said solemnly.

"It is...*rumored*..." Thorril said carefully, "that the baron's son, Kellith, was educated at the Magics Academy in the capital city."

"Kellith?" Rellen asked, surprised. "Not Kellith Hendron? The captain of the Guard?"

"The same," Thorril said. "Do you know him?"

"I just met him," Rellen said, his suspicions blossoming. "Thorril, this may be an awkward question, but what is the possibility that Captain Hendron is the Ravager?" He eyed Thorril's face, gauging the old wizard's response. "He has a knowledge of Azjerbahn, is in a position to manipulate the investigation, and would not be considered a suspect in something like this."

Without skipping a beat, Thorril shook his head. "Unlikely," he said. "I know for a fact that Hendron and his father were gone for two weeks in the middle of the month on a tour of a farming community to the south. One of my students accompanied them in an effort to improve crop yields."

"Could he have been involved with the other attacks?" Rellen asked.

"I suppose," Thorril said slowly. "But a spell like this would require there be only one caster for all iterations." He seemed to ponder something for a few moments. "I see what you're getting at, but Hendron has never struck me as a man who coveted power. He even turned down the baronial seat when his father was ill some years back. He insisted his younger brother take up the mantle in his stead."

So it can't be Hendron, Rellen thought, *but he could still be involved. If so, how? And why?*

For a moment he considered asking Thorril more, but he didn't want to put the chancellor further on the spot and, more importantly, he didn't want to risk giving himself away. As unlikely as it was, Thorril could be in on what was turning out to be a far-reaching Nissra conspiracy of some kind. For all he knew, Thorril was the spellcaster involved. But the captain being both the baron's son *and* a student of magic who knew Azjerbahn simply couldn't be a coincidence.

"Thank you for your help, Chancellor," Rellen said a bit hastily. "I appreciate the information, and you can rest assured that my oath shall remain unbroken."

"Thank you, Guardian," the chancellor said. "Should you need anything else, do not hesitate to reach out to me. Ever do I serve the king, above all."

"As do I," Rellen said. He gave a deep bow and strode from the room. As he walked down the long hallway, he contemplated the possibilities. Based on what he'd heard, it was likely that either Captain Hendron or Lieutenant Maddock were involved in the Ravager killings. It was also possible that both of them were, and even that one or both of them were actually undertaking the rituals themselves and not just covering up the crimes.

The shopkeeper who had tried to kill him and committed suicide was the key. The man had obviously been part of the Nissra cult. But how could he have come after Rellen if he was supposed to be locked up and destined for a purification ritual? Everything pointed to Hendron and Maddock.

But why? If they are involved, what's their endgame?

* * * * *

Six

With the door to his room once again magically barred, Rellen sat at the table with an assortment of items laid out before him. He rolled out a large sheet of vellum and drew a circle that reached nearly to its edges. Focusing his will, he placed Maddock's coin in the center of the circle and pulled out several eyelashes from his right eye. He carefully placed them upon the coin. Closing his eyes, he chanted a short spell as he drew a complex Bailian sigil at the top portion of the circle. He repeated the process with a different sigil beside the first, and then another and another, placing each one along the perimeter of the circle. The process took him several hours, and when he was done, the interior of the circle was filled with sigils that made a spiral all the way to the coin. He then drew a line from the coin to the exterior of the circle and placed one last sigil at the end of the line.

Opening his eyes, he watched the coin glow brightly. A gossamer filament of blue flowed out along the line, coursed its way over the last sigil, and extended quickly across the room to disappear through the wall at a downward angle.

"So there *is* a link," he said with a good deal of satisfaction.

Rising to his feet, he placed the coin in his pocket. The filament moved with it, and he knew he was the only one who could see it. He'd created a connection between the one coin he possessed and the other eleven that had been found with the body. He had a trail to follow, and he knew where it would lead, but he wasn't sure what he would find when he got there.

Moving quickly through the city, the filament led him straight back to the City Guard Tower and inside.

As he neared the tower, the filament did something he'd never seen before. It slowly separated into two filaments that seemed to lead to the same place, but only a few feet apart.

What the...? Rellen thought.

Upon entering, the filaments disappeared through the front desk, where a different lieutenant currently sat, and they passed through the wall toward where Captain Hendron's desk would be in the next room.

The lieutenant looked up from the desk. He was about to say something, but Rellen interrupted him.

"Captain Hendron," he called out. "It's Rellen of Corsia. May I have a word?"

"Come on back," Hendron called back.

The lieutenant glanced back to the open doorway, nodded once to Rellen, and then went back to a stack of vellum in front of him.

Rellen stepped through the door, and when he turned to face the captain, he stopped in his tracks.

Hendron sat behind his desk, his face raised to greet Rellen with a friendly smile. One blue filament from the coin went straight into the lower left-hand area of the desk, as expected. However, the other went straight into Hendron's heart. And that wasn't all. There were dozens more of the filaments running from the lower part of the desk and joining at the captain's heart.

Rellen was astonished. He hadn't expected to see something like that, but in an instant he pieced together a theory. Hendron was the mastermind, but he had someone working for him who was doing the actual killings. He immediately thought of Lieutenant Maddock, although the odds of Maddock being a spellcaster, let alone knowing Azjerbahn, was a stretch. There *must* be someone else.

"What can I do for you?" Captain Hendron asked.

How to proceed...? Rellen thought. *Do I start with the spell, the threads, the murders, or the shopkeeper?* He quickly made his decision and stepped up to the desk, intent on tripping the captain up.

"I was wondering what happens to the Nissra prisoners you bring in."

"They're given a choice," Hendron replied. "Stay locked up, or undergo a purification ritual that cleanses them of Nissra's taint. We performed it on the prisoners below yesterday."

"Were you there?" Rellen asked.

"No. I leave that up to whichever lieutenant is on watch."

"How does that all work?"

"The ritual requires a lawfully-aligned priest coupled with a mage. When we have a dozen or so prisoners, the priest purges the taint, while the mage places a...well, I guess you'd have to call it a curse...that makes the person violently ill if they're even in the vicinity of anyone with the taint of Nissra. It's similar to the constraint placed upon bounty hunters to obey the law. Once the ritual is performed, we keep them for three days, and then release them."

"And that includes the man they brought in yesterday?" Rellen asked. "The big fellow...long, wavy red hair and a nose you could plow with?"

"Shaylen Rual?"

"I don't know," Rellen replied. "His shop was on the main thoroughfare from the eastern gate."

"That's him," Hendron said.

"Is he still downstairs?"

"He should be," Hendron replied. "Let me check." He thumbed through a stack of vellum on his desk. "Here he is. He opted for the purification. It was performed not long after he came in, and he's waiting for his release."

"I don't think it took, Captain," Rellen said, "assuming it happened at all."

Hendron looked surprised.

"What makes you say that?"

"He tried to kill me last night, and then committed suicide…with this…" Rellen pulled the ring from his pocket and held it out.

"Gods…you can't be serious." Hendron looked genuinely appalled, recognizing the ring for what it was, and his reaction shook Rellen's theory about his involvement.

"You can ask the innkeeper at the Green Gryphon," Rellen said. "I paid him to arrange for three funerals, including Raul's."

"Are you certain?"

"I know what happened last night, but there's only one way to be certain it wasn't Raul. Let's go downstairs."

"I think that's an excellent idea," Hendron agreed. He rose from his seat, and Rellen watched as the dozens of blue filaments connected to Hendron's heart moved with him. "Follow me."

What can they mean? Rellen thought.

They quickly made their way through the rear door, along a series of empty cells, and down a spiral staircase at the end of the hall. They descended a single floor to find a tidy dungeon illuminated by lanterns hanging from the ceiling. There were fourteen cells in all, most of them occupied, and when they reached the end of the line, Hendron turned worried eyes to Rellen.

"Something wrong, Captain?" a blond-haired man in the cell beside him said with an air of devious delight.

Hendron scowled at the prisoner and turned to Rellen.

"He's not here," he said.

"I want to show you something," Rellen said. He pulled out the vellum with the sigils and handed it over. "I'm not sure what it means," he lied.

The captain looked at the sigils and was mildly surprised. "I haven't seen Azjerbahn for fifteen years."

"So you recognize it?" Rellen asked, a little surprised. It had been a perfect opportunity for Hendron to play dumb.

"Yes. It's been a while, but it looks to be part of a portal spell of some kind. It says, '*Bonds cut from seething flesh, tying mother and son, the mother breaks upon fullest night.*'" He looked up at Rellen with worried eyes. "Where did you get this?"

Rellen was an exceptional read of people, and the captain's responses all seemed genuine.

"It was carved into the chest of the last victim."

"What?" Hendron asked, immediately concerned. "Maddock didn't say anything."

"He said he didn't see it. I must admit, the victim's wounds were obscured with blood and covered by his tunic." Rellen took a deep breath. "Why was Maddock assigned to the Ravager murders?"

"It was his turn," Hendron said simply.

"So it was just blind luck?"

"I guess you could call it that. The lieutenant who would have been assigned came down with a nasty illness of some kind. Took a healer three days to get him back on his feet."

That can't be a coincidence either, Rellen thought. *Maddock must be involved somehow.*

"So how do you know Azjerbahn?" Rellen asked, hoping to catch Hendron off guard.

Hendron hesitated a moment.

"I spent a number of years at the Magics Academy in Corsia, not that I have much talent. My father felt it important I receive a rounded education. He's been shaping me to replace him someday, but to be honest, I don't have much interest in becoming baron."

"Really?"

"Politics and drafty castle corridors with little sunlight. I like the outdoors…and keeping the people of Calamath safe…especially now, with this Nissra cult gaining momentum."

"So you want to see an end to the cult?"

"Of course I do. Wretches like the Nissrans ruin a city…ruin the people in it. There's even a member of my father's council who thinks we should go easy on them. The damned fool. He suggested giving the cult a place in tomorrow night's Solstice celebration as a peace offering. Fortunately, my father turned him down…If it was up to me, he'd been in a cell and given the rite with the rest of these bastards."

"Did you consider having someone at the magic school try to trace the coins, or at least figure out what they're being used for?"

"I sent Maddock to do that with the coins from the third body," Hendron said. "He said they weren't able to scry anything and sent him back with them."

There it is, Rellen thought.

"Captain, what do you know about Maddock?"

"Maddock?" Hendron replied. "He's an old friend. I hadn't seen him for years, but when he returned to Calamath about eight months ago, I gave him a job with the guard."

"Eight months ago?" It was all starting to fit together. Rellen hesitated, wondering how Hendron would respond to what he was about to say. "Captain, I think Maddock is deeply involved with the Nissrans, and he's covering for them."

"What makes you say that?"

"A number of things. The way he handled the last body. His general disinterest in the clues. I'd bet a sack of gold he knew of the sigils on the victims' chests. And I just came from the Magic School. The chancellor said he hadn't been asked to get involved in the murders yet. The only thing I haven't figured out is who is casting this spell. Not everyone knows Azjerbahn, even if they have the gift."

Hendron's face paled, and he slowly locked eyes with Rellen. "Maddock went to school with me," he said, "and he learned Azjerbahn." He shook his head. "But he *hates* the Nissrans. His parents were part of the cult when he was a child. They tormented him terribly."

"Maybe they turned him?" Rellen offered, desperate to find Maddock now.

"They did more than that," a voice called from the far end of the dungeon. "They filled him with *me*."

Rellen and Hendron turned surprised faces to see Maddock standing at the base of the spiral stairs.

Rellen immediately reached for one of his falchions.

"Take them!" the thing calling itself Maddock shouted, eyes alight with fury.

The doors of every occupied cell burst open, and the nearest door slammed into Rellen just as he drew his blade. The impact caught him in the back of the head, and the lights went out.

* * * * *

Seven

Rellen woke to a freezing chill, surrounded by thick forest. In an instant, he realized three things. He was gagged, he'd been stripped down to just his leggings, and he was lashed spread-eagle to a large wooden cross. He looked up to where his hands were bound and saw several of the blue beetles that infested the region crawling along the wooden beam toward his hand.

Before him, a large, rough wooden table had been set in front of a burning pyre. Two dozen people in crimson robes kneeled around it, all of them facing Maddock. Maddock stood between the fire and the table, his body covered in robes of crimson and gold. Captain Hendron had been laid out upon the table, bound to the four corners with rope. Hendron had also been stripped down to his leggings, and surrounding him was a circle of silver coins. Each coin had a blue filament running from it straight into Hendron's heart, making it look as if he were at the center of a glowing wheel…or a *portal*.

The mother and the son, Rellen realized, and everything fell into place.

The demon inside Maddock was going to bring the goddess Nissra into the world and let her occupy Captain Hendron's body. Once she did, she could get rid of the baron and take his place…with an entire barony at her disposal. He looked around and spotted his armor and gear lying off to the side of the fire. Not that any of it would do him much good while he was bound to the cross.

"We stand upon the precipice," Maddock intoned, raising his hands above Hendron's body. "You shall all bear witness to Nissra's entry upon this world, and when she comes, she will raise all of us to the heights of demi-godhood. *Nothing* shall stand against her and those who serve her will." His eyes moved to Rellen. "Good, bounty hunter, you're awake. You, too, shall bear witness. Did you think it was stupidity that made me show you the moon signs? I left you breadcrumbs to bring you here...and for your meddling, you will be Nissra's first meal upon this world. Prepare for an eternity of agony!"

Maddock closed his eyes, lowered his hands, and placed them over Hendron's heart where the filaments joined together. His lips started moving, and although Rellen couldn't hear him, the intensity of the filaments grew brighter. He saw Hendron's mouth extend in a scream of agony, but no sound came out.

Rellen didn't have much time, and even if his plan worked, he didn't know how he could defeat two dozen cultists. He looked up and saw that one of the beetles was just within reach.

It's now or never, he thought.

He closed his eyes, focused his will, and gesticulated with both hands. He felt the magic course through his limbs. An instant later, the leather straps binding him loosened and slithered free of his wrists, dropping to the ground. Rellen grabbed the beetle with one hand and ripped the gag from his mouth, focusing his will once again. He blurted an incantation, made three quick motions with the hand holding the beetle, and then smashed the insect across his chest.

"He's free!" someone shouted. "The infidel is free!"

"Get him!" another screamed.

A whiff of the beetle's stench assailed Rellen's nostrils as he felt the spell flow from its crushed body across his skin. With a chitinous clattering, thick plates formed across his skin in a swirl of light, encasing him from head to toe. When he opened his eyes, he saw a half-dozen men and women in robes charging straight for him. The others were rising to their feet, while Maddock seemed immobile as he continued his incantation. The wheel of filaments around Hendron's body had darkened to near black with ethereal blue edges. Energy crackled along them, and a ruddy form was superimposing itself over the captain.

The first of the cultists reached Rellen, slashing with a long, curved dagger. Rellen raised his arm, and the blade clacked against the armor, cutting a deep gouge that found only a small purchase of flesh. Rellen sent a punch into the man's throat and felt a wet squelch. The cultist gurgled as a spray of blood erupted from his mouth.

Rellen stepped back to find that the horns of the beetle had manifested along his armor at knuckles, heels, elbows, knees, and back. He blocked the slash from another dagger and sent an elbow into the next attacker's face. The horn pierced flesh and bone before Rellen wrenched it free.

A cultist crashed into him, and then another, sending him to the ground.

"Don't kill him!" one of them shouted.

He kicked and punched as bodies piled on top of him. Daggers pierced and slashed at his armor, and some of the attacks got through. He felt blood seeping beneath the chitinous layer, and he realized he was done for. Strong arms pinned him to the ground, and then the mob lifted him to his feet, holding him in place as he watched the form of Nissra grow more solid around Hendron's body. She was hideous, with crimson skin like a dragon, horns rising above her head, and jagged tusks descending from her jaw.

Rellen struggled, but the hold the cultists had on him was unbreakable.

"Excuse me," a familiar voice said from behind him.

There was a crackle of electricity, and then a bolt slashed into the cultists holding him. He felt the energy tingle across his skin, most of it absorbed by the armor. The cultists, however, danced and trembled as lines of white electricity coursed across their bodies. Rellen turned to see Thorril, the chancellor of the magic school, standing a dozen paces behind him with his finger outstretched and the bolt of energy coming from it. Thorril lowered his hand, and the energy ceased, causing the cultists to drop to the ground, their bodies smoking.

"I believe you have a bounty to collect," Thorril said.

Rellen didn't hesitate.

He leapt forward, charging across the grass, and straight for Maddock, who was still casting his spell.

A tumultuous circle of black smoke had surrounded Hendron and Nissra, running along the circle of the coins.

Am I too late?

Rellen leapt over the table just as Maddock opened his eyes.

"NO!" Maddock screamed.

Their bodies slammed together, and then there was an implosion of magical energy that sent them flying. Their bodies hit the ground, but Rellen never lost his grip. They came to a stop a dozen yards past the table, with Rellen on top of Maddock.

Rellen raised a horned fist and sent it crashing down into Maddock's torso. He raised his other fist and sent it down. Again and again, Rellen pierced and tore at Maddock's body, opening wound after wound as the crazed servant of Nissra screamed in pain and horror.

When the grass surrounding them was covered in Maddock's blood, Rellen raised his fist one last time and sent his last blow into the center of Maddock's face. Maddock quivered once, and then his entire body shuddered as a smoky form seeped from his ruined mouth and nostrils.

"I believe I can attend to that," Thorril said from behind him.

Rellen turned to see the chancellor gesticulating as he cast a spell. A wash of magical energy passed through Rellen's body and latched upon the smoky form of the demon…one of Nissra's minions. The demon shrieked and struggled at the bonds that now held it in place.

Thorril stepped up, muttered another spell, and drew out the lines of a box in the air in front of him. Blue lines of energy formed around the twisting demon, encasing it in a prison of blue lines. Thorril shouted a final word, and the prison shrank. As it did, the energy cut into the demon's body. It hissed and spat and shrieked in agony. In moments the box shrank to nothing, leaving only the drifting smoke of a destroyed minion of evil.

"Come, Guardian," Thorril said, holding out his hand. "Let us attend to the good captain."

"Does he live?" Rellen asked.

"Indeed," Thorril replied. "And you interrupted Maddock's spell just in time to send Nissra back where she belongs."

"Thank the gods," Rellen said. "How did you know I was here?"

"I put a trace spell on that coin when you let me examine it," Thorril said simply.

"So what made you come find me?"

As they reached the table where Hendron lay unconscious, Thorril reached into his robes, withdrew a small, rolled up piece of vellum, and handed it over.

"I believe this will explain fully," he said as he began examining Captain Hendron.

Rellen unrolled the vellum.

Thorril, you served my father as a Guardian. I must ask you to take up the mantle once again and help my eldest brother Rellen. He is clever and brash, but he tends to get into trouble wherever it exists. Find him and lend what aid you can. ~ King Saren III

Rellen smiled and eyed the old wizard as he cast a simple restoration spell over Captain Hendron. *A Guardian, eh?*

"Thank you, Thorril," Rellen said.

"You needn't thank me," Thorril said without looking. "As I said, ever do I serve the King, above all."

"As do I," Rellen replied, moving over to where his armor and equipment lay. "As do I."

* * * * *

Eight

Rellen hooked two sacks of gold coins over Shaddeth's withers and pulled himself up into the saddle, wincing at the handful of small wounds he'd received the night before. Thorril had been kind enough to bandage them once Rellen's armor spell had dissipated. He turned in the saddle and looked to where Captain Hendron and Thorril stood in the doorway to the guard tower.

"Many thanks, Rellen of Corsia," Captain Hendron said. "You've done a man's job, sir."

"I couldn't have done it without the chancellor," Rellen replied. "Thanks again, old man," he added, winking to the elder Guardian.

"It was a pleasure," Thorril replied, nodding his head. "Where are you headed now?"

Rellen smiled. He reached into his tunic and pulled out the Eye of Tuluum. He held it before him and watched it swing toward the eastern gate.

"I have no idea," Rellen said, "but I'm sure I'll find out soon enough." He released the Eye and waved to them both.

"Farewell, gentlemen," he said.

"May the winds ever be at your back," Hendron said.

"And grant you every victory," Thorril added.

With a bow, Rellen pulled the reins and set Shaddeth moving toward whatever his next destination might be.

* * * * *

Quincy J. Allen Bio

Nationally Bestselling Author Quincy J. Allen is a cross-genre author with numerous novels under his belt. His media tie-in novel *Colt the Outlander: Shadow of Ruin* was a Scribe Award finalist in 2019, and his noir novel *Chemical Burn* was a Colorado Gold Award finalist in 2010. *Blood Oath*, Book 3 of the Blood War Chronicles, was released in February of 2019, and he is working on the fourth book in that six-book fantasy steampunk series, due out early in 2020.

He has co-authored *Reclaiming Honor* with Marc Alan Edelheit in their Way of Legend series, due out November 1st of 2019. He has also co-authored the novel "Enforcer" with Kevin Ikenberry in the Four Horsemen Universe Peacemaker series, due out late in 2019. He is currently working on a novel for Kevin Steverson in his Salvage universe based upon the short story *Vorwhol Dishonor* in this anthology.

His short story publications are numerous, including a pro sale appearing in Larry Correia's *"Monster Hunter: Files"* from Baen, published in October of 2017 entitled "Sons of the Father," as well as several stories appearing in Chris Kennedy Publishing's mil-sci-fi anthologies in and out of the Four Horsemen Universe.

He works out of his home in Charlotte, North Carolina, and hopes to one day be a New York Times bestselling author.

You can follow his writing endeavors at:

www.quincyallen.com and

www.facebook.com/Quincy.Allen.Author

# # # # #

About the Editors

A Webster Award winner and three-time Dragon Award finalist, Chris Kennedy is a Science Fiction/Fantasy/Young Adult author, speaker, and small-press publisher who has written over 20 books and published more than 100 others. Chris' stories include the "Occupied Seattle" military fiction duology, "The Theogony" and "Codex Regius" science fiction trilogies, stories in the "Four Horsemen" and "In Revolution Born" universes and the "War for Dominance" fantasy trilogy. Get his free book, "Shattered Crucible," at his website, https://chriskennedypublishing.com.

Called "fantastic" and "a great speaker," he has coached hundreds of beginning authors and budding novelists on how to self-publish their stories at a variety of conferences, conventions and writing guild presentations. He is the author of the award-winning #1 bestseller, "Self-Publishing for Profit: How to Get Your Book Out of Your Head and Into the Stores," as well as the leadership training book, "Leadership from the Darkside."

Chris lives in Virginia Beach, Virginia, with his wife, and is the holder of a doctorate in educational leadership and master's degrees in both business and public administration. Follow Chris on Facebook at https://facebook.com/chriskennedypublishing.biz.

Rob Howell is the creator of the Shijuren fantasy setting (www.shijuren.org) and an author in the Four Horsemen Universe (www.mercenaryguild.org). He writes primarily medieval fantasy, space opera, military science fiction, and alternate history.

He is a reformed medieval academic, a former IT professional, and a retired soda jerk.

His parents discovered quickly books were the only way to keep Rob quiet. He latched onto the Hardy Boys series first and then anything he could reach. Without books, it's unlikely all three would have survived.

His latest release in Shijuren is *Where Now the Rider*, the third in the Edward series of swords and sorcery mysteries. The next release in that world is *None Call Me Mother*, the conclusion to the epic fantasy trilogy *The Kreisens*.

You can find him online at: www.robhowell.org and his blog at www.robhowell.org/blog.

* * * * *

The following is an

Excerpt from Book One of The Balance of Kerr:

Burnt

_____

Kevin Steverson & Tyler Ackerman

Available Now from New Mythology Press

eBook and Paperback

Excerpt from "Burnt:"

Tog shrugged. "I like chicken," he said as he pulled out his dagger. Standing nearly seven feet tall and weighing nearly three hundred and twenty pounds, a dagger for him was a short sword to most men. He cut a piece off. He didn't bother blowing on it and poked it into his mouth. There was instant regret on his face. He began breathing through his teeth with the piece of meat between them, the sharpness of his incisors giving away that he was half Orc, if his size didn't already reveal it. He grabbed his mug and drained it.

Kryder shook his head, cut another piece for himself, and blew on it. Before he took a bite, he said, "If I had a copper for every time I've seen you do that, I could exchange them for a piece of gold. I'm talking about a whole coin and not a quarter piece."

Tog wiped his mouth with the back of his hand, ignoring the remark, and said, "So when are we going to be contacted? Besides the cost of mugs, this place isn't cheap. It's not like we have coin to spare. We should think about an inn more in line with our coin purses."

"I don't know," Kryder answered. "The old man said someone would contact us here. If we go across town, whoever it is may not find us."

"Well I…" Tog started to say when he was interrupted by a loud voice two tables away.

"Look here, halfbreed," a man dressed similarly to them, in leather armor covered with a travel cloak and a sword on his hip, said loudly. One side of his face had a scar stretching from eyebrow to lips. He was speaking to them. "I don't eat with such as your kind."

The three men sitting with him laughed. One wearing a half-helmet with leather flaps hanging on each side added his own loud insult, "Since the rape didn't kill his mother, surely bearing an Orc bastard did the deed." The group laughed even louder.

Kryder reached down to his side and drew another smaller, more ornate dagger with his free hand. He laid them both on the table. He stood, turned around, and looked at the four men. Tog, on his feet nearly as quickly, reached over his shoulder and grabbed the axe strapped to his back with one hand. It was dual-headed and meant for two hands when used by a normal-sized man. He placed it on the table beside his own large dagger. A hand's length of the worn leather-covered handle hung over the edge.

The four men realized the object of their harassment and his companion didn't intend to leave. They meant to fight.

* * * * *

The following is an

Excerpt from Book One of The Milesian Accords:

A Reluctant Druid

_____

Jon R. Osborne

Available Now from New Mythology Press

eBook, Paperback, and Audio Book

Excerpt from "A Reluctant Druid:"

"Don't crank on it; you'll strip it."

Liam paused from trying to loosen the stubborn bolt holding the oil filter housing on his Yamaha motorcycle, looking for the source of the unsolicited advice. The voice was gruff, with an accent and cadence that made Liam think of the Swedish Chef from the Muppets. The garage door was open for air circulation, and two figures were standing in the driveway, illuminated by the setting sun. As they approached and stepped into the shadows of the house, Liam could see they were Pixel and a short, stout man with a greying beard that would do ZZ Top proud. The breeze blowing into the garage carried a hint of flowers.

Liam experienced a moment of double vision as he looked at the pair. Pixel's eyes took on the violet glow he thought he had seen before, while her companion lost six inches in height, until he was only as tall as Pixel. What the short man lacked in height, he made up for in physique; he was built like a fireplug. He was packed into blue jeans and a biker's leather jacket, and goggles were perched over the bandana covering his salt and pepper hair. Leather biker boots crunched the gravel as he walked toward the garage. Pixel followed him, having traded her workout clothes for black jeans and a pink t-shirt that left her midriff exposed. A pair of sunglasses dangled from the neckline of her t-shirt.

"He's seeing through the glamour," the short, bearded man grumbled to Pixel, his bushy eyebrows furrowing.

"Well duh. We're on his home turf, and this is his place of power" Pixel replied nonchalantly. "He was pushing back against my glamour yesterday, and I'm not adding two hands to my height."

Liam set down the socket wrench and ran through the mental inventory of items in the garage that were weapons or could be used as them. The back half of the garage was a workshop, which included the results of his dabbling with blacksmithing and sword-crafting, so the list was considerable. But the most suitable were also the farthest away.

"Can I help you?" Liam stood and brushed off his jeans; a crowbar was three steps away. Where had they come from? Liam hadn't heard a car or motorcycle outside, and the house was a mile and a half outside of town.

"Ja, you can." The stout man stopped at the threshold of the garage. His steel-grey eyes flicked from Liam to the workbench and back. He held his hands out, palms down. The hands were larger than his and weren't strangers to hard work and possibly violence. "And there's no need to be unhospitable; we come as friends. My name is Einar, and you've already met Pixel."

"Hi, Liam." Pixel was as bubbly as yesterday. While she didn't seem to be making the same connection as Einar regarding the workbench, her eyes darted about the cluttered garage and the dim workshop behind it. "Wow, you have a lot of junk."

"What's this about?" Liam sidled a half step toward the workbench, regretting he hadn't kept up on his martial arts. He had three brown belts, a year of kendo, and some miscellaneous weapons training scattered over two decades but not much experience in the way of real fighting. He could probably hold his own in a brawl as long as his opponent didn't have serious skills. He suspected Einar was more than a Friday night brawler in the local watering hole. "Is she your daughter?"

Einar turned to the purple-haired girl, his caterpillar-like eyebrows gathering. "What did you do?"

"What? I only asked him a few questions and checked him out," Pixel protested, her hands going to her hips as she squared off with Einar. "It's not as if I tried to jump his bones right there in the store or something."

"Look mister, if you think something untoward happened between me and your daughter—" Liam began.

"She's not my pocking daughter, and I don't give a troll's ass if you diddled her," Einar interrupted, his accent thickening with his agitation. He took a deep breath, his barrel chest heaving. "Now, will you hear me out without you trying to brain me with that tire iron you've been eyeing?"

"You said diddle." Pixel giggled.

"Can you be serious for five minutes, you pocking faerie?" Einar glowered, his leather jacket creaking as he crossed his arms.

"Remember 'dwarf,' you're here as an 'advisor.'" Pixel included air quotes with the last word, her eyes turning magenta. "The Nine Realms are only involved out of politeness."

"Politeness! If you pocking Tuatha and Tylwyth Teg hadn't folded up when the Milesians came at you, maybe we wouldn't be here to begin with!" Spittle accompanied Einar's protest. "Tylwyth? More like Toothless!"

"Like your jarls didn't roll over and show their bellies when the Avramites showed up with their One God and their gold!" Pixel rose up on her toes. "Your people took their god and took their gold and then attacked our ancestral lands!"

"Guys!" Liam had stepped over to the workbench but hadn't picked up the crowbar. "Are you playing one of those live-action role playing games or something? Because if you are, I'm calling my garage out of bounds. Take your LARP somewhere else."

"We've come a long way to speak to you," Einar replied, looking away from Pixel. "I'm from Asgard."

"Asgard? You mean like Thor and Odin? What kind of game are you playing?" Liam hadn't moved from the workbench, but he had mapped in his mind the steps he would need to take to reach a stout pole which would serve as a staff while he back-pedaled to his workshop, where a half-dozen half-finished sword prototypes rested. From where he stood, though, he didn't feel as threatened. He knew a bit about gamers because there were a fair number of them among the pagan community, and he had absorbed bits and pieces of it. Maybe someone had pointed Liam out to Pixel as research about druids for one of these games—an over-enthusiastic player who wanted to more convincingly roleplay one.

"Gods I hate those pocking things," Einar grumbled, rubbing his forehead while Pixel stifled another giggle. "Look, can we sit down and talk to you? This is much more serious than some pocking games you folk play with your costumes and your toy weapons."

"This isn't a game, and we aren't hippies with New Age books and a need for self-validation." Pixel added. Her eyes had faded to a lavender color. "Liam, we need your help."

* * * * *

Get "A Reluctant Druid" now at:
https://www.amazon.com/dp/B07716V2RN

Find out more about Jon R. Osborne at:
https://chriskennedypublishing.com/

* * * * *